The Kiskeyano: A Taino Story

Rafael Morillo

ISBN: 0692903461
ISBN-13: 978-0692903469 (Caribbean Lion Publishing)

LCCN: 2017909231

I dedicate this book to my loving grandmother Venecia, may she rest in peace. I also dedicate this book to the Dominican community, and the Caribbean, and Latin American communities.

CONTENTS

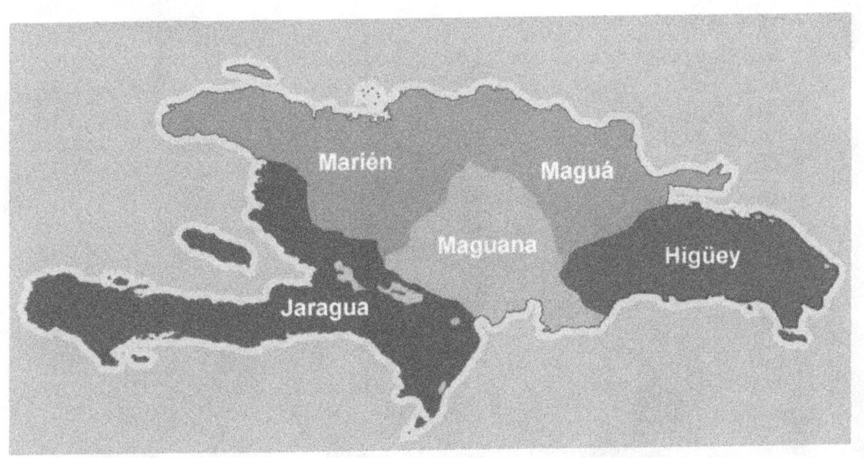

(Chiefdoms of Ayiti)

PROLOGUE: THE PEOPLE OF THE CARIBBEAN ISLANDS

Before the time of Jesus Christ, for thousands of years, the islands of the Caribbean have provided a home for various societies. People initially inhabited the island of Trinidad for over 600 years B.C., arriving from the Orinoco River valley. They travelled northward, inhabited successive islands, and eventually reached the main islands of modern day Cuba, Hispaniola (Haiti and Dominican Republic), and Puerto Rico. The Guanahatabey people were one of the earliest groups to continuously settle in the Caribbean islands, later inhabiting Western Cuba. The Igneri and Arawaks also inhabited the smaller Caribbean islands while moving upwards towards the Greater Antilles. The island of Ayiti (or Hispaniola) was soon inhabited by Taino, Ciguayo, and Macorix people while Cuba had Ciboney people or western Tainos. The Kalinago people, who were later referred to as island Carib, moved into the Lesser Antilles, sometimes coming into contact with other native groups—including the Tainos. The Tainos developed into an organized and peaceful society, which began to organize a network of trade throughout multiple islands.

At the time of European arrival to the Caribbean, there were four main native groups: the Tainos mostly in the Greater Antilles, the Guanahatabey of western Cuba, the Lucayans in the Bahamas, and the Kalinago or Caribs in the Leeward Islands and Windward Islands. The native Caribbean cultures and the incoming European cultures were set to clash when Christopher Columbus arrived in 1492, subsequently creating Spanish settlements which included the city of Santo Domingo in modern day Dominican Republic. The European arrival and subsequent settlement of the Caribbean would set into motion the collapse of various native civilizations and the arrival of African slaves to the island of Hispaniola. The wider Caribbean islands and what would be called the Americas would create new people and new cultures.

Our story begins in the island now called Hispaniola in the eastern region of Jaragua.

CHAPTER 1
AYITI

With tears in my eyes, I remembered a simpler time. A time of innocence enjoyed with my family and friends, uncomplicated and peaceful, with respect and empathy for others. A time where I enjoyed the songs of the various birds and delighted in the multitudes of colors their feathers displayed. A time where I ran and played with the other kids, free from want and despair. The island's treasures gave us everything we needed: water to quench our thirst, food that kept us full, and shelter from the rains and the hot sun. We lived simply, maintained a natural fair order, and avoided excess in our daily lives. The very same sea shells, stones, and metals that adorned nature adorned our own bodies and enhanced the beauty already inherent in ourselves.

Beauty was easily seen all around us; the waves crashing with their soothing sounds and the beauty of the breeze gently cooling our skin under the shade of pine trees. The beauty of a woman's eyes, her brown skin, and a smile that became large in laughter when you could make her laugh at a clever joke. My gift was finding the joys in everyday life and sharing them with my friends and the women who graced me with their time and conversation. It was a land so large and filled with large majestic mountains, long rivers, and beaches; a land filled with life and birds of all colors so numerous they would cover the skies when they took flight. The sounds of the people and their laughter, their pain, their hopes intertwined with the sounds from various animals of the land formed our common experiences as individuals and as a people.

My name is Amanex and I was born in this large island named Ayiti, meaning the land of mountains, which my family also called Kiskeya, meaning “mother of all lands”. I was born from the love of my father Maraguay and my mother Ana. At the time of my birth, seven years before the invaders arrived, my parents had moved to the southeastern region of Jaragua near the great sea in the southern region of our great island. The island was divided into five great regions called cacicazgos, each led by a chief called a cacique. The five major cacicazgos were Jaragua, Marien, Maguana, Magua, and Higüey. As a young boy, I had only travelled east to the cacicazgo of Maguana. My father however, had travelled to the other cacicazgos of Marién, Magua, and as far as Higüey.

My time was spent fishing in waterways and in the open sea in our canoa with my father and my friends. The canoa was made of hollowed-out tree bark and served for transporting my father and others to islands for trade and to promote good relations with other leaders called kassiquan, or caciques, who were the chiefs leading their respective societies. My older brother’s name is Amayao, born three years before me. Amayao was a strong confident person who always sought to protect me. My mother was named Ana because she was as beautiful as a flower in bloom, with deep bronze skin and black hair the color of midnight. She was born in the island of Xaymaca directly west from our island and our region of Jaragua. My father was born in Maguana and had moved to Jaragua shortly before my birth. He was a great farmer and he helped supervise the various plots of cultivated land called conucos. My father was a naboria, a laborer who established a good reputation among the chiefs and nobles or nitainos and the priests and medicine men called bohiques, which afforded him the luxury of travelling to other regions as a representative of his community. My father was muscular and his dark brown skin shined brightly in the sun. His courage and integrity were the template of how I wished to live my own life as a man. My father relished his various roles in society which allowed him to learn and associate with communities near and far.

Our society was fair and our people lived in peace and justice. My father helped in irrigation projects in effort to increase our crop production. Sometimes I joined my father in his duties, but most of my time was spent playing and hunting iguanas, hutias, and birds for myself and friends. I hunted larger animals—like the large turtles called jicoteas—alongside my father. I would also hunt large sea animals called manatees with my father and his friends. My mother created various fabrics out of cotton for herself and my dad while the children lived naked without any of the shame that the invaders displayed.

The men and women wore cloths to cover their painted and pierced bodies. My mother and the other women harvested our crops in our conucos such for garlic, fruits like mamey, anon, and guava, and various tubers like potatoes, yautías, and cassava or yucca. We lived in rounded houses made from palm wood and conical thatched roofs made from palm tree leaves called bohios. We shared our bohio with several families and slept on palm leaves or used a hamaca (hammock) to sleep in an elevated position. The sub chiefs and caciques lived in larger rectangular structures called caneys at the center of the village facing the batey, where we played our ball games, settled disputes, and held our ceremonies called batu. The batey was surrounded by stone and covered with symbols. We also carved stools to sit and talk with our family and friends, and weaved baskets for our food and used calabashes or gourds to carry and store our drinking water. We also used large calabashes in our canoas or canoes to bail them out, which was essential in longer voyages between islands.

We kept carved figures called zemis, which represented our gods and ancestors, in our homes and around our villages. The priests shared stories of our creation and our gods, such as the supreme Goddess Atabey who we worshipped as the goddess of the heavens, fresh water, and fertility. Atabey represents all bodies of water, the tides, and as the goddess of fertility women prayed to her during pregnancy. Atabey represents all that is tangible and she and the earth were manifested as Caguana the spirit of love, and Guabancex the violent fury of earthquakes, volcanoes, and storms. Atabey immaculately conceived two sons named Yúcahu the spirit of giver of cassava, and his envious brother Guacar who later renamed himself Juracan the god of destruction. These stories were taught to us by our parents and the priests and gave us a deeper sense of the nature which surrounded us. We preserved the history and stories of our ancestors who were related to and part of the Arawak people. Our ancestors had arrived from a great southern land and sailed from Guiana, the land of many waters and some of our ancestors arrived from the great landmass from the west.

I was excited because I would soon depart our island of Ayiti for the first time with my father and over a hundred other men east to the island of Boriken. My brother Amayao would remain with my mother during my travel. Our chiefdom of Jaragua was ruled by the powerful Cacique Bohechio and his main wife Yanuba, who ruled mainly from a region called Laguana. Cacique Bohechio ruled Jaragua, which was further divided into twenty-six nitainos. Cacique Bohechio's sister was the beautiful Golden Flower named Anacaona, who was recently married to Cacique Caonabo of the neighboring cacicazgo of Maguana. The unity of Bohechio and Caonabo strengthened our position on our island and led to a peaceful society. Our upcoming expedition, designed to bring greater unity within our island and others, delighted our cacique and our people. I was excited to embark east towards Maguana and then to the island of Boriken. I never expected how my life would change soon after.

CHAPTER 2
A GOLDEN FLOWER ON THE JOURNEY TO HIGÜEY

Amanex travelled east with the men and women, enjoying the sights and sounds of his beautiful island. They had reached Maguana, where they were expected to meet with Cacique Caonabo. The land was alive with the sounds, aromas, and motions of life. The expedition was a pleasurable experience for the young Amanex; he enjoyed meeting new people and visiting the villages each with their own sub-chiefs who ruled in place of their cacique. Every village was aware of the men and women undertaking their mission of goodwill and diplomacy and they welcomed the group with abundant food and sometimes jewelry. The evenings were filled with dancing and ceremonies called areyto. When someone fell sick, the local shamans (called bohuti) would purge them and cure them of their ailment.

Maguana was divided into twenty-one nitainos and the main mother goddess of this region was Apito, meaning the Mother of Stone. Cacique Caonabo was a powerful and famous leader and the young Amanex's excitement grew each passing day.

The beautiful Anacaona had married Caonabo just several months earlier in an elaborate celebration. Thousands of people came to see the beautiful and beloved

Anacaona marry their great cacique Caonabo. Anacaona was respected for her intelligence, grace, bravery, and beauty. Her deep brown skin glistened in the island sun and her dark hair flowed majestically in the wind. Her eyes were dark and deep when she was in her endless thoughts but sharp when dealing with the matters of society. Anacaona was near her seventeenth birthday and was trained from a young age to become a leader of her people. Anacaona's wisdom far surpassed her age and manifested itself in her leadership and creativity.

Anacaona had numerous suitors but she chose Caonabo, who she viewed as powerful, intelligent, and a man of principle. Caonabo would be a great husband and father to their children and Jaragua would be left to the sole leadership of her brother Cacique Bohechio. The wedding was large and celebrated among the people and all the minor chiefs in the land. There were thousands of dancers moving to the rhythms of hollowed out and dried fruit from the Higuera Tree, filled with pebbles and beans with a wooden handle called maracas, elongated, notched hollowed out gourds called guiras, drums made from thin wood and measuring up to a meter long and half a meter wide called Mayohavau, and the soothing sounds of wind instruments made from conch shells. The areyto informed the people of their shared history, their spiritual beliefs, and the celebration of the union of Caonabo and Anacaona. The people marveled at Anacaona's beauty and in the manifestation of her intelligence through her creativity as a song and poem composer. She captivated crowds with her compositions and through the tongues of her numerous admirers, her name travelled throughout the islands.

Amanex was thinking of the wedding ceremony and the large ceremonies as they approached the largest yucayeque or village he had ever seen. It was the seat of power of Cacique Caonabo and Anacaona, containing many thousands of people. The large group decided to stay the night at a local village before arriving at Cacique Caonabo's yucayeque. Amanex's mind swirled as night set in and he gazed at the stars in the island night, while a nice wind brushed across his body and put him at ease. Amanex's father Maraguay was nearby, conversing with the other men about their journey and their upcoming trip to Boriken. After a brief conversation with some of the men, Maraguay went over to his son, who lay pensive on the ground.

Maraguay curiously asked, "What thoughts wander in your mind, my son?"

Amanex replied, "I feel nervous, Father, as I have never been in the company of people of such high esteem and importance."

Maraguay comforted his son, explaining that the people were a reflection of their leader and leaders were a reflection of the people they led. If the leader was not of good character and wisdom they could not maintain leadership of a great people. Maraguay explained that all beings and all animals and plants had an important place and all served each other in life. As the men and women went to sleep Maraguay offered Amanex his hammock and observed his son fall asleep.

As the sun began to rise on the distant horizon, the men and women resumed their journey. Today would be the day they would all meet Cacique Caonabo, Caonabo's brother Manicaotex, and Anacaona. Amanex was slightly anxious as he gazed in awe at the many thousands of people greeting them now. The music filled the air long before Amanex reached Caonabo's seat of power. Thousands of dancers greeted the men and women as Amanex caught a glimpse of Cacique Caonabo alongside Anacaona. An elaborate ceremony was planned, extra food and jewelry was to be given to the travelers, and builders improved the canoes to allow an easier trip across the waters. Manicaotex approached the men as they entered the main batey, as they all observed his large muscular frame and determination. Amanex marveled at the large size of the rectangular court which previously held many of the famous ceremonies that fueled excitement and intrigue on the island.

Caonabo's house was large and was flanked by his family members and priests. There were numerous zemis depicting the various Gods. This was the first time the young Amanex, himself named after a cacique, was in the presence of a powerful cacique. Caonabo sat on a polished large wooden seat carved from the Guayacan Tree called a duho. The duho was decorated with many designs and was curved upwards in the figure of a naked man on all fours. Gold was shaped and placed on the wooden duho, a symbol of the cacique's power, making it glisten in the morning sun. Caonabo was just a few inches shy of six feet in height with a strong muscular body. His skin was dark brown and his eyes were focused and appeared like the night sky. Anacaona approached her husband, causing the music and dancing to increase with her appearance. Anacaona was indeed beautiful with long flowing black hair, bronze skin, and rich brown majestic eyes. She was adorned in gold piercings and a beautiful necklace made from gold, polished stones, and sea shells. She had a slender waist with strong legs and arms and a purpose to her stride. Anacaona surpassed her famed beauty when she was witnessed with one's own eyes and her empathy and kindness made her the favorite wife of Caonabo. The music and dancing stopped as Caonabo arose from his seat to address the crowd.

Caonabo's voiced pierced through the air as his people listened with much anticipation. "Welcome, my people. Let us host our esteemed travelers representing my wife's brother Cacique Bohechio. My marriage to Anacaona has solidified the unity between my territory of Maguana and the territory of Jaragua. Maguana is the center of this land and represents our Goddess Apito, the Mother of Stone. We have united with Jaragua and their mother Goddess Zuimaco to create a stronger, longer lasting union between our people. These men and women will travel east to Higüey and meet Cacique Cayacoa and this expedition will strengthen our bond with their land and their Goddess Atabeira, the mother of the Original Stone. Our guests from Jaragua will help fulfill our plans for unity not only in our land but in our island neighbor Boriken to the east. These travelers will visit a few of the major leaders in the island of Boriken, including Aymamón, Urayoán, and Cacique Agüeybaná. We will strengthen our relationships and bring harmony to our lands and provide a better future for our children."

Anacaona listened to her husband speak and addressed the audience once he had concluded his opening remarks. "I am proud to be the new wife of your courageous leader and I am proud to host our guests from my brother Bohechio's territory. We have strengthened the bonds between our people and we will seek to bring our land and the other islands together and create an example of a good society and a peaceful coexistence."

Anacaona was known for her creativity manifesting in a series of poems and songs crafted from her thoughts; Amanex was excited to witness Anacaona's ballads in person. Anacaona began to lead an areyto, displaying her lovely words and voice. Many of the minor chiefs were in attendance, smoking and drinking fermented corn beer called chicha.

The region northeast of the island was called Magua and was led by Cacique Guarionex; it was divided into twenty-one nitainos. The people of Magua were inhabited originally by Ciguayos, who spoke another language, and the Macorix people, who spoke a language similar to the Ciguayo people, although they were mostly absorbed by Arawaks who arrived later. Caonabo wished to solidify a relationship with Guarionex due to the growing tensions with Cacique Guacanagaríx. He led the region called Marien, which was divided into fourteen nitainos and located in the northwestern region of Ayiti. Cacique Guacanagarix ruled from Guarico and his land was represented by the mother Goddess Lermao, meaning Body Stone. He was challenged by various chiefs from the region of Mairena. It was believed that Caonabo was supporting rivals to the rule of Guacanagarix, however, the young Amanex was not interested in politics. Caonabo did not mention Guacanagarix in his speech, focusing on his general objectives of forming stronger alliances and maintaining the peaceful harmony which was a way of life for his people.

The tekina was the leader of the areyto who followed Anacaona in leading the dancing and music which would continue for several days. Maracas, drums, conch shell horns, and other instruments were used along with call and response songs helping to welcome everyone involved in the celebrations. Tubers such as cassava and sweet potato were harvested from numerous large conucos belonging to Caonabo, and fruits like pineapples, guava, and palm nuts were also harvested from the surrounding tress. The conucos were raised roughly three feet above the ground and were routinely irrigated. The crops in the conucos were planted with a coa or wooden hoe. Maiz (corn) was also planted in simple fields created with slash and burn techniques.

The men brought back meat from hunting and fishing before and during the celebrations; Caonabo also had large of amounts of live animals in captivity. Various lizards, hutias, birds, manatees, snappers, iguanas, along with mussels and oysters from the mangroves were all prepared with chili peppers and other spices. Fish were caught using lines hooked to suckerfish or remora fish and attached to the canoa. The suckerfish would attach itself to larger fish and sea turtles, then the men would dive into the water and catch their prey. Sometimes men would shred the poisonous stems and roots of the senna shrub and toss them into streams and rivers, which would stun the fish who consumed it. The fish remained edible and would be gathered and cooked high over a fire on top of a wooden grate in a process called barbacoa (barbeque).

The celebrations continued for several days and games were initiated in the large batey using teams of up to thirty players each. The objective was to bounce the ball using the shoulder, elbow, head, buttock, the hips, or knees—never with hands—into the opponent's area. If the ball failed to be returned and came to rest, or if the ball travelled out of bounds, the opposing team would earn a point. The boundaries of the rectangular batey were lined with large stones with petroglyphs representing various gods. Games were won or lost based on the first team to reach a pre-determined score. Games were set up with competition between males against females, young against old, married against the unmarried, and other teams created based on the level of skill of the participants. People would wager on the outcome of these games with the highest bets placed on the higher skilled matches.

Amanex participated in some of the games with the other children while his father conversed and inhaled the smoke from burning plant leaves called kohiba, which were inserted in various tabako Y-shaped pipes and inhaled sometimes mixed with another plant. The leaves in the pipe was called tabako and was widely enjoyed while the sick would sometimes smell or rub the powdered or cut green leaves inside their mouth to relieve colds and headaches. The men enjoyed the smoke which they also used for religious rituals. The grounded leaf power called Kohoba was also snorted during religious rituals.

The men and women were in good spirits and Amanex was excited to have seen and heard from Cacique Caonabo and Anacaona. Amanex was also excited for what would be his first time leaving the island of Ayiti and meeting the people of Boriken. The next day they would continue their trip to Higüey.

In the morning, a large gathering took place awaiting Cacique Caonabo and Anacaona, who would send off the travelers with presents and well wishes. Caonabo provided some food for the ongoing journey and presented the travelers with gifts and jewelry. Amanex received a necklace made of gold and polished colorful stones ranging in color from light blue to dark blue that he often saw in his birthplace in Jaragua. There was a small celebration as the travelers began their journey east to Higüey.

The Caicimu-Higüey people lived in the easternmost portion of the island where the sun and its rays illuminated first upon the island. Higüey was the land where the sun originated and later spread throughout the rest of Ayiti. Amanex was excited to see the people of Higüey, their main leader Cacique Cayacoa, and their other leaders including Cotubanamá and their female leader Cacica Iguanamá. Maraguay had informed his son about these lands and their leaders and now Amanex would see them and hear them speak. The lands of Higüey were beautiful and the people were happy and loyal towards their Cacique Cayacoa. Higüey was divided into twenty-one nitainos, each ruled by respected leaders. The land was lush and green and the sound of the birds filled the air as Amanex and his father made their way towards the seat of power of Cacique Cayacoa. After several days of travel, they were met by Cacique Cayacoa, who welcomed them with music and food. These celebrations would last a few days, after which they would travel southeast and leave the island of Ayiti towards a smaller island and travel by canoe towards another small island before landing on Boriken. Cacique Cayacoa also planned to travel north towards Anamuya to meet with his family members and other regional leaders for a religious gathering and celebration honoring Goddess Atabeira.

Amanex noticed that some of the people in Higüey spoke a different language and his father informed him that they were part of the Macorix people who might have been visiting Cacique Cayacoa. Cayacoa was a strong and intelligent man who was delighted to host his new guests due to the importance of the expedition. Cayacoa also wished to send gifts and various messages to the leaders of Boriken to solidify his own relationships within the island of Boriken. He had already solidified his relationships within the eastern regions of Ayiti and had sought to strengthen his bonds with Caonabo and establish his region as a more efficient trade route between Cuba, Western Ayiti, and Boriken to the east.

After several days of celebration, Amanex and his father continued towards the southeast along with over 100 men and women towards the coastline, where they would meet the leader named Cotubanamá. The season of the violent rains and winds was almost to an end and now it was a relatively mild season. Perhaps Goddess Guabancex was pleased and did not wish to unleash her power manifested in the juracan or hurricane. Although the weather had been calm, Cotubanamá and the travelers would plan a cohoba ceremony to appease Goddess Guabancex. The travelers would leave the island of Ayiti and arrive to the small island of Adamanay before leaving in the large canoas towards the island of Boriken.

CHAPTER 3
BORIKEN, THE LAND OF THE VALIANT AND NOBLE LORD (DECEMBER 1491)

Cotubanamá's priest led a Cohoba Ceremony in efforts to provide the expedition a safe sea voyage. Seeds from cojobana trees were gathered, crushed, and burned along with some other plants to create an altered state for those who consumed it. It also helped them connect with the gods including the Goddess Guabancex, who the travelers wished to appease. Members of the group danced and sang for the favor of the gods and their ancestors who were physically manifested by large and small zemis crafted from wood, sandstone, clay, and stone that stood near the shoreline as they participated in their ceremony. Many of the zemis were shaped in the form of men and women, while some were animals including lizards, birds, and snakes.

As night embraced them, Amanex spoke to his father about the people of Boriken, the other small islands south of Boriken, and the people which inhabited them. These people were known as the Kalinago and were respected for their abilities in combat and trade. Amanex was taught that these Kalinago people came from a different region in the same large land in the south. The Kalinago came to occupy the smaller islands, merging their own culture with the previous inhabitants. They were fierce combatants, however they generally coexisted with their neighbors and Amanex and his people never experienced prolonged warfare from the Kalinago people. Usually rivals would settle their disputes through the judicial process in the batey and casualties were rare. Still, Amanex felt a little anxiety about the new people he might encounter along the way. As the night set in and the moon shone bright on the beach, the ceremonies ended. In the morning, they would prepare their canoes and begin their voyage into the open sea.

The sun was beginning to rise as travelers gathered in their large canoes and started the initial voyage a short distance south towards the island of Adamanay. The trip towards Adamanay was brief and they used this stop to relieve themselves and relax. Cotubanamá also travelled along to reach Adamanay to speak with the people there. It was during their short stay that Cotubanamá decided it was also in his best interest to visit Boriken and meet their caciques in person. Cacique Cotubanamá spoke with a young intelligent woman named Iguanamá who was being groomed to become a leader in Higüey. Cotubanamá encouraged her to take the journey to Boriken as well and she agreed. When the winds calmed the sea, two large canoes and one smaller canoe, carrying Cotubanamá and Iguanamá, set sail towards the middle island Amona.

The sea was still and the journey proved to be easy and swift and they quickly arrived at the small island of Amona. The people welcomed the expedition and were excited that Cotubanamá and Iguanamá were among the voyagers. Cotubanamá decided it was best to stay in Amona and postpone the journey for one night to enjoy the festivities and then depart east in the morning. Some of the men began fishing at the beach. The fish swam in shallow water and the ripples they made combined with the light from the moon made them easy to catch. Amanex marveled at the size of the iguanas on the island of Amona—some seemed half as large as him. Amanex stared at the night sky, remembering the tales of the gods and how they created the world and his people. The night was cool as it always was at this time of year and in the distance Amanex could hear the conversations of the men and women. A cool breeze brushed across Amanex's face as he climbed into a hammock provided by the local villagers and he began to think about Boriken. As Amanex drifted to sleep he thought about the gods and the stories Maraguay and the elders would tell.

The spirit of the ancestors and the power of the gods were all around, manifested in the natural elements and energies of the world. The two supreme gods were Yúcahu and Atabey. Yúcahu meant the spirit of cassava, and was the god of cassava and the sea. Atabey, who was the mother of Yúcahu, was the goddess of fresh waters and fertility. The cassava was important in the diet of the people of these islands and cassava and Baibrama aided its growth. Boinayel, the god of rain, had a twin brother Márohu, who was the god of fair weather. Guabancex was the goddess of hurricanes and she was aided by Guataubá, a messenger who created hurricane winds, and Coatrisquie who created floodwaters. Maketaori Guayaba was god of Coaybay, the land of the dead. God Opiyelguabirán was the guardian of the underworld who watched over the dead. Opiyelguabiran appeared slender and humanoid, but rested on all four limbs. The hero Deminán Caracaracol was admired by the Tainos and believed to be the ancestor from which all people descended. Macocael was worshiped as a god and had failed to guard the mountain from which human beings arose. These were the stories passed down through conversation and songs during celebrations in the batey.

Amanex was awakened by his father early the next day and the people set off for the western coast of Boriken right before the sun began to rise on the horizon. The water was calm and Amanex enjoyed dipping his hands in it while the canoa picked up speed. Everyone paddled as the large canoas cut through the air at a faster rate. Amanex's focus changed from the deep sea to the stories his father often spoke of. Amanex thought about Goddess Itiba

Cahubaba and her four children, including Deminán Caracaracol. To create the sea, the fish, the islands, its people and their procreation, the sacred four disturbed the secrets of the Yayá, the Original Spirit. Yayá would become Yúcahu Bagua Maórocoti, the elemental beginning of existence, the life-giving spirit, and the son of Goddess Atabey. Yucahu's son Yayael was expelled for several months due to his plot to kill his father Yúcahu. Yayael later returned but was killed by his father. Yúcahu placed his son's bones in a calabash, which later became fish and water. Deminán later broke the calabash, creating a large deluge that formed the sea.

Deminán Caracaracol later passed by his grandfather's home, the God of fire and shaman Bayamanaco. Deminán noticed Bayamaco carrying cassava and although Deminán and his brothers ate fish, their hunger remained unsatisfied and so Deminán attempted to steal Bayamanaco's cassava. Bayamanaco shot snot laced with Cohoba towards Deminan's back as he attempted to flee, causing his skin to swell. Later, Deminán's brother would remove a female turtle from his scarred back named Caguama. The four brothers married the turtle and their offspring were humans. The Goddess Caguama gave birth to the people and was respected as the creator mother turtle.

Amanex understood life was about balance and respect for the gods and goddesses who acted upon the world through nature. God Yúcahu Bagua Maórocoti was born directly from the Goddess Atabey without a father—a fact referenced by his last name Maórocoti It was important to appease God Yúcahu as well as the feared God Maboyas, who was nocturnal and destroyed crops. Elaborate sacrifices were made in an effort to placate him. Goddess Atabey left her two sons Yúcahu and Guacar to control the affairs of the world.

Yúcahu infused energy and life into the world, becoming the architect of the earth. The gods Boinael and Maroya later arose; Boinael controlled the sun and Maroya controlled the moon, illuminating the New World day and night and saving it from perpetual darkness. Yúcahu later roamed the earth, finding four gemstones which he made into four celestial bodies named Racuno, Sobaco, Achinao and Coromo, who reproduced and spread throughout the universe and later served to aid the deities. God Guacar, in a fit of jealousy, hid in the heavens and was never to be seen again. Yúcahu continued his work creating animals, teaching them how to live, and providing shelter for them. Yúcahu had a revelation informing him that another being that was not an animal or deity should complete his creation, and that being was the first man named Locuo. Yúcahu opened the heavens, created Locuo, and gave him the energy of life. He provided Locuo with a soul and then left the earth in the guidance of mankind.

Yúcahu rose to his residence high above the land on a mountain named Yuké. Yuké was located towards the eastern side of the island of Boriken; it was called the White Lands because of the thick white clouds surrounding the mountain. Amanex's excitement grew as he thought of visiting Yuké in the region of Yukiyu, where the God Yúcahu lived. Maraguay asked his son to help paddle and to prepare for landing as Amanex suddenly noticed the shores of Boriken approaching.

The shoreline was full of people celebrating the arrival of the people from Ayiti. The beach had black sands with calm waves; the weather was mild and the heavens were without clouds. They stepped out into the cool waters and on the land of Boriken and the Yucayeque of Yagueca. The territory of Yagueca was led by Cacique Urayoán on the western coast. It was bordered by the region of Aymamón, led by Cacique Aymaco of the north. To the south of Yagueca lay the region of Guaynia, led by the most powerful and respected leader named The Great Sun, Cacique Agüeybaná. Cacique Agüeybaná was the main leader representing the island of Boriken and highly respected by the people. The island had over twenty major leaders and Cotubanamá desired to meet with some of them—mainly Cacique Agüeybaná.

Cotubanamá and lguanamá arrived soon after in the second large canoe alongside the first. After a small celebration was held, Cotubanamá and Iguanamá asked for Cacique Urayoán, who was not far from the beach. The young boys caught fish and the food was barbequed. Amanex was happy to see the festive people of Boriken with their deep bronze skin and dark hair. The girls were all attractive in their own ways, playing among themselves or helping their mothers clean or prepare meals for the upcoming festivities.

Amanex was struck by the beauty of the island and its lush rainforests. He loved the pleasant weather and the sounds of the parrots and other birds circling the skies. As the sun began to set, the weather cooled, sending a chill to his skin. The children caught crabs near the beach and brought the fish back to a nearby village not far from the shoreline where Cacique Urayoán had recently arrived to welcome the travelers. Cotubanamá and Iguanamá led the travelers towards a large village filled with several thousand people. There they were welcomed by Cacique Urayoan. Urayoan was a man who was highly respected and had a close alliance with Cacique Agüeybaná. The women of the yucayeque provided a large feast as Cacique Urayoan addressed his guests.

Urayoan was a young man of medium build who spent his time hunting and in discourse revolving around policies to improve the lives of his people, nature, and the purpose of things. "I welcome Cacique Cotubanamá and Iguanamá on behalf of the people of Higüey and the Cacique Bohechio and his sister Anacaona, who I have been informed was recently married to Cacique Caonabo of Maguana. They also represent our people of the island of Ayiti, a large glorious land of the largest mountain peaks. They have made their journey to promote goodwill among our people and to form a stronger union between all of the islands. We are all one people and our customs have brought about knowledge, respect of the nature which surrounds us, and respect for one another. We all live in peace and our disputes are settled swiftly. We have been provided these islands and the fruits and animals that provide us with nourishment and for that we thank our ancestors and the gods which guide us. In the following days, other caciques, including Cacique Agüeybaná, will be joining us and our guests in celebrations."

The people were overjoyed and the young Amanex was excited at the chance to possibly meet the Great Sun, Cacique Agüeybaná.

Amanex and a few of the children sat and ate crab around a fire, listening to the sounds of the island as darkness enveloped the land. Through the silence, Amanex heard a sound he never heard before, a sharpness piercing the silence. *Co-qui, co-qui.* Amanex then heard other similar sounds surrounding him, and his surprised expression caused the children of Boriken to laugh. They led Amanex to the source of the noise and to his amazement, the sound was produced by a small maco—a greyish brown frog—sitting on a tree leaf. The male frogs were in the middle of their mating songs, interrupting the silence between conversations. Amanex and the other boys decided to go to the beach and bathe themselves after their meal. Amanex enjoyed his new friends and anticipated the upcoming day as he laughed and played at the beach under the comforting moonlight which bathed the surface of the water.

The next day began early as thousands began to arrive on the western coast of Boriken. Many chiefs met their guests from Ayiti and the young leaders Cotubanamá and Iguanamá. Various caciques arrived at Yagueca, including Cacique Aymamón of Aymaco and Cacique Hayuya, with more leaders set to arrive later. Amanex and the other children were excited to see so them. Each cacique greeted Cacique Cotubanamá and the young leader Iguanamá as the representatives of Ayiti. The chiefs of Boriken spoke well of Cacique Caonabo and Cacique Bohechio and sent their best wishes to Anacaona and the chiefs of Ayiti.

Cacique Hayuya was a strong intelligent leader who was thirty-one years of age and brought many of his family members and friends along with him. The leaders were anxious to meet with The Great Sun Cacique Agüeybaná. He arrived later in the evening accompanied by his family, including his brother Güeybaná and his eleven-year-old cousin Arasibo. There were also members of his family who were not yet leaders but would soon become them. Amanex and his father were excited to see Cacique Agüeybaná, who was respected throughout the island of Boriken. The festivities were now complete.

Agüeybaná was an impressive figure and Amanex was inspired by Agüeybaná in the fashion in which he led his people. Amanex participated in the games in the batey. He surprised himself at how well he played in leading his teams towards several victories, which caught the attention of many people, including Agüeybaná's younger brother Güeybaná.

The leader approached Amanex after one of the games, stating "You have a fighting spirit and love for this game. You play it with a level of skill above that of your peers. Perhaps you should play with older boys and showcase your skills at a higher level."

Güeybaná asked Amanex about his life in Ayiti and his opinion regarding his first visit to Boriken and Amanex responded with enthusiasm, confirming his love for the people and Boriken. Güeybaná presented Amanex with a necklace made from sea shells, polished stones, and gold. Amanex was honored to receive a gift from one of the major leaders.

After embracing Cotubanamá and Iguanamá, Cacique Agüeybaná addressed the crowd. "My spirit is filled with joy as I welcome my guests from Ayiti to our beautiful island of Boriken. I wish to extend my greetings to all the caciques of Ayiti and I plan to visit Ayiti, Xaymaca, and Cuba. Our people throughout these islands share a common bond and peace bestowed upon us by our gods and our respect for nature and one another. We have been blessed by our Goddess Atabey and our creator, God Yúcahu Bagua Maórocoti who resides at the Yuké Peak on the eastern end of our island of Boriken. Let us seek to solidify our relationships between the islands of Ayiti and Boriken and the other islands in our great sea. Let us live together in peace and bring peace to all people from the smaller islands to Cuba and farther north where the Lucayan people live."

Amanex also desired to visit the other islands, including Xaymaca, the birthplace of his mother Ana, and the island of Cuba, where fertile land was abundant. Amanex's thirst for travel increased after his visit to Boriken and he asked his father if they could visit the home of God Yúcahu at Yuké Peak. Maraguay however, decided they would save a trip to Yuké Peak for a later time and return to Ayiti. Some of the travelers would remain in Boriken while most decided to return to Ayiti along with Cotubanamá and Iguanamá. Cacique Agüeybaná, Cacique Urayoan, and Cacique Aymamón led the celebrations and later they asked the gods to give their guests a safe return to Ayiti. It was of vital importance that travelers respected Goddess Guabancex and the huracán when sailing between islands, a respect that was taught to the islanders from a young age.

The huracán was the violent storm that brought devastating winds caused by Goddess Guabancex. Guabancex was entrusted to Aumatex, the ruler of a mystical land, making him cacique of the wind. Aumatex would fail to appease Goddess Guabancex, who escaped to wreak havoc on the seas and land. Guabancex, the goddess of hurricanes, was aided by Guataubá, a messenger who created the powerful winds, lightning, and thunder as well as Coatrisquie, who created floodwaters. Caorao was a deity that was also related to storms that could summon them by playing a sea shell instrument called a cobo. These deities would arrive from beyond the eastern coast of Boriken and would clash with the mighty God Yúcahu Bagua Maórocoti on their westward travel. Guataubá would cover the sky with clouds, warning the people of the potential arrival of devastating storms that brought flooding, powerful winds, and rains. Food was offered and ceremonies were held to appease Guabancex as Amanex and his father prepared for their return voyage to the island of Ayiti. The fury of Guabancex was feared and respected but this did not prevent a mightier force that would soon arrive. An arrival that would change the lives of Amanex and his people forever.

CHAPTER 4
IN THE FOOTSTEPS OF MARCO POLO
(CHRISTMAS EVENING 1492)

The impact was sudden and devastating. The Great Admiral of The Ocean—the title he had requested for himself—had been awake for two days, finally succumbing to deep slumber. The Santa María de la Inmaculada Concepción (the Santa Maria of the Immaculate Conception) had wrecked on the northern coast of the island of Ayiti. The owner of the Flagship Santa Maria was Juan de la Cosa and the other two ships were the Santa Clara—nicknamed La Niña in Spanish or the little girl after its owner Juan Niño—and the smallest was called La Pinta (the painted in Spanish). The admiral had fallen asleep the night of Christmas Eve, leaving the steersman in charge of the ship. The night was calm and the steersman left a boy in charge of steering the Santa Maria—a practice that was strictly forbidden by the admiral.

"Cristóbal! Cristóbal!" the crewmen yelled, awakening the admiral as the Santa Maria crashed into a sandbank. The admiral was now accustomed to the Spanish version of his name Cristóbal Colón, although he preferred his Italian name Cristoforo Colombo. The English called him Christopher Colombus and he believed his name would become well known throughout Europe upon his return.

Efforts to save the Santa Maria were unsuccessful and Cristóbal decided to salvage his flagship for wood. In a display for the natives, he ordered his men to fire upon the Santa Maria after most of the wood was salvaged, leaving the remainder to sink into the sea. Cristobal captained the Santa Maria, a beautiful ship with three masts, the Pinta was captained by Martín Alonso Pinzón, and his brother Francisco Martín Pinzón was the first mate of the Pinta. The Niña was captained by Martin's youngest brother Vicente Yañez Pinzón. Cristóbal remembered the excitement and anxiety as he set sail from Spain on the third of August and subsequently re-stocked on the Canary Islands, departing on the sixth of September. Cristóbal promised a reward for the first man to see land and on October twelfth, Rodrigo de Triana, a sailor aboard the Pinta, alerted everyone that he had spotted some. Cristóbal later stated he saw a light or aura originating from the landmass before Rodrigo caught sight of land, lying and denying Rodrigo his reward.

Cristóbal was the admiral and first governor of the Indies. He was promised to receive ten percent of all revenue from all new lands claimed for Spain. His pursuit of a western route to the Ming Empire of China led him to various European kingdoms in search for a patron to fund his voyage. King Fernando II of Aragon and his wife, Queen Isabella I of Castile, eventually funded Cristóbal's voyage. Many of the Castilians secretly disliked him and resented that Cristóbal, who was from the Republic of Genoa, would seize the glories and riches of these lands for himself.

The decline of the Roman Empire led to a division into two regions: the eastern and Western Roman Empire. The expansion of the Roman Empire, the subsequent economic decline, and the ineffectiveness of rule from Rome led to civil wars and invasions from tribes of the north. The northern tribes—referred to as barbarians by the Romans—eventually overwhelmed the western side of the empire. Constantine the Great was granted the title of Augustus after the death of his father, Emperor Constantius

Chlorus. Constantine faced various challenges to his authority and defeated several rebellions—most notably the civil wars against Maxentius and Licinius, who controlled the Balkans. Constantine and Licinius had previously met to create the Edicts of Milan, allowing people the freedom to practice Christianity without fear of prosecution, following the previous Edict of Toleration by Galerius which stopped Christian persecution in 311A.D. Licinius reneged on the Edict of Milan in 313A.D., leading to civil war and an eventual victory by Constantine, who legalized Christianity and made Constantinople the new capital Under Emperor Theodosius I.

Hundreds of years afterwards, the Western Roman Empire fell, paving the way to the Kingdom of the Visigoths, the Kingdom of Gallæcia, the Britons, Anglo Saxons, the Ostrogoths, Frisians, and various other kingdoms. The Eastern Roman Empire became the Byzantine Empire until it fell to the Islamic Ottoman Empire in 1453. Western Europe began forming into the Kingdom of Aragon, Kingdom of Castile, Kingdom of Portugal, Kingdom of France, Kingdom of England, Kingdom of Ireland, and others. At the heart of Rome, republics formed, including the Republic of Venice, where Marco Polo lived for some time after his birth in 1254. Marco Polo's father Niccolò and his uncle Maffeo travelled to China and met the Great Khan Kublai Khan. Kublai Khan had extended the Mongol territory of his Grandfather Ghengis Khan into China, establishing the Yuan Dynasty. Niccolò and his brother Maffeo were merchants who established trading posts in Constantinople, Sudak in Crimea, and in the Western Mongolian Empire. Niccolò and Maffeo enjoyed diplomatic immunity and tax relief in the Roman and Catholic controlled capital of Constantinople created by leaders of the Fourth Crusade. Later, the brothers relocated to Soldaia, a city in Crimea, after the Greek Orthodox Emperor Michael VIII Palaiologos of the Empire of Nicaea Constantinople reconquered Constantinople from the former Romanian Emperors and restored the eastern Roman Empire.

Marco Polo's father and uncle returned in 1269 and met the young Marco Polo for the first time. At seventeen years of age, Marco Polo, his father, and his uncle departed through the ancient Silk Road once again in 1271. Marco Polo travelled through the lands of the Middle East and Central Asia, arriving at Kublai Khan's Summer Palace at Shangdu in 1275, spending time in the court and lands of Kublai Khan working as a tax collector for the Great Khan. After many years, the Polos were instructed to escort a young princess to her intended husband Arghun, the Mongol ruler of Persia. Arghun was deceased upon the arrival of the Polos and the princess married Arghun's son. Marco Polo returned to Venice in 1295—a year after Kublai Khan's death—but was imprisoned by Venice's rival Genoa.

In prison, Marco Polo dictated his travels to the writer Rustichello of Pisa, creating the manuscript called *Description of the World.* A Genoese-Venetian peace treaty in 1299 allowed Marco Polo to return home to Venice and later marry Doñata Badoer and have three daughters. Marco Polo died in January of 1324, but his travels would live on through his book and in the mind of young explorers. The travels of Marco Polo influenced many explorers and Cristóbal was no exception. He carried Marco Polo's book with him as he travelled westward, determined to find an alternate route to Ming China. Marco Polo's travels and biography deeply impacted Cristóbal and he desired for adventure and prestige and was willing to endure hardships to reach his goals of discovery, wealth, and fame.

Cristóbal Colón read about Marco Polo's travels as a child and the various descriptions of the wild animals, people, and culture found in foreign lands. Marco Polo described Kublai Khan and his palaces, paper money, coal, the postal service, eyeglasses and other inventions, and systems not yet found in Europe. These stories help motivate Cristóbal and his brothers as they sought funding for their voyage. While other explorers had sought routes around the coast of Africa, Cristóbal proposed a western route towards Japan and China. Prince Henry the Navigator had convinced his father, King John I, to conquer the Moorish Port of Cueta, which often used as a base of operation for Barbary Pirates who raided the Portuguese coasts and enslaved numerous Portuguese and Europeans to be sold for services in the Ottoman Empire. Henry was fueled by his curiosity of Africa, his lust of gold, and the legend of the Christian King Prester John, who was believed to reside in India or the ancient land of Ethiopia. As Grandmaster of the Military Order of Knights—the successors of the Knights Templar—he received funding for his voyage to the African Coast.

The Ottoman Empire controlled the Silk Road and the Mediterranean routes after Mehmed the Conqueror gained control of the Byzantine Empire in 1453. The Sultanate of Rûm's defeat by the Mongols and the fall of the Mongol Empire left the Ottoman Empire as the main regional power. Many explorers sought fortunes and titles for themselves while Kings and Queens tried to establish empires through the acquisition of colonies in Africa and India. The Portuguese nobleman, Bartolomeu Dias, reached the southern tip of Africa and the Indian Ocean, further fueling other explorers including Vasco da Gama and Cristóbal Colón.

In 1485, Cristóbal travelled to the court of King John II of Portugal and requested three ships which he would use to travel west to reach China and India. Seeking one tenth of all revenue and the title of Admiral to the Seas, King John II and his advisors declined Cristóbal's request because they believed Cristóbal's estimated distance of 2,400 miles was far too short. Cristóbal approached King John II once again in 1488, but he was rejected as interest grew for the efforts of Bartolomeu Dias, who had reached the southern tip of Africa. Cristóbal appealed to Genoa and Venice, who rejected his idea, before he decided to send his brother Bartolomeo Colón to the court of King Henry VII of England who also rejected Cristóbal's idea. Bartolomeo then travelled to the court of Charles VIII in France, who would not hear of Cristóbal's proposal. Cristóbal's fortune would change when he met with Fernando II of Aragon and Isabella I of Castile, who had recently united the kingdoms of Spain.

Cristóbal was granted 12,000 maravedis and in 1489, he was given free food and lodging anywhere within the Spanish Kingdom and territories. Cristóbal was excited but still restless to embark on his voyage. 1492, Cristóbal was equipped with three ships and the command of a crew. Cristóbal remembered his excitement at the beginning of his voyage and the feeling of relief once land was spotted after crossing the ocean. His determination and hard work would allow him to access riches for himself, his family, and the Spanish Crown.

The Emirate of Granada in southern Spain was ruled by the Nasrid Dynasty, after the defeat of Caliph Muhammad al-Nasir who led the Almohad Caliphate by the hands of several Christian Iberian Kingdoms on July 1212. The threat of a Muslim invasion from Maghreb Northern Africa pushed Pope Innocent III to call on groups including the Order of Santiago, Order of Calatrava, and the Knights Templar to join the fight against the Moors. The Nasrid Dynasty began with Emir Mohammed I ibn Nasr in 1232 and was heavily financed by Genoese Bankers looking to gain a piece of the gold trade arriving from Sub Saharan Africa. Portugal's access to several African trade routes by sea coupled by political strife within Granada and the strengthening of the Reconquista led to the fall of the Nasrid Dynasty. In January of 1492 Muhammad XII, called Boabdil, surrendered Granada to the Kingdoms of Castile and Aragon. Cristóbal remembered the sight of Sultan Muhammad XII and his wife Sultana Maryam bint Ibrahim al-athar as they led a procession consisting of almost 100 people on horseback and the royal Spanish banners were placed on the towers of Alhambra in Granada. It was a powerful moment for Cristóbal and for Spain, a kingdom that now looked to establish an empire.

Cristóbal made a moderate effort to conceal his origins and personal beliefs, adopting and championing the Catholic faith and the glory of the united kingdoms of Spain. Cristóbal chose to keep his close association with Judaism and he did not speak of family members believed by some to be Jews. Cristóbal's efforts were to attain titles and wealth for him and his family and he sought to create opportunities for his brothers and his eldest and only son Diego Colón along with his Portuguese wife Filipa Moniz Perestrelo.

Cristóbal married Filipa in 1479—a marriage that produced Diego. Filipa died suddenly in 1484 at the age of twenty-eight; it was a death that pained Columbus and he would sometimes ponder how she would miss his newfound success in obtaining financial support for his voyage west towards China and India. Cristóbal was now enjoying his new opportunity with Diego, his Spaniard companion Beatriz Enríquez de Arana, and their young four-year-old child Fernando Colón. The year was 1492 when the forty-one-year-old Cristóbal departed Palos de la Frontera, Spain on August 3 for the Canary Islands, leaving his twenty-five-year-old companion Beatriz, his brothers Bartolomeo, Giovanni Pellegrino, Giacomo, and his sister Bianchinetta on his voyage west. Diego was made into a page of the Spanish Court before his father departed.

On August sixth, the rudder on the Pinta broke and was later repaired in the Canary Islands; the lateen sails of the Niña were also refitted to square sails. Martin Pinzon could sail the Pinta despite its broken rudder. The owners of the ship, Gomez Rascon and Christoval Quintero, were suspected of sabotage—Cristóbal believed their ship had been forced into service against their will. Despite the setbacks, Cristóbal led his three ships and his men across the ocean while facing several conflicts amongst his crew. On one occasion, some of the least educated crewmembers began to panic as the needle on Cristóbal's compass shifted from the North Star. Cristóbal reassured the crew that the needle pointed towards another northern region on earth. He understood the reasons for the compass to point to the magnetic north as it had been established many centuries before in Europe and China. The Chinese had invented the magnetic compass over 200 years before the presumed birth of Jesus Christ and it had been in use as a navigational tool during the Song Dynasty during the eleventh century. This knowledge was available for men such as Cristóbal and he sometimes wondered about the numerous men who were uneducated about these facts and still believed in tales of monsters and other fantasies.

Cristóbal and his crew were reassured when they encountered a large flock of birds—a sign they were possibly near land. When Rodrigo de Triana claimed to have spotted land during the early night of October twelfth, Cristóbal made sure to state he indeed spotted land first in order to keep the 10,000 maravedís reward for himself. It was the first action among many others that would deepen the rift between Cristóbal and the men he intended to lead.

Upon landing on the beach, Cristóbal and his crew were overjoyed and their curiosity grew upon seeing many natives approach them. The Admiral Cristóbal landed in a smaller boat, which was armed, along with Martin Alonzo Pinzon, and Vicente Yáñez Pinzón his brother, the captain of the Nina. The Admiral bore the royal standard and the two captains each held a banner of the Green Cross, which all the ships carried. The standard contained the initials of the King and Queen on each side of the cross. Cristóbal pondered about his location and asked the natives of the island and was informed that it was called Guanahani and that it was just one of many islands in the region. Cristóbal's initial elation turned to confusion: the natives did not appear Japanese or Chinese. Perhaps he had miscalculated the distance to China and India. His confusion increased when the natives said they were Lukku-Cairi, meaning people of the islands. Cristóbal simply called them Lucayos or the Lucayan people and mentioned their similarity to the appearance of the Guanche people of the Canary Islands. The Lucayo people had brown skin that was the intermediate of the white skinned Europeans and the black color of the people of Africa.

Cristóbal was unsure of China's location and most importantly India, however he felt he was on some island nearby and believed the natives to be Indios and that they might be related to the mainland people of India. Cristóbal observed their short black hair and their slightly flattened heads. They were friendly and just as curious of their white skinned visitors as Cristóbal and his crew were of their brown skinned hosts. The languages spoken were foreign to Cristóbal as well as his translator Luis de Torres. Luis de Torres was a Jewish man who had converted to Catholicism and understood various languages including Hebrew, Aramaic, Arabic, and Portuguese. Luis was chosen by Cristóbal Colón to serve as his translator and a special bond formed between the two that other crew members didn't fully understand. Luis de Torres, also known as Yosef ben Levi Ha-Ivri to some, was a man who had proven his skills as the interpreter for the governor of Murcia in southeastern Spain. Cristóbal needed Luis' services because he desired to communicate with Jewish traders in Asia as well as the possibility of finding the ten lost tribes of Ancient Israel. However, after several days, Cristóbal and his crew never encountered any Jewish traders.

Cristóbal observed extensive trading and people arriving on ships of different sizes that the natives called canoas. Cristóbal carried the *Description of the World* and he often spoke with Luis and a few other Castilians regarding his interests in locating the Great Khan. Many of the natives shared their food with Cristóbal and his crew and gave them shelter. They tried to communicate with each other using hand signals and human touch; the Lucayans and the Castilians pointed to various objects and then identified them with a name in their respective languages. Cristóbal and his men were overjoyed and relieved at finding land and meeting their friendly hosts who provided them with food and relaxation. Even Luis de Torre, who was deeply angered regarding his recent conversion from Judaism to Catholicism and leaving his wife Catalina Sánchez in Spain, relished his experience. Cristóbal enjoyed his translator's first feelings of happiness since the beginning of the voyage.

Cristóbal met with a few of the leaders before he departed. He observed some of the native men inhaling smoke from dried leaves. Luis de Torre was unsuccessful in his communication with the natives despite his mastery of various languages and would spend most of his time engaging the natives in speech during their ceremonies. Cristóbal convinced some of the elders to let children travel with Cristóbal along with many adults. One young boy about the age of twelve named Guaikán joined Cristóbal. Guaikán was to be taught the Castilian (Spanish) language to help Cristóbal communicate and facilitate his goals in the region. Cristóbal began to write a journal to record everything he observed. He wrote of the many small and large bodies of water on several of the islands of Guanahani before he departed to the first island to the east on October fourteenth, which he named San Salvador. Separating the Pinta from the Niña and Santa Maria, Cristóbal covered a larger region in an effort to reach the larger island the natives had informed him about. Cristóbal named a second island Santa María de la Concepción, a third island he named Fernandina, and named a fourth Isabela. The island of Isabela was named Samoete by the natives. After a few days landing on a few islands, Cristóbal continued his travels, now changing directions towards south and southwest, visiting and observing islands that he named Islas de Arena, or Sand Islands. On October twenty eighth, Cristóbal and his crew landed on a large land, excited at the prospect of reaching a mainland peninsula which was an island that the natives called Cuba.

Juan de la Cosa, the owner of the Santa Maria, was busy making notes to craft an updated map for future reference. Cristóbal would keep a diary and assign others to aid in mapmaking and the documentation of the native people and their customs. Cristóbal was informed of two groups of people on the island of Cuba: the Ciboney and the Guanahatabey. Cristóbal learned that the Ciboney lived in small communities near the sea and that the Ciboney and Guanahatabey people had arrived long before. During the initial encounter with the natives, they observed the anxiety in the eyes of Cristóbal and his followers and stated they were men of good, or good people—the words were heard and translated to roughly Taino in the Castilian language. Guaikán and most of the natives belonged to the Arawak people that Cristóbal and his crew began identifying as the Taino. The Taino people and the earlier groups who spoke different languages coexisted and lived in peace as opposed to the endless wars Cristóbal Colón had witnessed throughout the European Kingdoms.

Cristóbal and his crew analyzed the Taino society and naturally compared it to their own. The Tainos decorated their bronze skin with dyes, including red which led to some of Cristóbal's men calling them "red skins". The men and women were healthy and even though they wore simple clothing and the young children walked naked, they were a beautiful people. They did not suffer from poverty and everything that came with it such as sickness and starvation. Cristóbal and his crew also observed that some Tainos wore more decorations than others: polished stones and sea shells worn as necklaces and belts. The land of Cuba had many caciques and they had even more ornamentations. Gold was one of the primary reasons for Cristóbal's voyage and his blood rushed with excitement as he saw it worn on the bodies of the Taino men, women, and even some children. The Taino were peaceful and seemed to be ignorant of European iron weaponry; a few natives cut themselves as they touched the sharpened blades. Perhaps they did not develop weaponry as deadly as the Europeans because they were not engaged in warfare to the deadly degree Cristóbal had observed throughout Europe. Cristóbal was somewhat surprised at their giving nature, even offering their gold when he requested it. He believed the Tainos could be forced into labor for the purposes of exploiting these lands.

"*Adonde estas el oro*?" Cristóbal asked as he pointed to the gold necklaces and other jewelry.

Some of the Tainos said, "*Caona? Caona?*"

Cristóbal responded, "*Si, el Oro*."

Some more gold was brought for Cristóbal. He was excited despite a growing rift between himself and Martin Alonzo Pinson. Martin Pinson had proposed several changes of direction for Cristóbal, and he initially followed some of them. However, when he ordered Martin to follow his recommended routes, Martin failed to follow. Martin had recently suggested a different voyage towards a land eastward and had encouraged Cristóbal to leave Cuba. Cristóbal was informed that the land of Cuba had roughly thirty regions governed by various caciques. He resumed his voyage, now travelling eastward on the northern coast of Cuba during the month of December.

A few days into the voyage, Cristóbal believed Martin disobeyed his orders when he learned that Martin and his ship separated the Santa Maria. When Cristóbal landed on an island the natives called Ayiti, a land of many mountains and many people, Martin—who had heavily funded Cristóbal's voyage and supplied Cristóbal with a considerable number of crewmen as well as his own personal ships the Niña and the Pinta—felt he deserved more influence in the direction of the voyages. The Santa Maria ran ashore after the ship crashed into reefs. Water began to flood Cristóbal's flagship and he gave up hope of saving it. Vicente Pinzon rushed to aid Admiral Cristóbal Colón and his crew as the Santa Maria began to sink.

Cristóbal and some of his crew were examined by the doctor of the Santa Maria, Juan Sanchez, after some of the crew suffered minor injuries. Most escaped the wreckage without being majorly hurt and Cristóbal decided to settle in northwest Ayiti. Cristóbal began speaking with some of his mates regarding his anger at Martin and some of the crew tried to diffuse the tension, stating that miscommunication led to the separation of Martin and his ship.

Rodrigo de Jerez offered some of the dried leaves the Taino people often burned and smoked to Cristóbal and the other crew members. Rodrigo found the practice of smoking these leaves in the tabako pipe relaxing and had initially began smoking upon landing in Cuba. The leaves were called cohiba and bundles of cohiba were called tabako by the Tainos however, Rodrigo de Jerez, and some of the other crew members began to call the leaves simply as tobacco. Cristóbal spoke to various Tainos who directed him to their leader Cacique Guacanagarix, who had arrived earlier in the day and briefly spoke with Cristóbal as the Santa Maria began to sink. After a few hours, Cristóbal questioned Guacanagarix regarding the location of gold on Ayiti. Guacanagarix stated that there was an abundance on the island and more gold would be provided for Cristóbal and his crew. Cristóbal ordered wood to be salvaged from the Santa Maria to be used in the building of his fort, which he named La Navidad because construction began in earnest on Christmas Day afternoon.

He wrote in his journal, *I have ordered a tower and fortress to be constructed and a large cellar, not because I believe there is any necessity regarding our protectiong from the natives. I am certain the people I have with me could subjugate all this island ... as the population are naked and without arms and very cowardly.* Cristóbal named Diego de Arana, a cousin of his mistress Beatriz Enriquez, as governor of La Navidad.

As the Navidad fort was being constructed, Cristóbal wondered where Martín Alonso Pinzón and the Pinta were. Cristóbal believed that Martin might have left for Spain or had found other lands in search of gold fueled by his own greed. There were others who secretly supported Martin and were not pleased with Admiral Cristóbal's leadership. Cristóbal understood that he was seen as an outsider by some of his crew and the direct challenges by some of his crew—including Martin—were eroding his legitimacy as the leader of this expedition.

Vicente Pinzon, the captain of the Niña and Martin's brother, were in a heated argument with Cristóbal regarding Martin's location. Vicente reminded Cristóbal that his brother prevented a previous attempt of a mutiny against him, however Cristóbal loathed the fact that Martin and his brothers held considerable influence among the crew.

The Pinzón brothers were from a prominent family from the port town of Los Palos de la Frontera in Spain. Martin was well known because of his previous participation in the War of Castilian Succession against the Portuguese. The war was fought between Isabella, who was married to Ferdinand, heir to the Crown of Aragon, and Joanna, who was strategically married to her uncle King Alfonso V of Portugal. France and Portugal both fought in favor of Joanna while Aragon and his supporters—including Martin Pinzon—supported Isabella I of Castile. In 1479, at the Treaty of Alcáçovas, Isabella and Ferdinand were recognized as sovereigns of Castile and they gained the Canary Islands. Martin Pinzon and his brothers had wealth and prestige and when the Catholic Monarchs asked the town of Los Palos to provide two caravels for Cristóbal's voyage, Martin provided half a million maravedís in coins as well as the Nina and Pinta. Although most people were opposed or indifferent regarding Cristóbal Colón's proposed voyage west, Martin Pinzon helped recruit a large amount of men of various talents—some of which his own family members—and enlist them in service of Cristóbal's voyage using his fame throughout the Tinto-Odiel region. Martin also enlisted the brothers Pedro Alonso, Francisco, Juan, and Bartolomé Alonso.

La Navidad fort was built at a rapid pace in preparation for a prolonged stay in Ayiti. Cristóbal boarded the Nina in search of Martin Pinzon on Friday, January fourth, 1493 and observed the Pinta arriving from the east two days later. Cristóbal and Martin Pinzon returned to La Navidad where Cristóbal addressed his crew and chose the men he would leave behind.

Before Cristóbal addressed the crowd, he spoke with Martin Pinzon once again, trying hard not to let anger get the best of him. "I appreciate everything you have done for me and my voyage, however we have had some differences in opinion. As you understand, I have been entrusted with leading this expedition into the Indies and into mainland India. I also will oversee the Navidad Fort and other regions of the Indies where we will soon settle. It is of high importance that we remain focused, organized, and without struggle amongst ourselves. We will leave thirty-nine men which I believe can work together and maintain my fort until we return.

Martin angrily responded, "You wish to leave these

men here in this strange land? How will they survive and maintain themselves and the fort without constant support?"

Cristóbal replied, "These are my commands, Martin. Remember I am appointed to govern these lands. With the loss of the Santa Maria, it is best we reduce the number of men we return with to the Nina and Pinta. It is also important that we establish a settlement here and communication with the natives so we can easily expand and access the gold upon our return."

One of the men Cristóbal would leave behind in Ayiti was his Jewish translator Luis de Torres. Cristóbal would take a few natives with him, including the young Taino Guaikán who was learning the Spanish language and would replace Luis as his new translator. Guaikán would become an adopted son to Cristóbal and was renamed Diego Colón. Cristóbal prepared his crew while taking some time to speak with Luis de Torres. Cristóbal observed Luis with his long hair, rounded cheeks flushed with frustration, and sharp pensive eyes as he walked towards him. Luis felt somewhat relieved to remain in Ayiti but was angered at the mistreatment of the Jewish people in Spain and his hurried conversion. As a Jewish man who converted to Catholicism, Luis was recognized as a converso, just as Muslims who recently converted to Christianity were called moriscos. The Alhambra Decree which expelled the remaining Jewish people weighed heavily upon the mind of Luis de Torres. Also, some whispered that Luis de Torres secretly practiced Judaism and he was referred to as a marrano. Marranos were despised for their alleged practices; however, Muslims were hated the most in Spain.

Luis de Torres quietly stated, "I am treated differently because of my beliefs just as you are treated differently because of your own beliefs and birthplace, Cristóbal. This discrimination is amplified when we are given positions of power, just as you have encountered problems as admiral and leader of these lands. Perhaps we are no better, you and I, because despite our differences with the rest of our Castilian crew, we still see ourselves as superior to these peaceful Taino people. Is this what God wanted for us? Is this the Lord's will? To treat each other with such disdain and to separate ourselves by class and belief? The Taino live free with little if any class divisions; they don't have any poor among them and all of them sleep with their stomachs full without want or need. If we are more civilized, why are there so many poor within our society and so few with so much? We call them nobles, Kings, and Queens and they bestow us with titles but ultimately it can be an illusion to further their own cause. Already I am seeing that we are treating our hosts with anger, lust, and in some cases violence."

Cristóbal responded, "Careful, my friend. We are here for a purpose. It is in our interest to establish our territories for Spain here in the Indies and later create trade routes for Spain. It will benefit us and our families as well as solidify the Catholic faith in these lands."

Luis replied, "The Catholic faith cares about power and allows our rulers to expand their empires to gain riches. Observe how our Catholic priests have treated the Muslims and the Jewish people. Will we force our faith on these people, or spread our beliefs peacefully? I will remain in Ayiti and shall await your return, and be at your service until I rejoin my wife."

Cristóbal spoke with Cacique Guacanagaríx and then addressed his crew, informing them who would remain to complete the Navidad Fort as he prepared to depart for Spain. Cristóbal claimed the Island of Ayiti for Spain and before he left the island he renamed it La Isla Española (the Spanish Island), which would be shorted to Hispaniola. Cristóbal Colón departed Ayiti and the Cacicazgo of Marién on January fifteenth, 1493, aboard the Niña along with a few Tainos who left voluntarily and many that were taken by force. Cristóbal also brought some gold, precious stones, tobacco, and the young Taino Guaikán who everyone called Diego. The crew enjoyed the native way of sleeping on hammocks and brought them aboard their ships.

After a violent storm, which the Tainos informed Cristóbal were named Juracan and caused by the Goddess Guabancex, the Spaniards subsequently called the storms Juracan. The storm separated Cristóbal and the Nina and Martin Pinzon and the Pinta once again. After landing in Portugal and meeting with King João II (John II), Cristóbal arrived in Barcelona Spain on March fifteenth, 1493 to a hero's welcome. Martin Pinzon had arrived earlier to Los Palos, sending a letter to the King and Queen of Spain not knowing of Cristóbal's whereabouts. Martin Pinzon died of fever that was made worse by the storm that previously had separated him from Admiral Cristóbal. Martin died and was entombed at the La Rábida Monastery, as he previously requested.

Cristóbal brought gold, pearls, and jewelry stolen from the natives as well as cotton, hammocks, fruits, and birds. Cristóbal also presented the King and Queen the tobacco plant and the pineapple. King Ferdinand II and Queen Isabella I were dismayed that Cristóbal did not bring expensive black pepper, ginger, or cloves, however Cristóbal displayed the ají, which he stated was the pepper of the native Tainos and more valuable than black pepper. Cristóbal and his crew were honored and he was given the title of Governor of the Indies. King John II of Portugal stated that Cristóbal broke the Alcaçovas Treaty signed in 1479, which both Portugal and Spain would seek to resolve with Pope Alexander VI and the creation of another treaty. Word travelled fast in Europe regarding Cristóbal's voyages and triumphant return and the invention of the printing press by Johannes Gutenberg of the Holy Roman Empire helped to spread the information. The race to establish new trading routes was heating up between Spain and Portugal while England, France, and other nations eagerly awaited news. Cristóbal would return with a larger fleet as Governor of the Indies and was recognized as the Marco Polo of his time.

CHAPTER 5
UPON THE ASHES OF LA NAVIDAD (1494)

Cristóbal left Cadiz Spain on September twenty-fourth, 1493 with a larger fleet of seventeen ships, including the flagship Marigalante. On November third, 1493, Cristóbal landed on a small Island named Wai'tu kubuli by the Kalinago natives, meaning "tall is her body" and renamed it Dominica (the Latin word for Sunday). Over the next several days, Cristóbal named several more islands: Karukera (the Island of the beautiful waters), Cristóbal changed to Santa María de Guadalupe de Extremadura or Guadeloupe, after a portrait of the Virgin Mary in the Spanish monastery of Villuercas in Guadalupe, Extremadura. Cristóbal also found another small island and named it Montserrat, and an island named Waladli by the native people which meant "our own", and renamed it Santa Maria de la Antigua after an icon of the Seville Cathedral. An island named Soualiga by the native Kalinago people (land of salt) was renamed Santa María la Redonda, and later they briefly stayed at an island named Aichi by the Kalinago or Carib people and Touloukaera by the Taino people which was renamed Marigalante or the Galant Mary after Cristóbal's flagship.

On November fourteenth, 1492, Cristóbal landed on an island named Ay Ay, which he renamed Santa Cruz. In Santa Cruz, Cristóbal and members of his crew were attacked by Kalinago people who wanted them off their island because of the violence of the Spanish. Cristóbal and his crew viewed various islands and sometimes explored them as some natives fled, leaving their homes behind and making it easier for Cristóbal and his crew to steal their food and possessions as they searched for gold. Cristóbal sailed to the other islands, renaming them Santa Úrsula y las Once Mil Vírgenes (or Saint Ursula) and the 11,000 Virgin (or the Virgin Islands) because of the numerous islands that lay close together.

One day, Cristóbal's childhood family friend, Michele de Cuneo, observed a canoa near the beach in shallow water with four Carib men and two of their women. Michele de Cuneo was aboard the flagship's smaller boat and they quickly approached the canoa. There were two castrated males—perhaps from another people. The Caribs began shooting arrows at them, which hit a few of the Spaniards—including one man who had an arrow enter deep into his chest and would later perish from his wounds. The Spaniards subdued the Caribs; one who was thought dead and thrown overboard quickly began swimming for shore and was subsequently axed near his neck and nearly decapitated.

Michele de Cuneo apprehended one of the Carib girls and brought her back to his cabin with Cristóbal Colón's permission. Michele de Cuneo was amazed by her beauty and his lust led him to try to force himself upon her. In retaliation, the Carib woman scratched him deeply, causing Michele de Cuneo to beat her with a rope which caused her to scream and alert everyone nearby. The rest of the crew abused the Carib girl and a few others. Cristóbal named this island Cape of the Arrow in recognition of the Spaniard who had perished.

Cristóbal and his crew were successfully repelled from further expansion into various islands due to the presence of Kalinago; the Spanish often accused them of the foul practice of eating human flesh. To justify future aggressions against them and the corruption of their name led to the word "cannibal". The spreading of false information regarding the Caribs struck fear in some of the Spaniards as well as hatred and anger. Cristóbal allowed his crew to inflict violence on the native people and began encouraging his men to take Kalinago women.

On November nineteenth, 1493, Cristóbal arrived on a larger island east of Ayiti called Boriken and renamed it San Juan Bautista in honor of Saint John the Baptist. Many of the Spanish were enchanted with the beauty of San Juan Bautista, including the young Juan Ponce de León. Juan was a proven fighter in the Spanish wars against the Moors and was a great asset for Cristóbal Colón. The young eighteen-year-old was strong and had a lot of grit and Cristóbal and the other Spaniards often commented on his desire to rise and make a name for himself in the Indies.

The relationship between the Tainos and the Spaniards was amicable at first but had rapidly degraded within the first few months of the construction of Fort Navidad. The lust and greed of the men at the Navidad manifested in violence towards the Tainos; some of the men began to quench their thirst for lust by forcing themselves on Taino women—a behavior that rapidly became frequent and commonplace. Some of the Spanish began to molest and hurt young Taino boys and girls, stealing jewelry from the homes of Taino villagers. The governor of La Navidad, Diego de Arana, was losing control of his colony as the relationship between the Spaniards and Tainos rapidly deteriorated. The Spaniards began to focus less on finding goldmines and more on theft and leisure.

The Spaniards did not fully understand Taino society, where poverty and where class distinctions did not exist. The Spaniards believed they were superior and regarded the Tainos as childlike, yet many secretly resented the Tainos because in many ways they lived better than they themselves. The power the Spaniards had in weaponry and warfare slightly eased their own self-doubt and they began openly disrespecting the leaders and violating the wives of the Taino, Ciguayo, and Macorix people. Cacique Guacanagaríx, who had welcomed these Spaniard guamikena (or the covered ones), now desired an end to any potential hostilities.

After the violation of some of Cacique Guacanagarix's wives, the Spaniards became even more emboldened despite their numerical disadvantage. Other major leaders like Cacique Guarionex and Cacique Caonabo became aware of these hostile visitors and their blatant disrespect for elders and Cacique Guacanagarix. Cacique Caonabo disliked Cacique Guacanagarix and his irresponsibility and weakness for allowing these Spaniards to settle the island of Ayiti and encouraged the Taino people to forcefully remove the Spaniards from their land.

By early August of 1493, the Spaniards were involved in open aggression amongst themselves as Diego de Arana was rapidly losing control of La Navidad. With Cacique Caonabo and his warriors within his territory of Marién and his own warriors supporting Cacique Caonabo, Cacique Guacanagaríx could not stop the attack on Fort Navidad. One afternoon in late August, while many of the Spaniards were fighting amongst themselves, the Tainos closed in. Luis de Torres, who was opposed to the irresponsibility of the Spaniards and their treatment of the Tainos, was now openly arguing with other men within the fort.

One of the men accused Luis of being a false Catholic and Luis replied, "Despite my services for the Spanish, I had to change my own beliefs to be accepted by men who call themselves Catholic yet engage in this despicable behavior. It seems our behavior will only become worse as we act as rulers here and perpetuate horrors upon these people who have welcomed us. Who will judge us? Will it be God or will it be the hands of men—perhaps the very men we have treated so horribly?"

Some men yelled at Luis, calling him a marrano, a cryptic Sephardic Jew, and false Catholic. Diego de Arana was busy trying to maintain order in his settlement and was ill prepared when the Tainos retaliated, killing most of the Spaniards despite their weapons. Fighting was short-lived but violent and by the next day, La Navidad was burned to the ground.

Cacique Guacanagaríx did not oppose the killing of the Spaniards and hoped Cristóbal would never return.

When Cristóbal returned on November twenty-second, he observed eleven of his men lay on the beach, their bodies rotten for over two months and more bodies near La Navidad, which was destroyed. Cristóbal Colón recognized some of the corpses, including his clerk Rodrigo de Escobedo, Pedro Gutierrez, and Diego de Arana, the cousin of his mistress with whom he had his youngest son Fernando Colón. Cristóbal tried to control his emotions to no avail as he silently cried. The Spaniards were nervous; as they believed further attacks were imminent. Cristóbal felt fear in his heart and a surge of anxiety which he tried hard to contain in front of the men he was to lead in a land that was not his. Many of his crew began to call for open retaliation for the killings of their fellow Spaniards, however Cristóbal did not seek to engage an enemy that could possibly manifest itself in a combined force from the natives that did not want them on the island of Ayiti. Cristóbal quickly sought to calm his crew members and choose a course of action until he met Cacique Guacanagarix.

The crew moved inland with Cristóbal, led by some Taino people towards their leader Guacanagarix. The nervous Guacanagarix did not want to endanger himself or his people and when Cristóbal inquired about the deaths of his men and the burning of Fort Navidad, he stated the rival Cacique Caonabo or perhaps some other native groups were responsible. The Tainos were also alarmed at the sight of horses that the Spaniards called caballos. Cacique Guacanagarix made sure not to inform Cristóbal that many of the people he led also participated in the attack of the Navidad. Cristóbal believed he should establish himself further on the island and concentrate his crew on the purposes of increasing the exploitation of the islands gold and minerals. Cristóbal publicly accepted Guacanagarix's account and sought to build a new settlement after sailing further east on the northern coast of Ayiti. This time

Cristóbal would name the new settlement La Isabela, after Queen Isabela I.

Cristóbal brought a large crew of 1,200 men with various skills: doctors, priests, map makers, carpenters, stonemasons, and merchants like Pedro de las Casas who had left a young son in Spain named Bartolome de las Casas. Cristóbal would now begin to build permanent colonies for Spain, search for gold, and establish trade routes for the Spanish Monarchy. The Spanish Crown supported the spread of Catholicism into their new lands and the natives who inhabited them. The natives were to be taught the ways of the Lord and Savior Jesus Christ and become good Catholic subjects for the services of the Spanish Crown.

Cristóbal and his crew quickly began to build La Isabela. Stonemasons erected stone buildings, including a church and over 200 thatched huts which were constructed similarly to the houses of the Taino. Cristóbal brought livestock and plants with him, including pigs, wheat, sugarcane, and coconuts. He also arrived with horses, which became a source of great curiosity and some fear amongst the Tainos when they saw the Spaniards riding on them. Seeds were planted and enclosures were built for the livestock as well as the horses.

Initially, the search for gold was not as successful as Cristóbal hoped nor as Cacique Guacanagaríx had previously stated it would be. The failure of the search for gold and the increasing restlessness of Cristóbal and his crew led to harsher treatment of the Taino, Macorix, and Ciguayo people. Cristóbal received word that his brother Bartolomeo Colón, who had missed Cristóbal's second voyage to the Hispaniola, had recently arrived. After several days, the brothers were reunited and Cristóbal asked Bartolomeo to join him in exploring the islands called Cuba and Xaymaca. Cristóbal travelled with Diego Velázquez de Cuéllar, a nobleman who was a close friend of Bartolomeo Colón and who would help Cristóbal in governing Hispaniola. He also entrusted Alonso de Ojeda to lead fifteen soldiers into the center of the Hispaniola in search of Caonabo and his warriors. They desired revenge and Cristóbal wanted to establish control as governor by making example of Caonabo.

Amanex and his father Maraguay returned to their home the previous year and began to observe a difference in their way of life. The people began to speak of clothed visitors with pale skin who had brought misfortune upon them. In Jaragua, life continued with little disturbance. However, people were slowly arriving from surrounding territories—mainly Maguana. Stories of exotic beasts and pale skinned men mystified Amanex and the other children. Maraguay did not wish to alarm his family, but he was worried about the treatment of his people. Already tales of viciousness, torture, and murder by the hands of the foreigners had been spread. These people were seeking precious stones, spices, and most importantly the Caona—the gold these Spaniards called oro. They placed human lives below that of a simple metal that you could not eat, did not provide shelter, and did not supply heat nor cold. Gold was a metal that did not love or hate you, but was simply an ornament to be worn on the body. Yet these foreigners were unleashing the worst of the human condition upon a people that had welcomed and sheltered them.

It had become known that Cacique Caonabo, with the support of his wives and the Cacica Anacaona, had supported an attack on Fort Navidad led by Diego de Arana in the region of Marién. Cacique Bohechio also supplied warriors to help Cacique Caonabo in his battle in the north. Some of the Tainos who fled from the north stated that Diego de Arana ruled in place of another man named Cristóbal Colón and others who had returned. The relationship between with Cacique Guacanagarix and foreigners who returned was unknown, however many people assumed the worst. It was also unknown exactly where the foreigners had moved but it was generally believed that it was east along the northern coast of Ayiti. Tensions began to rise between Cacique Caonabo and

Cacique Guacanagarix regarding the violence of the foreigners.

As the months went by, more people from other regions began arriving to Jaragua with horrific tales of violence and Tainos being forced into manual labor by the Castilians. The people of these islands worked for themselves or their families and each family member labored for the benefit of their society, however this forced labor was controlled by the Spaniards. These foreign Guamikena people were believed to be moving towards the interior of Ayiti which they had already named Hispaniola. Cacique Guarionex maintained a fragile relationship with Cristóbal and the Spaniards in Maguá and it began to strain as more men and young children were recruited to seek out gold and work in goldmines. More mining sites were to be constructed with Cristóbal seeking to establish a relationship with various chiefs to enable an increasing supply of laborers. Cristóbal desired to maintain the original Taino tribute system in place, which he believed could be used to facilitate the recruitment of new laborers throughout the island for the purposes of the Spanish Crown and his own enrichment.

It was rumored that Cristóbal Colón, the man responsible for the first settlement at La Navidad, had returned and Cacique Caonabo and Anacaona were preparing to launch an attack. Some Tainos had encountered the Spaniards led by a man named Alonso de Ojeda, who had attacked some of the villagers weeks prior. Caonabo then sent some scouts to explore the northern regions in hope of discovering Spanish settlements. Cacique Bohechio was also preparing to help his sister Anacaona and her husband Cacique Caonabo in a united attack against the Spaniards. Maraguay was conflicted regarding joining a battle against an enemy he had yet to witness or fleeing the island with his family to Boriken. It was yet to be known to what extent the Spaniards had infiltrated Ayiti, Boriken, and the other islands, and this only increased Maraguay's indecisiveness.

The elders began debating as to the best response to

the rising Spanish presence on the island. The Tainos were aware that the Spaniards had already renamed the other islands, including theirs. Ayiti had been renamed Hispaniola by the white-skinned foreigners and they desired to take the land for themselves. The foreigners were moving aggressively into the interior of the island and the elders believed they ultimately desired to violently remove the Taino people. They had lived peacefully for countless generations among the Ciboney, Macorix, Ciguayo, and Guanahatabey people. These foreign invaders were nameless and faceless to many of the Taino people of Jaragua but their presence could be felt through fear, anxiety, and anger. Amanex simultaneously grew nervous about these foreigners and their exotic beasts and curious about the appearance and origins of the foreigners. The elders would hold various Cohoba ceremonies where they would contemplate the origins of these pale-skinned foreigners. The only thing that was certain to the Taino of Jaragua was that Cacique Caonabo had already begun to move forward in an attack against the Spaniards with the support of other caciques, including Cacique Bohechio.

Cristóbal had already begun the construction of a new fort in a region the Spaniards called Ciba-o, which meant Stone Mountain in the Taino language. The region was filled with potential gold mining sites and Cristóbal sent builders who rapidly constructed Fort Santo Tomas. Despite his initial failure to find Caonabo, Cristóbal still respected Alonso de Ojeda as a soldier and leader and declared him mayor of Fort Santo Tomas. Alonso de Ojeda was a skilled fighter who was strong, swift, and had experience with the sword and other weapons. Alonso de Ojeda was slightly shorter than the others, however, he possessed more courage than most and despite his cruelty he was a deeply religious man. Alonso took his role as mayor of Fort Santo Tomas seriously and led with focus and determination. Alonso and his quest for power and gold led him to treat the Taino people with increasing levels of cruelty.

The Spaniards were now within Cacique Caonabo's

territory. However, Caonabo's scouts were able to find the Spaniards before they could spot his location. Caonabo would take a more active role in the attack of Fort Santo Tomas and he discussed this attack with various elders and chiefs. Caonabo's brother Manicaotex as well as Anacaona agreed that the Spaniards were hostile to their way of life. Anacaona was aware of how the Spaniards mistreated the Taino men and abused the women and young children and she feared this hostile existence among these barbaric people for herself, her husband, her people, and her two-year-old baby daughter Higüemota. Anacaona initially struggled with her husband's decision to kill the Spaniards and burn Fort Navidad but the actions of the Spaniards justified Caonabo's attack. Anacaona realized that her husband had to move quickly and with deadly force against La Isabella.

Anacaona desired the company of her intelligent uncle Matunheri, whose name meant the highest one. Matunheri's wisdom would aid her and Caonabo in dealing with Cristóbal Colón and the Spaniards. Anacaona advised Caonabo to enlist various chiefs from Jaragua, Higüey, and other regions, but they had to attack swiftly in order to inflict the initial offensive. Anacaona remembered her various family members and chiefs who had influenced her own decisions and the decisions of Jaragua. Matunheri previously led Jaragua and his advice was needed now as Caonabo led thousands of warriors north towards Fort Santo Tomas. Caonabo began to move towards Fort Santo and planned a subsequent raid on Fort Isabela and the capture or killing of the Spanish leader Cristóbal.

Caonabo, leading thousands of Tainos, descended upon Fort Santo Tomas and engaged the Spaniards in battle. Caonabo pierced into Santo Tomas from various directions, leaving a segment of his archers in reserve to shoot any Spaniard who chose to retreat. Caonabo led his main force into Santo Tomas, delivering a vicious initial attack, however the Spaniards were more numerous and better prepared than the Spaniards that were defeated at La Navidad. The leader of Santo Tomas, Alonso de Ojeda, ordered his soldiers to fire at Caonabo's center formation. Bullets ripped through Caonabo's forces, inflicting many casualties and quickly reversing Caonabo's initial success. The Spaniards aimed their arquebuses at the charging Taino forces, killing and injuring many and dealing devastating damage to the psyche of the confused Tainos. As one group of Spaniards shot their large arquebus rifles, another would load their weapons and fire while the other group reloaded. Caonabo encouraged his warriors to fight with bravery and charge forward despite the Spaniards and their weapons.

Some Tainos began to flee in fear and Spaniards on horseback cut them down as Caonabo's forces splintered. Caonabo began ordering his archers to shoot their arrows towards the center of Alonso de Ojeda's soldiers. Alonso ordered his men to shoot towards the archers, killing most of them while the others began to flee into the mountains. In desperation, Caonabo ordered some of the Tainos to send word to his brother Manicaotex for reinforcements as the battle quickly turned in favor of Alonso de Ojeda and the Spaniards. Alonso, realizing Cacique Caonabo was leading his troops, ordered his soldiers to capture Caonabo to gain valuable information and to present him to Cristóbal Colón. Spaniards on horseback chased after the fleeing Tainos and sent their dogs after those who ran into the mountains and surrounding trees. Caonabo, who initially escaped intending to return and kill Alonso, was later fooled into a trap and imprisoned. Caonabo was heavily beaten by the Spaniards and brought to Alonso de Ojeda. Tainos who supported Cacique Guacanagarix were among those supporting Alonso de Ojeda and the Spaniards at fort Santo Tomas, which confirmed their alliance to the much disappointed Caonabo; he had suspected Cacique Guarionex and other regional chiefs as being complicit in a Spanish alliance with Cacique Guacanagaríx.

Caonabo and many of his Taino soldiers were imprisoned and beaten to extract information about other Taino chiefs and their potential war plans against the Spaniards. Alonso correctly expected a retaliatory attack on Santo Tomas, which came several days afterwards led by

Caonabo's brother Manicaotex. Cacique Manicaotex was now the active leader of Maguana in place of his brother. Manicaotex decided on a quick and strong full-frontal attack on Fort Santo Tomas despite some objections from other chiefs who advocated for a more strategic response. Anacaona believed that a larger alliance with her brother Bohechio and the other chiefs would be more effective but in fear of her husband's safety, Anacaona agreed with Manicaotex in a quick attack and rescue of Caonabo.

Manicaotex's attack was met by a stronger Spaniard counterattack which quickly defeated his efforts. Spaniards with lances killed the Taino fighters who managed to evade the heavy fire power. The fighting was brutal as Manicaotex encouraged his fighters into close combat in an effort to avoid the Spanish weapons and despite the Spaniard's armor, the Tainos could kill many who were weakened because of the climate. Manicaotex attempted to spread the fight away from Fort Santo Tomas to exploit the ignorance of the Spaniards regarding the land of Ayiti. Manicaotex's efforts came to avail with his capture and the deaths of his soldiers and he was imprisoned alongside his brother Caonabo and various minor chiefs. Alonso de Ojeda commanded his soldiers to transport Caonabo, Manicaotex, and the other chiefs towards La Isabela, where Cristóbal Colón would decide their fate.

Cristóbal Colón had returned from his trip to Cuba and Xaymaca, which some of the Spaniards began referring to as Jamaica. Cristóbal was excited to meet the great Cacique Caonabo, whose name meant king of the Golden House; he could lead Cristóbal towards more gold and riches and would help Cristóbal gain further control of the island of Hispaniola. Despite the pleading of many of the Taino people in efforts to release their chiefs, Cristóbal executed many of them by burning them alive as an example to other Tainos who would take up arms against him and the Spanish. However, Cristóbal decided to keep Caonabo and Manicaotex alive and send them to Spain alongside enslaved Tainos. Cristóbal desired to maintain the fragile Taino hierarchy and continue to use this system for his benefit until he could create a more efficient system and establish a more developed system of his own administrators.

Cristóbal began ordering the constructions of other forts within Hispaniola near goldmines for easier access for gold mining including Fort La Concepción in a region Cristóbal named La Vega Real because of its exceptional beauty. Fort Magdalena was constructed near the territory of the Macorix people where Cacique Guatigara lived. Numerous rebellions began to occur after the capture of Caonabo, including a rebellion by Cacique Guatigara, which resulted in the deaths of ten Spaniards. Cristóbal feared a unified rebellion prompting him to quickly retaliate against the smaller rebellions before they became stronger. The expeditions would also result in the killings and abuse of women and young children and the forceful bondage of Taino for labor. Cristóbal did not want the Catholic priests to Christianize the Taino population—he did not want to legitimize the Taino as Catholic Spanish subjects; he wanted to keep them firmly below Europeans. Cristóbal began crafting a letter to Queen Isabela to legitimize his plans for mass slavery of the natives. He believed he could avoid conflict with Queen Isabela by enslaving the Kalinago people.

Other forts, including Fort Esperanza, Fort Santa Catalina, Fort Santiago, and others, were quickly constructed. Cristóbal began to enforce a partition of Taino people and initiated the Encomienda System where Tainos were assigned plots of land to cultivate as well as quotas of gold which were strictly enforced. Cristóbal however, not only faced Taino revolts but also increasing restlessness among the Spaniards he led. One Spaniard who became increasingly vocal against the Governorship of Cristóbal Colón was Francisco Roldán, and many others began to join Francisco in open opposition against Cristóbal.

Another large Taino rebellion would occur near Fort La Concepción, which was crushed by the Spaniards. The superior weaponry of the Spaniards and aid of Taino chiefs including Cacique Guacanagaríx helped splinter support for the Taino rebellion. In addition, a sickness began to blanket the island, causing many Tainos to weaken, die, and give up their motivations to rebel. The Spaniards believed it to be a cause of divine intervention. Cristóbal began to quickly enslave Tainos as well as authorize the building of new forts and excursions into surrounding villages in an effort to gain more slaves for gold mining, farming, and construction. Although it was known that Queen Isabela did not approve of massive enslavement of the Tainos, Cristóbal proceeded to place the Tainos into the encomienda system in order to increase gold mining and shipments for the Spanish Crown and to secure further colonization in Hispaniola and other islands. Cristóbal summoned various caciques—including Caonabo and Manicaotex—to gather further information from them.

Cristóbal called his Taino interpreter Guaikán to translate his words to the Taino leaders. "Caonabo, the great leader of the Indios. We want to form an alliance with you and your people and therefore, you will sail to Spain and meet our King Ferdinand and Queen Isabela."

Caonabo responded, "I only respect those who challenge me in the field of battle or those who have led like Alonso de Ojeda. However, even Alonso has disgraced himself for his misconduct as the victor in battle by defiling our innocent women and children. Therefore, I think less of you and your purpose in Ayiti. I do not recognize you or your people and the only purpose I serve for you is to help strengthen your legitimacy, which is not recognized by the Taino people and is even questioned by the Castilians you desire to rule. You pretend to be a Christian man, however you and your people do not worship your God or the examples that your Jesus Christ made well known. Your God is the very gold that drives you to behave with such brutality towards me and my people. We welcomed you with open arms, supported you, and now you seek to divide us and cause conflict among my people in order for you to further seek to destroy us and exploit our lands. If your God approves of you and your people's behavior in our land, then that is a God we will never accept. If justice exists, you will receive your punishment in this life or the next, Cristóbal."

Cristóbal was angered, but he secretly feared Caonabo's words. His legitimacy was being threatened and the numerous Taino deaths, although helping his efforts to rule the island, were at the same time hurting his efforts in gaining sufficient Taino laborers for his mines. Cristóbal expanded punitive expeditions into various regions, including expeditions into the lands of the Macorix people, resulting in the capture and assassination of Cacique Guatigara. These expeditions created increasing numbers of Taino and Macorix laborers for Cristóbal despite the rapidly diminishing Taino population. However, Cristóbal faced potential rebellions from Taino allies and many of the Spaniards which he suspected might be forming alliances against him. Cristóbal had imprisoned several Spaniards, including Bernal Díaz de Pisa, who had plotted against him and his governance. A suspected potential alliance between Cacique Guarionex and Francisco Roldán and other Spaniards also troubled Cristóbal as he sought to further expand his control in Hispaniola.

Cristóbal himself was afflicted with a sickness and began to entrust his brother Bartolomeo Colón with most of the important affairs of the island, including the building of new cities. Cristóbal planned for more slaves and gold to be shipped to Spain before his own departure for Spain, leaving Bartolomeo to rule Hispaniola. Cristóbal planned a quick return to Spain, as he suspected many of the Spaniards might attempt to undermine his efforts in the Hispaniola and surrounding islands, deny his legitimacy, and break his contract with the Spanish Crown. Cristóbal also needed to establish control of various forts and punish the Spaniards who refused to work.

Maraguay and his family received information regarding the enslavement of the Taino people and the shipment of Taino slaves towards an unknown land, including Cacique Caonabo and his brother Manicaotex. The violence, the failure of rebellions, the capture of Taino leaders, and a sickness that rapidly blanketed the island like clouds before a hurricane led to many Tainos fleeing Ayiti towards other islands. Maraguay began to make plans to flee along with his family east towards the island of Boriken; perhaps they could make a united effort against the Spanish invaders there. Maraguay had lost some relatives and friends in the previous battles against the Spanish invaders and he did not trust some of the Taino leaders who had allied with the Spaniards, suspecting that other Tainos were secretly allied with Cristóbal and would work against future rebellions. Leaders held a Cohoba ceremony asking the Gods for intervention against the brutality of the Spaniards. Amanex nervously cried, holding onto his mother as he asked the Gods to punish the invaders and free them from their bondage and the sickness they had brought to him and his people.

CHAPTER 6
SANTO DOMINGO DE GUZMÁN (1498)

On July of 1495, Cristóbal Colón witnessed a ferocious hurricane rip through his beloved fort La Isabela as the Taino natives ran for shelter into the mountains. The Goddess Guabancex unleashed her fury upon the island of Hispaniola in the form of powerful storms which the Spaniards identified as Juracan, the Taino deity of chaos. Many of Cristóbal's ships sank, his flagship the Marigalante among them. The hurricane's path ripped through Cristóbal's fleet, including a ship carrying Caonabo, Caonabo's brother Manicaotex, and other chiefs who all drowned beneath the violent waves, freeing them from Spanish bondage and torture.

Cristóbal began to lose influence as more Spaniards openly rebelled against him. Francisco Roldán led the largest Spanish rebellion against Cristóbal Colón as he left for Spain. Scurvy and other diseases ripped through the Spanish populations and crops began to fail. The amount of gold found was far less than Cristóbal had predicted and many Tainos had died from overwork and diseases or had fled themselves. Numerous expeditions failed to produce large amounts of gold and instead resulted in the enslavement of over a 1,600 Tainos. The Tainos that remained began to fight with the Spaniards. As Cristóbal's control weakened, Francisco's rebellion gained support. This rebellion survived several years, increasing in power as Bartolomeo Colón failed to suppress Cristóbal's primary rival.

Caonabo's Maguana territory was now under control of the Spaniards and Anacaona and her daughter Higüemota relocated to Jaragua to rule alongside her brother Cacique Bohechio. Bartolomeo Colón could not rule efficiently; he was preoccupied with Francisco Roldán's rebellion and the establishment of his regime in western Hispaniola. Guarionex and other chiefs were allied with Francisco Roldán against Cristóbal and Bartolomeo—alliances that Bartolomeo swiftly sought to break. Bartolomeo awaited the arrival of Cristóbal Colón's arrival before any decision was made against Francisco Roldán and his opposition.

The Treaty of Tordesillas, authored by the corrupt Roderic Borgia who was now named Pope Alexander VI, was created in Tordesillas Spain and later ratified in July 1494 in Spain and September 1494 in Portugal. The division would be marked halfway between the Portuguese Cape Verde islands and the islands entered by Christopher Columbus on his first voyage. King João II was now succeeded by his first cousin and brother in law, King Manuel, who would use this Treaty of Tordesillas to expand Portugal's Empire in competition with Spain, although Portugal was limited to the east of the line and excluded from the territories Cristóbal Colón had claimed for the Spanish Crown. King Manuel was nicknamed the Fortunate for avoiding various conspiracies such as the death of his older brother Diogo, Duke of Viseu by the king himself, and rising to the Portuguese throne after the death of Prince Afonso and the failure of King João II to appoint his illegitimate son Jorge de Lencastre, Duke of Coimbra. The Treaty of Tordesillas helped legitimize Cristóbal and the Spanish Crown's claims to the lands Cristóbal conquered.

Bartolomeo Colón helped create a new city in the south next to a river and near the sea which he believed would become an important port. The Port City was named La Nueva Isabela after La Isabela; however, the city would be renamed Santo Domingo after Saint Domenic—a priest who was widely regarded as the founder of the Catholic Dominican Order and the patron saint of astronomers. Other cities were being constructed while Cristóbal was in Spain, but Santo Domingo was built for the purposes of creating a central city and focal point of Spanish power on the island of Hispaniola and beyond. Bartolomeo Colón began enforcing the Encomienda System within the city and continued to send soldiers in search of Tainos to help in gold mining, agriculture, and further construction. Bartolomeo and various Taino leaders agreed to bring Tainos into Santo Domingo to work and in return the Taino leaders would maintain their roles. Bartolomeo felt Santo Domingo would be secure and profitable, although almost half of the total Spaniard population had defected for the regime of Francisco Roldán. Cristóbal Colón's impending arrival and the weakening alliance between Roldán and Guarionex would give Bartolomeo and Cristóbal an upper hand in their efforts to solidify control of Hispaniola.

Maraguay and his family secretly believed their Cacique Bohechio would not be able to mount an effective offense against the Spaniards. Maraguay feared that the Spaniards had grown powerful—evidenced by the defeat of Cacique Caonabo and his forces as well as the defeat of Caonabo's brother Manicaotex. The return of the powerful Cacica Anacaona, in an effort to aid her brother Bohechio in the governance of Jaragua, did little to assuage the growing fear and anxiety within Maraguay for his beloved family. Cayacoa had become the most powerful cacique in Hispaniola after Caonabo's death and rumors of his defeat echoed throughout the island. Maraguay believed Cristóbal Colón's return would further strengthen the Spaniards if he was successful in defeating Francisco Roldán.

Maraguay's decision to move eastward towards Boriken was questioned by his wife Ana and his son Amayao. Ana believed it would be wise to flee westward towards Cuba while Amayao desired to remain and fight for Jaragua and the island of Ayiti.

Maraguay exclaimed, "Many have shed their blood to defeat these Spanish invaders in our land and failed. Some of our leaders have taken the side of our enemies and have undermined our efforts. Guarionex has allied himself with Francisco Roldán against Cristóbal and Bartolomeo, but this is only an alliance of convenience for Francisco Roldán— the Spaniards only argue about the best way to exploit us and our lands and who keeps most of the spoils. Guarionex is a pawn of Roldán and many other leaders have advised him to break his alliance. When Cristóbal returns, he will only seek to regain full control and continue to divide and make us weaker. You see, my son Amayao, we remain divided among ourselves while the Spaniards will remain united against us. These Spaniards have already renamed our lands and they will seek to remove us completely. I am a brave man but I fear for you, for Ana, and for Amanex. My family is my immediate priority, so it is best we continue our life and our fight in Boriken."

Amayao angrily replied, "Father, these invaders will continue to kill us and take from us and our lands in Ayiti, Boriken, and the rest of the islands. We must stay and fight for our people and our land; we cannot let these invaders take them."

Maraguay responded, "My son, I will protect you and my family but we lack organization. I do not anticipate our leader Bohechio will engage Cristóbal in battle. Caonabo and his brother have been killed and now the story of Cacique Cayacoa's death have reached my ears. Perhaps Cacique Cotubanamá will lead a rebellion, but I cannot wait while my family's safety is uncertain. These invaders say they have a God but the only God I see them worshipping is our gold. I also fear the great sickness that has inflicted our people; it seems our Gods have left us at the mercy of their weapons and this great disease. I will fight with my people; however, it must be a united effort. We now understand their motivations and later we can successfully defend ourselves, but I need to protect you. When you have a family of your own, Amayao, then you will understand my words."

Maraguay did not wish to leave for Cuba; he feared Francisco Roldán and other Spaniards who were moving westward. Maraguay believed he could go through the mountain and avoid the major Spanish Forts and reach Higüey in the east. He thought Higüey was relatively safe and there he could decide to fight or flee to Boriken. He and his family should leave soon before Cristóbal's arrival, and they began preparations along with several families to leave Jaragua in several days. Maraguay did not trust the invaders or any alliance between Tainos and Spaniards—particularly after the Spanish invaders revealed their brutality. Amanex also was told of these things, which manifested into fear, unlike the bravery his older brother Amayao often displayed. Amanex was proud of his older brother but understood his father's reasoning. He was saddened to leave Jaragua, their Cacique Bohechio, and his beautiful and intelligent sister Anacaona. After several days, Maraguay and his family joined several other families as they left Jaragua with hopes of a safe arrival to Higüey and Boriken.

Cristóbal Colón was celebrated in Spain and the rest of Europe and despite growing criticism against him, he received support for his third voyage back to the islands. Cristóbal explored new lands and attempted to solidify his control of Hispaniola. he was dismayed that Queen Isabella I rejected his idea of mass enslavement of the Tainos who she regarded as her vassals. However, Cristóbal sought to strengthen the Encomienda system and increase his exploitation efforts. Cristóbal was commissioned to find new trade routes to the orient and he set sail in May of 1498, splitting his fleet of six ships. Three ships were to head straight to Hispaniola while the other three—the Santa María de Guía, the Vaqueños, and the Correo led by himself—would take a southern route.

After spending time with the Portuguese captain João Gonçalves da Câmara, Cristóbal stopped at the Cabo Verde archipelago off the coast of Africa in search of cattle and was unsuccessful. Cristóbal then sailed a southern route towards the island he had named Dominica. After observing some native canoes, he landed on an island with three hills which he named Trinidad after the Holy Trinity. Cristóbal landed on a southwestern point of Trinidad which he named Punta de Arenal on August fourth of 1498. After gathering water and taking some much-needed rest, Cristóbal observed two more islands which he renamed Bella Forma and Concepcion. Cristóbal subsequently sailed south, landing on the northern coast of a large landmass which was never documented. Cristóbal believed this landmass was connected to China and despite his growing sickness, he was energetic with enthusiasm.

Upon his return to Hispaniola on August nineteenth, 1498, Cristóbal Colón publicly hung Spaniard crewmembers for disobedience. Cristóbal also became aware of the Spanish and Taino rebels as well as the rebellion of Francisco Roldán. Cristóbal began to organize a movement to bring an end to Francisco Roldán's regime. He quickly suppressed previous rebellions, including the one led by Bernal Diaz de Pisa, however, Cristóbal understood the power of Francisco Roldán could sustain an effective rebellion and he had attracted nearly half of the Spaniards.

A nobleman by the name of Adrián de Moxica who had accompanied Cristóbal had joined Francisco Roldán's rebellion and took many Spanish nobles with him. Cristóbal also feared potential alliances between Francisco Roldán and the native chiefs and spoke with his advisors about a quick and effective resolution to maintain his fragile governance of Hispaniola. Cristóbal understood Roldán's demands and insisted on a possible agreement. Francisco Roldán and his supporters requested the right to search for gold for personal profit and the ownership of forced Taino laborers. Although Francisco Roldán and his supporters refused to work for the Colón family, they requested back pay and they also demanded to take Taino wives for themselves. Cristóbal, fearing the growing force of Francisco Roldán and his followers along with Taino rebellions and facing the weakening of his control, decided to discuss terms with Francisco Roldán.

Maraguay and his family had successfully fled Jaragua before the arrival of more Spaniards and the return of Cristóbal. Several days into their eastward journey, Maraguay received information of large amounts of Spaniards to Jaragua and he understood that if he had remained on the island now named Hispaniola, he and his family would have soon confronted the hostile invaders. Maraguay moved his family swiftly, avoiding any of the sprouting Spanish cities on the island as he advanced towards Higüey. Maraguay was surprised to see the increasing number of Spaniards and the rapidly decreasing amount of Tainos as he observed from the mountains.

The sun was setting on a hot summer day when Maraguay smelled a scent that was foreign to him. He realized there was a group of Spaniards that had surprisingly found their location; Maraguay assumed a Taino had betrayed him—the Spaniards remained ignorant of most of the geography on the island.

"*Como te llamas*?" one asked. "*Como ustedes se llaman y cual Fortaleza ustedes pertenecen?*"

Maraguay did not understand and simply motioned that he was not hostile and simply wanted to keep moving eastward. Some other Spaniards approached Maraguay's family, causing growing unease in Maraguay. When one of them aimed their weapon at him he struck the Spaniard and disarmed him. Other men from other families joined in as weapon fire began raining on the group, killing a few and injuring Maraguay. A young man around eighteen years of age struck a few of the Tainos with his sword injuring and killing innocent Tainos with visible glee. As he approached, another Spaniard yelled "Ya Basta!" causing the Spaniard to cease his thirst for blood. Ana, Amanex, and Amayao were apprehended by other Spaniards, who brought them back as Maraguay pleaded for their safety. The thirteen-year-old Amanex was not as brave as his fifteen-year-old brother Amayao; he trembled and cried.

Amayao went to strike the young Spaniard, who hit him and broke his nose. Someone called the Spaniard, revealing his name to be Radamés Cesar Milfuegos.

Radamés laughed as Amanex sobbed while he dragged the more aggressive Amayao by his feet with a rope behind his slowly galloping his horse. A smile spread across the menacing young face of Radamés when his eyes gazed upon Amanex's necklace and he took the prized possession for himself.

As they approached the city, Amanex was surprised to see the white invaders practicing some Taino customs. Some Spaniards were now smoking their leaves—which they incorrectly called tobacco—and cooking meat above a fire in the fashion of a Taino barbeque. Amanex also observed many of the Spaniards using Taino words with their own language, although they had slightly corrupted some words. Amanex and his family also noticed many Taino laborers and some Tainos who were speaking the language of the Spanish people they called Castilian. Amanex believed he should learn this exotic language at once to understand where these violent invaders originated from, their culture, and the purpose for their selfishness and lust. Some of these thoughts raced through Amanex as his tears dried in the summer heat. Amanex and his family were counted and their names were recorded as they entered the city of Santo Domingo. They were chained and held near a Taino style home where some Spaniards were ordered to look after them. They were lucky; the other families imprisoned with Amanex were suffering the loss of murdered family members. Amanex ceased being a child and saw life through a new and terrible reality as their way of life came to the end.

In the morning, the Spaniards awakened Amanex and his family from the little sleep they managed to get and began searching for gold among their possessions. They demanded Amanex and the other Tainos remove their jewelry; Amayao and some others who refused were quickly beaten and threatened with death which resulted in their compliance. Maraguay attempted to comfort his family, stating that they should comply and await a safer opportunity to flee their situation. The plan was to wait for the arrival of Cristóbal Colón and continue their labors until the Tainos could respond with a legitimate rebellion. Cristóbal was already on the island, initiating his negotiations with Francisco Roldán and travelling to Santo Domingo. Maraguay secretly hoped that Cristóbal and Francisco Roldán would engage in open warfare so Spanish control of the island would be severely weakened. His immediate concern was to learn as much as he could of these foreigners for the safety of his family.

Santo Domingo was becoming a large city, and one of vital importance to the business of the Spanish Crown in the region. Daily abuses were commonplace; Maraguay and his family were ordered to search for gold for their Spanish masters in nearby mines which entailed arduous labor in the hot summer sun from early morning to late afternoon. He instructed his family to work diligently and remain vigilant for an opportunity for an organized escape.

A few weeks after Amanex and his family were imprisoned in Santo Domingo, Cristóbal Colón finally arrived to Santo Domingo, welcomed by his brother Bartolomeo and the other Spaniards excited about news from Europe. It was the first time Amanex and his family saw the Colón brothers and Amanex mistakenly believed the healthier and stronger Bartolomeo was Cristóbal. Cristóbal Colón appeared far older than his age due to sickness and stress. He squinted at times because of his poor eyesight and some parts of his body were swollen—particularly his legs. Bartolomeo spoke loudly, addressing the crowd and pleased at the progress of the city of Santo Domingo and the arrival of Cristóbal Colón. The Colón brothers sought to end the conflict with Francisco Roldán and unify Spanish Control of the Hispaniola under their rule.

Cristóbal Colón's hair turned white early in life and although he was tall, he did not stand at his full height, which was perhaps from the same ailment that made his walking difficult. Cristóbal was light skinned, although the constant sun and weather of the region had given him slightly reddish skin. He appeared worn by the heavy weight of governing an entire region, nevertheless, he appeared overjoyed with the city of Santo Domingo. Using his adopted Taino son Guaikán as his translator, Cristóbal delivered a message to the Spaniards and Taino alike.

Cristóbal exclaimed, "I thank my brothers Bartolomeo and Giacomo Colón for keeping order in the face of Taino and Spanish rebellion. We still have work to do and we will maintain order and continue to build our cities for the glory of the Spanish Crown and for the Glory of God."

He proceeded to punish Tainos and Spaniards who disobeyed his leadership and the orders of the Colón family. Spaniards were hung publicly, but Tainos were punished in a more brutal fashion. Some Tainos were accused of stealing corn and other crops and Cristóbal cut their ears, hands, and fingers off, publicly parading them to the horror of Amanex. Maraguay desired open warfare between Francisco Roldán and Cristóbal, however, a year later Cristóbal and Francisco Roldán agreed to terms. Cristóbal would soon capture and arrest Spanish rebels including Adrián de Moxica. Cristóbal hung him and managed to arrest the other conspirators: Pedro de Riquelme and his followers in Bonao and Hernando de Guevara. They were arrested and executed in the city of Santo Domingo before Cristóbal and Francisco Roldán agreed to end their war.

Facing growing anger against him and the rising strength of Francisco Roldán, Cristóbal agreed to Francisco's terms. The Former Alcalde Mayor (or the mayor of La Isabela) Francisco Roldán could gain power for himself and other a greater portion of wealth from the exploitation of the Tainos. Francisco Roldán also moved to Santo Domingo, where he would have a more prominent role in the affairs of the city. Cristóbal Colón could keep himself in power in Hispaniola, however, his power was severely eroded and the stories of his abuse, tensions arising from his refusal to baptize the Taino people, and the expansion of slavery led to the arrival of Francisco de Bobadilla.

Francisco de Bobadilla was part of the Order of Calatrava: the first military order founded in Castile. Bobadilla was proud of his order in that it could guard the Castle Calatrava from the Muslims—a castle that the Templar Knights were not able to defend. Bobadilla often spoke about his order and their battles against the Almohad Caliphate and he believed he upheld the principles of his order and desired to bring these principles to Hispaniola.

Cristóbal had sent a letter to the Spanish Crown for someone who could help him lead and instead received his replacement. Francisco held a trial between Cristóbal and the accusations of Francisco Roldán and his followers. Cristóbal was surprised to be found guilty and was publicly shamed and imprisoned along with his family. The Spanish Crown was angered at Cristóbal's actions, his failure to maintain control of the island, and his losing battle against Roldán—which was seen as a lower-class victory over the ruling class. Francisco de Bobadilla sent the Colón brothers back to Spain as prisoners in chains—an embarrassment that would remain etched in the mind of Cristóbal Colón. Francisco de Bobadilla quickly took the position of Governor of the Indies and pardoned the previous actions of Francisco Roldán. Francisco de Bobadilla eliminated the mining tax on gold to stimulate gold production and overall economic growth, which was also viewed negatively by the Crown.

Amanex noticed the vile Radamés Cesar Milfuegos, who seemed to enjoy the arrest of Cristóbal and his brothers. Radamés Cesar Milfuegos remained abusive; sometimes this resulted in the death of Tainos. Many things angered Radamés, particularly the nickname other Spaniards called him. "El Moro" they would yell to gain the attention of Radamés and even when he successfully hid his anger, it would still end in increased beatings of innocent Tainos.

Francisco Roldán continued to hold significant

power in the island of Hispaniola but would soon return along with the Governor Francisco de Bobadilla in 1502. The power of the deity of chaos Juracan arrived in a large hurricane ripping through a large fleet of ships, leading to the deaths of Francisco Roldán and Francisco de Bobadilla. July of 1502 saw the destruction of twenty ships out of thirty-one, including the Flagship El Dorado in the passage between Hispaniola and the island of Boriken renamed San Juan Bautista. Ironically, one of ships that survived the devastating hurricane was the Aguja, which was the weakest in the fleet as well as the one that carried the gold that Cristóbal Colón was owed. This led to various conspiracy theories, including allegations that Cristóbal performed magical spells to influence the hurricane and the survival of the Aguja.

Maraguay and his family continued to work in the goldmines. Although many Catholic Priests objected to the harsh working conditions and the increasing violence against the Tainos, the behavior of the Spaniards continued. Maraguay believed that the best opportunity for himself and his family to flee would arrive soon; the island was not under complete control and the Spaniards did not have a strong leader to manage the affairs of the Spanish. Cacique Cotubanamá was gaining strength in Higüey in eastern Hispaniola and Maraguay believed he would challenge Spanish control of the island. The Taino people's misfortunes would soon increase and send Maraguay and his family through terrors never seen even through the brutal rule of Cristóbal Colón.

CHAPTER 7
THE BRUTALITY OF GOVERNOR NICOLÁS DE OVANDO Y CÁCERES (1506)

Nicolás de Ovando y Cáceres became the third Governor of the Indies in September of 1502. He was a noble and a Knight of the Order of Alcántara appointed by Queen Isabella I of Castile. On the thirteenth of February 1502, Nicolás sailed towards Hispaniola commanding a fleet of thirty ships and over 2,500 colonists from various classes to establish a permanent colony for Spain in this New World.

The arrival of Nicolás brought new horrors for the Taino people as he sought to crush rebellions and to make an example of any who dared question his authority. Nicolas arranged a meeting with leaders including Cacique Bohechio and the beloved Cacica Anacaona. It was organized to be a dinner of two distinct cultures—two peoples who were to agree to an improved coalition between Spaniards and Taino in a feast of Thanksgiving. Maraguay and many other Tainos understood that the barbaric nature that the Spaniards had displayed would never stop and would only worsen with time. The Taino leaders did not want the complete destruction of their people and they agreed to a large dinner in 1503, a year after the arrival of Nicolás Ovando y Cáceres. Amanex remembered in horror when many Tainos and Spaniards gathered together in the village of Yaguana in Jaragua for the honor of Cacica Anacaona.

Anacaona believed that a new Spanish Administration could improve upon the administration of the Colón brothers. She did not trust the Spaniards but thought that a coexistence could develop without the brutality. Perhaps a negotiation could occur where Nicolás would obtain his gold and other precious minerals while the native Taino could continue their lives peacefully. Anacaona understood she could not mount a strong and united revolt against Nicolás and the Spaniards without uniting the caciques from her island and others. The Spaniards carefully observed communications between the caciques on Hispaniola and particularly any communications involving the strong and influential leader Cacique Cotubanamá. Anacaona knew her power was limited and sought to try to maintain a temporary agreement and peace until she and her brother Bohechio could gather strength and negotiate from a position of power.

Anacaona and her brother could maintain cordial relations with Cristóbal and his brother Bartolomeo and they agreed that Tainos should pay the Spaniards a tribute of food and cotton. They also were guests on Cristóbal's boat as they sailed in the bay of western Hispaniola. The Spaniards brought their exotic animals, including the pig that had a delicious flavor and was much loved by many Tainos. Over eighty-six chiefs gathered in honor of Anacaona and Bohechio along with hundreds of Spaniards. As the dinner began, armed Spanish soldiers secretly closed in on the Taino chiefs and upon Governor Nicolás' orders, they signaled the other Spaniards at the dinner to move out of the way. The large meeting house was set on fire and any Taino that managed to escape were shot. Most of the chiefs were burned alive where they ate, along with Taino women and children. Cacique Bohechio was killed in an attempt to fight back and many of his wives would also perish from violence and disease. The screams and cries were met by the laughter of the Spaniards, who watched as the flames consumed the Taino Chiefs and their families. Anacaona was spared and imprisoned.

Anacaona and her daughter Higüemota were rescued by other Tainos but a Spanish search party recaptured her several months later. Anacaona and several Tainos were then paraded in front of the Spaniards. The Tainos loved the leadership of Anacaona and admired her beauty, intelligence, and empathy for her people. The Spaniards understood the importance of keeping Anacaona alive and Governor Nicolás de Ovando y Cáceres offered Anacaona to one of the noble Spaniards who desired her most. The marriage of Anacaona to a Spaniard noble could maintain the obedience of the Tainos who respected her and thus maintain the stability of the Spanish Government in Hispaniola. As a light rain began to fall in the late afternoon, Anacaona looked at her subjects and then the Spaniards before she rejected the offer of marriage, sealing her fate.

Anacaona was offered clemency but refused as she exclaimed in a loud, powerful voice, "I'd rather leave this world alongside my Taino people than spend another day as a concubine to a Spaniard man in a Spaniard society."

Tears began to fall on the faces of the Taino as she stood triumphantly as the noose was fastened around her neck. Amanex and his family saw from a distance as Anacaona quickly left the world an image that would remain engraved in their minds for as long as they lived.

The horrors of the Spaniards continued in Higüey, where the peace between both people would quickly dissolve. A local cacique was helping load cassava for transport by caravels to Santo Domingo and several other cities. The cacique supervised the Tainos with his scepter (or vara, as the Spaniards called it), which called the attention of one of the dogs held in chains by a Spanish captain named Salamanca. Captain Salamanca tried to hold back his attack dog as the cacique unknowingly continued to wave his scepter.

One of the Spaniards jokingly said, "It would

indeed be funny if we let the dog upon this Indio!"

Some Spaniards who had overheard this comment motioned towards the attack dog, sending him upon the cacique and dragging Captain Salamanca. At once the dog disemboweled the cacique as his screams shocked the other Tainos. Captain Salamanca and the rest of the Spaniards loaded the cargo onto the ships and proceeded their business as if no incident had occurred. As if an animal had perished rather than a man. However, news spread of this foul deed, reaching the ears of the powerful leader, Cacique Cotubanamá.

Cotubanamá ordered the other Taino leaders to organize and attack Spanish garrisons in Higüey. When Taino rebels overran one, Governor Nicolás ordered Juan Ponce de León and Juan de Esquivel east towards Higüey and placed a small army of Spaniards under their command to destroy the Taino force. Juan Ponce de León and Juan de Esquivel had previously arrived during the Cristóbal's second voyage to Hispaniola and both men were now trying to gain prominent positions of authority in the exploitation of the Taino people in the Hispaniola. Juan Ponce de León moved quickly, seeking to gain a higher standing in the eyes of Governor Nicolás. Cacique Cayacoa's widow—now called Doña Inés de Cayacoa—alongside Cacique Cotubanamá and the Cacica Iguanamá had united a strong Taino rebellion against the approaching Juan Ponce de León and Juan de Esquivel.

Leading 400 Spaniards, Juan de Esquivel marched ahead of Juan Ponce de León towards the location of Cacique Cotubanamá. Juan de Esquivel and Juan Ponce de León led their respective units on horseback as the Spanish soldiers marched for about five days with heavy armor and the island sun working together, causing some to slow down and collapse from heatstroke. The Spaniards ate whatever they could from the plants that Hispaniola produced: yucca, maize, and small animals like the hutia and agutí which the Spaniards hunted after learning the techniques of the Tainos. The location of Cacique Cotubanamá in Higüey was betrayed by other Tainos who did not want to rebel against Governor Nicolás de Ovando y Cáceres. However, Taino scouts alerted Taino leaders through smoke signals. At once the fight began initially in the favor of Spaniards, who had surprised the Tainos. However, Cacique Cotubanamá called on Taino reserves which carved through the Spanish lines and divided the Spaniards into several segments, eventually leading to an intense, close quarter combat. The Tainos managed to insert fear into the hearts of the Spaniards as their anger and bravery manifested in the temporary retreat of the Spanish lines. Retreating Spaniards cut down Tainos with their swords while the Spaniards who were at a safe distance fired upon those in the rear and advanced towards the area of battle, quickly turning the fight in favor of Juan de Esquivel.

The region of Higüey was mountainous and some Taino leaders, along with women and children, took refuge in the numerous caverns in the mountaintops while the Taino warriors attempted to defeat the advancing Spaniards. Cotubanamá was farther east, leading his own Taino warriors. A Spanish force could reach Cacique Cotubanamá, who at times engaged the heavily armed Spaniards in combat himself. The Spaniards were in awe of the size of Cotubanamá: his skill and his ability to kill a few Spaniards by managing to disarm and dig their own swords through their chests. Some of the Tainos were able to kill Spaniards despite being shot and pierced with multiple swords strikes. However, as the Spaniards continued eastward, Cacique Cotubanamá realized he was unprepared and sent minor chiefs to negotiate a peace treaty with Juan de Esquivel and Juan Ponce de León. After negotiations, Juan de Esquivel and Juan Ponce de León agreed for a peace treaty and invited Cacique Cotubanamá to discuss terms. Juan de Esquivel did not want to engage in further war and wished to gain the territory of Higüey and additional Taino slaves for Governor Nicolás de Ovando y Cáceres. Juan de Esquivel observed the ferocity of the Tainos in defending their lands against the Spanish swords and guns and believed they would all fight to their death despite the odds and therefore he and others welcomed Cacique Cotubanamá's offer.

This peace was short-lived, however. The Spaniards continued their brutality against Taino women and children—including those of the Taino chiefs. The Spanish garrison left behind by Juan de Esquivel and Juan Ponce de León became the target of vengeful Tainos seeking to reclaim the honor of their women and children.

The native custom was for leaders to exchange names as part of peace agreements and thus Juan de Esquivel took the name of Cacique Cotubanamá and Cotubanamá took the name of Esquivel in the Taino tradition of guatiao. The Spaniards however, did not honor this ceremony. Juan de Esquivel and Juan Ponce de León were taken aback by the large frame of Cotubanamá, whose strength, height, and muscularity was far above other Tainos and most of the Spaniards. After the destruction and the killing of the Spaniards in Higüey, Governor Nicolás de Ovando y Cáceres ordered a larger force—now led by Juan de Esquivel commanding the Spaniards of Santiago, Juan Ponce de León leading the Spaniards of Santo Domingo, and Diego de Escobar leading the Spaniards of Concepcion de la Vega. Governor Nicolás de Ovando y Cáceres also sent an additional Auxiliary force of Tainos and declared that Juan Ponce de León would become Governor of the eastern region of Higüey following a successful defeat of Cacique Cotubanamá and the Taino leaders. The Governor also ordered for the mass killing and executions of all Taino leaders and the Taino people as he angrily exclaimed, "Sword and Fire to all the Tainos."

The Spaniards marched forward alongside their Taino supporters. This time the brutal Radamés Cesar Milfuegos was ordered to march under the command of Juan Ponce de León. Juan Ponce de León was short in stature—just an inch below five feet. However, what Juan Ponce de León lacked in height, he exceeded in perseverance, violence, and ambition. Juan de Esquivel was ordered to kill as many Tainos and their leaders as he could and the Tainos spared would be subjected to the rule of

Juan Ponce de León. The Governor ordered Cotubanamá to be captured alive and returned to Santo Domingo where he would be questioned, humiliated, and executed. Governor Nicolás de Ovando y Cáceres understood that Cacique Cotubanamá represented a large threat to his governance just as Cacique Caonabo had represented a threat to Cristóbal Colón's administration in Hispaniola. The public display of Cotubanamá's execution would serve as a warning to any Tainos who desired to challenge Governor Nicolás de Ovando y Cáceres and so his capture was of vital importance.

As they marched forward, the Spaniards encountered small bands of Tainos who would fire arrows from mountaintops, which inflicted some damage. Shots from the arquebuses pierced the island air, hitting Tainos who fled in fear as their friends and family fell around them. The Spanish march continued; some villages were empty as the Tainos fled to the hills and some had Taino warriors who were cut down by Spanish fire. The vile Radamés Cesar Milfuegos took pleasure in the mass killings and torture of innocent Tainos after Spanish victories in the battlefield.

Despite the horrors that the Tainos faced, they refused to reveal the location of their chiefs. However, they were eventually found— Ines de Cayacoa among them. Cacica Iguanamá had fled to the southeastern reaches of Higüey along with Cacique Cotubanamá. Radamés called for the torture and deaths of the chiefs and Tainos after they revealed important information about the whereabouts of Cacica Iguanamá and Cacique Cotubanamá. Juan de Esquivel partially agreed with Radamés, however Juan Ponce de León believed that if the mass executions persisted he would rule the land of Higüey without any subjects.

The Spanish arrived at the southeastern point of Higüey after receiving information that Cacique Cotubanamá and possibly Iguanamá were now holding for a final stand on the island Cristóbal Colón had renamed Isla Saona. Juan Ponce de León remained in Higüey in an effort to break any remaining Taino rebellions, while Juan de Esquivel would initiate the final offensive against Cacique Cotubanamá. Despite their growing advantage, some of the Spaniards feared the strategically capable and fierce Cotubanamá and tales of his best Taino fighters with two and three bone-tipped arrows. Jose de Esquivel reassured his men that if they had been successful in conquering Higüey, they could easily conquer this small island. Jose de Esquivel understood that most of the major caciques had been captured or killed in battle. The few major caciques in custody would later be brought to Santo Domingo for further interrogation and execution. Still, a few caciques were still free, including Cacique Guarionex who many believed had escaped to the neighboring island to the east now renamed San Juan Bautista. Governor Nicolás de Ovando y Cáceres knew he had to take full control of the island of Hispaniola before he could turn his attention to Cuba and San Juan Bautista.

Juan de Esquivel led a little over fifty Spaniards into Isla Saona during the night, moving swiftly and with violent aggression for fear that the elusive Cacique Cotubanamá would escape. The Spaniards found some Taino spies who were tortured for the purpose of uncovering Cacique Cotubanamá—one of which was stabbed in the heart while the other Taino agreed to lead the way towards the location of Cotubanamá. At once, large amounts of three tipped arrows descended upon the Spaniards, causing panic and confusion. Juan de Esquivel ordered his men to fire on the Tainos, which forced them to flee. Juan de Esquivel grew more sadistic and ordered gibbets to be built close to the ground to prolong the hanging of the Tainos by letting their feet slightly touch the ground. The Spaniards then separated into small groups, killing men, women, and children along with the sick and the elderly from caves.

A young twenty-year-old Spaniard named Bartolome de las Casas, who was accompanying Juan de Esquivel's expedition, grew increasingly appalled at the brutality of the Spaniards upon the Taino people. Despite

Bartolome de las Casas and his criticism of Spanish brutality, they continued to brutalize any Tainos they found under the orders of Juan de Esquivel.

One of the Taino prisoners who led the Spaniards across the island revealed that Cacique Cotubanamá was nearby, but before they arrived to his hiding place, the Taino prisoner jumped from a cliff and lost his life on the jagged rocks below. A strong and fast Spaniard named Juan Lopez was the first to observe a group of Tainos in a thick wooded area. Juan Lopez ran towards the group and alerted the other Spanish soldiers, who followed quickly behind him. The Tainos separated into two rows, revealing the strong and tall Taino leader Cotubanamá. Cotubanamá ordered his fellow Tainos to fight as he countered the advancing Juan Lopez with a strike, knocking the powerful Spaniard to the ground. While Juan Lopez tried to regain his balance, Cotubanamá reached for his bow to kill him and defend himself against the other Spaniards. Cotubanamá fired an arrow while ordering the hesitant Tainos to engage them in battle. Juan Lopez lunged at Cotubanamá as he prepared to kill him, knocking the famed cacique to the ground. Juan Lopez sliced Cotubanamá across his arms, partially missing his chest as the cacique tried to shield himself from further injury. Cotubanamá managed to disarm Juan Lopez and after striking him across his face, he began to choke him to death. Juan Lopez was overpowered and only survived because of other Spaniards swarming the cacique, beating him into submission. The enraged Juan Lopez and his group threatened the cacique with death.

In response, Cacique Cotubanamá yelled, "I am Juan de Esquivel!"

The Spaniards held Cacique Cotubanamá until the arrival of Juan de Esquivel, who ordered the cacique to be interrogated and transported alive back to Santo Domingo along with other chiefs. Cacique Guarionex was now believed to have escaped to the island of San Juan Bautista with other chiefs, however most of the major leaders in Hispaniola were now captured or killed. A further search of

Isla Saona revealed that the female chief Iguanamá was still at large in Higüey. Juan de Esquivel believed her forces had been greatly reduced from constant Spanish raids of Higüey and as soon as he arrived on the Hispaniolan mainland, he ordered Juan Ponce de León to capture her alive. The great Cacica Iguanamá, through the stress of leading a rebellion against a growing Spaniard force, had grown older in appearance.

Juan de Esquivel ordered any native who did not comply with the Spaniards to be executed. This was followed by many of the Spaniards, most notably Radamés Cesar Milfuegos. Radamés and his killing of Spaniards paled in comparison to his thirst for Taino blood. He enjoyed the torture of the Tainos, often taking part in interrogations. Radamés found joy in impaling the young Taino children in front of their parents and would sometimes drown them in the local rivers. Sometimes the Spaniards would send their dogs to chase fleeing Tainos and watch as they tore the flesh and limbs from bodies. After several weeks, the great leader Iguanamá was captured.

Always defiant, she did not recognize the rule of Governor Nicolás de Ovando y Cáceres and exclaimed, "No matter how many of us you kill and how much of our history you destroy, if the God you worship is a just God then you will face punishment for your transgressions against me and my people."

Iguanamá would not be taken to Santo Domingo, threatening the Spaniards and trying to kill any who approached. Juan Ponce de León ordered her to be executed by hanging to maintain the peaceful transport of the other Taino chiefs back to Santo Domingo. The respected leader Iguanamá, fighting until the end, hung until dead on a single gibbet erected for her alone. Her body was to remain there for many months until Juan Ponce de León ordered it cut down. Juan Ponce de León would remain in Higüey to oversee the construction of new cities and to begin to organize his administration and building of several cities, including the expansion of Salvaleón de Higüey, which would now include a church as Juan Ponce de León began his role of Provincial Governor of Higüey.

Amanex remembered the day they brought the feared and respected Cacique Cotubanamá to Santo Domingo. The Governor was relieved when Juan de Esquivel entered Santo Domingo with Cacique Cotubanamá; he was the last major threat to the rule of the Governor Nicolás de Ovando y Cáceres. The governor ordered the public hanging of the chiefs and other Tainos were burned alive in a sadistic form of celebration while Cotubanamá would be saved for a final public execution. The Spaniards had threatened to burn Cotubanamá alive several times, but Esquivel reminded them that Cotubanamá would be spared for the purposes of quenching the Governor's thirst for vengeance. Amanex recalled the loud laughter and excitement among the Spaniards in Santo Domingo as Cotubanamá was paraded around for everyone to see. Cotubanamá was a large man who was widely respected; now he was reduced to an object of an entertainment.

When Cotubanamá was brought in front of the Governor, he said, "Who are you who pretends to be the owner of our lands? Your governance has no legitimacy in the eyes of the Taino people on the island of Ayiti or any other islands. I made peace with Juan de Esquivel yet the Spaniards continued to rape our wives and children and hurt and kill our people, so I punished them by burning them to death. You punish me for simply punishing the Spaniards who broke our peace. We offered you peace when Cristóbal Colón arrived and instead your people offered only hatred and violence in return. So, I will leave my life among the lies and hatred that is your people because this is no life for me."

The Governor replied, "Your life will soon be over and you will disappear along with your race."

Cotubanamá was hung, and with his death the last major challenge to Governor Nicolás de Ovando y Cáceres was extinguished. The Governor turned his attention to

Cristóbal Colón. The Governor prevented the Colón family from landing on the island of Hispaniola and now the Governor would desire Cristóbal's death.

Amanex, who was a better student than his brother Amayao, had developed a larger vocabulary in the language of the Castilians and would secretly interpret for his parents who anxiously awaited the words of their tormenters. Through his knowledge of the Castilian language, Amanex informed his parents of Spanish affairs and the current news of Cristóbal Colón's return to the region.

The Spanish Crown imprisoned Cristóbal Colón along with his brothers in the year 1500, embarrassing Cristóbal, who believed he deserved respect and titles for his work in conquering and governing these lands for the young and enlarging Spanish Empire. Cristóbal and his brothers were there six weeks before finally being released. After this, Cristóbal Colón's sailed westward along with his brother Bartolomeo Colón, Diego Mendez, and his youngest son Fernando. Cristóbal departed Cádiz, Spain on May twelfth, 1502 leading four ships: the Gallega, Vizcaína, Santiago de Palos, and his flagship the Capitana. After hearing that Portuguese sailors were attacked by moors, Cristóbal arrived at Arzila to rescue them, departing Africa and arriving On June 15, 1502 to the island named Jouanacaëra-Matinino by the Tainos, named Jouanacaëra by the Kalinago people, and now renamed as Martinica. The famed island of the Iguanas was the last stopping point before Cristóbal Colón turned his attention once again to the island of Hispaniola.

Cristóbal arrived in Santo Domingo on June twentieth, 1502, but Governor Nicolás de Ovando y Cáceres denied him port. As a powerful hurricane began to arrive, Cristóbal asked the governor to avoid sending a departing fleet to Spain and to allow him shelter in Santo Domingo. Governor Nicolás de Ovando y Cáceres denied this as well and much of the fleet was destroyed.

Cristóbal Colón would be denied entry to Santo Domingo and the entire island of Hispaniola. He subsequently sailed to the island of Jamaica, where he stopped at Guanaja and spent two months. Bartolomeo found a large canoe full of cargo and gold, which excited his brother, who was overjoyed to find such richness in these new lands. The natives were shipping gold to large cities—cities of the Maiam—which Cristóbal and his brothers began referring to as the Mayas. Cristóbal continued his explorations, later travelling south and discovering a narrow pass where the natives stated an entire large body of water just west of this region was named Veragua by the native Ngäbe or Guaymí people. There he met a leader named Urracá, who the natives and Spaniards also called El Quibían. Cristóbal entrusted Bartolomeo to make a peace agreement with El Quibían and it was successful. However, the peace would soon be broken.

Cristóbal encountered a river named the Yebra and renamed it Rio Belén after the day of the Epiphany—the date of his arrival to this region on January sixth, 1503. Cristóbal founded a settlement which he named Santa María de Belén and he instructed his brother to govern the settlement and lead eighty Spaniards while he returned to Spain for reinforcements to subjugate the Ngäbe people and exploit their resources. Cristóbal believed he could establish a far more profitable settlement and surpass Governor Nicolás de Ovando y Cáceres and the city of Santo Domingo in Hispaniola. However, when the Spaniards crossed a section of a river that El Quibían instructed them not to, El Quibían began calling on all the chiefs—including his enemies—to unite against the Colón brothers. Bartolomeo, who had been suspicious of El Quibían, discovered his plot and invited the powerful chief and his family and friends to his boats to discuss further negotiations. Bartolomeo tied up El Quibían and apprehended his family, later throwing El Quibían overboard and incorrectly assuming he drowned.

Cristóbal Colón's dreams of creating a new settlement was destroyed when El Quibían led a united native revolt which resulted in the destruction of Santa Maria de Belen, the death of Spaniards, and injury to

Bartolomeo. Cristóbal and his family managed to escape, leaving his and burning settlement behind and one of his ships destroyed. Bartolomeo had barely escaped with his life along with the embarrassed and humbled Spaniards aboard the ship. They hung El Quibían's family members and friends who had failed to flee. Cristóbal and his crew attempted a return to Hispaniola, but storms and termite damage led the weakened fifty-two-year-old to dock in the bay of Jamaica along with his brothers and his frightened son Ferdinand.

He suffered from various ailments and could barely walk, confining himself to his ship and walking along the Jamaican shore during the day to speak to Tainos who could aid him and his crew in getting water, food, and wood to rebuild his ships. In a desperate state, Cristobal sent Diego Mendez and others to the island of Hispaniola in an effort to seek entry, but Governor Nicolás de Ovando y Cáceres denied him once again.

However, Cacique Ameyro, who ruled eastern Jamaica, and a Taino named Guani approached Cristóbal and his crew and provided Diego Mendez with a canoe so he and the Spaniards could travel to the island of Hispaniola. Cristóbal was secretly interested in Taino knowledge of the sea and stars which they depicted through their art and rocks. The Tainos were able to teach Cristóbal about the seas and the weather, warning him about hurricanes. They helped Cristóbal find the other islands and tried to inform him of the great landmass he failed to reach. Nevertheless, he sought the good graces of his Taino hosts in Jamaica; he wanted to impress them with the accuracy of his own knowledge of Astronomy.

Cristóbal went to his ship and gathered some materials from his study regarding the works of a German polymath named Johannes Müller von Königsberg (or simply known as Regiomontanus), which detailed astronomical patterns and predictions. In his Ephemeris (or navigational notes provided by Regiomontanus), it detailed an upcoming Lunar Eclipse on February twenty-ninth, 1504. For several days, Cristóbal sent word to different

Taino leaders on the island of Jamaica to gather around and witness the Lunar Eclipse, which was correctly predicted. Many of the Tainos were overjoyed and through Cristóbal's translators asked him to share his notes regarding the celestial bodies. Cristóbal thus remained on the island with plenty of food and water and materials for his ship until the Governor of Hispaniola finally sent him aid, allowing Cristóbal and his family safe passage back to Spain on November seventh, 1504.

Cristóbal began to realize he never landed in Japan, Korea, or the Indies. The Tainos had corrected Cristóbal and educated him about the geography of this New World and he came to the realization that the world might be larger than he originally believed. However, he would not make another voyage. Governor Nicolás de Ovando y Cáceres finally cemented his power on the island and removed all rivals while the man he hated, Cristóbal Colón, finally passed away at the age of fifty-four in Valladolid, Spain, on May twentieth, 1506.

The Tainos in Hispaniola had died in massive numbers through disease and violence. Many of the women were married to Spaniards or used as concubines while many others were raped and tortured. The work became more unbearable and many Tainos were killed. Amanex soon believed there would be no more Tainos to supply the work that the Spaniards needed to operate their colony. Maraguay began to advise his children to either join the Taino military forces under the Spaniards or to escape to another island. Amayao followed his father's advice and because of his abilities, he made himself available to fight alongside the Spaniards. However, his father pleaded with his children that they escape whenever they found the opportunity to do so. Amanex did not wish to leave his parents as tears rolled down his face, but the memories of all his friends and family who had perished and the many thousands of Tainos who had been killed or passed away made him understand escape was necessary. Some of the Tainos had killed their own children and committed suicide to escape this hell on earth. Amanex knew the replacement of the Taino on the island of Hispaniola was now a certainty as a new people under Spanish bondage began arriving to Santo Domingo.

CHAPTER 8
AFRICAN ARRIVAL (1508)

In 1501, the Spanish Monarchs granted permission to the Spanish conquistadors to begin bringing African slaves to Hispaniola and other islands under Spanish control. Later in 1501, the first Africans began arriving. Some argued that the Africans would make bad Christians and bad slaves in Hispaniola while many Spaniards supported an increase in African slavery because the Taino population was rapidly declining. After 1502, African Slaves began arriving in increasing numbers. The slaves were initially purchased cheaply from the French and Portuguese. Some Spanish African conquistadors also arrived, serving the Spanish Crown with promises of emancipation including Conquistador Juan Garrido who arrived in Santo Domingo and would serve in various Spanish expeditions including the conquests of Cuba, San Juan Bautista, and the Aztecs. Other Spanish African conquistadors would later include Sebastián Toral, Juan Bardales, Juan Beltrán, and Juan Valiente who would later serve under Pedro de Almagro in Guatemala and subsequently Pedro de Valdivia's company in Chile.

Amanex remembered just a few years prior the arrival of a people with dark skin the color of midnight as they entered the city of Santo Domingo. Now a tall and strong twenty-three-year-old man, he looked upon his own people with pity and sadness as the Taino continued to be exterminated and many of the royal family had been executed. Anacaona left behind her young nephew named Guarocuya, and the twelve-year-old was under the care of the Spaniard named Bartolome de la Casas. He was renamed Enrique Bejo but was commonly called Enriquillo. Enriquillo's father was named Magiocatex and he was burned alive along with other Taino leaders in the massacre of Jaragua. Amanex wondered about the life of young Enriquillo under the protection of Bartolome de las Casas; living amongst the Spaniards who executed his family members and thousands of Taino people.

The men, women, and children with dark rich skin began arriving more frequently from a region the Spaniards called Africa. Amanex had become fluent in the language of the Spaniards, however he made sure they believed he only had limited knowledge. Amanex learned that the Moros were Africans who the Spaniards sometimes used as slaves. Their religion is like that of the Catholic Spaniards, but their God is called Allah.

Slavery had existed in Europe and Muslim Spain for centuries. The institution of slavery also extended into Africa, where African people would work and gain their freedom at a later date. The Moors had also enslaved Christians, but the process was reversed after the fall of Muslim Spain and the rise of the Spanish Empire. Now Catholics enforced slavery on the Muslims who had previously enslaved them. The Africans first arrived to Hispaniola in 1501 and were already enslaved in Spain and spoke the Spanish language—the same language as their masters. The Taino secretly communicated with the Africans in the same language as their common oppressors. Amanex began to see more of them as the years passed and now these Africans began to work alongside him in the goldmines.

Africans were beaten regularly by Spaniards. They understood the worst part of Spanish society and practices, as they were enslaved long before the Taino and other native island peoples. The Africans came from a land mass with many riches, tribes, and nations; they spoke to Amanex and other Tainos about their ancient history and individual cultures. The practice of systematic forced bondage to the scale of the Spaniards and their European Rivals were unknown the Tainos. The Africans were enslaved in Spain and in various Portuguese posts around Africa. Through his conversations with the Africans and Spaniards, Amanex realized there were other white empires colonizing other parts of the world. Amanex had learned that the Portuguese had conquered a land called India in 1506 with the help of Francisco de Almeida, and Amanex believed these Indians lived near the same region in which Cristóbal Colón mistakenly believed he had arrived.

Amanex observed a hierarchy of races brought over from Africa and Europe. The Africans who lived in Spain and other mixed people who arrived were more resistant to the diseases the Spaniards brought to Hispaniola. The people who were mixed with African and Spaniards were named Mulattoes by the Spaniards and appeared in different shades of brown similar to the complexion of the Taino people. The Spaniards began to label the different mixtures, including the children of the Taina women and Spaniards who were called Mestizos. Many Africans came from the Kingdom of Kongo. Other Africans arriving belonged to various groups of people including the Igbo, Mandingo, Kalabari, Akan, Aja, and Yoruba. Africans who had been enslaved in Spain were often used as translators and were treated slightly better than those arriving directly from central and Western Africa.

Amanex's mother and father were growing sick and could no longer work. The abusive Spaniards spared Amanex's parents because he worked harder and provided more gold than others and his brother Amayao had become a good Taino aid and translator for the Spanish soldiers. For the first time, Amanex was alone during his work in the goldmines while his father did minimal construction work in Santo Domingo. For many years, Maraguay had helped

Amanex improve as a laborer and lifted his self-esteem. Maraguay, sensing the end of his life was near, had informed his children to escape and seek a life of their own on another island. He had planned to escape along with his children but had grown weak and planned to protect his wife in Santo Domingo if he failed to escape.

The Africans helped replace the dwindling Taino population and Amanex personally experienced the increasing amounts of Africans at the goldmines. For the first few years, most of the Africans worked in agriculture and construction in Santo Domingo then began moving to copper mines. However, soon they began to replace the sick and deceased Tainos in the goldmines, including the goldmine where Amanex worked. His anger at the Spaniards grew and dwindled everyday but remained a shadow everywhere he went. Some days were better than others but the brutality of the Spaniards and their constant harassment of Taino men, women, and children instilled a constant hatred and fear within Amanex and others. He wanted to remain with his parents but he also wanted to flee the island of Hispaniola like his brother Amayao was now determined to do.

Amayao hated his work as an aid for the Spanish soldiers but made sure to analyze the men he deeply despised as he waited for his moment of escape. Amayao was a twenty-six-year-old man who had become a skilled fighter and now had learned to contain his short temper. Despite the strengthening Spanish control of Hispaniola, Amayao and other Tainos were aware of Taino chiefs on the island who refused to submit to Spanish rule. Amayao did not want to kill any Taino he encountered during patrols, but he assisted in various retrievals of Taino runaways which culminated in punishment and execution. The actions of the Spaniards solidified Amayao's resolve and his plans of escaping. He believed other chiefs had already fled east to the island of Boriken and would plan an attack on the island, as it had now become the headquarters of Spanish power in the region. Amayao's plot would materialize when he was ordered to accompany the Spanish soldiers east towards Higüey, where he would serve Juan Ponce de León.

Amayao's departure brought sadness to his parents and his brother Amanex, however his father Maraguay was excited about the increasing possibility of his son's escape. After his brother's departure, Amanex began to think of his own plan and the possibility of freeing his parents from slavery. He was motivated by the open retaliations of Africans against their Spanish masters. Amanex befriended an African from the Kingdom of Kongo named Elombe Masombo, which meant "brave one" in his native Kikongo. Elombe was a tall, strong man who had a high level of intellect and was able to read Spanish literature during his previous stay in Spain under a benevolent master. Elombe had two other siblings a younger sister and an older brother who remained in Spain as slaves. Amanex was interested in Spanish literature as well as the rich African literature that Elombe often spoke of; he enjoyed his overall conversations with Elombe Masombo whenever they were free from close Spanish observation.

Elombe spoke of his kingdom, its capital city of Mbanza Kongo, and the kings of Kongo who held the title of manikongo. Their society had grown powerful in the Central African region and began hundreds of years prior in 1390 with their celebrated King Lukeni lua Nimi in. Elombe Masombo was three years older than Amanex and the same age as Amayao. He was born in 1482, a year before the Portuguese arrived to the Kingdom of Kongo. At the time of Elombe's birth, the manikongo was a leader by the name of Nzinga a Nkuwu who was baptized into the Christian religion and renamed João I Nzinga. The successor to the throne of Kongo would be Mvemba a Nzinga, who was baptized and given the name Afonso I Mvemba a Nzinga. The Portuguese were working to establish deeper ties with the Kingdom of Kongo and the subsequent ruler Afonso I Mvemba a Nzinga.

The Portuguese were developing the slave system within Africa while continuing to enlarge their empire. The Spanish began purchasing African slaves from the

Portuguese and sending them to the island of Hispaniola to help replace the shrinking Taino population and to further exploit the natural resources of the islands to inflate the riches of the Spanish Crown. Elombe was from the province of Nsundi in 1492 when the Portuguese stole him and his brother from their family. He was ten. Elombe was well read in Spanish literature, which exposed him to the culture of the Muslim, Jews, Christians, Middle Eastern, and Far Eastern people. His favorite piece of literature was called *El Cantar de mio Cid* (or *The Song of my Cid*). *Song of my Cid* was an epic poem about the Castilian hero named El Cid during the time of the Reconquista war against the Moors in Spain.

Elombe improved in the Castilian language which was sometimes identified as Español or Spanish, because it was the language mainly spoken by the Spaniards. Elombe also spoke Catalan and some Portuguese and helped Amanex learn them daily during their work at the goldmine. Elombe inquired about the islands and the history of Hispaniola and the surrounding islands. Amanex explained that the Taino were a kind people who had lived in peace with various native groups on the islands including the Ciguayo, Macorix, Lucayans, and the Guanahatabey. Amanex spoke of the Kalinago, who the Spaniards referred to as the Carib, as people the Taino would have conflict with, but Amanex stated that his people never had experienced violence, brutality, and widespread slavery until the Spaniards came.

Amanex understood that the Spaniards, Portuguese, and other white people were entering Africa and the islands of the Taino people; he suspected that Santo Domingo would be used to expand Spanish and European power into other civilizations of the mainland using help from the native people. Amanex believed the Taino revolts in the island now called Hispaniola were nearly extinguished and future rebellions would have to start from the surrounding islands, however he still had hope. The Spaniards sporadically spoke of chiefs who remained free and would potentially create future rebellions. There was also a growing possibility of a massive revolt on the island of San Juan Bautista to the east. Amayao informed Amanex about the growing movement on San Juan Bautista headed by the Supreme Leader Cacique Agüeybaná I against Spanish rule. When the two men were not within earshot of their Spanish masters, Elombe exclaimed, "I think a revolt is the only way we can achieve a life of peace and freedom. In Africa, we still have our great civilizations and cities but they are slowly being corrupted by the growing power of the Spanish, Portuguese, and other kingdoms. Your Taino people don't simply face corruption and slavery, but total elimination from the earth. We should form an alliance between all Africans, Tainos, and Caribs despite our tribal differences. If we work together we can overcome slavery and create a new society for ourselves free of Spanish domination."

Amanex replied, "I believe we can do it, but I do not wish to leave until my parents can come with me. We can possibly escape towards Puerto Rico or another island. I am unsure if we can stage a successful revolt in the island of Hispaniola now, as communication between the different tribes has been difficult with Spanish intervention. Perhaps in the future we will be able to form a formidable rebellion."

The two men quickly changed the conversation as a Spaniard yelled, "Keep quiet, you animals and continue your labors or I shall beat you close to death."

Maraguay rejoined his son in the mines as soon as he got a little healthier. He and Amanex learned more about the Africans they worked amongst: some came from the Kingdom of Mali and spoke of the great city of Timbuktu and the famous library which educated their people and visitors who desired to learn. The Mali Empire had a rich history and was strategically positioned in western Africa in the vast savanna grasslands south of the Sahara Desert and north of the coastal rain forests. The Mali Empire rose above the previous Empire of Goa and the Empire of Ghana and was founded by the prince and leader named

Sundiata Keita.

Sundiata Keita was born in Niani which became the capital of the Mali Empire. In 1235, as the leader of one of the state of Kangaba, he defeated his main rival—the neighboring kingdom of Susu—and began consolidating power in the region. Sundiata Keita expanded his territory and gained control of the gold bearing lands of Bambuk and Bondu of the south, pushed north to Lac Débo, and northwest. subduing the Diara.

Sundiata Keita's successors increased the Malian Empire's territory towards the western coast of Africa. The emperors of Mali were called Mansa and Musa Keita I (known as Mansa Musa). He became legendary in the minds of many who heard of his power and wealth. Amanex marveled at the story of Emperor Mansa Musa—how he could control his vast resources, enabling him to bring great wealth to himself and his people. Africans explored the western oceans before, including Abu Bakr II (also known as Mansa Qu), who appointed Mansa Musa as his deputy as he ordered hundreds of ships to sail the limits of the ocean—a mission he never returned from, leaving Mansa Musa in power. Mansa Musa acquired the influential trading cities of Timbuktu and Gao, the important South Saharan city of Walata in the south, and the salt rich Taghaza region in the north. Mansa Musa also extended his empire eastwards towards the Hausa people and subdued Takrur, the lands of the Fulani, and Tukulor peoples.

Mansa Musa later embarked on a famed pilgrimage to Mecca to fulfill his Islamic religious duty. His wealth and power made him well known in Africa and the Middle East and in July of 1324, he visited the Mamluk sultan of Egypt, Al-Nasir Muhammad. Amanex was amazed at the tale of Mansa Musa's journey and the amount of wealth and influenced he possessed. Mansa Musa sent ambassadors to various civilizations, including Morocco and Egypt, and invited many scholars from Egypt to Timbuktu, where he also erected a Great Mosque named Jingere-Ber. Maraguay was also curious about the great

African societies and he asked Elombe many questions about his life in Africa and Spain.

Elombe asked Amanex and Maraguay about the societies on the islands and the cities the Spaniards had yet to encounter. Maraguay, speaking through his son Amanex, informed Elombe about the Taino and their relations to the Arawak people in the southern mainland. Maraguay spoke about civilizations in the mainland, including the Mayas that sometimes contacted the Tainos for the purposes of trade and intellectual exchange, and other civilizations with large complex cities. Maraguay stated that the Taino were a simpler people who chose to live their lives in peace rather than war. Amanex was unaware that his father had such an extensive knowledge of the civilizations on the mainland and believed that through his diplomatic duties for various caciques, his father had learned about these different people and their cultures. Maraguay believed Santo Domingo was used to expand the power of the united Spanish Crown by the future conquests of other civilizations in the mainland. Elombe's tales of white expansion into Africa solidified Maraguay and Amanex's fears that if the enslaved people did not unify they would face the violent eradication of their peaceful way of life not only in Hispaniola, but in every land the conquistadors reached.

Elombe spoke of the death of Queen Isabella I in 1504 and her husband, King Ferdinand II ruling as the regent for their daughter Joana, the queen of Castile. Joana was deemed mentally ill and called Juana la Loca, (or Joana the mad). The House of Trastámara and their rule of Spain appeared to be coming to an end and the House of Hapsburg began rising with the rule of Juana's husband, King Philip I of Castile. Queen Juana and King Philip I had an eldest son named Carlos, who at the young age six had inherited the Burgundian territories—part of the Holy Roman Empire—in 1506. Elombe confirmed what Amanex and his parents had heard from some of the Spaniards regarding their rulers in Spain. Amanex was angered that these monarchs yielded so much power and spread their brutality to the peaceful Taino way of life. These monarchs and nobles left the Taino and other native people at the mercy of the ruthless Spaniards who determined their fate by sword and gun.

Amanex wanted to learn more about the African people and the kingdoms including the Igbo and Mandingo people, who had now begun arriving at a greater number and equaled and in some mines surpassed the amounts of Tainos. Amanex marveled at the stories of the Great Pyramids, the Sphinx, and the legendary pharaohs of Kemet in the region of Africa the Spaniards called Egipto (or Egypt). He desired to learn how to read in the many languages of the Africans and Middle Eastern people to unlock their knowledge and history. Elombe also spoke about a great plague that had devastated the lands of the white people that also reached the Middle East and Egypt, where it killed many people in several African cities including Alexandria. Amanex believed the Spaniards brought this curse with them and along with their violence, these diseases helped kill many of his fellow Taino. Amanex secretly desired another plague to kill off the Spaniards and stop the brutality that the Africans and Tainos faced. Amanex and his parents wondered about Amayao and his current situation in Higüey under the direction of Juan Ponce de León. They hoped he remained safe and if he could escape, they wished for a safe passage and freedom.

Amayao had reached Higüey accompanied by many Spanish soldiers, including the hated Radamés Cesar Milfuegos. Radamés, along with other Spaniards, would kill and torture any Tainos who did not agree to the rule of Juan Ponce de León. They would take pleasure in violating young Taina girls—a horror that Amayao could not bear observe any longer. Their actions strengthened Amayao's resolve to escape to the island of Boriken now renamed San Juan Bautista. Juan Ponce de León was developing his capital city named Salvaleón and was given the direct order by King Ferdinand II to conquer all remaining Tainos in Higüey and use them for slave labor. Juan Ponce de León had recently married an innkeeper's daughter named Leónora and had begun building a large stone house in Salvaleón for his wife and the children he planned to raise there. Juan Ponce de León sent expeditions to the eastern coast of Hispaniola.

Amayao and a few other Tainos planned their escape to Boriken. It was believed the supreme leader of Boriken, Cacique Agüeybaná, alongside his brother Güeybaná and other caciques would create a formidable rebellion. Under these conditions, Amayao and other Tainos planned to overpower the Spanish soldiers and escape to Boriken to join the resistance.

CHAPTER 9
AGÜEBEYBANÁ II AND THE WAR FOR BORIKEN
(1511)

Amayao and a group of Taino followers had planned an escape during an eastern expedition. They overpowered the Spaniards and took their swords and guns, killing them quickly before they were met with retaliation led by Radamés Cesar Milfuegos. Amayao and hundreds of Tainos rebelled against their Spanish masters in a ferocious attack, killing many Spaniards as they secured large canoes at the eastern coastline of Hispaniola. Radamés and his friend Jose Sanchez faced a brutal onslaught as the full weight and vengeance of the Tainos overwhelmed the Spaniards. Amayao wanted to kill Radamés and the rapist Jose Sanchez, but was only able to strike a glancing blow to the face of Radamés. The sword strike ripped open Radamés' right cheek and pierced his chest as he fell in a desperate attempt to grasp for his gun. Radamés was saved by the gunfire of his fellow Spaniards as the Tainos fled towards the island of Boriken. The Spaniards escaped back to the city of Salvaleón to meet with the governor of Higüey, Juan Ponce de León, who had just returned from an expedition on the island of Boriken.

Juan Ponce de León had made two expeditions—the first one a secret since the Spanish Crown previously commissioned Vicente Yáñez Pinzón to explore and govern the island in 1505 but his commission was revoked in 1507. On July twelfth, 1508, Juan Ponce de León led an expedition of fifty men on one ship, explored the island of San Juan Bautista (formerly Boriken) and created a city near roughly two miles inland from the bay and named the settlement Caparra. King Ferdinand II granted Juan Ponce de León the right to settle the island of San Juan Bautista and his official exploration for gold was deemed a success. The Governor of Hispaniola, Nicolás de Ovando y Cáceres, named Juan Ponce de León the Governor of San Juan Bautista on August fourteenth, 1509.

Upon his return trip to Higüey, Juan Ponce de León learned about the rebellion in Higüey and the escape of hundreds of Tainos to the island of San Juan Bautista. He grew angry at the failure of Radamés Cesar Milfuegos and publicly reprimanded him, referring to Radamés Cesar Milfuegos by the nickname he hated: el Moro.

There was a challenge presented to Juan Ponce de León's position on the island the Tainos still referred to as Boriken, and it was led by the strong, charismatic, and determined leader Cacique Agüeybaná I and his brother Güeybaná. Cacique Agüeybaná (also known as the Great Sun) quickly began solidifying his power throughout the island and forming a coalition with the other caciques of Boriken and the Kalinago people, setting aside their differences and unifying against their common Spanish enemy.

Cacique Agüeybaná remembered in 1508 when he had received Juan Ponce de León in his village of Guaynia. Agüeybaná practiced the guatiao Taino custom where he took the name of Juan Ponce de León and Juan Ponce de León took the name of Agüeybaná. Afterwards Juan Ponce de León baptized Agüeybaná's mother and gave her the name Doña Inés.

To maintain peace, Agüeybaná helped Juan Ponce de León explore the island of Boriken and even allowed him to build the settlement of Caparra. After his stay in Boriken, Juan Ponce de León invited Cacique Agüeybaná to the island of Hispaniola, where he was received by

Governor Nicolás de Ovando y Cáceres in the city of Santo Domingo. The peace would be only temporary; Agüeybaná had previously received information regarding the brutality of the Spaniards. He believed Juan Ponce de León had designs on the complete conquest of Boriken which they had already renamed San Juan Bautista. Agüeybaná originally believed the Tainos should attack the stronghold of Santo Domingo but he was advised by his brother Güeybaná that a large coalition of Tainos and Kalinago should defend the island, where they were in a position of strength.

Agüeybaná still advocated for peace, although other caciques—including his brother— advised him to prepare for war. Juan Ponce de León was determined to take the island of San Juan Bautista by force and his return to Boriken brought further destruction to the Taino people through the slave labor of the encomienda system. The Spaniards brought more sickness to San Juan Bautista, which was exacerbated by slavery and violence. The epidemic of various diseases, including small pox and measles, devastated the Taino people and Juan Ponce de León ordered the killings of any who resisted his rule as governor. Juan Ponce de León also sought leaders of the small rebellion which had occurred in Higüey, publicly blaming Cacique Agüeybaná for providing safe harbor for the Tainos who had revolted. Although Juan Ponce de León did not have evidence that Cacique Agüeybaná had provided safe harbor, it gave him legitimacy to attack Agüeybaná I and make an example of him.

Amayao and many of the other Tainos had previously met with Agüeybaná I and were farther north under the protection of Cacique Urayoán when the Spanish onslaught began. Cacique Urayoán and many of the Tainos under his direction—including Amayao—fled inland after the sudden death of Cacique Agüeybaná I. News of the death of the Great Sun spread quickly among the Taino people and the regional chiefs rallied around Agüeybaná's brother Cacique Güeybaná. Cacique Güeybaná immediately solidified his rule and renamed himself

Cacique Agüeybaná II. Cacique Agüeybaná II allied himself with many of the regional chiefs, among them the southern caciques of Boriken Urayoán, Coxiguex, Yauco, Jumacao, Orocobix, Loquillo, Guayama, and a cacique named Luis by the Spaniards. Cacique Guarionex, who had fled Hispaniola years before, was informed of the pending revolt of Cacique Agüeybaná II. Cacique Agüeybaná II then moved inland towards the territory of Cacique Hayuya, where Amayao and hundreds of other Tainos from the island of Hispaniola were now gathered.

Juan Ponce de León and his position in the island of San Juan Bautista was not only threatened by a potential rebellion under Cacique Agüeybaná II, but also his rival, Diego Colón. Diego Colón, the eldest son of the deceased explorer Cristóbal Colón, replaced Governor Nicolás de Ovando y Cáceres as governor of Hispaniola in 1509. Governor Diego Colón challenged Juan Ponce de León's position and this increased Juan Ponce de León's determination to swiftly put an end to any potential mass rebellion. King Ferdinand II favored Juan Ponce de León, however some of the favorable developments between Diego Colón and the Spanish Crown helped place Diego Colón as governor of Hispaniola. Diego Colón initially had planned to marry Mencia de Guzman, the daughter of the Duke of Medina Sidonia. However, he was encouraged to marry María de Toledo y Rojas, the cousin of King Ferdinand II and the niece of Fadrique Álvarez de Toledo, the second Duke of Alba.

Cacique Agüeybaná II was now plotting a rebellion against Juan Ponce de León and the Spaniards and received an opportunity to spark the revolt when Juan Ponce de León sent a conquistador named Diego Salcedo to explore other locations in the interior of San Juan Bautista and speak with Cacique Agüeybaná II. In reality, he was to report back to Juan Ponce de León regarding the military capabilities of Cacique Agüeybaná II, who was known as El Bravo or the Brave One. Diego Salcedo travelled towards Hayuya's region alongside other Spaniards, including Jose Sanchez. Diego Salcedo made a habit out of abusing the Taina women and Jose Sanchez did as well, often leaving young girls and boys seriously injured or dead to appease his forbidden depraved appetite. Diego Salcedo disrespected female subjects of Cacique Agüeybaná II, which angered the great leader. He made a habit of riding Taino men as he would ride his horse to dehumanize them in front of their wives and children. Amayao recognized Jose Sanchez and remained out of sight as he observed him abusing children and laughing without a care in the world. The Spaniards went to sleep happy and content as they anticipated another day where they would continue their hedonistic adventure and then gather intelligence for their high-ranking officers, including Cristóbal de Sotomayor.

Diego Salcedo was one of the first Spaniards to awaken the following morning and he asked to be taken to a local river to quench his thirst. Cacique Urayoán led Diego Salcedo to the river as Diego laughed and talked about Tainas and inquired about the location of gold. Amayao had spoken to Cacique Urayoán and Cacique Agüeybaná II and identified himself as the elder brother of Amanex. After ingratiating himself with the caciques, he explained various rebellions in the island now called Hispaniola and how he had personally killed the Spaniards during his escape from Higüey, which helped inspire the caciques to take action.

When Diego Salcedo got on one knee to drink water, Jose Sanchez—who trailed behind—spotted Amayao and other Tainos and alerted his comrades, shouting, "There is that scoundrel Amayao and the rest of the savages that escaped Higüey!"

As Diego Salcedo stood, he was struck down by Cacique Urayoán and beaten by other Tainos who held his head underwater until he drowned. The nearby Spaniards were quickly killed, including Jose Sanchez, who was impaled with his own sword by the hands of Amayao.

Some Tainos spoke about the Spaniards having god-like abilities, some bringing up the Catholic religion and their belief of resurrection and of the god they called

Jesus Christ who himself was believed to have arisen from death after three days. Cacique Urayoan and Cacique Hayuya suggested they wait three days to prove they were mortal men whose only advantage was their superior weaponry. The mortality of the Spaniards was confirmed and used as motivation for a Taino rebellion, as the bodies of Diego Salcedo, Jose Sanchez, and others remained lifeless after three days, rotting in the tropical weather. On the fourth day, after several days of strategic discussions, Cacique Agüeybaná II sent messengers to the other caciques on the island of San Juan Bautista to attack various Spanish settlements to catch the Spaniards by surprise.

The first attack would take place on the fort of the high ranking Spanish officer and Chief Marshall Don Cristóbal de Sotomayor. Cristóbal de Sotomayor had previously sent the translator Juan González to spy on an areyto involving Cacique Agüeybaná and other caciques, where he uncovered the plot of a potential attack on Cristóbal de Sotomayor. Juan González informed Cristóbal de Sotomayor and Juan Ponce de León, which led to preparations for departure of Cristóbal de Sotomayor and a several hundred of his Taino slaves he had received from a local cacique.

Although Juan Ponce de León was previously informed about a possible Taino rebellion, he mistakenly did not believe that Agüeybaná II could mount a large force in a short period of time. Agüeybaná II's war declaration spread quickly throughout the island as Taino warriors ripped into the settlement led by the Cristóbal de Sotomayor. Cristóbal de Sotomayor was the subject of much hatred and gossip throughout the island for his relationship with a native Taina named Guanina, which helped fuel Taino revenge. Guanina was viewed as a traitor by many of the Taino people, including Amayao, who could not understand why native women would willingly initiate relationships with the same men who were oppressing them. Guanina's brother, Cacique Guaybana, was involved in the initial attack on the settlement. It came early as Cristóbal de Sotomayor was beginning his journey towards the capital city of Caparra for a meeting with Governor Juan Ponce de León. Natives encircled Cristóbal de Sotomayor, killing the Spaniards around him and cutting him off from his settlement. The Spaniards were only able to fire a few shots as the arrows rained down into the settlement, killing most of the Spanish soldiers and over eighty people. Juan González and a few other Spaniards barely escaped the attack, however Cristóbal de Sotomayor was injured and captured. After Cristóbal de Sotomayor was identified, he was executed and his girlfriend Guanina was later found dead near his body. The caciques had previously advised that Guanina be spared and simply punished; some Tainos were unsure who killed Guanina while some believed she had committed suicide.

The Taino war against the Spaniards began as Juan Ponce de León named Juan Gil as the replacement for Cristóbal de Sotomayor as Chief Marshall. Any Tainos who were not killed were to be captured and enslaved, forced to work to exploit the island of Boriken. Cacique Agüeybaná II quickly sent messengers to other islands in canoes, seeking to unify the Kalinago and Taino into a united coalition against Juan Ponce de León and the Spaniards. In February 1511, Juan Ponce de León led the first offensive against the Tainos at Cayabo. Hundreds of Spaniards fired their arquebuses at the Taino warriors, cutting hundreds of them down as a relentless number of arrows hit the Spaniards, injuring many and killing some. Juan Ponce de León desired to kill as many Tainos as he could and capture their leaders to stop the war before other islands could resupply and send more native warriors.

The battle was violent as Ponce de León exclaimed, “Find their leader El Bravo. I want Agüeybaná II to be made into an example for others who wish to rebel against me.”

The Spaniards’ first offensive strike proved to be a quick victory, as many of the Tainos retreated in the face of superior weaponry. Another battle waged under the leadership of Cacique Guarionex was successful on the western coast of San Juan Bautista; he had surprised a Spanish settlement, killing most of the Castilian soldiers by outflanking the soldiers and breaking through their frontline. Cacique Guarionex was instructed to head inland to help Cacique Agüeybaná II confront Juan Ponce de León in a massive Taino offensive with the purpose of eliminating the growing Spanish threat. It would take place at Yahuecas within the region of Cacique Urayoán.

The battle or Yahuecas began on March eleventh, 1511. Cacique Agüeybaná II was successful in enlisting more of the Kalinago people, including ones from islands north of Hispaniola. Despite the efforts of the Spaniards to block communications, Cacique Agüeybaná II was able to contact other caciques within Hispaniola who were still revolting against Spanish control, a young and brave cacique named Hatüey among them. Cacique Agüeybaná II desired a victory against Juan Ponce de León and subsequently to form a wider coalition between the islands and eliminate the Spanish. Agüeybaná II sent messengers to islands, including Ay Ay—now renamed Santa Cruz or Saint Croix—in an effort to increase momentum for a large native coalition against the Spanish Crown. Juan Ponce de León descended upon the coalition of Tainos and Kalinago.

Thousands of Tainos engaged Juan Ponce de León and his commanders as Juan Ponce de León frantically rode on his horse, galvanizing his troops to fire in rotation to prevent the failure of the initial battles. Poisoned arrows rained down as Cacique Agüeybaná attempted to break through the superior weaponry of the Spaniards. Some Tainos were also equipped with arquebuses taken from the bodies of Spaniards from previous battles. Amayao was in the reserve unit led by Agüeybaná II's cousin Cacique Orocobix. Amayao helped teach Tainos how to fire the weapons and how to handle their swords—a skill he gained by observing Spanish soldiers and aiding them in Hispaniola. The Spanish gunfire ripped through the Taino frontlines as Cacique Agüeybaná II desperately pushed to outflank Juan Ponce de León. Agüeybaná II was known as El Bravo and he lived up to his name as he was able to successfully outflank Juan Ponce de León's soldiers, causing momentary panic among the Castilians as they made a strategic retreat.

Agüeybaná killed a few Spaniards, capturing some of their weapons and horses as he advanced, but Juan Ponce de León's reserve units moved forward as well, firing at the advancing Tainos. Juan Ponce de León lacked height but did not lack determination as he encouraged the Spaniards to capture El Bravo. Taino leaders were shot and killed; Agüeybaná II himself was shot and injured as he retreated. Agüeybaná II ordered a tactical retreat inland towards the center of Boriken as Cacique Urayoan, under the direction of Agüeybaná II, ordered Amayao and other Tainos to fire their arquebuses on the advancing Spaniards. The last defensive move by the Tainos allowed the survivors to retreat inland. Agüeybaná II would continue to build his coalition between all native islanders and wait for an opportunity for a counterstrike. The battle of Yahuecas became a major victory for Ponce de León and the Spaniards, however Agüeybaná II was able to escape.

Governor Diego Colón and his relationship with the Spanish Crown and Juan Ponce de León worsened as the Taino rebellion continued the island of San Juan Bautista. Juan Ponce de León sent a letter to the Spanish Crown, who later appointed Juan Cerón as Governor of San Juan Bautista and named Miguel Diaz as Chief Constable. King Ferdinand II and Diego Colón continued their court battle concerning the promises made to Cristóbal Colón and the Colón family: land titles and ten percent of all riches involving the territories explored by Cristóbal Colón. These lawsuits were called the Pleitos colombinos, or the Columbian lawsuits, which caused King Ferdinand II to send Juan Ponce de León to seek the rumors of an unexplored mainland to the north for fear that Diego Colón would gain control of the mainland territories as well. These developments created a growing friction between Diego Colón and Juan Ponce de León as the battle for San Juan Bautista continued.

Amanex and his parents were unaware of the full

extent of the war on the island of San Juan Bautista, but it was rumored that Cacique Agüeybaná II remained fighting and elusive. Amanex and his father were careful to speak about any of the rebellions for fear of being punished and Amanex worried that he or his parents would be punished for the actions of his brother Amayao in Higüey. Amanex and his parents believed that Amayao had escaped to San Juan Bautista, however they were unsure if he was currently alive. Governor Diego Colón grew restless and was angered with the ongoing war. Although two confirmed caciques had agreed to cease fighting against the Spaniards, most of the caciques continued to rally around Cacique Agüeybaná II. Other native people including the Kalinago from the southern islands were travelling to San Juan Bautista in canoes, causing Juan Ponce de León to ask for ships to block any possible assisting of the Taino war effort.

Within the island of Hispaniola, the Spaniards tightened their control of the Taino and African slaves and tried to stop any information from reaching their ears. The Spaniards began increasing labor in an effort to increase sugarcane harvests and cattle ranching. Other exotic animals and plants arrived to the island of Hispaniola, including the coconut tree which began appearing throughout the island close to various bodies of water and produced large coconuts that provided food and water. Amanex was transferred to labor in large sugarcane fields along with many African slaves and the punishments and workload increased along with Spanish brutality. Some of the Spaniards began openly speaking out against the violence. The biggest Spanish voice of dissent was a Dominican friar by name of Antonio de Montesinos.

Antonio de Montesinos was among the first Dominican friars to arrive to Hispaniola under the leadership of the Inquisitor Pedro de Córdoba on September 1510. Antonio de Montesinos became a Dominican friar at the convent of Saint Stephen in Salamanca where he occasionally studied. Antonio de Montesinos embraced the Catholic Dominican Order that was founded in France in 1216 by a Castilian priest named Domingo Félix de Guzmán (also known as Santo Domingo or Saint Dominic). Born in Caleruega Spain to his mother Juana of Aza and father Felix Guzman, Dominic was named after Dominic of Silos, the patron saint of prisoners, pregnant women, and shepherds. In 1215, Dominic and six followers establish themselves in a house given to them by Peter Seila, who was a rich resident of Toulouse. Dominic envisioned his organization would combine dedication and systematic education with greater flexibility than either monastic orders or secular organizations. He travelled to Rome to seek written approval from Pope Innocent III and after his death, in 1217 Pope Honorius III gave Dominic written authority for the Dominican order named the Order of Preachers. Domenic became the Patron Saint of Astronomers and the order encouraged intellectual pursuits. The Dominican Order was proudly represented by Antonio de Montesinos in the city of Santo Domingo on December twenty-first, 1511.

On December 21, 1511, during the fourth Sunday of advent, Antonio de Montesinos gave an impassioned speech against Spanish brutality and slavery:

"I am the voice of one crying in the wilderness. In order to make your sins known to you, I have mounted this pulpit—I who am the voice of Christ crying in the wilderness of this island. Therefore, it behooves you to listen to me, not with indifference but with all your heart and senses; this voice will be the strangest, the harshest and hardest, the most terrifying that you ever heard or expected to hear. This voice declares that you are in mortal sin, and live and die therein by reason of the cruelty and tyranny that you practice on these innocent people. Tell me, by what right or justice do you hold these Indians in such cruel and horrible slavery? By what right do you wage such detestable wars on these people who lived mildly and peacefully in their own lands, where you have consumed infinite numbers of them with unheard of murders and desolations? Why do you so greatly oppress and fatigue them, not giving them enough to eat or caring for them when they fall ill from excessive labors so that they die or rather are slain by you so you may extract and acquire gold every day? And what care do you take that they receive religious instruction and come to know their God and Creator, or that they be baptized, hear mass, or observe holidays and Sundays? Are they not men? Do they not have rational souls? Are you not bound to love them as you love yourselves? How can you lie in such profound and lethargic slumber? Be sure that in your present state you can no more be saved than the Moors or Turks who do not have and do not want the faith of Jesus Christ."

The speech caught the attention of other friars, including Bartolomé de las Casas, and the message spread among the Taino and Africans. Many of the Spanish Conquistadors were angered at the speech, King Ferdinand II and Governor Diego Colón among them. Amanex and the other Tainos and Africans were happy with the speech although it did little to save them. Amanex wondered how the Spaniards could use their God and belief of Jesus Christ to justify goodness or cruelty. The Holy Bible and its words could be twisted to justify actions that could be vastly different from each other and was now used to advocate for peace while at the same time the conquistadors used the Bible to justify slavery and murder. Another leader named Cacique Hatüey emerged to lead a rebellion on the island of Hispaniola, and he also observed the hypocrisy of the Spaniards and their Catholic religion.

CHAPTER 10
HATÜEY (1512)

Cacique Hatüey, who ruled the region of Guahabá in Hispaniola, could not maintain and continue a successful rebellion, which led him to the island of coabana (now called Cuba by the Spaniards) in 1511. Hatüey entered the island of Cuba with a combined force of over 400 Taino and over 100 Africans in canoes in an effort to warn the Tainos, Ciboneys, and Guanahatabeys about the impending danger at the hands of the expanding Spaniards. Diego Colón had become Viceroy of the Indies in 1511 and he ordered Diego Velázquez de Cuéllar to lead the conquest of the island of Cuba. Hatüey believed he could organize a successful counter attack against the Spaniards and advise various caciques in Cuba about the brutality on the island of Hispaniola.

After a few months, Cacique Hatüey gathered over 300 Tainos and some escaped African slaves armed with stone axes and wooden lances called macanas, ready to fight and led by Diego Velázquez de Cuéllar. They were skilled with the macana and they prepared for a prolonged battle as Hatüey and other leaders discussed various battle strategies.

Cacique Hatüey spoke of the horrors the Spaniards inflicted on the Tainos of Hispaniola and with gold in his hand, he exclaimed, "This gold is the God of the Spaniards, and they will commit atrocities to our people because they kill their own people for this gold." Hatüey continued forcefully, "Here is the God the Spaniards worship. For these they fight and kill; for these they persecute us and that is why we have to throw them into the sea. They tell us—these tyrants—that they adore a God of peace and equality, and yet they usurp our land and make us their slaves. They speak to us of an immortal soul and of their eternal rewards and punishments, yet they rob our belongings, seduce our women, and violate our daughters. Incapable of matching us in valor, these cowards cover themselves with iron that our weapons cannot break." Cacique Hatüey planned to continue his fight against the Spaniards in the island of Cuba and he believed he could mount a successful counterattack with a larger Taino offensive.

The island of Cuba which Cristobal Colón believed to be an Asian Peninsula was circumvented four years prior in 1508 by Sebastián de Ocampo, proving that Cuba was an island and the existence of unexplored territories to the north and west. This led Diego Colón to send an expedition under the leadership of Diego Velázquez de Cuéllar. Diego Velázquez de Cuéllar travelled to Cuba with three ships and a battalion of over 300 men and created a settlement on the eastern tip of Cuba in Baracoa, which he re-named Nuestra Señora de la Asunción de Baracoa. Diego Velázquez de Cuéllar was accompanied by Pedro Alvarado, Bernal Díaz del Castillo, Juan de Grijalva, Francisco Hernando de Córdoba, Bartolomé de las Casas, and a young man named Hernando Cortés. When Diego Velázquez de Cuéllar entered the island, he began raiding the villages of the Tainos and killing its people. As this continued, more Tainos joined Hatüey's rebellion against Diego Velázquez de Cuéllar and Pánfilo de Narváez.

The violence caused by Pánfilo de Narváez spread fear and anger throughout the islands of Cuba and Jamaica. Cacique Hatüey and his powerful ally Cacique Caguax, who also fled the island of Hispaniola, decided to strike the Spaniards first. Cacique Hatüey launched an attack on an isolated section of about fifty Spanish soldiers, killing several men and forcing a tactical retreat. Caguax encouraged Hatüey to destroy the Spanish settlement of Baracoa, however Spanish weaponry kept Hatüey on the defensive. Cacique Hatüey used a series of short and ferocious attacks on small groups of Spanish soldiers until he could receive reinforcements from other caciques.

Hatüey continued to increase his guerilla warfare tactics, victorious in many battles and always retreating to the mountains when the Spaniards received reinforcements. He remembered the depraved abuse of young Taino children and the mistreatment of Taina wives. Some Spaniards fed the Tainos to their war dogs as they laughed with glee after severely beating them, which helped Hatüey's recruitment efforts. Hatüey was successfully able to stop Spanish expansion to the rest of Cuba, restricting Diego Velázquez de Cuéllar and the Spaniards mainly to their initial settlement of Baracoa.

Many months passed and Cacique Hatüey continued to be successful, but reinforcements from other islands failed to arrive. The Spaniards had begun intercepting canoes arriving in Cuba and San Juan Bautista. Diego Velázquez de Cuéllar requested the aid of Pánfilo de Narváez, who began organizing a small army of Spaniards on the island of Jamaica in an effort to help cripple Hatüey's Taino rebellion in Cuba.

Hatüey was to lead an attack against Diego Velázquez de Cuéllar and planned a separate attack on the approaching Pánfilo de Narváez, however he was betrayed by a Taino he had previously disagreed with. Some Tainos believed the continuous fight against the Spaniards would lead to their complete demise, but they failed to understand Hatüey's warning regarding the level of depravity of the Spaniards and their continuous broken agreements. A devastating offensive crippled Cacique Hatüey's war effort and he was eventually captured and sentenced to death. Stripped of all his gold and possessions and publicly beaten, Cacique Hatüey remained defiant in the face of his Spanish oppressors. A fire was started designed to consume his body for the crime of defending his Taino people and their way of life.

On February 1512, Hatüey was brought in front of Diego Velázquez de Cuéllar, who inquired as to the location of gold and other Taino warriors and caciques. Hatüey refused to help the Spaniards and their greed, vowing that the Taino people would continue to fight even after his death. After a few days, a pyre had been prepared for the execution. As the fires grew, a Franciscan Friar named Juan de Tesín approached Hatüey in an attempt to convert him to Christianity so his soul could find peace in his salvation. Hatüey did not let the fear of being burned alive, influence his convictions. The friar explained aspects of the Christian faith and retold stories found within the Holy Bible as Hatüey listened carefully.

Another friar by the name of Olmedo approached Hatüey and spoke about the sweetness of heaven, to which Hatüey asked, "Are Spaniards found in your heaven?"

Olmedo responded, "Yes, if they are good and accept Jesus."

Hatüey replied, "Then I do not wish to go to your heaven."

As everyone looked on, the friar Olmedo stated that if Hatüey chose the Christian God he would avoid the eternal torture of the inferno and a painful existence in hellfire. Hatüey said to the Friar Juan de Tesín and Olmedo: "I would prefer to go to hell because I do not want to be where the Spaniards are. I do not wish to spend eternity with such a cruel people. To be in a place with the brutal Spaniards is a form of hell just as the Spaniards have changed our society into a living hell today."

The fire burned Hatüey's body as he turned his head and stared directly at the Spaniards, showcasing his large, broad shoulders and prominent jaw line, happy to finally be removed from a life under Spanish rule.

Cacique Caguax was now the leader of the rebellion in Cuba, however the rebellion under Caguax was not as effective as his former leader. More Spaniards entered the island of Cuba as Pánfilo de Narváez continued to push westward with extreme violence. In Caonao, Pánfilo de Narváez put to the sword all Taino men, women, and children who approached him in peace and fear for their lives. to the horror of Bartolomé de las Casas, Pánfilo de Narváez had beaten and bloodied the Tainos of Caonao. Between the screams of agony and loss, Pánfilo de Narváez asked Bartolomé de las Casas, "What do you think about the actions of our Spaniards?"

Bartolomé de las Casas quietly responded, "I send both you and them to the Devil!"

It brought a slight smile to Pánfilo de Narváez's face.

Pánfilo de Narváez now commanded a large battalion as he moved into the Cuban interior in search for Cacique Caguax. Equipped with horses, arquebuses, crossbows, swords, and other weapons, Pánfilo advanced towards Bayamo where Cacique Caguax and his Taino were positioned. After the violent subjugation of Taino villages, a large clash ensued between the Taino forces of Cacique Caguax and the Spaniards under Pánfilo de Narváez. The fight quickly turned in favor of the Spanish conquistadors, causing the Tainos to flee as a second group of Spaniards approach from the side. After several days of fighting, thousands of Taino were killed or made slaves and Cacique Caguax was captured and executed.

Pánfilo de Narváez continued his advance westward, where he captured and executed Cacique Camagüebax and threw his cadaver from the highest peak in the region—over 1,000 feet above sea level. Diego Velázquez de Cuéllar then ordered additional conquistadors to join the efforts of Pánfilo in a westward offensive to conquer the entire island of Cuba. The horrors the Spanish committed during the Cuban westward offensive strengthened Bartolomé de las Casas' resolve in favor of the human rights of the Taino and other native people. Bartolomé de las Casas agreed with his fellow Dominican Friars, including his mentor Pedro de Córdoba, and Antonio de Montesinos.

The Spaniards continued their push westward and by 1514 they had found seven important cities near Taino villages, including Bayamo, Trinidad, Sancti Spiritus, Puerto Principe (or Camaguey), Santiago, and San Cristóbal de La Habana. The battles also continued to proceed in the island of San Juan Bautista. A Spanish settlement named Añasco was burned to the ground by the

Tainos and ordered to be rebuilt by the Spanish Crown. Añasco was an important settlement needed to carry out mining and exploitation of resources from the Otoao region. The Spanish Monarchy authorized Governor Diego Colón to continue his war against the Taino and the enslavement policy by branding Tainos on the forehead. Caciques were captured and killed, including Cacique Aymaco and Cacique Guarionex at the battle of Aguada. This left a cacique named Don Alonso by the Spaniards to continue the fight in the Otoao region.

In 1512, the southeastern part of San Juan Bautista remained outside of Spanish control, allowing for escape and re-entry routes for Tainos and Kalinagos throughout the ongoing war. Juan Ponce de León led incursions into Saint Croix and Guadalupe while Miguel Díaz led incursions into the island of Trinidad. On February twelfth, 1512, on the island of San Juan Bautista, the Spaniards advanced inland led by the governor of San Juan Bautista Juan Cerón. Governor Juan Cerón ordered Hernando de la Torre to target and fight the first cousin of the deceased Agüeybaná, Cacique Orocobix and his wife Cacica Yaya, who were defeated and captured while the search continued for their daughter (renamed Catalina) and Cacique Orocobix's young brother Cacique Oromico.

On June tenth, 1512, Álvaro de Saavedra entered the lands of Guayama. The captured natives—including Cacique Orocobix and his wife Yaya—were auctioned and enslaved at Villa San Germán.

Juan Gil, Juan Lopez, and Luis de Añasco led repeated horseback slave hunts in Agüeybaná II's domain, killing and capturing many of the Tainos and some of the escaped African slaves in the months of July and August of 1512. Caciques including Cacique Mabodamaca were able to resist and escape Spanish domination; Cacique Mabodamaca refused to submit to the Spaniards and began a rebellion leading initial successful attacks on Spanish settlements. Don Diego Salazar used spies to discover the location of Cacique Mabodamaca and over 600 Taino warriors. After nightfall, as most of the Tainos rested,

Diego Salazar attacked. The Spaniards fired their arquebuses, killing and injuring many Tainos, however little visibility allowed the Tainos to engage the Spaniards in hand to hand combat. The Taino responded with speed and ferocity against the conquistadors as they fought throughout the night. At dawn, over 150 Tainos were dead with many other wounded and enslaved. Cacique Mabodamaca and the remaining Tainos were able to retreat further inland. Amayao had been transferred by Agüeybaná II to fight under the leadership of Cacique Mabodamaca, who hoped to stop the Spaniard eastern advance.

Radamés Cesar Milfuegos became increasingly violent towards the Tainos, Africans, and Kalinago he encountered in battle and often preferred torturing and killing the natives instead of enslaving them. Radamés Cesar Milfuegos was in desperate search of Amayao—he had killed his friend and scarred his face. Diego Salcedo launched a devastating attack when his spies revealed the location of Cacique Mabodamaca and several hundred of Taino, Kalinago, and African fighters. The fight was brutal and Amayao led a counteroffensive where Spanish weapons were used against the Spaniards themselves. Amayao and the other Tainos fired their arquebuses at the advancing Spaniards, causing them to temporarily halt their advance and help the Tainos regroup. The Spaniards responded with their own gunfire in an effort to capture Cacique Mabodamaca. As the Spaniards began to advance, the Tainos dispersed and retreated—including Amayao, who was spotted by Radamés in the distance.

Radamés approached the fleeing Amayao on horseback as he escaped into the mountains behind Cacique Mabodamaca. Entering a heavily wooded area, Radamés foolishly left his horse and pursued Amayao on foot.

As he gave chase, he shouted, “I will punish you for killing my friend and scarring my face! I will kill you and feed you to my dogs!”

As they approached a clearing, Amayao suddenly turned around and charged Radamés before he could shoot his arquebus, throwing him to the ground as he tried to reach for his sword. Radamés was able to escape from Amayao's grasp and lunged forward. In his anger, Radamés failed to attack the elusive Amayao and left himself open for a counterattack. Amayao struck Radamés and continued to pummel him as the Spaniards approached. Amayao reached for Radamés' sword in an effort to kill him as the Spaniards began firing upon Amayao, saving his life as the Tainos fled. The Spaniards pursued killing many Tainos and also injured Cacique Mabodamaca, who continued to escape towards the mountains. As he reached the edge of a ridge, Cacique Mabodamaca's injuries tired him and made him lose his footing. He fell to his death in the river below. Some Tainos were able to get away, including Amayao, much to the anger and frustration of Radamés.

In January 1513, the Spaniards—led by Diego Salcedo—positioned themselves at Guánica and began processing mined gold and capturing Tainos, Africans, and Kalinagos at San Germán to be enslaved. On March fifteenth, 1513, Salazar attacked Yauco and Coxiguex, and Sancho de Arango attacked Cacique Coxiguex. The Spaniards continued their raids and violence in an effort to capture and kill the Taino, Kalinago, and African slaves who had escaped the island of Hispaniola. The Tainos also attacked the female Cacica known as Luisa, who had allied with the Spaniards, and killed her along with two Spaniards named Garci Fernández and Pedro Mexía. The Cacique Cacimar of Bieke was also killed in the exchange while a similar attack was carried out at Salinas, where the Spanish ally Cacica Cayaguax (renamed Isabel) was targeted. Eyewitness accounts by various Spaniards of Cacique Agüeybaná II convinced Viceroy Diego Colón to depart Santo Domingo and travel to San Juan Bautista with over 200 Spanish soldiers in an effort to capture and kill the supreme leader called El Bravo.

While Viceroy Diego Colón was on the island of San Juan Bautista, a large counteroffensive began on the eastern part of San Juan Bautista which led to the burning of the capital city Caparra. Eight caciques led a force of over 350 warriors of the native alliance (including

Amayao) into Caparra, burning the city down and killing eighteen Spaniards. Juan Ponce de León's family narrowly escaped. Amayao helped loot the settlement and take guns, ammunition, horses, and other supplies. Over 4,500 pesos worth of gold were taken, agricultural fields, and over thirty buildings were burned to the ground; the Bishop's house, the Church, the monastery, and the gold processing building were among them.

Viceroy Diego Colón quickly sent Spanish conquistadors towards Caparra and his lieutenants to punish the Tainos and native alliance forces. A Spaniard named Juan González stated he had seen Cacique Agüeybaná II during the burning of Caparra as he eluded capture and hid in a building during the attack. The Spanish offensive ripped through the eastern side of San Juan Bautista and caciques were captured and sent to Hispaniola for execution, including the caciques Guayervas, Mabo, Yabey, Cayey, Guariana, Guayaboa, Guayama, Hayaurex, Baguanamey, and Yauco. The caciques and Tainos captured revealed the locations of others, leading to an offensive led by Francisco Vaca on July tenth and Pedro Dávila on July nineteenth. Juan Enríquez and Marcos de Ardón would continue the offensive on August 10, 1513, a week after Cerón led his own. Diego Colón and Juan González led successful attacks and the caciques Bairex, Aymaco, and Guayervas fell to Spanish aggression with their subjects enslaved.

On September second, 1513, Pedro de Espinosa attacked various caciques along with hundreds of Spaniards, defeating the Tainos and enslaving them as he advanced. As the Spaniards pressed eastward, Amayao failed to escape the island of San Juan Bautista and was involved in a massive battle. Radamés Cesar Milfuegos was part of the final punch, where Amayao was captured after a gunshot wound to his leg.

Radamés Cesar Milfuegos had finally captured Amayao, inflicting horrors upon his mind and body. For several days, he hung Amayao and beat him repeatedly until he was exhausted. When he was ordered to take the

Tainos back to the capital in Caparra and other settlements for enslavements, he chose to execute Amayao by decapitation. The Spaniards continued their domination of the island of San Juan Bautista. On September seventeenth, 1513, Alonso de Mendoza entered the lands of Hayuya and later that month, Luis de Añasco would continue the offensive. October of 1513 began with another incursion against Cacique Hayuya, this time led by Alonso Niño and Cristóbal de Mendoza, who intended to eliminate the population of the island of Bieke (which the Spaniards called Vieques) to the east of San Juan Bautista. The Spaniards were now winning the fight for San Juan Bautista, however the supreme leader Cacique Agüeybaná remained elusive and still in command of the united native forces.

CHAPTER 11
A MACORIX ROMANCE (1515)

Amanex worked grueling long days in the sugarcane fields and his only respite came from spending time with his parents and speaking with a woman he had met two years prior named Tayamari. Tayamari belonged to the Macorix people of northern Hispaniola and at twenty-five, she was five years younger than Amanex. She spoke her native Macorix language as well as Spanish—she spoke it better than Amanex and would help him improve. Tayamari's family were subjects of a Macorix chief named Cacique Guatigara, who was captured and executed by the forces of Cristóbal Colón from nearby Fort Magdalena. The Macorix people were enslaved and Tayamari's parents and elder brother died from disease and overwork, leaving the young Tayamari under the care of her uncle Hayanao. She and her uncle were transported to the city of Santo Domingo several years prior and Tayamari and Amanex quickly formed a bond.

Tayamari was a beautiful woman of a dark brown complexion, dark long hair, dark eyes, and not far above five feet in height. She was smart, graceful, and careful with her speech and possessed many of the same qualities that Amanex enjoyed in his mother Ana. Tayamari's uncle Hayanao had begun working with Amanex's father Maraguay at the mines and through their friendship,

Hayanao recommended that her niece meet Amanex. Hayanao respected Maraguay and the man that his son Amanex had become and desired him for his niece Tayamari.

Life was dreadful for Taino and African men and even more dreadful for Taina and African women. Life was alienating for the Macorix and Ciguayo minority populations, whose way of life and people had already been nearly wiped out. Enslaved women were a target for sexual violence and other abuses and often subjected to shameful acts. Many of the women committed suicide and killed their own children, fearing for their safety. Tayamari's arrival to the city of Santo Domingo brought new fears and uncertainty, however Amanex helped calm them. Amanex and Tayamari began spending most of the little time they had available outside of their labors together. Their time together was the most enjoyable part of their day and Amanex began to look at Tayamari as a potential lover and possible wife.

The days were always brighter for Amanex with Tayamari by his side and his troubles momentarily vanished with a simple gaze from her beautiful eyes or the sound of her laughter. Amanex helped Tayamari escape from her dread of the Spaniard conquerors at least momentarily through his sense of humor and his courage in the face of uncertainty. He had learned how to maintain a sense of self-respect and calm through adversity from his father Maraguay. Amanex always contemplated before speaking or taking action just as his father and opposed to his brother Amayao, who was quick to retaliate. Amanex and Tayamari found solace in each other and their happiness spread to their family members.

Amanex had liked other women before but his feelings never developed as deeply and as quickly as they had for Tayamari. As the months passed, Amanex would speak to his parents about possibly marrying Tayamari—a union that Maraguay and Ana approved of. He also planned on speaking to Hayanao about the possibility of marriage to his niece as he contemplated his future while laboring in the growing sugarcane fields.

The sugarcane fields were becoming a source of high revenue for Spain and Europe, as the price of sugar rose along with its demand.

Sugar was priced as high as if not higher than nutmeg, ginger, cloves, and pepper. Amanex became a very good laborer in the field, cutting the sugarcane cleanly and quickly with his machete and outworking the other men. He worked alongside the growing population of Africans, including a few African women forced to labor for long, strenuous hours. Amanex made a few friends among the various slaves from Africa. Amanex's closest friend Elombe remained in the goldmines along with Maraguay and Hayanao.

Row after row of sugarcane stalks seemed to reach towards the heavens, temporarily shielding the laborers from the rays of the hot island sun. Amanex and other Tainos and Africans cut the sugarcane at the base, separating the stalks from their roots underneath. The cutting created a rhythm in the worker and a rhythm in sound. Amanex and the other slaves were sometimes allowed to chew on the sugarcane stalk and drink the sweet juice it produced in order to temporarily quench their thirst. The sugarcane was cut, crushed, and boiled, producing molasses and crystallized sugar. Sugarcane experts from West Africa, the Canary Islands, and Madeira instructed the Spaniards, Africans, and Taino on ways of improving sugarcane cultivation and processing as they prepared the first large shipments of sugar out of Hispaniola in 1516. The Spaniards contemplated the expansion of sugarcane cultivation into the other surrounding islands like Cuba and Jamaica. The dead Tainos were continuously replaced with more slaves from West Africa.

The encomienda system was barbaric and continued despite the appeals to end the system by various Spanish friars. The encomienda system was used by the Roman Empire in Hispania or united Spain and was reintroduced by the Spanish after their defeat of the Moors. Ecomendar—the Spanish word meaning to entrust and the practice of the encomienda system—returned after the Spanish defeat of the Islamic State in southern Iberia. The Adelantado was a title held by Spanish nobles who had been granted the right to extract tribute from Muslims or other peasants in areas they had conquered and resettled. The encomienda system continued in an extreme fashion in Hispaniola and its neighboring islands. The Dominican friar Antonio de Montesinos and other Spaniards rallied against Spanish abuse of the Tainos, helping to bring about the Laws of Burgos on December seventh of 1512 in Burgos, Kingdom of Castile. These were the first codified laws placed to govern the Spaniards and their behavior towards the natives within the island of Hispaniola with a potential to expand to the other islands. The laws implemented payments for the native laborers, including provisions, basic living quarters, maintaining basic hygiene, and freedom from forced labor for native women who were at least four months pregnant. Leaders of the estate named encomderos were allowed forty to 150 native laborers to work in their establishments. The Tainos who previously sometimes practiced polygamy were now only allowed one wife, as the Laws of Burgos prohibited Bigamy and they were ordered to be catechized so they could learn the Catholic sacraments. Amanex and his family learned Catholic Doctrine and were expected to perform los sacramentos (or Sacrament), including baptism.

Despite the Laws of Burgos, the Tainos and Africans continued to suffer under the Encomienda system and many of the laws were rarely enforced. The only respite from the grueling existence of slavery was wine. Wine was a major part of Spanish society in Hispaniola and at times red wine was combined with various herbs provided by the Tainos, which became popular on the island. Amanex occasionally engaged in drinking wine with herbs whenever the Spaniards permitted him to do so. At times, he would drink heavily as his anxiety flared when he thought of discussing marriage with his love. Amanex would nervously wonder about their future together and a possible family under the dangerous and uncertainty of

Spanish rule. He and his family were fortunate however, as they were transferred to a new Spanish master who did not share the extreme abusive nature of other conquistadors.

Encomendero Pedro Ramirez was now the master of Amanex and his parents Ana and Maraguay. Pedro Ramirez was entrusted with over 100 Taino and African slaves after his successes in the conquest of the island of Jamaica under the leadership of Pánfilo de Narváez. Pedro Ramirez had extensive experience in sugarcane cultivation in the Canary Islands, and Governor Diego Colón believed he could help increase sugar shipments for European consumers. Pedro Ramirez viewed the Tainos and Africans as people who were below him but people who did not deserve to be abused unnecessarily. He was particularly lenient with Africans and Tainos who worked harder than others, often allowing them additional leisure time. Pedro Ramirez was an astute and observant man who read the Bible at the end of each day—a practice he had begun the previous year. Pedro Ramirez had married a Taina woman of noble birth who gave him a mestiza daughter who he named Maria after the Virgin Mary. Pedro had a Catholic wedding and his Taina wife was baptized and renamed Valeria. In these horrific conditions, Amanex and his family believed serving Pedro Ramirez was a respite from the more vicious encomenderos. Amanex feared a public Catholic marriage with his love Tayamari and discussed a private Taino wedding with his parents, but Ana did not want her son to be punished if the Spanish friars discovered that he engaged in what they deemed as pagan activities.

One evening Amanex approached Tayamari as she was leaving her master's quarters. Tayamari's encomendero was Joaquín Montero an unpredictably violent man who was often found drunk beating upon Tainos and Africans who he believed were lazy.

Amanex anxiously but confidently asked in the Spanish language, "Tayamari, you have shared memories with me and you have comforted me throughout these painful times. I hope I have made you happy as you have continued to make me happy and I would love to share this life with you in a lifetime bond with each other. Will you marry me, Tayamari?"

Tayamari laughed nervously as tears made their way down her soft brown cheeks. "Yes, I will be your wife, for I have never known a man who was not my uncle or father to provide me with a sense of security and happiness as you have."

Amanex was overjoyed, however Tayamari questioned their life together as she quietly stated, "I love you, Amanex, but how can we love each other fully when our people are killed like animals? How can we bring children into this violent world of the Spaniards? How will we live with a family under their rule? Will we live with the constant stress of losing our own children like our own families do?"

Amanex responded, "Perhaps we can live under the relative safety of my master until we can have better laws to protect us. Perhaps I can speak with the Franciscan or Dominican Friars about our conditions and they can help mediate a common agreement with respect between the Tainos and Spaniards. The only thing I can guarantee is that I will sacrifice my life for you and our children, if we are blessed with them. I will give my own life before anything happens to you, Tayamari."

Tears fell down Tayamari's face as Amanex kissed her and held her as if he was holding the earth and the heavens together.

Amanex spoke to his parents and Tayamari's uncle about their wedding as they prepared themselves for the wedding date. He desired to be married the Taino way, although he believed informing Pedro Ramirez would result in a Catholic wedding and a possible transfer of Tayamari and her uncle as servants for the more lenient Pedro Ramirez. Having Tayamari living with him under Pedro Ramirez would be beneficial for them as opposed to being under the service of the other more brutal encomenderos. Amanex also believed Pedro Ramirez would show some empathy, as he was married to a Taina and had a daughter who was both Spaniard and Taino. Amanex and Tayamari were able to share a brief moment with their families and one evening in July of 1515, they were wed in a Taino ceremony.

Surrounded by their family members, Amanex sang the songs of his people, asking the Gods to bless their marriage. They celebrated their union as one heart together in this life to improve upon each other's weaknesses. Amanex and Tayamari were then given herbs to consume and drink and herbs rubbed in powder spread on their bodies. Maraguay and Ana exclaimed, "Taino, Ti. May the Great Spirit be with you," as Amanex and Tayamari embraced each other.

The celebration was quick, quiet, and performed away from the eyes of the Spaniards. Amanex was excited but understood he could only live with his new bride if he had a Catholic wedding. A Catholic wedding would provide Amanex and Tayamari with official recognition under the Catholic Church—a reality that disturbed Amanex, but it was necessary.

One evening after working in the sugar fields, Amanex spoke with Pedro Ramirez regarding his desire to marry Tayamari.

Pedro Ramirez questioned Amanex. "Were you baptized by your previous masters and have you taken the sacraments and read your Bible?"

Amanex replied, "I have read the Bible and if you offer me one I will be proficient in their lessons; however, I have not been baptized and neither has my family members or Tayamari."

Pedro Ramirez said, "You are a great servant, Amanex, and you have never caused me any grief. You have caused me happiness and increased my sugarcane profits. I will ask a friar to help set up a Catholic wedding in the eyes of Jesus Christ."

Amanex also suggested that Tayamari and her uncle Hayanao be moved to his quarters, to which Pedro Ramirez responded, "I will ask Joaquín Montero to move them under my direction."

Amanex was excited as the wedding preparations moved quickly and they were married the following week after Amanex and Tayamari were baptized. Some of the other Spaniards objected to the baptism of Amanex's parents and Tayamari's uncle, as they were not learned in Biblical teachings. In reality, many of the Spaniards believed the Tainos to be unworthy of receiving the teachings of Jesus Christ and it also excused the Spaniards' brutality towards the Tainos and Africans.

The Catholic wedding was presided over by a Franciscan Priest named Ignacio Muñoz. He opened the ceremony with a prayer, asking God to bless the wedding day of Amanex and Tayamari. After several prayers, they exchanged vows and the couple were married under the Catholic Church. Ignacio Muñoz carried on with other prayers as the wedding culminated in an embrace between Amanex and Tayamari. Ignacio Muñoz exclaimed Amanex should be renamed Abrahán after his baptism. Observing the wedding were various friars and Bartolome de las Casas who was accompanied by the deceased Cristóbal Colón's adopted Taino son Guaikán.

Amanex desired to engage in conversation and spoke with Bartolomé de las Casas and Guaikán. Pedro Ramirez's wife Valeria also observed the wedding and after Valeria's conversation with the young couple, she helped convince her husband to speak with Joaquín Montero to quickly transfer Tayamari and her uncle. After the wedding ceremonies, Amanex was welcomed into the catholic faith, however Amanex secretly maintained his traditional Taino beliefs.

Several months prior, in January 1516, King Ferdinand II of Aragon died, leaving Juana la Loca as ruler with her teenage son Carlos I vying to gain power and legitimacy as king. As the Crown was caught in a power struggle, the wars raged on in San Juan Bautista in 1514 as the Spaniards continued their mining efforts near the long mountain ranges in the central part of the island. Jerónimo de Merlo led incursions into San Juan Bautista, which resulted in various wars, while the capital of Caparra was attacked by Tainos on July 26, 1514. A secondary attack at Caparra returned several months after this, as the native and African coalition of 300 injured the Spanish ally Cacique Cacibona, but they were later repelled by the Spaniards. In 1515, the caciques Humacao, Loquillo, and Daguao led another offensive against the Spaniards which resulted in defeat. An attempt at a peace treaty between the Spaniards and by a nephew of Agüeybaná II failed and he was targeted for capture.

The caciques Daguao and Agüeybaná II were aided by the arrival of over 150 natives in canoes, creating a coalition force of over 400 combined with growing African forces which engaged in battle near the river in northeastern San Juan Bautista. The battle resulted in an initial success for Cacique Agüeybaná II, but the cacique popularly nick-named El Bravo suffered a severe loss in the next two battles, forcing him into a retrea to the adjacent islands with heavy reinforcements. A force of Spaniards stated they cornered the Supreme Leader Cacique Agüeybaná II in the island of Guadeloupe but the Spaniards suffered many losses and retreated as Cacique Agüeybaná II remained alive and elusive. The Spaniards continued to capture, enslave, and execute all the caciques on the island of San Juan Bautista while entering the lands of the caciques Loquillo and Humacao. Although the Spaniards were marching deeper into Taino territory, many of the natives and Africans continued to fight, resulting in a high number of Spanish casualties in the year 1517.

Ponce de León, who had secured three ships in 1515 from the King Ferdinand II of Aragon, left on May fourteenth of 1515. He had survived several battles with the Kalinago who he called Caribs, including a small battle on the island of Guadalupe. After King Ferdinand II's death, Juan Ponce de León had little support, including from the regent of Castile Cardinal Francisco Jiménez de Cisneros. Without authorization to land in San Juan Bautista and spies sent by his rival Viceroy Diego Colón, Juan Ponce de León set his sights on a land he had previously explored on

April second, 1513. A land he had secretly explored and falsely believed to be another island during the Easter Season. This influenced the name La Pascua Florida. It was a land green with lush vegetation and trees which Juan Ponce de León called La Florida.

CHAPTER 12
DOMINICAN INTERVENTION (1517)

King Carlos I and the Hapsburg dynasty had increased in power in Spain and across Europe as his mother Juana la Loca was sidelined. The House of Hapsburg, under the seventeen year old King Carlos I, was now on the verge of taking power from the ruling House of Trastámara in unified Spain. King Carlos I was heir to Europe's leading dynasties, which included the Houses of Valois-Burgundy of the Netherlands, the House of Habsburg of the Holy Roman Empire, and the House of Trastámara of Spain. At six years old, Carlos I inherited the Burgundian Netherlands to the north from his father Philip I of Castile, and the Franche-Comté as heir of the House of Valois-Burgundy. King Carlos I was also elected to succeed his Habsburg grandfather, Maximilian I, as Holy Roman Emperor—a title held by the Habsburgs since 1440. With his rise to power in Spain, King Carlos I was set to control all the territories in the city states of Italy, including the Papal States and the territories of the New World with discussions about possible expansions into Asia.

The island of Hispaniola was often the base of operations of conquest for the Spaniards and King Carlos I. Amanex and his new bride were finally allowed to live together after their master Pedro Ramirez convinced Joaquín Montero to trade Tayamari for two of his African slaves, but Tayamari's uncle Hayanao remained under the control of Encomendero Joaquín Montero. Amanex was determined to find a way to get Hayanao transferred under Encomendero Pedro Ramirez, and he believed that his growing friendship with Guaikán and some of the friars, including Bartolome de las Casas, could possibly influence Hayanao's transfer. Amanex was now speaking with Guaikán and other friars who informed him of the civilizations of Europe. He was interested in learning more about the Spanish people; their monarchs and their relationship with other societies in that region of the world.

Guaikán had described to him in detail about the cities of Europe and details of Spanish exploration and other ancient societies. He informed Amanex of the young King Carlos I, who ruled many lands, including the growing Spanish Empire and was positioning himself to become the Holy Roman Emperor. He described the English Kingdom on an island separated from the mainland and the ruler of England King Henry VIII. Guaikán also explained the growing tensions between King Francis I of France and the solidifying alliance between King Henry VIII and King Carlos I and the territories of Italy where Admiral Cristóbal Colón was from. Amanex was informed of the Great Ottoman Sultan Selim I, who had expanded the Ottoman Empire and had recently defeated the Mamluk Sultanate of Egypt under the leadership of Sultan Al-Ashraf Tuman bay II. In January of 1517, Sultan Selim I captured Cairo, including the lands of Al-Hijaz, the Levant, and Tihamah, while his Vizier Hadım Sinan Pasha died during battle. Sultan Selim I was also granted the title of Protector of the Two Holy Cities, which made him responsible for two holiest mosques in Islam: the Sacred Mosque named Al-Masjid al-Haram in Mecca, and the Prophet's Mosque named Al-Masjid an-Nabawi in Medina. Guaikán told Amanex about Prophet Muhammad, who was believed to be the last Prophet of Islam. Amanex desired to learn about the religion of Islam despite the fact that the Franciscan and Dominican Friars viewed the Islamic religion negatively and forbade Muslim African slaves from openly practicing.

At thirty-seven years of age, Guaikán was a man

who seemed to have lived several lifetimes. Amanex, who was soon to become thirty-two, could only hope to experience everything Guaikán had. However, Guaikán's life had been under the submission to Spanish power. Guaikán excelled in the spoken and written aspects of the language of the Spaniards. The Castilian language which they generally referred to as Spanish was poetic whenever Guaikán spoke, revealing his thoughts and vast knowledge. As their friendship grew, Guaikán asked Amanex's Encomendero Pedro Ramirez to allow Amanex a day of respite on Sundays. Pedro Ramirez allowed Amanex more freedom due to his hard work in the sugarcane fields and his increasing profits. Amanex began bringing his wife Tayamari with him to the monastery, where he began conversing with the Dominican Friar Bartolome de las Casas.

Amanex and his wife learned more about the Catholic religion and although he secretly kept his Taino beliefs, he was interested in learning about the Spaniards and their beliefs that seemed to both justify and reprimand their brutality. Within the monastery, Amanex met various Tainos who were of royal lineage, including the descendants of Cacica Anacaona, Cacique Caonabo, and Cacique Bohechio. Bartolome de las Casas introduced Amanex to the daughter of the deceased Anacaona named Higüemota. Amanex marveled at the intelligence of Higüemota, who had the beauty of her mother and the determination of her father Caonabo, despite her pseudo-captivity. As Amanex began speaking with Higüemota, he was also introduced to Anacaona's nephew Guarocuya, who was recently married in a Catholic wedding to Anacaona's Mestiza niece Doña Mencia. Amanex was pleasantly surprised; it was the first time he had been formally introduced to Guarocuya and Doña Mencia, who was nearly as beautiful as the great leader Anacaona.

Guarocuya had been renamed Enrique—nicknamed Enriquillo for his short stature. Guarocuya was born in 1496 as the Spaniards continued to conquer the island now called Hispaniola. Guarocuya was a small but strong twenty-one year old man who was well versed in Spanish culture and history; he also had a great command of the Spanish language. Enriquillo was spared much of the details regarding the murders and execution of his family members, however he had witnessed the brutality of the Spaniards on the Taino and African slaves despite his privileged position in Spanish society. Enriquillo also heard brief stories of the executions of his family members, including his father Magiocatex and Anacaona's daughter Higüemota. This caused a growing sense of pain and helplessness in his heart of Enriquillo despite his guardianship under the secular priest Bartolome de las Casas and friars from the Franciscan and Dominican Orders. Despite Enriquillo's privileged status as compared to the other Tainos, he still belonged to Encomendero Don Francisco de Valenzuela. Enriquillo questioned Amanex about his great aunt Anacaona and Cacique Caonabo and the chiefdoms in the former island of Ayiti, including the territories of Maguana and Amanex's birthplace of Jaragua. As Amanex and Enriquillo spoke about the details of Spanish conquest, Bartolome de las Casas and other friars nervously interrupted them.

Bartolome de las Casas directed Amanex and his wife Tayamari to the areas of the monastery and library when he observed the growing child within the belly of Tayamari.

Bartolome quietly stated, "Excuse my curiosity, but it seems that our Lord has blessed Tayamari with a child."

Amanex replied, "Yes, the child is over four months old now so my wife was granted leave from her duties so she can relax and concentrate on the upcoming birth."

Bartolome de las Casas was genuinely happy and spoke about how the teachings of Jesus Christ could help form a better society between the Tainos and Spaniards. In the previous year of 1516, priests of the Order of Saint Jerome were sent to Hispaniola and the surrounding islands to observe and report on the native situation. The Order of Saint Jerome—also called the Hieronymites—carried the legacy of the fifth century hermit and biblical scholar Saint

Jerome, who had translated the Holy Bible into Latin. The Hieronymites arrived wearing their white tunics with brown, hooded scapular and brown mantle and reserving their brown cowls for Liturgical services.

Cardinal Francisco Jiménez de Cisneros sent a small party of three monks of the Order of Saint Jerome to Hispaniola, including their leader Luis de Figueroa who became the co-governor of the island of Hispaniola. In 1515, Bartolome de las Casas had renounced his Encomienda, releasing his personal Taino slaves and advocating on behalf of the Tainos against Spanish brutality to King Carlos I. Despite the rising Spanish criticism of the Encomienda system, Amanex and many of the Tainos and Africans were still suffering through slavery and executions. Nevertheless, Amanex was excited to speak to Spaniards who treated him with at least a basic level of respect.

Bartolome de las Casas believed he could influence Viceroy Diego Colón through his relationship with Luis de Figueroa and Diego Colón's wife María Álvarez de Toledo. Diego Colón's power was rapidly declining with his previous loss of direct rule in Cuba and his deepening feud with Juan Ponce de León and the Spanish Crown. Cuban Governor Diego Velázquez de Cuéllar convoked a general cabildo which was the local Cuban government council, which was duly authorized to deal directly with Spain, and therefore removed Velázquez and the settlers from under the authority of Diego Colón. The Spaniards in Cuba had a public celebration after Governor Diego Velázquez de Cuéllar diminished Diego Colón's power in Cuba. Bartolome de las Casas and the other priests believed they were in position to alter the relationship between Spaniards and the slaves into a more peaceful coexistence. Amanex believed even with improvements in their relations, they would remain below the Spaniards.

Amanex inquired about the books in the library and Bartolome de las Casas began to explain the scientific papers, philosophies, and works of fiction. Amanex enjoyed learning about the past of the people who behaved so brutally towards his own people; he believed understanding their history could help explain their nature. He secretly pondered about the apparent paradox of the Spaniards, who were warlike yet believed in Jesus Christ who preached benevolence and empathy for others.

Amanex learned about Jesus Christ's teachings and the Samaritans and their differences with the Jewish people. The Samaritans were thought of as inferior by many of the Jews because they believed the Samaritans were imperfect believers in Judaism who also practiced paganism. The Samaritans equally disliked the Jewish people and they accepted only the first five books of the Bible as canonical, and their Samaritan temple was on Mount Gerazim instead of on Mount Zion in Jerusalem. Although both the Samaritans and Jewish people worshipped Yahweh, they remained divided and the Jewish people avoided Samaritan towns when travelling between Judea to Galilee by crossing the river Jordan and bypassing Samaria by going through Transjordan. Jesus Christ decided a new attitude should be taken in regard to the Samaritans and he purposefully walked through the lands of the Samaritan people and provided an example for his fellow Jewish people. Amanex questioned Bartolome de las Casas. How could the Spaniards truly one day practice the words of Jesus Christ even when they continued to overshadow God in their worship of gold?

He enjoyed the verses involving Jesus Christ and the Samaritans. Particular verses that Amanex liked were found in *The Book of John Chapter Four*.

Verse nine and ten of *John Book Four* read: "The Samaritan woman said to him, 'you are a Jew and I am a Samaritan woman. How can you ask me for a drink?' For Jews do not associate with Samaritans. Jesus answered her, 'If you knew the gift of God and who it is that asks you for a drink, you would have asked him and he would have given you living water'."

Verses nineteen through twenty-six continued, "'Sir', the woman said, 'I can see that you are a prophet. Our ancestors worshiped on this mountain, but you Jews claim that the place where we must worship is in Jerusalem.' 'Woman,' Jesus replied, 'believe me, a time is coming when you will worship the Father neither on this mountain nor in Jerusalem. You Samaritans worship what you do not know; we worship what we do know, for salvation is from the Jews. Yet a time is coming and has now come when the true worshipers will worship the Father in the Spirit and in truth, for they are the kind of worshipers the Father seeks. God is spirit, and his worshipers must worship in the Spirit and in truth.' The woman said, 'I know that Messiah is coming. When he comes, he will explain everything to us.' Then Jesus declared, 'I, the one speaking to you—I am he."

Amanex believed in the words of Jesus Christ and his ability to bring communities together although they were hostile to each other, but he also believed many of the Spaniards were using division as a weapon and were not practicing the words of Jesus Christ.

As the months passed, Amanex continued to speak with Bartolome de las Casas, Guaikán, and the Enriquillo family. He disliked his Catholic name Abrahán and convinced Bartolome de las Casas, Guaikán, and Enriquillo to call him Amanex during private conversations while he tried hard to conceal his disdain for his Catholic name particularly from Spaniards who could use his anger against him. Amanex developed a close friendship with Bartolome de las Casas and Enriquillo and their respect for Amanex allowed for good conversations. Through these conversations, Amanex learned about the culture of other ancient civilizations and how they interacted with each other. However, peace between the Tainos and Spaniards seemed unattainable despite the hopeful words Bartolome de las Casas. The Taino populations were quickly decreasing with another outbreak of diseases which frightened Amanex as he observed his mother Ana weaken with disease as well as Anacaona's daughter Higüemota.

African slaves were arriving in increasing numbers to the island of Hispaniola and in even higher degrees in the surrounding islands of Cuba and San Juan Bautista.

Juan de Esquivel founded the first Spanish settlement in the northern coast of Jamaica and named it Sevilla la Nueva in 1509 and later Juan de Esquivel passed away in the island of Jamaica in 1513. However, Jamaica remained a small military base without a large Spanish presence due to the unsuccessful search for gold on the island. The second Royal Governor of Santiago (commonly referred to as Jamaica) brought extreme brutality to the Tainos there as he extended sugarcane plantations and sent Taino slaves to the goldmines of Cuba. Governor Francisco de Garay also began to grow pigs and enslaved thousands of Tainos to herd his swine.

Bartolome wrote a report to the Spanish Crown regarding Juan de Esquivel during the Higüey massacre of 1503. This brutality was now visiting Amanex and his family with the return of Conquistador Radamés Cesar Milfuegos to the city of Santo Domingo. Bartolome also spoke against Governor Francisco de Garay and his genocide of the Taino people in Jamaica. Amanex secretly hoped for Radamés to meet his demise in the wars in San Juan Bautista and his fear of Radamés increased the idea of fleeing from Hispaniola and taking his family with him. As the month of November came to a close, Amanex reached her ninth month of pregnancy and Amanex's family happily awaited the birth of the child. On December fifth of 1518, Tayamari gave birth to a healthy son.

Amanex and his family held a small celebration and Encomendero Pedro Ramirez encouraged the child to be baptized in the Catholic faith and given a Spanish name. Amanex's son was named Simon Pedro after one of the twelve disciples of Jesus Christ. Amanex also gave his son the name of after Cacique Haübey, who had protested the brutality of the Spaniards against the Taino people, for which he was burned alive. Amanex did not witness the execution of Haübey as he had witnessed the executions of the other caciques, but he admired Haübey's bravery in the face of death and chose to name his son after him.

Amanex was now working in the large boiling vats where the sugarcane was processed. He helped chop the wood used to burn and heat the sugarcane juice and convert it to molasses which was later converted to sugar. Amanex was also ordered to help in the burning and fertilization of the sugar cane fields to prepare the soil for future cultivation. One Afternoon, Amanex was accompanied by Africans from the same tribe as his friend Elombe to help in the burning of a sugarcane field. As they observed the growing flames, Conquistador Radamés Cesar Milfuegos approached Amanex and the frightened Africans.

As he grew closer, Radamés smiled and got off his horse, aiming his three-foot sword at Amanex as he exclaimed, "Your brother Amayao and his followers betrayed Juan Ponce de León in Higüey and fled to San Juan Bautista. Amayao participated in the wars in San Juan Bautista along with other caciques and personally fought alongside Cacique Agüeybaná II. Amayao murdered my friend Jose Sanchez and he helped Cacique Urayoán drown Diego Salcedo. Your brother also helped burn down the city of Caparra in San Juan Bautista, however I was able to strike him down and torture him slowly until I ended his life by decapitation." Radamés pointed at his right check and his chest and stated, "Your brother scarred me for life and for that perhaps I will scar you and your family—a small price to pay for the actions of Amayao."

Amanex began to sob. "I do not believe you have killed him!"

Radamés replied, "I executed that wild animal you call your brother with the same ease I kill a wild pig. If you do not believe my words you can review our records listing all the caciques, Africans, Tainos, and Caribs we have killed."

Some of the Africans protested Radamés and he responded in brutal fashion, loading his arquebus and firing upon the them, killing two African slaves and injuring several Tainos. As more Africans came to the aid of their fallen friends, Radamés alerted other Spaniards, who brought Radamés his armor and prepared to massacre them all. Another Spaniard named Simon De La Cruz, who worked as an overseer for the sugar cane plantations of

Pedro Ramirez, attempted to stop what was about to happen.

Simon pleaded with Radamés, "Please do not kill these laborers! They have always worked hard for Don Pedro Ramirez—particularly Amanex. Do not make him answer for his brother's failures."

Radamés replied, "Some of you Spaniards have grown weak among these savages we are supposed to rule over. You and Don Pedro Ramirez choose to even marry the Taina women and have mestizo children who should not inherit what we have worked so hard to establish here away from civilization. Pedro Ramirez used to stand with us and now he believes what these Catholic friars and priests teach them regarding a false idea of mixed community in peace. I have fought these Tainos and the more barbaric Carib natives along with the African slaves who hate us simply for helping create civilization where there was previously none. Now we marry with these Tainos. Will we marry African slaves next and create bastard mulattoes? Many of these Africans and Tainos have fled and formed their own communities free from our guidance and have created sambos who hold the same hostility for us that their parents have."

Amanex responded, "This is no civilization, what you have brought to our native lands. You have killed before and now you kill innocent slaves with your weapons and you justify your murder through the words of your God and his book *The Holy Bible*. The Spaniards have brought disaster, disease, brutality, and murder and your God is not Jesus Christ but the gold that motivates you to take the lands of others and murder, steal, and rape our women and children. That is why Spaniards like your friend Jose Sanchez have met a violent demise by an honorable man like my older brother Amayao. However, how can I be certain you murdered my brother? The Spaniards have proven to be liars and dishonorable men who break their agreements and promises. Perhaps these new people born from the Spaniards, Tainos, and Africans will not inherit the brutality of the Spaniards and perhaps they will receive the goodness of the Tainos and Africans. Perhaps these children will learn to continue the small amount of kindness I have seen from some Spaniards like the friars but even they do not do enough to stop the advancing Spanish armies into other civilizations."

Radamés angrily rushed towards Amanex and kicked him to the ground, aiming his sword at his neck when suddenly he was stopped by some Franciscan and Dominican friars—including the friar Bartolome de las Casas.

Bartolome de las Casas spoke on behalf of Amanex. "This man has been a great worker and a smart man and has learned much from our society. Amanex will not cause any problem as he is a new father as his wife welcomed a new baby into this world. My desire is for our people to live in harmony as we build this new society."

Simon De La Cruz interjected, "These sugarcane fields have created major profits for Pedro Ramirez, Viceroy Diego Colón, and the Spanish Crown. You have already murdered workers here who have contributed to our success and you do not want to further anger Viceroy Diego Colón."

Radamés let his anger get the best of him and he understood he was in conflict with Viceroy Diego Colón and his family. Radamés departed as quickly as he arrived, and left the burning sugarcane field along with the other conquistadors but not before he made sure to put on Amanex's necklace within sight of Amanex.

As the sun set on the horizon, rumors spread of the incident in the sugarcane. Amanex gathered enough strength and he told his father and sick mother about the death of their son while sparing them the gruesome details. Maraguay lowered his head as he tried to console Ana who was crying uncontrollably. Amanex held his wife and his son as tears ran down his cheeks as his pain multiplied with every cry from Ana's broken soul. Amanex secretly planned his escape from Santo Domingo and privately spoke to Maraguay.

Many Tainos continued to die from disease and

murder at the hands of the Spaniards and the Spanish court never delivered justice for the Taino people. African slaves and Tainos were fleeing more frequently as Viceroy Diego Colón's personal feud with King Carlos I and the regional officials increased. The Spaniards were about to launch further invasions into other civilizations and various Spanish officials vied for a power within the expanding Spanish Empire. Amanex understood the Taino people were not welcome in this New World order and thoughts of escape frequented his mind. He understood the importance of his family's safety and he calculated a method of escape as the terrors already witnessed by Amanex and his family were to pale in comparison with the horrors to come.

CHAPTER 13
WAR CRY (1519)

Established in 1511, The Spanish Audencia in Santo Domingo on the island of Hispaniola was the first court of the islands and had jurisdiction of the surrounding islands. The regular judges of a criminal case were called Alcaldes de Crimen of Mayors of Crime and the regular judges form civil cases were called oidores or hearers. The presiding officer of the audencias were the gobernador or regentes, which meant the governor or regent. Radamés Cesar Milfuegos was placed under trial in the audencia (or Spanish court) a few weeks after his murders of African and Taino slaves at the sugarcane fields which belonged to Encomendero Pedro Ramirez. Amanex nervously awaited the ruling of the Audencia on Radamés Cesar Milfuegos but anticipated injustice on behalf of a corrupt court. The natives rarely received justice and Amanex expected more injustice regarding a case involving the murder of African slaves. Elombe, who had lost several of his friends at the hands of Radamés, also feared an unjust ruling.

Viceroy Diego Colón's wife Doña María Álvarez de Toledo had previously ruled on her husband's behalf in 1515 and had considerable influence in the welfare of the Taino people. Diego Colón's disdain for the recklessness and violence of Radamés and the loss of slaves and profits for Ramirez and the Spanish Crown put pressure on the audencia to punish Radamés. However, the audencia sent Radamés to the lower civil court after the judges blamed the African slaves for inciting violence and causing their own deaths. Many of the Spaniard eyewitnesses fabricated their stories, stating that although Radamés verbally threatened Amanex, the African slaves surrounded and threated Radamés physically.

Amanex exclaimed, "This man Radamés threatened me and taunted me regarding the death of my brother Amayao by his own hands. Radamés subsequently fired upon the African slaves who never physically assaulted him. Many of our people just want to live in peace and perhaps the policies of the best members of your society should be implemented if you desire to continue living in our lands. We welcomed the Spaniards to our lands and the Spaniards continue to push for gold and other resources at the expense of the original inhabitants. The best way to move forward in an integrated society is to deliver true justice under the law for all peoples—including the Tainos, Africans, and Spaniards—to restore faith in our system and to follow the example of the best and brightest among our combined communities. If the aforementioned cannot be met we will continue on the path of violence and injustice."

Viceroy Diego Colón believed he would soon be replaced due to his ongoing conflict with King Carlos I and the other regional nobles. Diego Colón would soon face a residencia (or judicial review) and did not want to leave on bad terms; he also pressured the court to punish Radamés not for the murder of the African slaves but particularly for the loss of profits of Encomendero Pedro Ramirez, himself, and the Spanish Crown. Radamés was to be fined for the African slaves lost until replacements arrived and was forced to pay a fine to Pedro Ramirez for loss of property. Radamés also would temporarily lose minor leadership positions and his interactions with Africans and Tainos would be limited. The ruling angered the Tainos and African slaves, including Elombe, and further revealed and cemented the corrupt Spanish court system. Although he never faced incarceration for murder, Radamés, who expected to be cleared of all wrongdoing, was angered that he had to pay fines. The ruling also partially helped Diego Colón, who would face questioning by the Tainos and Spaniards during the residencia regarding his tenure. This included the Radamés and Amanex case and he would face little backlash from his disdain for the African slave community.

After the trial's conclusion, Bartolome de las Casas spoke with Amanex. "Why do you remain saddened? Radamés will pay for threatening you and your master will defend you."

Amanex replied, "The African men Radamés murdered received no justice. Are their lives not worth as much as a Taino or a Spaniard when they toil the land every day for the benefits of the Spaniards?"

Bartolome de las Casas quickly answered, "These African slaves were brought to Hispaniola from Spain and other lands for the purpose of labor just as they provided slave labor for the Spaniards and Portuguese in Africa and Europe and just as they provided labor for the Arabic people and the Muslims. My main concerns are the good Taino people who live well such as yourself. The Tainos are good people and many of you live better than the poor Spaniards in Spain. This is why in 1516 I wrote, *Memorial de Remedios para las Indias*, detailing an improvement of Spanish policies regarding the Taino people."

Amanex said, "You are a better man than most of the Spaniards I have known; however, you cannot speak against Spanish brutality without acknowledging the faults of African slavery as it makes your positions weak."

Amanex was provided the Bartolome de las Casa's book *Memorial de Remedios para las Indias* (or *the Memorial of Remedies for the Indies*), which was Bartolome de las Casa's solution to stop the abuses of the Taino people and the evil he felt permeated the colonies in order to maintain peace and improve the republic. Amanex read some of Bartolome's proposals the first one being a temporary prohibition of native forced labor and to allow the native people to recover and regain their dignity until improved regulations were implemented. Bartolome de las Casa's believed the rate of the exploitation of the Tainos would lead to their destruction as a people if corrective measures were not soon taken. Bartolome also advocated a change in the labor policy where instead of owning the labor of a specific number of natives, the Spaniards would only have a right to man-hours to be provided by no specific person. The Tainos could form their own communities and regain self-governance and provide the labor force to the Spaniards, allowing the Tainos to care for the sick and overworked and maintaining a healthy work and rest balance. In his writings and speeches, Bartolome de las Casa tried to establish more rights for the native people and sought to limit the power the Spaniards had over the original inhabitants.

Bartolome de las Casas also expressed his desire to reorganize native society in relation to Spaniard society. Bartolome argued that native settlements could be scattered, populated with roughly 1,000 natives called pueblos and therefore they could be better protected from Spanish brutality and converted into the Catholic faith. Each pueblo would have a Royal Hospital with four wings the shape of the Holy Cross which would help cure the natives from disease and stop the widespread death. Bartolome stated that maintaining this new system would be inexpensive as the Tainos provided for the work and their own products and the potential gold and extraction of resources would provide a profit while providing for people of various trades, including administrators, clerics, advocates, surgeons, doctors, pharmacists, ranchers, miners, muleteers, hospital workers, pig herders, and fishermen. Amanex appreciated Bartolome de las Casa's efforts, but he doubted most Spanish officials would adopt his policies. Amanex also emphasized the fact that Bartolome excluded the plight of the African Slave in his thoughts and proposals.

Amanex asked Bartolome to provide him with books from the library; he had increasingly found a passion in Spanish literature and was particularly interested in the works of the Ancient Greeks and Romans. Amanex also asked for a popular Spanish Epic Poem called *El Cantar de Mio Cid or El Poema del Cid.* The Poem or Epopeya was written about a historical Castilian figure who lived during the eleventh century named Rodrigo Díaz de Vivar and was highly regarded as a valiant warrior and hero among the Castilians. *The Song of my Cid* was also briefly read by Enriquillo, who approached Amanex and Bartolome during their discussion. Enriquillo was aware of the injustice of the Spanish court system and the unjust ruling of the Amanex case and arrived to console his friend. Amanex privately explained the danger his family was in as long as Radamés Cesar Milfuegos remained in the city of Santo Domingo. Enriquillo reminded Amanex that he remained relatively safe under the protection of Encomendero Pedro Ramirez—a position that even Enriquillo and his family did not enjoy under Encomendero Francisco de Valenzuela as their relationship was quickly deteriorating. Amanex informed Enriquillo that Tayamari's uncle Hayanao was also in a bad situation under his master. There was little Enriquillo could do to help Amanex and his family, as he himself was under a precarious situation.

As the months passed, Viceroy Diego Colón was locked into a legal battle with King Carlos I as he sought to keep the family titles and claims to the island of Jamaica and other lands in legal battles known as the pleitos colombinos continued. King Carlos I now claimed the throne of the Holy Roman Empire after the death of his paternal grandfather Maximilian I, the King of the Germans, Romans, and the Holy Roman Emperor, and the earlier death of his father Felipe El Hermoso or Philip I The Handsome in 1506. After bribing various German princes, on June twenty-eighth, 1519, King Carlos I was renamed Carlos V—or Holy Roman Emperor Charles V. Viceroy Diego Colón's power was in serious decline as his rival Governor Diego Velázquez de Cuéllar of Cuba was subsequently declared the fifth Governor of the Indies. As Charles V solidified his power and Hispaniola experienced a power shift, the thin veil of protection that shielded

Amanex and his family quickly evaporated in the month of August in 1519.

A few weeks earlier, in July, a scandal rocked Santo Domingo as the highly respected Enriquillo and his wife Doña Mencia were disgraced by Encomendero Francisco de Valenzuela and his son Andrés de Valenzuela. Jealousy arose in the heart of Andrés as he observed Enriquillo's intelligence and the respect he held among his Taino people and the African slaves—a respect Andrés lacked in the eyes of his fellow Spaniards and even his own father Francisco de Valenzuela. Andrés urged his father to curtail some of Enriquillo and his family's freedoms by insisting that his friendships with Bartolome de las Casas, Amanex, and Guaikán would cause problems among the Tainos and Africans. One night drunk, on wine, Andrés stripped Doña Mencia and violated her, leaving her naked and enraging Enriquillo and his family. When Enriquillo angrily confronted Francisco de Valenzuela about his son's actions, the embarrassed Francisco de Valenzuela physically assaulted Doña Mencia in an attempt to break Enriquillo's anger and re-introduce Enriquillo to his proper place in Spanish society. Enriquillo went to the audencia to make a case against his encomendero and his son.

Amanex warned Enriquillo that the Spanish courts were corrupt and he would never receive the justice he deserved. He tried to keep his conversations with Enriquillo private as he did not want to place his own family in danger, however Amanex and his family were now under close observation and on one hot summer afternoon as Amanex briefly paused from his labors in the sugarcane fields, some conquistadors led by a violent Spaniard named Pedro Mujica ordered him and others on a long march outside of the city of Santo Domingo. To Amanex's surprise, his parents Maraguay and Ana later joined him in the march.

Amanex's mother was sick and bedridden with a rapidly worsening disease and angrily requested she be given bedrest, to which Pedro Mujica replied, "You all will have eternal rest before this day is over."

As the march ended, Ana began to vomit and could barely move as she had intense pain in her stomach and back and she felt hot to the touch. Ana's fear made her symptoms worse as she called for her husband and son. Ana struggled as she stated, "I love you, my husband Maraguay and my youngest son Amanex. It has been my greatest joy having a brave, loving husband and a smart, loving son. I am too sick now and welcome death and my only wish is for you both to escape and save yourselves."

Amanex began to cry as the familiar voice of Radamés Cesar Milfuegos broke the uneasy silence.

Radamés Cesar Milfuegos dragged Amanex towards the gallows with thirteen hangman nooses. "These are meant for your twelve disciples and the thirteenth for you, the false prophet. Originally, they were meant for your little king Enriquillo, however my friend Andrés de Valenzuela wanted to humiliate Enriquillo and now his father is convinced that animals such as you, your Taino people, and African slaves should never be given the opportunity to be educated and live among us as equals. We should not expect much of a fight from you and your people as you are now native mansos—a bunch of natives and African slaves to meek and broken-hearted to fight back and rebel."

As Radamés left the area to retrieve rope and wood to burn the corpses after executions, Amanex's mother fell to the ground, too weak to stand. Maraguay ran towards his wife as a startled young Spaniard left to guard the Taino prisoners opened fire on him.

Pedro Mujica exclaimed, "Aim your arquebuses at these wild beasts."

Amanex gathered the little courage he had left and charged Pedro Mujica, knocking him to the ground, taking his sword, and burying it deep into his chest. The other Spaniards opened fire as some Tainos managed to flee, but Amanex and his parents Maraguay and Ana were all struck.

As the sun began to set, Amanex awoke from his daze and realized he was losing blood. he knew his parents were dead and he was below the other Taino cadavers who had been killed in the shooting. A few of the Spaniards were also dead, including Pedro Mujica, who remained on the ground with his own sword through his chest and his face frozen in deathly fear. Amanex checked on his parents' bodies and with tears in his eyes vowed to have his revenge as he managed to escape the Spaniards and flee before Radamés returned with extra wood. Some of the Spaniards began to burn the cadavers while others dug a massive grave.

Upon his return, Radamés Cesar Milfuegos angrily asked one of the Spaniards if they had identified all the bodies before they burned them, noticing that Amanex was not among the dead. Radamés Cesar Milfuegos sent a search party in search of Amanex as he loudly said, "You coward! You are not half the man your brother Amayao was. At least he had enough spirit to confront me man to man. I know you have escaped, but I know despite your fear that you must return to Santo Domingo, for your wife and son remain there. Perhaps I should take the liberty of getting to know your wife in the same fashion as my friend Andrés de Valenzuela and his father Francisco familiarized themselves with Doña Mencia. Your dead brother killed my friend Jose Sanchez and now they have informed me that you have killed my friend Pedro Mujica, and for this payment will be the torture of your family."

Amanex watched from a distance as the Tainos—including his parents—were burned as the sun began to set on the horizon.

Amanex began gathering other Tainos as they evaded various Spanish search parties. Some had learned about Amanex and the humiliation of Enriquillo and the great Cacique Tamayo sent Amanex reinforcements of weapons and soldiers. The Spanish court expectedly did not deliver the justice Enriquillo deserved and for weeks the Spaniards ridiculed Enriquillo. Despite Bartolome de las Casa's pleas for peace, in early September 1519 Enriquillo and many of the Tainos decided to flee the city of Santo Domingo. Amanex, in his excruciatingly deep fear that his wife Tayamari was in danger, decided to return quickly.

Amanex believed Encomendero Pedro Ramirez would not protect his family from Radamés Cesar Milfuegos. Radamés had begun openly criticizing Pedro Ramirez because of his Taina wife and mestiza daughter, stating that a new order had now come under the Adelantado of Cuba and now Governor of the Indies Don Diego Velázquez de Cuéllar. Radamés became emboldened after a few weeks, but he was patrolling for runaway Taino and African slaves when Amanex and his soldiers ripped through Santo Domingo.

Amanex split his men into two large groups, leading part of his Taino soldiers into the quarters of Encomendero Pedro Ramirez.

In fear Pedro, Ramirez exclaimed, "Abrahán, I have treated your family and son as if they were my own family. I have defended your family despite the fact that you ran away and killed the Spaniard Pedro Mujica. You chose to kill; however, I chose to protect your wife Tayamari, her uncle Hayanao, and your son Simon Pedro Haübey. Please do not take your vengeance upon me and my wife Valeria and daughter Maria. I am a Spaniard yet I chose a Taina wife so I am not like these other Spaniards who have abused your people."

Amanex responded, "My name is not Abrahán. My name is Amanex, and my parents were killed along with other Tainos at the hands of Pedro Mujica and Radamés Cesar Milfuegos. Am I not a man like you; perhaps your wife Valeria should have taught you that we are equals as men. Your own people look down on your mestiza daughter yet you continue to ignore this fact and you still own over 100 slaves. I have also not forgotten about your history as a conquistador and the Taino lives you have taken during your adventures in Cuba. I will take my family with me and live in freedom and I will spare your life and the life of your wife and child but remember this luxury is not enjoyed by my people. This has always been our land of Ayiti and now we live under domination in your Hispaniola. I understand you have treated my family well despite our slavery and for that I will spare your life and I have instructed my warriors to do the same, but do not interfere in our battle tonight or I will make sure if we cross paths again that I will kill you and all those you hold dear."

Amanex took his scared wife and child and instructed his men to take the horses and Spanish weapons as they killed any Spaniard that stood in their way. Riding his horse, Amanex raided the home of Encomendero Joaquín Montero, looking for Hayanao as the African slaves ran outside. In panic, Joaquín Montero positioned a sword at Hayanao's neck, begging him to let him live.

Tayamari cried out, "Let my uncle live and my husband will spare your life! All we desire is freedom."

Hayanao attempted to break free, screaming, "My niece, go with Amanex! Live free and forget about my life," as he attacked Joaquín Montero.

Joaquín Montero fired upon Hayanao but not before Hayanao knocked him off his feet, leaving him defenseless as Amanex cut his neck while instructing Tayamari to shield her eyes from the violence. Enriquillo confronted his old Encomendero Francisco de Valenzuela and was able to injure him with a stolen Spanish sword and take his wife Doña Mencia before Spanish soldiers arrived. The Spaniards took Higüemota captive as Enriquillo and Doña Mencia escaped and joined a large contingent of African slaves and Tainos from Jaragua. Amanex liberated many of the African slaves, including his good friend Elombe, who valiantly took up arms along with the other Africans. Enriquillo began his search for Diego de Valenzuela as Amanex finally joined forces with Enriquillo and they began to search for Diego.

Amanex sent over 100 Taino and African fighters towards the outskirts of the city of Santo Domingo in an attempt to cut off reinforcements and to capture Radamés Cesar Milfuegos. Many of the Spanish conquistadors who were not killed died from their injuries, including Francisco de Valenzuela, who succumbed to his wounds a month later in October. Enriquillo and his wife Doña Mencia and Amanex and his family escaped the city of Santo Domingo as the sun set and darkness enveloped the island, killing any Spaniard that confronted them. Radamés' men were violently defeated on the outskirts of Santo Domingo and Radamés was able to barely escape with his life. Amanex and Enriquillo took as many arquebuses and Spanish swords as they could carry and freed hundreds of Tainos and African slaves as they left the city of Santo Domingo. The next morning, the city and its growing population of Spanish women and children were shocked at the events that occurred the night before.

Governor Diego Velázquez de Cuéllar received reports of expeditions to the Aztec Empire from Juan de Grijalva as well as the Yucatan from Francisco Hernando de Córdoba; he had authorized them both in 1518. Hernando Cortés gathered his men and against the order of Governor Diego Velázquez de Cuéllar, he would set sail towards the Aztec Empire while other conquistadors set their focus on the lands south of the isthmus of Veragua. In early 1519, The Holy Roman Emperor Charles V authorized the conquering of new lands as other navigators sailed east to Asia, including Ferdinand Magellan, who set sail in September 1519 to increase the eastern reaches of the empire of Emperor Charles V. Governor Diego Velázquez de Cuéllar was determined to conquer the island of San Juan Bautista and capture the elusive Agüeybaná II, however he was troubled at the strength of Cacique Enriquillo, who was gathering Tainos, African slaves, and other natives into a powerful coalition within Hispaniola. War had begun on the island of Hispaniola and Governor Diego Velázquez de Cuéllar realized he could lose control if he could not subdue Enriquillo.

For several months, Enriquillo repelled Spanish offenses and won several battles, forcing the Spaniards to retreat. Enriquillo suggested that the Taino rebellion would succeed in Jaragua and he easily convinced the Tainos and Africans to move their war against the Spaniards to the west. Jaragua would become the stage for the resurgence of the Tainos and a large-scale coalition between natives and Africans against the Spaniards. Amanex and his family hoped this would be the start of a fight that would bring the end of violent rule under the Spaniards. The Tainos reaffirmed their stand under the leadership of Enriquillo and legitimized his rule as cacique as the fight continued in Jaragua and throughout the island of Hispaniola.

CHAPTER 14
LA FLORIDA (1521)

Juan Ponce de León had finally returned to the land he named La Florida with two ships and over 200 men, including farmers, priests, artisans, over fifty horses, pigs, and other domestic animals and farming equipment. Juan Ponce de León believed he now had more control in his colonization efforts as his rival Diego Colón had been removed as viceroy and replaced with Governor Diego Velázquez de Cuéllar. The conquistador previously had failed to colonize the lands of Florida after being expelled by warriors of the native Calusa Tequesta tribes. He also suspected that Diego Colón had sent spies to track his movements in Florida—particularly Diego Miruelo, who had suffered a shipwreck in 1516 and later returned to Cuba, losing some of his mental faculties. On previous expeditions to Florida, Juan Ponce de León encountered large turtles, monk seagulls, and observed many thousands of seabirds. He was informed about many tribes that lived in Florida, including the Mayaimi people who lived around a large freshwater lake.

Many other explorers had made a name for themselves, including an Italian explorer named Amerigo Vespucci. Born in the Republic of Florence in 1454 to his parents Anastasio, a Florentine notary and Lisabetta Mini, Amerigo Vespucci sailed extensively to the islands previously explored by Cristóbal Colón and proved that the large southern landmass and the islands conquered by Cristóbal Colón were not on the outskirts of east Asia but a new land with new people and civilizations. Amerigo Vespucci's contributions and his expertise in the area of cartography impressed King Ferdinand II, who made him a Spanish citizen. After Amerigo's death in Sevilla Spain in 1512, a cédula real (or royal decree) dated May twenty-second, 1512, granted his widow, Maria Cerezo a lifetime pension of ten thousand marvedis per year deducted from the salary of Amerigo's successor. Amerigo's accomplishments appeared to surpass that of Cristóbal Colón as his son Diego Colón and the rest of the family continued their lawsuit against the Spanish Crown. Juan Ponce de León observed men who had carved out land and riches for themselves in the past and present and compared how each had succeeded and failed. Juan Ponce de León had governed the island of San Juan Bautista three separate times previously, replacing Governor Cristóbal de Mendoza, and Juan Ponce de León was subsequently replaced in 1519 by Governor Sánchez Velázquez, who was himself replaced by Governor Antonio de la Gama.

San Juan Bautista was now under the leadership of Governor Pedro Moreno, who persisted in the Spanish wars against the united native and African coalition. Natives continued to arrive to the island of San Juan Bautista on canoes and El Bravo Cacique Agüeybaná II remained elusive and was suspected to still be in control of the native and African coalition. Some of the Spaniards jokingly referred to Agüeybaná II, who was commonly referred to as Cristóbal, was believed to be alive in some of the smaller southern islands, particularly the island of the Guadeloupe. The native and African coalition forces appeared to have been quelled in the islands of Cuba and San Juan Bautista, however Cacique Enriquillo's successful rebellion on the island of Hispaniola threatened the city of Santo Domingo, which was now the capital of Spanish Imperialism in the New World.

Juan Ponce de León desired to carve out his own

lands and gain riches for himself and his wife and his children. Juan Ponce de León was informed of the growing rebellion led by Cacique Enriquillo that was devastating the island of Hispaniola. Enriquillo's rebellion formed a growing coalition of Tainos and other native groups and African tribes. Several of the conquistadors under leadership of Juan Ponce de León had spoken to Spaniards in Santo Domingo who desired to expand their war against Enriquillo, including some who believed a man named Amanex was still alive and helping to incite violence against the Spanish settlements in Hispaniola. Several of the Spaniards, including Diego de Valenzuela and Radamés Cesar Milfuegos, asked for the help of Juan Ponce de León and other conquistadors to stop Cacique Enriquillo, Amanex, and another cacique named Tamayo who raided Spanish settlements and defeated Spanish forces in the central and northern regions of the island. Juan Ponce de León had little respect for some of the Spaniards in Santo Domingo and held Radamés Cesar Milfuegos, who he often called El Moro, with least regard. However, Juan Ponce de León considered the possibility of defeating rebellions in the islands and possibly consolidating his power after his conquest of Florida.

Several months into the expedition, Juan Ponce de León sent conquistadors to read the Requerimiento to tribes in Florida. The Requerimiento (or requirement) was written by the Council of Castile Jurist named Juan López de Palacios Rubios and was declared by the Spanish monarchy, giving Castile divinely ordained right to take possession of the territories of the New World and to subjugate, exploit, and occasionally fight the native inhabitants if they resisted. Juan Ponce de León believed he would succeed in conquering Florida and possibly establish an entrepreneurial venture with the brewed beverage of the Bahamian love vine, which along with gold, would produce large amounts of wealth for himself and his family.

The Spaniards were confronted by warriors of the Calusa tribe during a brief stop at a river in southwestern Florida. Juan Ponce de León attempted to use a translator from the Calusa tribe to inform them of his desire to have peaceful relations, however the Spanish diseases—including small pox—had devastated native populations of Florida and the Calusa were well aware of the brutality of the Spaniards from previous encounters and attacked. Initially, Juan Ponce de León and the Spaniards found success against the Calusa but as the day progressed, the Calusa warriors engaged in close combat, severely limiting the effectiveness of the advanced Spanish weaponry. Juan Ponce de León called a retreat, leaving the Spaniards open to arrows from Calusa archers. he himself was pierced deep in his thigh by a reed arrow coated in poison from the sap of the manchineel tree, which the Spaniards named manzanilla de la muerte—or little apple of death—as they could not be consumed. The manchineel tree was so poisonous to humans that simply standing beneath it during rain would cause blisters to form upon the skin. The Spaniards quickly sailed in desperation to the island of Cuba where Juan Ponce de León died in extreme agony on July of 1521, leaving behind his wife Leonor Ponce de León and his children Juan, Maria, Juana, Isabel, and Luis Ponce de León. His death also hurt the potential coalition between Juan Ponce de León and various Spaniards including Radamés, who sought financial support and a larger army to suppress Enriquillo's continuing war in Hispaniola. However, Spanish conquest would continue throughout the New World despite the objections of various Spanish priests and Tainos, including Cacique Jumacao, who previously wrote a letter to Holy Roman Emperor Charles V in an attempt for the emperor to enforce the laws of protections for the natives. The Spaniards largely ignored these laws and continued practicing the Encomienda system.

CHAPTER 15
CONQUEST OF THE AZTECS & DECLINE OF THE MAYAS (1522)

The Aztec Empire was weakened by food shortages and Spanish diseases before the arrival of Hernando Cortés. The Spaniards formed alliances with the Totonacs of Cempoala and the Nahuas of Tlaxcala. The Aztec Empire was composed of the Triple Alliance between altepetl (also called city-states) named Mexico-Tenochtitlan, Mexico-Texcoco, and Mexico-Tlacopan. The Tenochca Mexica people and their city of Tenochtitlan took the leadership position above the other two Mexica cities of Texcoco and Tlacopan. The language was Nahuatl, which merged with the Spanish language as the Spaniards conquered the Mexica people. The ninth tlatoani (or ruler) of the state of Tenochtitlan was King Motecuhzoma Xocoyotzin (also named Moctezuma II), who was the son of King Axayacatl.

Tales from the explorations of Cristóbal Colón reached Spain and intrigued the young teenager Hernando Cortés, who left his Latin studies under his uncle-in-law in Salamanca. Hernando Cortés travelled to Santo Domingo in 1504 and registered as a citizen of Hispaniola, earned an Encomienda, and became the notary of the city of Azua de Compostela. Tales of the Mayan Civilization were spreading throughout the islands as Spanish conquistadors explored the Yucatán Peninsula. These tales of the complex Mayan Civilization and its incredible riches enticed Spaniards, including the thirty-three year old Hernando Cortés in 1518, while the conquistador lived in Cuba. Hernando Cortés had established himself as Alcalde of the city of Santiago and lived a decent life in Cuba owning slaves and cattle. His position in Cuban society helped him gain followers for his expedition to the Yucatan.

After Governor Diego Velázquez, de Cuéllar revoked Hernando Cortés' charter due to disagreements such as Hernando Cortés' romantic affair with Diego Velázquez de Cuéllar's sister-in-law Catalina Juarez, Hernando Cortez was able to raise over 500 men, and charter eleven ships, and set sail towards the Yucatan Peninsula after securing his marriage to Catalina Juarez. Hernando Cortés landed in Mayan territory in the Yucatan peninsula and met several Spaniards who escaped Mayan bondage, including the Spanish Franciscan priest named Geronimo de Aguilar, who had survived a shipwreck followed by a period in captivity where he had learned the Chontal Maya language and served Hernando Cortés as his translator. After several battles against tribes, Hernando Cortés captured over twenty native women, including a Nahua woman named Malintzin who the Spaniards called La Malinche and Doña Marina. She became Hernando Cortés' mistress.

Hernando Cortés was joined by conquistadors who held expeditions in Terra Firma and had experiences in Mayan Territory, including a conquistador named Bernal Díaz del Castillo. Hernando Cortés then formed alliances with Aztec tributaries who were against Aztec domination, the Totonacs, Chinantecas, and Zapotecs among them. Hernando Cortés subsequently created the first Spanish settlement in May 1519 near the eastern coastline and renamed it Villa Rica de la Vera Cruz, due to the abundance of gold and the Holy Cross. This coastal region had many cultures: the Huastecs and Otomis in the north, the Totonacs in the north-center, and the previous great Olmec civilization. Hernando Cortés then began his march westward in an attempt to capture the Aztec capital city of Tenochtitlan.

Moctezuma II assumed rule in 1502 and expanded the Aztec Empire as far south as Xoconosco and the Isthmus of Tehuantepec, however his empire now faced its largest threat. La Malinche understood Aztec and Mayan languages and was a vital asset for Hernando Cortés and his plans to subdue the Aztec Empire. As he continued his march, he clashed with various tribes, but he was successful with the aid of the brutal commander Pedro de Alvarado. Pedro de Alvarado had reddish hair and this along with his aggressive personality earned him the nickname Tonatiuh, named after Ōllin Tōnatiuh, the fifth Aztec Sun God who had replaced the fourth Sun God. Hernando Cortés and other conquistadors realized the importance of increasing their native coalition against the formidable Aztec Empire, including an alliance with Xicotencatl II Axayacatl, the son of the old ruler Xicotencatl I. Xicotencatl II Axayacatl was the prince and war leader of the state of Tlaxcallan. He had initially inflicted high casualty rates on the Spanish conquistadors and forced them to retreat despite Hernando Cortés' efforts for a peace treaty. Maxixcatzin, the ruler of Ocotelolco, also desired a peace treaty with the Spaniards and decided to cease his war against the Spaniards, forcing Xicotencatl II to accept the treaty and a coalition with Hernando Cortés, the Spaniards, and the native coalition against the Aztecs.

La Malinche helped to uncover various plots, one of them being a possible unification between the people of Cholula and the Aztecs. He alerted Hernando Cortés, who led his Spanish and native coalition in a large-scale slaughter of the people of Cholula and the burning of their city. News of the slaughter reached the Aztec capital of Tenochtitlan on November eighth, 1519. Hernando Cortés led his Spanish army of over 1,000 infantrymen and 100 cavalrymen, with a coalition of over 400 Cempoala warriors—over 200,000 Tlaxcala warriors and additional native troops joined the war effort as well—against the fifty-two year-old ruler of the Aztecs, Moctezuma II. The

Aztecs, devastated by diseases from the Spaniards and facing the advanced weaponry, the speed of the never before seen horses, and a growing native coalition against them, allowed a segment of Hernando Cortés' coalition into the capital city and religious center of Tenochtitlan.

The Spaniards were amazed at the immensity and complexity of the island city of Tenochtitlan, which was situated in Lake Texcoco and surrounded by smaller islands; Lake Texcoco was the largest of five interconnected lakes. A levee was constructed under the leadership of Nezahualcoyotl, which was close to ten miles in length and was completed around 1453. The levee kept fresh spring-fed water around Tenochtitlan and kept the brackish waters beyond the dike, to the east. Nezahualcoyotl was a wise ruler who contributed to the rise of the Aztec triple alliance and brought the rule of law, scholarship, and artistry to Texcoco. He was a strict ruler who adopted the Mexica legal system while enacting over eighty laws. Nezahualcoyotl designed a code of law based on the division of power, which created the councils of finance, war, justice and culture. Nezahualcoyotl was a pious man but also regarded as a religious sceptic who questioned gods who required religious human sacrifices. He constructed a temple which within his city which prohibited human sacrifices and tried to encourage other cities to convert to his faith.

The people believed in cleanliness and usually bathed at least twice a day—a practice the Spanish deemed abnormal—while Moctezuma II was known to bathe multiple times a day. The city had various causeways which connected the city to the north, south, east, and west. The causeways could also be retracted in an effort to protect the city of Tenochtitlan. The city was dominated by an immense pyramid called the Temple Mayor, which served the Aztec gods named Huitzilopochtli and Tlaloc. The Spaniards were in awe of the city—Bernal Diaz del Castillo included—and they conversed with each other regarding the riches, the large buildings, and the amount of people numbering well over 200,000. The city was laid out in a grid pattern and had a large stone aqueduct. The streets and canals were numerous and narrow and food and materials were transported through them by small boats and canoes. Tenochtitlan had numerous willow trees, flower gardens, and white-plastered monuments divided into four major residential quarters. The Spaniards also observed Moctezuma I's old residence and the palace of Axayacatl. There were smaller flat-roofed stone residences for nobles and officials and small adobe brick and reed homes where the lower classes lived. Jade, chocolate, and vanilla were sold and stones and gems including obsidian were polished.

The center of the Sacred Precinct of the city had around eighty different structures including the pyramid of Tezcatlipoca—in the southwestern corner stood the Sun Temple of Tonatiuh and the temple of Quetzalcoatl. There was also a temple dedicated to the Earth Goddess named Tonantzin and the Coateocalli building, which contained artwork predating Aztec society as well as artwork belonging to the Olmec people. The Temple Mayor was called Hueteocalli by the Aztecs and had two flights of steps, reaching almost 200 feet into the sky. The north side shrine was dedicated to the god of rain named Tlaloc and marked the summer solstice and rainy season, and on the south side the shrine was dedicated to the god of war named Huitzilopochtli, which marked the winter solstice, the dry season, and warfare. The steps leading up to Tlaloc's temple were painted blue and white symbolizing water, and the steps leading up to Huitzilopochtli's temple were painted red to symbolize blood and war. At the base of the temple stood a large ten-foot diameter stone structure of Goddess Coyolxauhqui—goddess of the moon and Milky Way—who was butchered by her brother Huitzilopochtli.

The wonders of the city amazed the Spaniards and the ritual sacrifices performed by the Aztecs frightened some of the Spaniards and Catholic priests. The Spaniards, who themselves treated the natives brutally, now felt they were justified in taking the city of Tenochtitlan and the Aztec Empire. Many of the sacrifices were taken from native tributary states and the Spaniards used this knowledge to gain more native allies. The Spaniards used effective propaganda as they began to exaggerate the Aztec practice of ritual sacrifice and warfare to justify their own brutality as they began to coerce the Aztec ruler Moctezuma II. In the spring of 1520, Hernando Cortés was informed that a Spanish force was sent to stop him led by Pánfilo Narváez, authorized by the Governor of the Indies Nicolás de Ovando y Cáceres. Hernando Cortés left the Spaniards under the leadership of conquistadors—including the brutal and quick-tempered Pedro de Alvarado and Rodríguez de Ocaña. Hernando Cortés defeated Pánfilo de Narváez, injuring him in his eye during a night attack, and convinced his soldiers to join his efforts to conquer the Aztec Empire and lure the Spaniards with promises of gold, riches, and power. On May twenty-second, 1520, Pedro de Alvarado massacred men, women, and children during the celebration of Toxcatl, as the people honored the god Tezcatlipoca.

The Spaniards severed heads, limbs, and disemboweled the Mexica people as they celebrated. The Spaniards were drunk on power, greed, and brandy and when they ran low on brandy they drank the native *pulque* drink of the Agave plant and would distill Agave to create a drink later known as Tequila. Some of the few that managed to climb the city walls quickly informed the other Aztec communities of the massacre that occurred at the Great Temple. The Spaniards closed the gates of the patio; the Gate of the Eagle in the smallest palace, the Gate of the Canestalk, and the Gate of the Snake of Mirrors. Armed with swords and shields, they began to violently kill all of the native Mexica and laughed as they murdered those who could not climb the walls and failed to escape. The Mexica people called for the aid of the Aztec warriors who had been defeated by the Spaniards. When Hernando Cortés returned, the Spaniards stated that the Mexica had plotted to sacrifice innocent people to their gods and murder and evict the Spaniards from the capital of Tenochtitlan.

Hernando Cortés desperately tried to maintain the

peace as unrest grew among the people. Moctezuma II, who had ruled and expanded the Aztec Empire since 1502 to its greatest boundaries, was now a puppet of Hernando Cortés. Moctezuma II convinced the Spaniards that his younger brother Cuitláhuac could help persuade the Mexica people to dispose of their arms, but the Aztec people elected Cuitláhuac as tlatoani or ruler of the Aztec people while his older brother Matlatzincatzin kept his position of cihuacoatl (or president) of the Aztecs. The Aztec war expelled Hernando Cortés and the Spaniards from the Aztec capital city of Tenochtitlan by force on the night of June thirtieth. The Spaniards lost the battle and many were killed when the feared Aztec Eagle Warriors identified them and attacked as the Spaniards, weighed down by the large amounts of gold they carried, drowned along with the riches they attempted to steal. Hernando Cortés managed to escape along with a few women, including his mistress La Malinche, the interpreter Doña Luisa, and a Spanish woman named María Estrada. Hundreds of Spaniards were killed by Aztec warriors or drowned and thousands of the native Spanish allies perished as well. Montezuma II's son Chimalpopoca was killed along with the Tepanec prince Tlaltecatzin, King Cacamatzin, and his three sisters and two brothers. The Aztecs lost thousands of lives on the night of July first, 1520, which the Spaniards called La Noche Triste or the Sad Night.

Hernando Cortés later defeated the Aztecs in the field of battle with heavy use of his horses in repeated attacks by his cavalry and the Tlaxcalan infantry, resulting in the death of the Aztec commander Matlatzincatl, who was recognized by his rich armor, headdress and flag. Hernando Cortés, Gonzalo de Sandoval, Pedro de Alvarado, Cristóbal de Olid, Juan de Salamanca, and Alonso Dávila led the advance and Juan Salamanca killed. Hernando Cortés then returned to the city of Tenochtitlan and held a siege of that city, restricting its access to food and water as the population suffered a large-scale smallpox epidemic, which also claimed the life of the Aztec ruler Cuitláhuac, who was replaced by Aztec ruler Cuauhtémoc.

The siege continued for eight months and after constant bombardment, disease, fires set by the Spaniards, and an allied native force numbering over 200,000 warriors, the capital city of the Aztecs fell on August thirteenth, 1521. Hernando Cortés expelled the surviving Aztec people and captured the Aztec leader Cuauhtémoc and his advisor Tlacotzin, who was baptized and renamed Juan Velázquez Tlacotzin. After the Spaniards and their native allies were victorious, Hernando Cortés and the Spaniards moved to place their former allies under their control and Xicotencatl II Axayacatl was hung after a false accusation of treason by the Ocotelolcan war leader Chichimecateuctli. The former Aztec Triple Alliance was now in the process of integration into the greater Spanish Empire and was re-named New Spain under the governorship of Hernando Cortés, as Hernando Cortés and the Spaniards turned their attention south towards the Mayan Civilization and the other smaller surrounding tribes.

Cristóbal de Tapia was sent to investigate the conduct Hernando Cortés in New Spain and served as the second Governor of New Spain from Christmas Eve in 1521 until the thirtieth, however the conquistadors of New Spain did not accept Cristóbal de Tapia and Hernando Cortés was legitimized as Governor. Hernando Cortés and his native mistress La Malinche had a first born named Martín Cortés (also called El Mestizo due to his mixed races of Spanish and native). La Malinche—affectionately called Doña Marina—helped Hernando Cortés and the Spaniards in their wars against the Mayas. The Franciscan Friar Geronimo de Aguilar also helped Hernan Cortés by detailing what he had learned from Mayan culture during his previous years in captivity. Geronimo de Aguilar explained his arrival at the colony of Santa María la Antigua del Darién in 1510 located in the isthmus that the Spaniards began calling Panama from the Kuna word of bannaba meaning far away and distant land. In an attempt to reach the islands of Jamaica and Hispaniola Geronimo de Aguilar and a few others were shipwrecked in the Yucatan Peninsula and captured by the Mayas.

Geronimo de Aguilar spoke about the Mayas and their complex art, mathematics which included the number zero, their scientific knowledge, and his fascination with their calendar systems following the sun, moon, Venus, and other heavenly bodies. Geronimo believed the Mayas were far more advanced than the Spaniards. The Mayan hieroglyphs was in extensive use hundreds of years before the birth of Jesus Christ and their science, mathematics, poetry, history, and general culture was heavily documented. They had various Mayan languages including Petén and Yucatán, some of which Geronimo de Aguilar could speak. The Mayan history revealed complex relationships with other societies such as the Olmecs, Mixtecs, Teotihuacan, and Aztecs.

The Mayan civilization was suffering from Spanish epidemics as Hernando Cortés and the Spaniards pushed into the lands, including what they had named Guatemala after the Nahuatl word Cuauhtēmallān, meaning place of many trees. Captains Gonzalo de Alvarado and his brother, Pedro de Alvarado, initially allied themselves with Kaqchikel nation to fight against the K'iche' nation then turned against the Kaqchikel nation. The Spaniards continued into the lands they identified as Belize from Mayan word belix, meaning muddied water, the land named Guaimura (or Honduras) by the Spaniards, meaning the depths in Spanish, and the eastern edges of the Mayan Civilization, where Pedro de Alvarado renamed Provincia De Nuestro Señor Jesus Cristo, El Salvador Del Mundo (Spanish for the Province of our Lord Jesus Christ, the Savior of the World)—or simply referred to as El Salvador. Despite the superior weaponry of the Spaniards and the weakened Mayan which lacked strong central unification, the Spaniards could not conquer the entire civilization and were locked into a continuous war.

The information of the Spanish expanding wars reached the island of Hispaniola and Cacique Enriquillo and his coalition fighters as the Enriquillo war continued. The Spaniards tried desperately to capture Enriquillo, Tamayo, and other cacique leaders and African slaves who were joining the Tainos in increasing numbers. Other native groups managed to infiltrate the island of Hispaniola and the Spaniards feared the rebellion could topple various Spanish settlements, including the capital of Santo Domingo, and serve to encourage rebellions in the surrounding islands—particularly Jamaica, San Juan Bautista, and Cuba. The war against Enriquillo's coalition forces drained the finances of the Spanish officials in Hispaniola as the islands became part of Greater New Spain and Governor Diego Velázquez de Cuéllar was replaced by the Governor of New Spain Hernando Cortés in 1524.

CHAPTER 16
THE PHILIPPINES & THE TRIUMPH OF LAPU-LAPU (1524)

The Spanish Crown sought an expansion eastward in an effort to increase their access to eastern markets and surpass the wealth and power of their European rivals and the Ottoman Empire, which was now ruled by Sultan Suleiman I The Magnificent, the tenth Ottoman Emperor. Holy Roman Emperor Charles V had increasing tensions with the French King Francis I, which resulted in ongoing wars for territory in many republics of Italy. Charles V and King Henry VIII formed an alliance, and Pope Leo X switched his alliance from Francis I to Charles V. Pope Leo X was born Giovanni di Lorenzo de' Medici, and was the second son of the ruler of Florence, Lorenzo de' Medici or Lorenzo the Magnificent. The grandfather of Lorenzo de' Medici was Cosimo de' Medici, who was the first member of the powerful Medici family, who merged the Medici family and their control of the Republic of Florence and the Medici Bank. A political theorist, writer, and Renaissance man named Niccolò di Bernardo dei Machiavelli, a bureaucrat in the Republic of Florence, would write *Il Principe* (or *The Prince*) in hopes of reestablishing himself in Medici controlled Florence. *The Prince* was later published five years after his death in 1532, under the

Medici pope Clement VII. *The Prince* would be compared with Machiavelli's later work, *The Discourses on Livy*. After the death of Pope Leo X in 1521, he was replaced by Pope Adrian VI, who would die in 1522. He was succeeded by Giulio di Giuliano de' Medici, who became Pope Clement VII in November of 1523, despite the opposition of King Francis I. The Spaniards took Milan from the French in 1521 and returned it to the Duke of Milan, Francesco Sforza in 1522. The French continued to be outmatched by the Spaniards in the battles of Bicocca on April 27, 1522 and the battle of Sesia against the Spaniards led by Fernando de Avalos on April 30, 1524.

As Emperor Charles V continued to defeat Francis I and his French Army, the Portuguese skilled naval officer Fernão de Magalhães—or Ferdinand Magellan—set out towards the East Indies in 1519. Ferdinand was named captain and led a fleet of five ships named the Fleet of the Moluccas, and commanded his flagship named La Trinidad, which was accompanied by La San Antonio under the command of Juan de Cartagena, La Concepción under the command of Gaspar de Quezada, La Victoria under the command of Luis de Mendoza, and La Santiago under command of Juan Rodríguez Serrano. Ferdinand Magellan sailed westward in an effort to find Maluku Islands commonly called the Spice Islands, traveling south past the southern mainland of the New World into a strait they named the Estrecho de Todos los Santos (or Straight of All Saints) because they passed through on All Saints' Day: November first, 1520.

After initially avoiding a naval detachment sent by Portuguese King Manuel I, Ferdinand Magellan suppressed a mutiny involving three of his ships after creating a temporary settlement called Puerto San Julian on March 30, 1520. On April first and second, a mutiny broke out involving three of the five ship's captains and Magellan took quick and decisive action. Luis de Mendoza the captain of Victoria was killed by a party sent by Magellan, and the ship was recovered. After Concepción's anchor cable had been secretly cut by his forces, the ship drifted towards the well-armed ship of the Trinidad. As a result, Concepcion's captain de Quesada and his inner circle surrendered. The leader of the mutineers and commander of the San Antonio Juan de Cartagena subsequently gave up. Antonio Pigafetta reported that Gaspar Quesada (the captain of Concepción) and other mutineers were executed, while Juan de Cartagena the captain of San Antonio and a priest named Padre Sanchez de la Reina were marooned on the coast. Most of the men, including Juan Sebastián Elcano, were needed and forgiven.

On March sixteenth, Magellan reached the island of Homonhon in the Philippines, with 150 crewmembers remaining. Magellan and his crew were spotted by the subjects of Rajah Culambu of Limasawa, who were allied to the Datu of Zubu, and guided him to his territory where Hindus, Buddhists, and Animists lived. The Rajahnate of Cebu was founded by a half-Malay, half-Tamil prince of the Chola dynasty who invaded Sumatra in Indonesia on behalf of the Maharajah but established his own independent Rajahnate. Through his translator Enrique, Ferdinand Magellan befriended Rajah Humabon and persuaded the natives to swear allegiance to Emperor Charles V. Ferdinand Magellan baptized the Rajah and his wife, giving them the names of Carlos and Juana along with over 700 natives and a gift of the Santo Niño (or the Child Jesus) to the Rajah's wife. Subsequently, Magellan erected a large wooden cross on April fourteenth, 1521 on the shores of Zubu, which the Spaniards called Cebu.

Ferdinand Magellan's adventure was largely a success; however, King Lapu-Lapu of Mactan Island was a rival of the Rajahs of Cebu and fought against their combined forces. After Lapu-Lapu's refusal to submit and pay tribute to Ferdinand Magellan and Emperor Charles V, Ferdinand launched an offensive against Lapu-Lapu and dispatched forty-nine armored men with swords, shields, axes, crossbows, and guns, and sailed for Mactan on the morning of the twenty-eighth of April 1521. The shores were rocky and Magellan left the rest of his soldiers to guard the boats along with the Rajah Humabon and Zula.

Magellan was confronted by three divisions of Lapu-Lapu's army, numbering over 1,500 men. After they shot their arquebuses, the natives advanced against Magellan's conquistadors, aiming for their unshielded legs. He ordered his men to burn down the natives' houses but it only angered Lapu-Lapu's army and he quickly recognized Ferdinand Magellan, knocking his helmet off twice.

Lapu-Lapu's army advanced against Ferdinand Magellan as he was defenseless, unable to bring his ship's cannons upon Lapu-Lapu due to the rocky, coral shores. Lapu-Lapu's men's arrows rained on Magellan's retreating conquistadors and killed the Spaniards with their iron and bamboo spears and Kampilan swords—among them was Ferdinand Magellan. Humabon and the Spaniards ordered Lapu-Lapu to return the bodies of Magellan and some of his crew who were killed in exchange for as much merchandise as they wished, but Lapu-Lapu refused. Some of the Spaniards who survived the battle were later poisoned by Humabon at a dinner in Cebu. Ferdinand Magellan was replaced by his lieutenant Juan Sebastián Elcano as commander of the expedition, ordering his crew to return to Spain after Humabon's betrayal and completing a circumnavigation of the world. The circumnavigation expanded the Spanish Empire and brought wealth, power, and glory to Charles V.

The subsequent expansion into the East Indies and the Aztec and Mayan civilizations increased the power of Emperor Charles V. In the wars against King Francis I and the French, Charles the V succeeded in re-capturing Milan in 1522, when Imperial troops defeated the Franco-Swiss army at Bicocca. After Francis I crossed his army into Lombardy, several cities—including Milan—fell under attack with only the city of Pavia holding on. On the twenty-fourth of February 1525, on King Charles V's twenty-fifth birthday, Charles V's Spanish forces captured Francis I and crushed his army in the Battle of Pavia, yet again retaking Milan and Lombardy and capturing all Italian territory. Francis I was imprisoned in Spain and a special envoy sent by Francis I's mother Louise of Savoy to

Suleiman the Magnificent resulted in an ultimatum by the Ottoman Empire. Sultan Suleiman the Magnificent used this opportunity to invade the Kingdom of Hungary, defeating Charles V in the Battle of Mohács on August twenty-ninth, 1526, however Francis I was forced to sign the Treaty of Madrid in January 1526. The Treaty of Madrid surrendered Francis I's claims to Italy, Flanders, and Burgundy to secure his release from prison.

CHAPTER 17
MAROON IN JARAGUA (1526)

In 1522, a major African slave rebellion ripped through eastern Santo Domingo at a Sugar Factory led by over twenty African Muslim Slaves who originated from the Kingdom of Jolof. Through the mayhem some Tainos were able to release Anacaona's daughter Higüemota from her captivity and brought her to Enriquillo in 1523. The Wolof created their own maroon, forming a community of free African people—some travelled to join Enriquillo's rebellion. Some of the Wolof Islamic people joined Enriquillo's rebellion, including a young man named Mamadou Dieng and his young sixteen-year-old sister Arjana Dieng, who became close to Amanex and his family. The runaway African slaves were called cimarrones (from the Spanish word Cimarron, meaning wild and untamed). The African slaves were regarded as subhuman and animals and the runaways were regarded as untamed people which posed a threat to Spanish authority with their growing alliances with the native Tainos.

Amanex's son Simon Pedro Haübey was now seven years of age and Amanex and Tayamari had a second son who was two years old. Amanex named his second son Adán Hatüey after Adam, the first man in the Holy Bible and after Hatüey, who led the native rebellions in Hispaniola and Cuba. Amanex fought constantly during the initial years of his escape from Santo Domingo, however life in the settlement became more peaceful as Enriquillo's forces experienced numerous victories in the battlefield. Enriquillo, his wife Doña Mencia, and his forces moved to the mountains of Bahoruco and formed a large and well-structured settlement free from Spanish bondage.

Enriquillo led his Taino and African coalition in a series of guerilla maneuvers during the first several years but recently had begun to beat Spanish forces in open battle. Amanex led a series of battles against the Spanish forces resulting in various Spanish defeats and retreats. Enriquillo also led raids into Spanish settlements, emancipating the Tainos and African slaves and capturing Spanish horses and weaponry and increasing his military might. Amanex actively sought Radamés Cesar Milfuegos within the Spanish armies sent to confront Cacique Enriquillo, who had not been seen after the Jolof slave rebellion of 1522 in the sugar plantation of Diego Colón on the outskirts of Santo Domingo after he suffered an injury in battle trying to stop the escaping Wolof slaves and their Taino allies. Amanex believed Radamés was in the central and northern regions of Hispaniola trying to stop Tamayo and other Taino leaders who were raiding Spanish settlements, but he believed the Spaniards would soon learn of Enriquillo's general location and he would have to confront Radamés.

Despite the looming Spanish threat, life continued in Enriquillo's maroon settlement and men became fathers and women became mothers. Amanex's friend Elombe had married a younger Taina woman in 1522 named Magdalena who was now twenty-two years of age and had a young four-year-old daughter he had named Malundama Masombo. The main language of communication within the settlement was Castilian, however various African and native languages were also spoken. There were African people in Enriquillo's settlement including the Kongo, Yoruba, Igbo, Bran, Bambara, Fulbe, Zape, and most recently the Wolof. After the Wolof people rebelled within and near Santo Domingo, restrictions were placed on the transportations of slave from the Jolof Empire. Most of the natives were Tainos from Jaragua, but there were other native people in Enriquillo's settlement, including a few Ciguayos and Kalinago people including some Macorix people such as Amanex's wife Tayamari. The settlement was peaceful and most of the Africans and native people united against Spanish colonialism. Within Enriquillo's growing maroon community, there were also children who were mixed—the product of African and Spanish parents which the Spaniards referred to as mulattoes. Some of the African women were taken by force by conquistadors and some of these women escaped with Cacique Enriquillo, where they were free to raise their children as equals with the other African, native, and Mestizo children.

Amanex was disgusted by the behavior of the Spaniards in regard to mixed children and how they were treated differently depending on their particular ancestry. Amanex did not believe in the society of the Spaniards and he thought the other white men who were arriving to these islands would only bring more devastation. Amanex somewhat agreed with the society that some of the Spaniards—including Bartolome de las Casas—desired to create, however he believed even under Bartolome de las Casas' ideal society the native and African peoples would remain as an underclass to the Spaniards.

Bartolome de las casas and Chancellor Jean de la Sauvage were previously appointed by King Carlos V to write a new plan for reforming the governmental system of the Indies in 1517. Bartolome de las Casas advocated for native self-governing townships which would live free and pay tribute to the Spanish Monarchy while Africans would be brought to the Indies for slave labor. Bartolome de las Casas advocated for Spaniards of the peasant class to settle into the Indies and work as farmers and ranchers in order to establish peaceful Spanish and native relationships but after the death of Chancellor Jean de la Sauvage Bartolome de las Casas received less support for his ideas and small amounts of Spanish peasants with little provisions were sent to the Indies. Bartolome de las Casas subsequently petitioned for a land grant in the settlement of Cumaná in northern Venezuela which involved a lengthy legal battle with Bishop Fonseca and his supporters Gonzalo de Oviedo and Bishop Quevedo of Tierra Firme. Bartolome de las Casas was able to build a few settlements but native attacks, the prohibition of gold and pearl extraction, and finding investors willing to provide three years of unpaid work proved impossible and propelled Bartolome de las Casas to travel to San Juan Bautista in 1521. On January of 1521, Bartolome de las Casas learned that the Dominican convent at Chiribichi had been sacked by natives and that the Spaniards of the islands had launched a punitive expedition, led by Gonzalo de Ocampo, into the land Bartolome de las Casas wanted to settle peacefully. The natives attacked the settlement of the monks because of the repeated slave raids by Spaniards operating from the island of Cubagua near the mainland of Venezuela. As Ocampo's ships began returning with slaves from the land Las Casas had been granted, Bartolome went to Hispaniola to complain to the Audencia Real to no avail.

Bartolome de las Casas returned to his settlement of Cumaná but was constantly harassed by the Spanish pearl fishers of Cubagua Island who traded slaves for alcohol. Early in 1522, Las Casas left the settlement to complain to the authorities. While he was gone, the native Kalinago (or Caribs) attacked the settlement of Cumaná, burned it to the ground, and killed four of Las Casas' men. Bartolome de las Casas was initially rumored to be one of the men killed and the Spaniards used these attacks to justify their enslavement of the native people.

Amanex was informed that Bartolome de las Casas was frustrated and depressed after the failures of his ideas and he returned to Hispaniola in 1522 to join the Dominican monastery of Santa Cruz in Santo Domingo as a novice. He finally undertook his holy vows as a Dominican friar in 1523. Bartolome de las Casas began studying the philosophies of Saint Thomas Aquinas as he searched for a new avenue for his thoughts in the New World. Amanex learned that Bartolome de las Casas had relocated to a northern settlement of the Hispaniola for the purposes of overseeing the construction of a new monastery. Amanex desired to speak with Bartolome de las Casas once again, however he understood that Bartolome's dreams of Spanish and native unity would eventually fail as long as natives remained subservient and the Africans remained slaves in Bartolome's vision of a Spanish society.

The arriving Tainos and Africans informed Enriquillo of the recent information regarding Spanish affairs and he would often hold talks with his community and rebel leaders regarding the Spanish military and community affairs. Through the information of emancipated Africans and Tainos, Cacique Enriquillo and Amanex learned much from the new arrivals, including the latest conquests of the Spanish Empire. Amanex learned about the Spanish and native coalition and their victory over the Aztec Triple Alliance as well as the ongoing Spanish wars against the Mayan Civilization. Amanex also became aware of the famous Portuguese explorer named Fernão de Magalhães (also named Ferdinand Magellan) who helped organize the Castilian expedition for Emperor Charles V to the East Indies in 1519.

Cacique Enriquillo observed the common strategies of the Spanish Empire throughout their expansions across the world. The conquistadors were encouraged to find the weaknesses of the civilizations and seek alliances with their enemies they desired to subjugate. The Spaniards would defeat their enemies at war and subsequently break their previous alliances, securing their position at the peak of their new societies. Civilizations which were more complex and warlike were subjugated by superior weaponry, disease, and the divisions fomented and exploited within each society and between societies by the Spaniards. The Aztecs were now ruled by Hernando Cortés through political puppets, along with the larger surrounding territories including the Hispaniola and the surrounding islands now called New Spain.

Enriquillo often would stress the importance of cohesion and communication among his communities.

Enriquillo respected the various languages and cultures within his communities but stressed the importance of people learning additional languages and the establishment of a general language within his communities to facilitate organization within his communities and military. It was important that the African freed men, women, and children remain united despite their cultural differences along with the Tainos and other natives who had joined Enriquillo's fight against the Spaniards. Enriquillo respected the cultures of the people within his communities and understood the importance of synergy and a unifying purpose for everyone within his community. Various interconnected communities were created for the needs of the elderly, children, and family. Enriquillo and his advisors began to construct irrigation systems and farming systems with small and larger conucos; Africans and natives worked different shifts to provide for their families. Men and women worked freely to feed themselves and their families and because they believed in the community created by Enriquillo, free from Spanish domination. For the first time, Amanex enjoyed his labor because it benefitted his family, himself, and maintained the greater good and freedoms enjoyed in Enriquillo's communities.

Cacique Enriquillo began to solidify his people into a confederacy throughout the Bahoruco Mountains near the largest lake in Hispaniola while decreasing the communication capabilities of the Spanish settlements of Hispaniola. Enriquillo also increased his advanced military outposts which would conduct reconnaissance and advance raids into various Spanish settlements which involved burning their crops, destroying Spanish equipment, and taking Spanish weaponry to reinforce Enriquillo's increasing military. Enriquillo's scouts also learned about the presence of other white men from Europe—particularly French pirates disrupting Spanish sea transportation. Enriquillo's efforts began to succeed in limiting Spanish profits in Hispaniola and he turned his attention to various gold mining efforts in the northern region of Hispaniola.

Some of Enriquillo's raids also yielded books that

Enriquillo and other African and Tainos who could read Spanish would use them to educate and entertain themselves. A favorite of Amanex's was *El Cid,* which he read as well as Ancient Greek books that were translated into Spanish. Amanex would spend his leisure time reading to his children and sometimes to other Tainos and Africans whom he would converse with about philosophy and different ideas and global affairs. Amanex often spoke about El Cid the story of Rodrigo Díaz de Vivar, the legendary hero of the Castilian people. Some of the Africans belonging to the Islamic faith identified El Cid as being the Arabic words sîdi or sayyid, meaning lord or master, and some identified El Cid as Rodrigo Díaz el Campeador, meaning the battlefield master.

El Cid was born in 1043 in Castillona de Bivar, a small town about six miles north of Burgos (the capital of Castile). Despite his mother's aristocratic background, El Cid became a hero to the peasant class. El Cid fought against the Moorish stranglehold of Zaragoza which made Emir al-Muqtadir a vassal of Sancho, who soon became King Sancho II of Castile known as El Fuerte (or the strong) after the death of his father Ferdinand. Later, El Cid Rodrigo Díaz fought for King Sancho II and emir al-Muqtadir against Ramiro I of Aragon and the Argonese, defeating Ramiro I and the Argonese Army. The childless King Sancho II was later believed to have been assassinated by his brother King Alfonso VI and his sister Urraca. Rodrigo's position as armiger regis was later taken away and given to Rodrigo's enemy, Count García Ordóñez. Rodrigo Díaz was sent to Seville to the court of al-Mutamid to collect tributes for King Alfonso VI. In 1079, at the Battle of Cabra, El Cid rallied his troops and turned the battle into a rout of Emir Abdullah of Granada and his ally García Ordóñez. However, El Cid's unauthorized expedition into Granada greatly angered King Alfonso VI in May 1080 and El Cid Rodrigo Díaz was later exiled.

Rodrigo Díaz went to Barcelona, where the brothers Count Ramon Berenguer II and Count Berenguer Ramon II denied his services. Rodrigo Díaz was subsequently recruited by the Moors and later led the armies of Taifa of Zaragoza, defeating the Argonese Army at the battle of Battle of Morella in 1084 and receiving his title of El Cid. In 1086, the El Cid was triumphantly led his Moorish forces along with the coalition of Almoravid Berbers of Northern Africa, the Andalusian Taifas, and the armies of Badajoz, Málaga, Granada, Tortosa, and Seville against the northern Iberian coalition armies of the Kingdoms of León, Aragón, and Castile. Rodrigo Díaz was recalled from exile by King Alfonso VI in 1087 but chose to create his own territory in the Kingdom of Valencia, ruling shortly alongside his wife Doña Jimena Díaz. El Cid and Doña Jimena lived peacefully in Valencia for five years until the Almoravids besieged the city and El Cid's death on June 10, 1099. Doña Jimena would rule until 1102.

The story of El Cid fascinated Amanex and it revealed the complex political history of the Spanish Kingdom. Enriquillo also spoke about the Moorish exploitation of European division which paralleled the current exploitation of native division. Amanex believed the Spaniards would seek to divide native as well as African groups to solidify their own positions in the new society they sought to build while using the skeleton of the original for their benefit. Hernando Cortés now ruled New Spain using the hierarchal system of the Aztec Civilization through puppet leadership throughout the former Aztec territories. Hernando Cortés' mistress Doña Marina had given him an illegitimate mestizo son named Martín Cortés who was born in the Aztec capital in 1523. Martín Cortés was left under the care of Hernando's cousin Juan Altamirano as Hernando Cortés and Doña Marina left on an expedition to Honduras. Enriquillo understood the Spanish Empire was expanding, however he believed their grip on Hispaniola and the surrounding islands was weakening as the conquistadors sought lands with more riches.

Amanex was drinking coconut water and eating kenepas after his dinner of barbequed fish when Enriquillo asked him to lead a division of his military south near the lake where a small Spanish military force had gathered. Amanex was reluctant to lead in battle for fear that he would be recognized and vengeful friends of Radamés Cesar Milfuegos would seek to harm him and his family, but Cacique Enriquillo prohibited his fighting men and women to use their actual names among the Spaniards in battle or when speaking to Spanish hostages. Enriquillo's advance posts had notified the cacique and he ordered three separate divisions numbering over 100 men each to encircle the estimated 500-man Spanish force as they waited for a nighttime attack. The initial attack was led by an African Igbo woman in her late twenties named Onyekachi—usually called Onyeka. Onyeka's name meant "who is greater than God?" It was a question Enriquillo often pondered in the wake of Spanish domination and a question he desired to pose to the leaders of the Spaniards who stole the bulk of the spoils of war. The Spaniards believed they were gods as they treated the natives, Africans, and the mixtures of people born to them as below themselves. However, Enriquillo could live free from Spanish enslavement and build a civilization with the original native inhabitants just as they had built their own civilizations in Africa. Enriquillo also proved that he could repeatedly defeat Spanish armies despite their superior weaponry with the help of his capable lieutenants which included Onyeka who came from a family of brave Igbo war strategists.

Onyeka led the initial attack as the moon was high in the Hispaniolan summer night sky. Onyeka approached the Spanish camp on the northeastern edge of the large saltwater lake with a secondary unit of fighters led by Amanex and Elombe several miles south, and a third unit several miles west on the northern shores of the lake led by Cacique Enriquillo. The initial attack was devastating; Onyeka and the Taino and African forces ripped through the unprepared Spaniards as they desperately tried to reach for their swords and arquebuses. In the close combat, many Spaniards lost their lives as Onyeka and her forces took the arquebuses and began firing upon them while Amanex and Elombe quickly approached from the south. A few archers with poisoned arrows fired upon the rear of the Spanish forces, killing and injuring many before Amanex and Elombe confronted them. As the Spaniards began firing upon Onyeka's forces, Amanex and Elombe approached them from the south, rendering their weapons useless. Hundreds of Spaniards died and the few who retreated into the mountains were killed by awaiting Tainos as the rest retreated westward where Enriquillo waited with over 100 of his forces heavily armed with Spanish weaponry.

Enriquillo hid his forces until the Spaniards were within 100 feet and quickly set his men in three rows of twenty fighters armed with Arquebuses, enabling them to fire and move to the rear to reload while another row fired in rapid succession. Enriquillo sent forty of his fighters towards the center of the lake where they awaited any Spaniards trying to escape while ten of Enriquillo's men observed in the island near the center of the lake. Over 100 of the remaining Spaniards desperately tried to swim away from the carnage, but Tainos in canoes fired their arquebuses at them. Many drowned due to their injuries and under the weight of heavy armor. At the end of the battle, 143 of Enriquillo's forces lay dead with most of the Spanish killed with eight hostages and a few that escaped, resulting in one of Enriquillo's largest victories, emboldening his coalition, and weakening Spanish domination in Hispaniola. By sunrise, only a few were able to escape only to be captured later along with the few hostages gathered near the shores of the lake to be taken to Enriquillo for questioning.

Amanex spent the next several days personally observing the dead Spaniards in the hopes of seeing the body of Radamés Cesar Milfuegos without success, however Elombe had spoken to one of the Spanish hostages named Jose Manuel Palacio. Jose Manuel Palacio, under threat of execution, mentioned a secondary expedition to the center of Hispaniola which included Radamés Cesar Milfuegos. Amanex later learned that Radamés married a Castilian woman of a lower class who was now called Paulina Milfuegos and had a young son named Maximo residing in the city of Santo Domingo. He understood that his family's safety rested on Enriquillo's defeat of Spanish forces and the death of his foe.

CHAPTER 18
DREAMS OF VENEZUELA (1531)

Enriquillo's war in the island of Hispaniola continued successfully against the Spaniards and other smaller rebellions were threating Spanish power in the surrounding islands. On the island of Cuba, a Taino leader named Cacique Guamá continued an ongoing war of over eight years against the Spaniards. Guamá was influenced by the legendary Hatüey and had devastated Spanish forces in the mountains of Baracoa in eastern Cuba. Amanex believed Cacique Enriquillo should expand his successful war and solidify his alliance with Cacique Tamayo in Hispaniola and Cacique Guamá of Cuba. An increase in recruitment efforts among Africans and Carib natives was necessary, as disease had continued to kill the Taino people, including Higüemota, who had passed away recently. Enriquillo had become the most important Taino resistance leader after the death of Cacique Agueybana II was finally confirmed by Taino messengers in 1528, although the knowledge of Agueybana II's passing had eluded the Spaniards.

Cacique Enriquillo decided that Amanex and Elombe should lead their own community in the southeastern regions of the Bahoruco Mountains which was near Amanex's birthplace. Amanex was joined by his wife Tayamari and his two sons Simon Pedro Haübey and Adán

Hatüey. Elombe Masombo was accompanied by his wife Magdalena and young daughter Malundama Masombo. The two Wolof Africans, Mamadou Dieng and his sister Arjana Dieng, also joined Amanex in forming his new community. Amanex was confident in the success of Enriquillo's ongoing war as the Spaniards continued to suffer military defeats at the hands of Enriquillo and Tamayo. In northern Hispaniola, the Tainos, Ciguayos, and Macorix allied with escaped African slaves and leaders. Hernandillo el Tuerto continued to score victories against the Spaniards, including multiple raids into various Spanish cities across the island of Hispaniola. In desperation, Emperor Charles V appointed General Francisco de Barrionuevo, who was a veteran of numerous battles in Europe, in an effort to defeat Cacique Enriquillo's Rebellion.

As the war continued the, Spaniards in Hispaniola were angered at the increased taxes on meat and wine in an effort to fund the efforts against Cacique Enriquillo. General Francisco de Barrionuevo found himself at a disadvantage in the strategic intelligence of Cacique Enriquillo and feared that unity between Enriquillo, Tamayo, and possibly other caciques in the surrounding islands would result in a devastating defeat for the Spanish forces. The Spaniards also feared that the coalition of Africans and natives could influence mestizos and mulattoes to join the fight against the Spaniards and Francisco de Barrionuevo suggested that young mestizos should be sent to Spain. Enriquillo and his African and native coalition were succeeding and Enriquillo's confederacy had increasing numbers of African, native, Mestizos, and Mulatto children, which were uniting against the Spaniards. Enriquillo was a product of Spanish education and society, which gave him a tactical advantage—he had studied their methods of exploitation.

Enriquillo discussed the possibility of Spaniards attempting to foment anger between Africans and native groups. Enriquillo often spoke about the necessity of unity between different people against Spanish brutality. Amanex observed how the African and native cultures began to intertwine with the Spanish culture within communities in Hispaniola. Religions including Christianity, Islam, and the African and native beliefs began to combine and some Catholic Saints began to be identified with African and native Gods. Amanex enjoyed the conversations he had with Elombe, Mamadou, and Arjana Dieng regarding their cultures, the Islamic religion, and the history of their people.

Amanex often thought about the new culture that would arise from the ashes of Enriquillo's war in Hispaniola and the Spanish wars against the native civilizations of the mainland. He desired a new, peaceful society where natives, Africans, and Spaniards could live together and use the strengths of their communities to improve. Amanex believed the ideal society proposed by Bartolomé de las Casas, however he understood the Spaniards would continue to be slaves to their greed and thirst for power. Amanex and Enriquillo had previously discussed the irony of Spanish society as the poor Spaniards committed most of the violence against the Africans and natives, but the Spanish nobility and their monarchs reaped the majority of the riches, essentially exploiting their own subjects. Despite the expanding power of the Spanish Crown, most Spaniards suffered from exploitation and poverty—a reality that was occurring in other European Kingdoms. Enriquillo previously discussed that a crushing blow to the Spanish Empire would come from rival European powers as well as a class rebellion. However, Amanex observed that the lower-class Spaniard was usually the most violent and abusive towards the Africans and natives; it was an anger that Amanex believed should be directed towards the Spanish nobility and monarchy.

Amanex and Elombe would converse about global affairs every evening and sometimes Mamadou and Arjana would speak about the Spaniards and their affairs in Africa. Amanex took an interest in the Jolof Empire and other African civilizations and their interactions with the Spanish Empire and other European Kingdoms. Ahmad Abu Bakr (also called Ndiadiane Ndiaye) was the founder of the Jolof

Empire established in 1350. Mamadou spoke about the legend of Ndiadiane Ndiaye and his dispute with other leaders over wood near a lake.

The Jolof Civilization started as a vassal state of the Mali Empire and later became independent during a conflict between two rival royal lineages within the Mali Empire's royal bloodline. The Jolof Empire was a confederacy of various kingdoms including the Waalo, Kayor, Baol, Sine, and Saloum and the ruler of the Jolof Empire was known as the Bour ba, who governed in the capital called Linguère. Each Wolof State was governed by its own ruler appointed from the descendants of the founder of that state while the Bour ba of the Jolof Empire was chosen from a college of electors and Wolof State leaders.

Mamadou and his sister Arjana were originally from the Kingdom of Waalo, which had previously agreed to join the Jolof Empire. The Portuguese had previously infiltrated the Jolof Empire after 1444 and they began to influence the politics of Jolof. Prince Bemoi had previously ruled the empire in the name of his brother Bur Birao, however he was tempted by Portuguese trade and decided to move the seat of the Jolof government to the coast to take advantage of the new economic opportunities. This led to his assassination by rival princes.

Jolof society had castes including nobles of royal and non-royal birth, free men, indentured servants, blacksmiths, jewelers, tanners, tailors, musicians, and griots. The griots served important roles in Jolof society: serving as historians, storytellers, praise singers, musicians, and as oral historians, political commentators, and sometimes political advisors. Slaves served the Jolof Monarchy as agricultural workers, soldiers, and administrators. Slavery was shunned by people of the Jolof Empire, including Muslims, who grew increasingly angry and condemned the monarchy for the enslavement of fellow Muslims and the consumption of imported alcohol. The Jolof Empire traded slaves for firearms, textiles, iron bars, alcohol, and manufactured goods. In the eyes of Wolof Muslims, the king and the court were pagans who were cooperating with the Europeans to expand slavery within Africa. Mamadou and Arjana often spoke against the royal families within the Jolof Empire who were profiting from the expansion of the slave trade. Amanex learned that the coastal kingdoms and their growing trade with Europeans were growing stronger and acquiring wealth and power, undermining the authority of the eastern landlocked Jolof Kingdom.

Another state in Western Africa was the Songhai Empire, founded by Ali Kolon (also known as King Sonni Ali). Sonni Ali was the successor to Sonni Suleiman and the fifteenth ruler of the Sonni Dynasty. He helped expand the Songhai Empire, conquering the territories of the former Akwar Empire (or Ghana Empire) and the declining Mali Empire and their important city of Timbuktu in 1468. Emperor Sonni Ali organized fleets to patrol the large river known by various names which included the Isa Ber River. Emperor Sonni Ali was believed to have drowned there in 1492. Sonni Ali's son, King Sonni Abū Bakr Dao, ruled shortly until he was overthrown by his father's general, Muhammad Ture of the Soninke people, who ruled as Askia Mohammad I of the Askia Dynasty. Emperor Askia Mohammad I accused Sonni Abū Bakr Dao of being weak and not being a faithful Muslim. Emperor Askia Mohammad I helped improve education and literacy rates in the Songhai Empire by expanding and improving the universities, including the university at Timbuktu. He became Askia the Great, and also helped foster Islamic and scientific scholarship, standardized trade measures and regulations, improved the empire of Songhai's bureaucracy, and he expanded the Songhai Empire by acquiring surrounding states such as Hausa. Askia Mohammad I was overthrown by his own son, Emperor Askia Musa, in 1529; he killed several of his brothers and over twenty-five of his rival cousins to obtain the thrown only to be overthrown himself by his brothers and the current ruler of the Songhai Empire, Emperor Askia Mohammad Benkan, in 1531.

Amanex enjoyed learning about the African civilizations and their interactions with the European

Kingdom. He also lived among people of the Songhai Empire in his community free from Spanish domination. Economies that flourished due to salt, gold, and the European slave trade which Amanex believed would eventually bring the ruin of these impressive African societies just as it had to Taino society. Amanex was proud of Enriquillo's growing confederacy of free communities and enjoyed learning about the Igbo and Yoruba people and their traditions and religions. The Africans were free to practice in their beliefs and were widely celebrated within Enriquillo's confederacy.

Amanex learned about the orisha spirit which reflected the three manifestations of the Supreme Creator of the Yoruba Religion named Eledumare, Olorun, and Olofi. The Yoruba people believed in reincarnation and the elevation of the spirit. Orishas such as Orunmila were celebrated, representing wisdom, knowledge, and divination. Eshu was the trickster, a master linguist, and the orisha of chance, accident, and unpredictability. Orisha Ogoun represented iron and metallurgy, and Orisha Yemoja was the Mother of Waters, also representing the female breasts, the fluid of the womb, and the protective energy of femininity. Orisha Shango represented virility, masculinity, fire, lightning, stones, Oyo warriors, and magnetism. Orisha Oshun was the second wife of Shango, representing cool water, induction of fertility, and control of the feminine essence. Orisha Oya was the third wife of Shango and represented the tempest, guardian of the cemetery, winds of change, storms, and progression.

Amanex also learned about the beliefs of the Igbo people who believed in a single Creator God named Chukwu represented by the sun. There were five aspects of Chukwu as the force and existence of all beings: Anyanwu as the sun revealed everything so Chukwu was the source of knowledge, Agbala was the fertility of Earth, its people, and its spiritual world full of sub-deities. Chi was a sub-deity functioning as a personal spiritual guide, and Okike was the creator of laws that govern the visible and invisible. The Igbo also believed in Ala, representing the mother of all crops, was in an important dualistic relationship with Chukwu. Amadioha was the god of thunder and lightning similar to Shango; Agwu the trickster god was similar to Esus and the god of the Akan people, Anansi; Ekwensu was the evil spirit which could possess people and make them commit evil acts.

Amanex enjoyed speaking to his family and his friends Elombe and Mamadou about the similarities of these African beliefs and those of the Taino and other native groups. Arjana would also join in excitement in speaking about her culture and people. As the year came to an end, Amanex and Elombe planned a raid on several Spanish settlements as Christmas Eve approached. Amanex believed the Spaniards' will to fight against Enriquillo was weakening and an attack on them during Christmas Eve could encourage the other caciques to attack the Spaniards and form a stronger coalition throughout the island and extend to those nearby. Amanex laughed to himself as he thought about the origins of the Christmas holiday and how it was incorporated from an earlier Roman celebration that started on December seventeenth in honor of God Saturnalia, who the Greeks called Kronos. Saturn (or Kronos) was the father of Jupiter, who the Greeks called Zeus and Saturnalia was a time of festivity where social norms were overturned, gambling was permitted, and slaves were allowed freedoms only masters enjoyed. Amanex observed how different religions were incorporated into that of the Roman Catholics and how it spread to Europe and subsequently how these beliefs were now mixed forcefully and sometimes passively with the native and African belief systems.

The Spaniards were weakening in Hispaniola—they were more interested in the riches of the mainland. Amanex and Elombe successfully led several raids during Christmas Eve of 1531 that emancipated hundreds of Tainos and Africans and further crippled the Spanish forces. Amanex requested an audience with Taino leaders including Cacique Enriquillo and Cacique Tamayo in an effort to strengthen African and native alliances and to further devastate the Spanish armies of General Francisco de Barrionuevo. The dream of Bartolome de las Casas' society in Venezuela or any peaceful society among the Spaniards, Africans, and natives had failed and only the certainty of a nightmarish existence persisted if Enriquillo's war failed.

CHAPTER 19
FALL OF THE INCAS (1532)

The Spanish continued the expansion of their American Empire, however some setbacks occurred with the drowning of Pánfilo de Narváez 1528, who was made Adelantado of Florida. Still, the expedition continued with others, including Álvar Núñez Cabeza de Vaca in 1528. In the year of 1530, Charles V had received a Papal Coronation and was officially recognized as Holy Roman Emperor by Pope Clement VII in Bologna. Emperor Charles V subsequently continued the expansion of the Spanish Empire towards the east and the west and in the New World he authorized the invasion of one of the largest empires in the world: the Incan Empire. The leader of the Incas was called the Sapa Inca, meaning "The Only Inca" in the Incan main language of Quechua. The Sapa Inca was considered the son of the Sun God Inti and the Moon Goddess Mama Killa with the Supreme Creator Viracocha (or Apu Qun Tiqsi Wiraqutra) and Kon-Tiki. The first Sapa Inca was the mythical Manco Cápac, who founded the Kingdom of Cusco. In 1438, under the leadership of Sapa Inca Pachacuti-Cusi Yupanqui the Earth Shaker, the Incas began to expand and acquired surrounding territories, which included the tribe of Chancas. Pachacuti-Cusi reorganized his empire into the Tahuantinsuyu, which consisted of a federalist system with the provinces of

Chinchasuyu in the northwest, Antisuyu in the northeast, Kuntisuyu in the southwest, and Qullasuyu in the southeast. Sapa Inca Túpac Inca Yupanqui further expanded the Incan Empire, conquering the Kingdom of Chimor and continuing the construction of the city of Machu Piccho.

Sapa Inca Huayna Capac and his sister and wife Coya Cusirimay produced no heirs, however Huayna Capac had over fifty sons with other women, including Atahualpa, Túpac Huallpa, Manco Inca Yupanqui, General Atoc, Paullu Inca, and Quispe Sisa. Huayna Capac's sister and second royal wife Araua Ocllo produced children—a son named Tupac Cusi Hualpa, (also known as Huáscar) among them. Sapa Inca Huayna Capac was aware of the Spaniards landing off the coast of his empire since 1515, and was alarmed at the violence and the millions of deaths caused by diseases in surrounding territories. After 1527, Sapa Inca Huayna Capac, his brother Auqui Tupac Inca, and successor and eldest son, Ninan Cuyochi contracted measles and smallpox and died. Huayna Capac died at the age of 63, leaving his son Sapa Inca Huáscar Inca ruling the southern region; the Incan capital of Cuzco and Atahualpa, the northern portion centered on Quito. Huáscar and Atahualpa ruled their regions for a little over four years before their rivalry resulted in civil war as the Spaniards attempted to invade.

Conquistador Francisco Pizarro González of Trujillo Spain led an expedition into the Incan Empire. Francisco through his father was the second cousin, once removed, of Hernán Cortés. Previously in 1522, Pascual de Andagoya searched the gold-rich territory called Virú, which was on a river called Pirú (which the Spaniards called Peru). The Peru region and the surrounding lands and its abundant riches and stories of El Dorado (or the Golden One) encouraged Francisco Pizarro to lead several voyages south from Panama. El Dorado was said to be a mythical tribal leader or zipa of the Muisica native people who ritualistically covered himself in gold dust and submerged himself in Lake Guatavita. Pizarro formed a partnership with a priest named Hernando de Luque and a soldier named Diego de Almagro to explore and conquer the south and Pizarro would lead the journey. After several expeditions to the south, Pizarro was given approval by the governor of Castilla del Oro and Nicaragua, Pedro de los Ríos y Gutiérrez de Aguayo. Pizarro later held an audience with Emperor Charles V, who legitimized his role in the conquering of the southern civilizations—including the Incan Empire.

Civil war raged within the Incan Empire between the forces of Huáscar and Atahualpa. Huáscar saw himself as the legitimate successor and had the support of the Incan nobles, however Atahualpa had the support of many of the generals and warriors within the Incan Military, including generals Chalcuchimac, Quizquiz, and Rumiñawi and created his new northern capital of Quito. The northern Kañari people supported Huáscar and contributed over 100,000 warriors for his war efforts and his army of roughly 400,000 warriors which attacked and initially defeated Atahualpa in the city of Tumebamba. Huáscar's generals Atoc and Hango captured the cities of Tumebamba and Cajamarca and imprisoned Atahualpa. Atahualpa escaped with the help of a woman during the drunken celebrations of Huáscar's military and mounted a counter attack. Atahualpa commanded close to 100,000 warriors, but Atahualpa and his generals proved to be better war strategists. Near the city of Ambato in the plains of Mochacaxa, Atahualpa defeated Huáscar's armies and captured and killed General Atoc. Atahualpa continued to win battles, including ones at Bonbon, Jauja, Pincos, and Andaguayias, and executed several of Huáscar generals—Hango among them. After Atahualpa's victory in several more cities (Limatambo, Mullihambato, Chimborazo, and Ichubamna), Atahualpa ordered his generals Chalkuchimac and Quizquiz towards the capital of Cuzco, where Huáscar and his remaining forces were defeated and captured. Atahualpa executed thousands of Kañari people and others who supported the Kañari and increased his army to over 250,000 warriors. Atahualpa remained in Cajamarca with 40,000 troops when he was declared the victor in 1532. As

Atahualpa's army celebrated their victory, Atahualpa received information that the Spaniards had travelled within Incan territory and were approaching Cajamarca.

Holy Roman Empress Isabella of Portugal signed the Capitulación de Toledo on July sixth, 1529, granting Francisco Pizarro the authority to conquer Peru and other surrounding territories. Francisco Pizarro was joined by his brothers Gonzalo, Juan, Hernando, his cousin Pedro Pizarro who served as his page, and a brother from his mother named Francisco Martin de Alcantara who later decided to join. Francisco Pizarro's expedition involved over 180 men and twenty-seven horses when he arrived to Peru in 1532. Francisco Pizarro landed at Cajamarca on the fifteenth of November 1532 with a force of 110 foot soldiers, sixty-seven cavalrymen, three arquebuses, and two falconets. Francisco learned about the Incan civil war and the millions who had perished due to diseases and believed he could ally himself with rivals of the Incan Empire in an attempt to defeat them by exploiting their weaknesses. Atahualpa was relaxing in the nearby thermal Incan Baths when he sent Cinquinchara, an Orejon warrior, to the Spanish to serve as an interpreter. Francisco Pizarro sent Hernando Pizarro and Hernando de Soto to meet with Sapa Inca Atahualpa, who agreed to rendezvous with Francisco Pizarro the next day in Cajamarca.

The Dominican friar Fray Vincente de Valverde and native interpreter Felipillo approached Atahualpa in Cajamarca's central plaza. They spoke of Christianity as the one true faith and the need for Atahualpa to pay tribute to Holy Roman Emperor Charles V, however Atahualpa replied, "I will be no man's tributary."

Friar Vicente joined the conversation holding a crucifix in his right hand and carrying a breviary in his left, asking Atahualpa to renounce his gods and choose Christianity, but Atahualpa refused as the conversation became strained due to the difficulty of the translations between Spanish and Quechua. The conquistadors were anxious and angry and launched a strike at Atahualpa, eventually capturing and imprisoning the Incan leader.

Spanish artillery, guns, and cavalry gave the Spaniards victory in Cajamarca while the captured Emperor Atahualpa was forced to fill several rooms with gold, silver, and other riches.

Atahualpa filled one room measuring twenty-two by seventeen--feet with gold and two other rooms with silver. Despite the riches delivered to Francisco Pizarro, Atahualpa was accused of various crimes, including plotting against the Spaniards and the killing of his brother Huáscar. On August twenty-ninth of 1533, Atahualpa was given a choice of execution by fire or garrote and he chose the latter in the hopes of preserving his corpse for mummification in the Incan tradition. Atahualpa's young wife Cuxirimay Ocllo was renamed Doña Angelina and was groomed to become Francisco Pizarro's mistress. Pizarro marched into Cuzco leading over 500 conquistadors and subdued the city and burned Chalcuchimac at the stake. He then named Atahualpa's younger brother Túpac Huallpa as a puppet Emperor of the Incas.

Túpac Huallpa died in Jauja in 1533 and was replaced with Sapa Inca Manco Inca Yupanqui, who was used by the Spaniards to exploit Incan resources and precious metals like gold and silver. The Spaniards also desired their vassal leader Manco Inca Yupanqui to engage the Incan rebel general Quizquiz, who continued to fight the Spaniards. The Spaniards marveled at the cities which were larger than many of the cities in Europe. The Spaniards also observed record keeping administrative strings and knots the Inca called khipus (which the Spaniards renamed Quipu). Francisco was awed at the complex system as well as the riches found in the Incan Empire and this fueled him and the Spaniards to continue their conquest of the Inca. Francisco Pizarro remained in control of the Incan conquest despite reprimands against his actions, including the execution of Atahualpa by Hernando Pizarro, Hernando de Soto, and Emperor Charles V. The Spanish Empire continued to expand, however rebel forces such as the territories of the Aztecs, Mayas, Incas, and Asia continued to fight Spanish control. Hernan Cortés sent his son Martín Cortés el Mestizo (the son of his mistress named Doña Marina) to Spain while Hernando Cortés' legitimate son was born in 1532 and named Martín Cortés y Zúñiga, who he had with his second wife named Doña Juana de Zúñiga. Hernando Cortés' authority declined, however he increased his wealth in owning mines and discussed exploration of a new territory further north. In Peru, Manco Inca Yupanqui was continuously mistreated and plotted against Francisco Pizarro and the Spaniards while Enriquillo continued his successful war on the island of Hispaniola.

CHAPTER 20
CACIQUE ENRIQUILLO'S WAR (1533)

Amanex felt optimistic about the defeat of the Spaniards on the island of Hispaniola. Cacique Tamayo and Cacique Enriquillo now had the freedom of open coordination and began solidifying and expanding Enriquillo's confederacy of free natives and Africans. Amanex advised Cacique Enriquillo regarding the need to increase raids and recruiting efforts and build a wider coalition throughout the surrounding islands of Cuba, Jamaica, and San Juan Bautista. Enriquillo initially agreed with Amanex and Tamayo, particularly after Enriquillo and Tamayo's united effort in several victories over Spanish military forces and the capture of Spanish hostages.

By late 1531, Enriquillo and Tamayo had cornered hundreds of Spanish conquistadors near the southern region of Bahoruco, north east of Jaragua Lake. Amanex was summoned to reinforce Enriquillo and Tamayo's forces and brought his eldest son Simon Pedro Haübey. To the dismay of his wife Tayamari, Amanex had begun to involve his son in campaigns against the Spaniards. Amanex did not wish to involve his wife and children in direct combat, however he understood that the Spaniards were capable of barbarity unseen by natives who had not had contact with them and so he desired to teach his children how to defend themselves. He understood that he had to instruct his children in the art of warfare to keep themselves safe. Throughout the wars, the families within Cacique Enriquillo's Confederation had strengthened their bonds despite their cultural differences into a single community against Spanish oppression. Enriquillo's son Simon Pedro Haübey who was twelve and Elombe's eight-year-old daughter Malundama had grown close in their friendship; Simon Pedro was always close to Malundama whenever she feared the dangers of the ongoing wars. Amanex was proud of the bravery Simon Pedro had displayed at the young age of twelve and how he comforted the other children. It was a bravery that Amanex himself had not shown at the same age, but he had seen it from his deceased brother Amayao. The pain of losing his parents and his eldest brother was somewhat relieved when he saw the traits of his family members within his children.

Close to 200 Spaniards had retreated into a cave near the base of the Bahoruco mountain range and as Amanex approached, he observed no Spanish reserve forces in the area. Despite this, he left Elombe in charge of over 100 fighters as he travelled along with his son and Mamadou Dieng to meet Enriquillo and Tamayo and observe the interrogation of the Spanish hostages. The Spaniards were overwhelmed by Tamayo's forces and Enriquillo helped to push many of them into the cave where their weapons were confiscated and they stood shaking in fear awaiting Cacique Enriquillo to decide their fates. Amanex searched the Spaniards to see if Radamés Cesar Milfuegos was among them and to his dismay, he was not.

Cacique Tamayo called for execution of the Spaniards because he believed it was too dangerous to let them leave alive, while Cacique Enriquillo decided to extract as much intelligence from the Spanish captives before possibly freeing them.

Amanex angrily exclaimed, "My cacique, I have always respected you and your esteemed family, but I find it hard to accept your decision regarding these Spanish prisoners. Would Spaniards show the same generosity with Taino or African prisoners of war? We must keep these prisoners as prisoners until the end of this war and we must gather all the other native leaders surrounding and on the island of Ayiti and mount an offensive in Santo Domingo. If we are able to crush the Spaniards in Santo Domingo, we can motivate the other caciques to successfully defeat the Spaniards elsewhere and liberate Ayiti. We can aid Cacique Guamá in Cuba and begin to reclaim these islands from the Spaniards."

Cacique Enriquillo calmly replied after formulating his thoughts for a moment. "We have been largely successful in our war against the Spaniards, however I was raised by them and have been privy to their tactics and culture. If they cannot beat us outright they will turn us against ourselves. Diseases have killed millions of our people throughout these islands and only a few thousand Tainos will remain in the next generation. How long can we maintain our native and African coalition if Charles V rededicates his energies towards these islands?"

Cacique Tamayo said, "We have other Taino leaders and African recruits that are willing to fight to the death against the Spaniards and follow you, Enriquillo. Amanex is right. We should not release these hostages, but where I disagree is keeping them as hostages for a prolonged amount of time. If even one Spaniard escapes and informs General Barrionuevo of our whereabouts it will force us to quickly relocate our communities and possibly reveal ourselves to the Spanish."

Cacique Enriquillo replied, "Tamayo, General Barrionuevo understands he is defeated and his Spanish army lacks the resources to pay their conquistadors to continue the fight. The Spaniards are seeking their fortunes in the mainland, however I have Spanish intelligence that informs me that Emperor Charles V desires to continue his fight to keep Hispaniola and the surrounding islands and without a European rival kingdom challenging Charles V, he will continue to mount attacks on my army despite our continuous victories. We need a large force and we also need to get through their naval blockades in order to reclaim our island. I am not sure how long the other caciques in Hispaniola and Cuba will be able to maintain their respective rebellions. I believe we should negotiate with the Spaniards from a position of strength rather than weakness."

Amanex, Tamayo, and many of the freed Africans were particularly upset at Enriquillo's statements as the summer months of 1532 passed. Amanex observed Enriquillo's health begin to decline; perhaps he was exhausted from his war efforts. Amanex did not believe in negotiations with the Spaniards who repeatedly broke their agreements—particularly when Spanish control was weakening. However, Cacique Enriquillo was correct. The native and African coalition required more recruits and a wider effort to not only defeat the Spaniards in battle but to reclaim their lands. Amanex was convinced they needed a decisive victory at Santo Domingo to gain a final victory against General Barrionuevo and Emperor Charles V. Elombe and Mamadou strongly doubted a possible agreement between Enriquillo and the Spanish forces; they believed the Africans would be returned under the yoke of slavery. Many of the Africans desired to continue the fight under the leadership of other native leaders like Tamayo or under African leadership.

Amanex spoke to Tayamari about the possibility of fleeing the island of Hispaniola if Enriquillo chose to negotiate. Elombe Masombo wanted to remain and fight, however he was also pondering the safety of his wife Magdalena and his daughter Malundama. Amanex believed if Enriquillo negotiated with the Spaniards it would fragment the native alliances throughout the island and weaken resistance against the Spaniards. To the surprise of many, Enriquillo released all the Spanish hostages as Christmas approached in 1532. Cacique Enriquillo subsequently called for a meeting with the other caciques of Hispaniola to discuss his plans to negotiate with the Spaniards in early 1533.

Cacique Enriquillo gathered caciques Villagrán, Matayco, Incaqueca, Gascón, Vasa, Maybona, and Tamayo in one of his main camps at the Bahoruco Mountains. After speaking privately with his lieutenants for several days, Cacique Enriquillo made a public statement about his decision to negotiate with General Francisco de Barrionuevo.

Enriquillo announced, "I have been approached by Spanish messengers who have informed me Emperor Charles V wants our war to end and he has instructed General Francisco de Barrionuevo to cease Spanish hostilities towards the Tainos and Africans who live freely and have fought bravely for many years. I have led you towards victory in battle and freedom from Spanish slavery and towards a good life in our confederacy. We have worked together and all natives and Africans have lived in general peace with little dispute under our way of life. General Francisco de Barrionuevo will meet with me several months from now at a location of my choice to discuss terms that will give us rights and freedoms free from Spanish harassment and rule. If I believe General Francisco de Barrionuevo's terms are just and good for natives and Africans, I shall accept this agreement to live freely side by side with the Spaniards. Now we have been successful in war, however I do not believe we have the manpower to maintain a rebellion for several generations, nor do we have the overwhelming power to reclaim the island of Hispaniola and the surrounding islands. My desire is for my people to be both physically free as well as live mentally free—a freedom from fear and freedom from constant warfare and worry."

Cacique Enriquillo's speech delivered mixed results; many natives who tired of fighting agreed with him while many believed the Spaniards were not trustworthy—particularly the Africans, who thought they would place them under bondage once again. Cacique Tamayo was Enriquillo's main critic and called for natives and Africans to continue their war against the Spaniards.

Cacique Tamayo replied, "I have respected your leadership, Cacique Enriquillo, but we cannot agree to terms with the Spaniards. Since their arrival to our lands they have only brought a trail of blood and misery and this will not end despite the noble and generous actions you have displayed in times of peace as well as war. If you choose to negotiate with General Barrionuevo and the Spaniards, I will support your decision. However, I will continue to wage war against the Spaniards and I welcome any cacique who wishes to continue their fight as well as any Africans and natives who wish to join me. I will depart from Enriquillo's camp and continue my fight to the north and I will wish you and those who choose to follow you in whatever your decision may be."

A slow, growing murmur rippled through the crowds of Africans and natives each in their own languages as well as Spanish as men, women, and their families discussed what decision would benefit them.

As the summer months approached in 1533, Cacique Enriquillo agreed that the location of his meeting with General de Barrionuevo would be on the island of the large Jaragua Lake. Cacique Enriquillo would position over a thousand of his best warriors on the shores of the lake and a reserve unit on the island in case the Spaniards betrayed him. Several caciques sympathetic to Cacique Enriquillo's potential peace agreement were also in attendance as the Spaniards began arriving to Lake Jaragua, outnumbered by the large native and African presence.

Emperor Charles V had summoned General Francisco de Barrionuevo, authorizing him to speak with Cacique Enriquillo and bring an end to the war between the forces of Cacique Enriquillo and the Spaniards. General Francisco de Barrionuevo arrived early in the morning to meet the great Cacique Enriquillo along with hundreds of conquistadors. The Tainos prepared a canoa for them to arrive at the island in the center of Jaragua Lake where Cacique Enriquillo was waiting for them. It was the first time they had stood in front of each other.

Cacique Enriquillo initiated the conversation. "Welcome, General Francisco de Barrionuevo. My desire is that we can come to a compromise that allows my people to live freely in our own communities without Spanish intervention. If we can come to a compromise where my people will be guaranteed their freedom we can put an end to this war, but we will defend ourselves if you break our agreement."

General Barrionuevo replied, "You have proven to be a great leader and although you have defeated many Spaniards in battle, you have been honorable in war and just to your Spanish prisoners. The Holy Roman Emperor Charles V has authorized me to make this agreement between your people. We desire to maintain our way of life on the island of Hispaniola and that requires you cease your war against the Spaniards and we will grant you and your people freedom to live in your communities as you have always done, and free to practice your beliefs as you see fit. You will be offered the lands of Boyá in the settlement of Santa María de Azua, where you can relocate and live in peace among your people."

The Spaniards remained with Cacique Enriquillo for several days while the agreement was discussed and certain changes were adopted. Francisco de Barrionuevo desired to complete the agreement quickly to stop Enriquillo's wars and asked him if he could instruct other caciques, particularly Cacique Tamayo, to stop their attacks against the Spaniards. Cacique Enriquillo made sure to inform Francisco de Barrionuevo that he could not stop the other wars throughout Hispaniola, as he believed that at the signing of his agreement with Barrionuevo he would stop being the war leader in Hispaniola. Francisco de Barrionuevo was excited to end his costly wars against Cacique Enriquillo, however he was dismayed he could not encourage Cacique Enriquillo to aid the Spaniards against the other caciques in Hispaniola. By September, the agreement was signed and Enriquillo's fourteen-year war against the Spaniards was over.

Amanex did not attend the meeting but had learned about Cacique Enriquillo's final decision. He was in his childhood home to the west of Azua where Enriquillo and his followers would be resettled to live freely. This agreement was the first major one between native and free Africans and the Spanish Crown, but Amanex did not believe the Spaniards would honor it. Even if Emperor Charles V demanded the Spaniards to do so, many Spaniards would eventually disobey their own leader. Amanex gathered his family, the family of Elombe, and Mamadou and his sister Arjana as he discussed his plans of escaping Hispaniola. He still had Spanish enemies, including Radamés Cesar Milfuegos, who would only be encouraged by the end of Enriquillo's war to inflict harm on the Tainos and Africans. Amanex also believed Radamés might still believe that he was alive and would seek vengeance against him and his family. Amanex now believed a decisive attack on Santo Domingo would not occur under Cacique Tamayo or other caciques who did not have the organization nor the manpower that Cacique Enriquillo previously did.

Elombe, Mamadou, Arjana, and many of the Africans living in Amanex's community agreed with him and his plans for escape, but some Africans believed they should remain in Hispaniola and continue their fight against the Spaniards and free their friends and family members who were still enslaved. Simon Pedro Haübey agreed with his father's escape plans and with his mother Tayamari, who also believed the Spaniards would break their agreement with Cacique Enriquillo. However, Amanex's youngest son Adán Hatüey thought the family should follow Cacique Enriquillo.

"This is your land and our island," he said. "Why should we flee from our ancestral homeland?"

Amanex replied, "My son, you are still young and you have not seen the horrors of the Spaniards as you were born and raised free. You have not experienced warfare against the Spaniards as I have for many years. I also have enemies in Santo Domingo and on this island who might know I am still alive and these enemies might not only seek vengeance against me but you and our entire family. I do not believe the Spanish will honor their agreement with Cacique Enriquillo. The Spaniards' lust for gold overwhelms their humanity."

Amanex discussed various routes of escape and

islands where he and his family could find peace and a future. He recruited the help of elder Taino navigators, who would use the stars to travel in the cover of darkness away from Spanish ships and French pirates. Amanex wanted to move west and avoid the Spanish dominated eastern regions of Hispaniola and decided to possibly find a haven with Cacique Guamá and perhaps escape from the island of Jamaica. The destination was debated; some argued to head for the island of Guadeloupe, some argued in favor of the island of Dominica and surrounding islands. Amanex believed he could continue the peace the Tainos and Kalinago had created in Hispaniola during the war and bring it to these smaller islands with the help of some of the Kalinago people who had lived among the Tainos in Hispaniola.

Cacique Enriquillo was invited to the city of Santo Domingo and a large celebration was held for several weeks. He was given a title by the Spaniards and now referred to as Don Enriquillo Bejo. The Spaniards celebrated the end of the Enriquillo war and Cacique Enriquillo wrote a letter in Spanish to Emperor Charles V, which legitimized the agreement between Don Enriquillo and the Spaniards. The Spaniards and Tainos smoked, drank wine, and danced the night away in honor of the end of the war. The celebrations lasted throughout the year and there was another large one during Christmas of 1533, the time when over 100 Africans and natives followed Amanex westward towards Cuba and then towards Jamaica as they planned their escape towards the islands in the southeast. Don Enriquillo had secretly met with Amanex and promised he would not reveal his plans. As Don Enriquillo began to move his community towards Azua in early 1534, Amanex and his followers had successfully fled the island of Hispaniola towards the southeastern mountains of Cuba. Many of the Spaniards observed the Tainos and Africans who celebrated in Santo Domingo and were now moving to Azua, including Radamés Cesar Milfuegos.

CHAPTER 21
ESCAPE THROUGH JAMAICA (1534)

Early in 1534, Amanex, his family, and over 100 Africans and natives had reached Cuba. Cacique Guamá had maintained a rebellion against the Spaniards in Cuba for ten years but before Amanex could meet with Cacique Guamá, he was informed he had been assassinated by his own brother Oliguama, who had buried an axe into Cacique Guamá's head while he slept. The rumor was that Cacique Guamá had an affair with the wife of Oliguama, however Amanex believed that was a tale fabricated by the Spaniards. Cacique Guamá's widow Casiguaya continued the rebellion against Governor Manuel de Rojas and the Spaniards in Cuba, but as Amanex moved towards the mountains of south eastern Cuba he learned that Casiguaya had been apprehended and executed by Manuel de Rojas, leaving Brizuela of Baitiquirí as the leader of the Taino rebellion in Cuba.

Brizuela of Baitiquirí helped Amanex and his family leave the southeastern coast of Cuba safely on their way to Jamaica. Several of Brizuela's followers asked Amanex and Elombe questions regarding Cacique Enriquillo and his agreement with Emperor Charles V and the Spaniards. Many of the Tainos were proud of Cacique Enriquillo in his successful war against the Spaniards, however many were also disappointed with his agreement because they believed it weakened other ongoing wars for freedom. Brizuela expressed her opinion on this matter as she prepared Amanex and his followers for travel to Jamaica.

"I am proud of Cacique Enriquillo and his strategic excellence in battle," she said, "but just like you, Amanex, I do not believe the Spaniards will respect the terms of the agreement. The Spaniards have proven to be a greedy and vengeful people and if they cannot defeat the natives or Africans on the battlefield they will foment and exploit divisions among ourselves to further weaken us and set us up for genocide and exploitation. It is possible they might use Cacique Enriquillo to further weaken other ongoing resistance movements in Hispaniola, Cuba, and other islands. I believe in continuing our fight no matter how hopeless. I also agree with the decision you made to escape to the other southern islands where there is no Spanish presence. I desire the best for you, your family, and the community you wish to create, but a day will come when the Spanish or French or other European invaders will seek to conquer the islands in the southeast. Even if you do not fight, perhaps it will be your children or your grandchildren, so you must create an alliance with the Kalinago people. Move swiftly through Jamaica and sail directly towards your destination before the season of hurricanes arrives."

Amanex ate and celebrated and early in the morning they left on the same two large canoes that they had arrived to Cuba on and an additional large canoe supplied by Cacique Brizuela of Baitiquirí. Amanex rejoiced; he and his family were among the first to step on the northern beaches of Jamaica. Amanex's son Simon Pedro Haübey and Elombe's daughter, both fifteen years of age, were excited to leave the dangers of Hispaniola and Cuba and had grown close through their shared experiences in Enriquillo's free community. Many of these children had grown to adulthood throughout the war between Cacique Enriquillo and the Spaniards and although they were raised as free men and women, they still had lived under uncertainty and horrors. The children were overjoyed as Amanex led them towards Jamaica and a life free from war and conquistadors. Amanex reminded his family that Jamaica was his mother's homeland, which was now partially inhabited by Spanish conquistadors. Jamaica was currently part of the negotiations between the Spanish Crown and Diego Colón's son Luis Colón and Diego Colón's brother Fernando Colón, in the ongoing Pleitos colombinos. The Royal Prosecutor argued against the Colón family, trying to establish the idea that the so called West Indies were indeed discovered by Martín Alonso Pinzón. Fernando Colón had lived the life of a scholar in Spain and created a vast library which contained over 15,000 volumes with the riches gained from his father's lands in the New World. Fernando Colón was also fighting the Spanish Crown alongside his nephew for titles and territories, including the island of Jamaica. Luis Colón would later be granted the titles of First Duke of Veragua, First Duke of la Vega, First Marquis of Jamaica, and Third Admiral of the Indies. Through arbitration, in June of 1536, the president of the Council of the Indies, the bishop García de Loaysa, along with the president of the Council of Castile, Gaspar de Montoya, also granted the island of Jamaica as a fief for the Colón family—a territory of 25 leagues square in Veragua, the title of alguacil mayor or High Sherriff of Santo Domingo, and 500,000 maravedíes per year were to be paid to each of the sisters of Luis Colón, and 10,000 ducats annually to the heirs of Colón. The major lawsuits were settled, but minor ones would continue between the Spanish Crown and the Colón family.

The island of Jamaica was the land of proud Taino leaders such as Cacique Huareo, who had rebelled against the invading Spanish in the early 1500s. There were few communities of Africans and Tainos who had run away from sugar plantations into the mountains of Jamaica. Some of the Africans and Tainos also joined Amanex as he travelled eastward through the mountains of Jamaica. The Africans and Tainos there spoke Spanish, making it easy for everyone to communicate among themselves as they approached the large mountain ranges of southeastern Jamaica. Amanex stayed away from the new Jamaican capital of Villa de la Vega (or Santiago de la Vega) and the Jamaican governor Gil González de Ávila. Some Africans believed Amanex should liberate some of the slaves in Spanish settlements, however Amanex as well as others believed it would focus unwanted attention on their escape.

Amanex decided that the destination should be towards the island that was renamed Saint Vincent. He and his group now numbering over 150 gathered near the Jamaican coastline by a southern bay. As the sun began to set, Amanex led his followers out into the bay, placing his best navigators in the front of the three large canoes. Amanex embraced his family as well as Elombe's family as they began to set sail towards what many of them believed to be their final destination. The water was calm and the night was cool upon the skin. There was a quiet but noticeable murmur within the large canoe as people were excited about their new destination filled with new possibilities. Some feared not only Spanish ships, but French pirates who roamed Spanish territories in uninhabited areas of Hispaniola and other islands. The Frenchmen would adopt the same practices of the Tainos and the Kalinago or Carib people of roasting meat on top of a wooden frame the Tainos called a buccan. The Tainos and Caribs usually roasted manatees on the buccan and the French would also roast feral cattle and pigs. The French pirates were later associated with the buccan and would be referred to as buccaneers.

Emperor Charles V had proven himself superior to European such as Frederick III, Elector of Saxony and his two successors named Johann, Elector of Saxony and Johann Frederick I, Elector of Saxony. The King of France, Francis I, was encircled by Emperor Charles V's growing empire and had allied himself with Sultan Suleiman the Magnificent and the Ottoman Empire in 1533. The alliance between France and the Ottoman Empire was the first between Christian and Non-Christian power, which angered much of Europe and helped Charles V fuel negative propaganda against France and Francis I. The Protestant Reformation initiated by Martin Luther spread throughout Europe, causing political divisions after Martin Luther was excommunicated by Pope Leo X on the third of January 1521. The Edict of Worms authorized by Emperor Charles V on the twenty-fifth of May 1521, declared Luther an outlaw. Frederick III subsequently sheltered Martin Luther, where he continued his writings translating the Bible from Latin to German and influencing other translations of the Bible such as from Hebrew and Greek to English by William Tyndale in England.

Tyndale's Bible was translated by the Greek Bible written by Erasmus and older than the Latin written by Jerome, but he angered the Pope and King Henry VIII, who had him executed in 1536. King Francis I used the political divisions between Catholics and Protestants against Charles V. King Francis I executed protestants in France during the Affair of the Placards in October 1534, where he confused Protestant demonstrations against Catholic Mass as a plot against his throne.

King Francis I began exploring the New World by authorizing sailors like Giovanni da Verrazzano to the northern mainland and claiming a settlement named New Angoulême. He also sent Bertrand d'Ornesan, who explored the southern mainland. King Francis I also began to encourage naval officers to attack Spanish ships—which they often did during the night—and these privateers or buccaneers placed added fear upon Amanex and many of his followers. They were only relieved once they reached their destination of Saint Vincent. Amanex and his family rejoiced as they sought to make peace with the island's Kalinago population and create a new settlement between Taino, Kalinago, and other natives as well as the Africans and children of these people into a new community free from Spanish domination. At the age of forty-nine, Amanex believed he had finally found freedom as he looked forward to celebrating his fiftieth birthday with his family and out of the reach of the Spanish Empire. However, Amanex's peaceful settlement and peace of mind would be shattered just a few years later.

CHAPTER 22
TREACHERY IN AZUA (1540)

After his agreement with Charles V two years earlier, Cacique Enriquillo passed away in 1535. Nearly in his fourth decade, Enriquillo appeared older and sickly from diseases which had taken his life along with thousands of other Tainos in the previous few years. As a result, the Taino rebellions on Hispaniola were failing. Many of the Spaniards were angered that Emperor Charles V had made an agreement with Cacique Enriquillo and called for a destruction of Enriquillo's free community in Azua. The Spaniards coerced Africans and Tainos to hunt runaway slaves and combat Taino and African rebellions, however many of the Tainos and Africans preferred not to fight those among them who emancipated themselves. Most of the Africans and Tainos secretly supported Cacique Enriquillo's rebellion and others, including Cacique Tamayo's, which had stretched throughout the Cibao region.

Some Spaniards welcomed the peace agreement between Spaniards and Enriquillo just as many Tainos and Africans. Franciscan and Dominican Priests embraced a greater peace between Spaniards, Africans, and Tainos, including Don Pedro Ramirez, his wife Valeria, and daughter Maria Ramirez, who was now a beautiful thirty year old woman. Don Pedro Ramirez had given up his

Encomienda, encouraged by the words of Amanex several years after his escape from Santo Domingo to the anger of Radamés Cesar Milfuegos. Radamés did not approve of men like Don Pedro Ramirez, who were wealthy and who had married Taina women. Don Pedro Ramirez had long retired from his life as a conquistador and an Encomendero and had managed to accumulate wealth after selling his sugarcane fields while Radamés had continued his life as a conquistador with poor finances and had only recently acquired land and a few African slaves. Radamés had lost his friends, but he believed in his ability to father additional children. However, he remained at the lower end of Spanish society.

Radamés had taken his frustrations out on the few slaves he directly controlled and sometimes his wife Paulina, who he would beat when he was drunk. Radamés' son Maximo was now eighteen and had grown resentful of his father's actions as well as his own status in life. After the agreement began failing between the Spaniards and over 4,000 free men, women, and children who followed Cacique Enriquillo and lived in Azua, Radamés began to threaten the people of the settlement. Radamés, who was now fifty-eight, had grown angry at the Spanish society that he felt had not fully compensated him for his work in pacifying the natives and Africans he believed were below him. Several Spaniards opposed Radamés and his abuses against the people of Azua, including Pedro Ramirez and Jose Manuel Palacio, who had once been a prisoner of Cacique Enriquillo but had witnessed his generosity and honesty—qualities he rarely observed among other Spaniards. After several violent raids into Azua, Radamés finally received the answer he was searching for: Amanex had fled to the southeastern islands where the Carib people resided. An area rarely visited by Spaniards.

Radamés did not question Cacique Enriquillo's wife Doña Mencia, nor any of his remaining relatives, but he identified several Tainos close to the Enriquillo family and forcefully coerced them to reveal Amanex's whereabouts by threatening their families. After the general location of

Amanex and his followers was revealed, Radamés encouraged his friends to set fires to their homes and kill the Taino and African people. The Spaniards openly encouraged the Tainos an Africans to retaliate so the Spaniards could have an excuse to openly kill the Africans and Tainos in Azua and confiscate their remaining weapons and riches.

In the subsequent years, several of Radamés' main Spanish opponents had left the island of Hispaniola for the mainland in search of wealth. His few detractors were silenced by other Spaniards who began to agree with Radamés in destroying what was their humiliation in Cacique Enriquillo's agreement and free community of Azua. Maximo Milfuegos had also participated in the raids against the settlement of Azua after Spanish officials began turning a blind eye towards his father's actions. In the year 1542, Radamés' primary Spanish rival Don Pedro Ramirez passed away, leaving his wife Valeria, daughter Maria, and Radamés without a main outspoken enemy. Radamés began to convince other Spaniards to travel to the southeastern islands that had been largely ignored in search of riches. Radamés lusted for more gold and land and sought an opportunity for himself and his son to elevate their status in Spanish society. He also thirsted for revenge and the hope that he would locate Amanex, Elombe, and their families to humiliate and kill them and their community. Radamés Cesar Milfuegos began to gather a sizeable force that supported his efforts to conquer land and riches in several of the southeastern islands as the year of 1545 approached.

CHAPTER 23
THE SUN NEVER SETS ON THE SPANISH EMPIRE
(1545)

Emperor Charles V sustained the expansion of his empire in the east and the west while Sultan Suleiman the Magnificent had continued to exert power in the Mediterranean. Suleiman ordered Pasha Hayreddin Barbarossa to build a large fleet in Constantinople. Over seventy galleys were constructed under the supervision of Pasha Hayreddin Barbarossa, which were manned by African as well as European slaves—those of Slavic descent were provided by the Crimean Khanate which succeeded the Golden Horde. The Crimean Khan exported slaves from Russia and Poland-Lithuania, which were added to the Ottoman Empire's war machine and the Ottoman fleet that included over 2,000 Jewish slaves in the Ottoman Navy. The Ottoman fleet, under Pasha Hayreddin Barbarossa, conducted raids along the Italian coast and eventually conquered Tunis and Ifriqiya in August 1534. This ousted the local leader named Muley Hasan of the weakened Hafsid Dynasty, who was subservient to Spain and Emperor Charles V. Charles V countered with over 30,000 soldiers, seventy-four galleys, and 300 sailing ships with over 360 bronze cannons to result in a Spanish victory and driving the Ottomans out of the region of Tunis.

Emperor Charles V retaliated against the alliance between Francis I and Suleiman the magnificent by forming an alliance with the Ottoman Empire's Islamic rival, the Persian Safavid Dynasty ruled by Shah Tahmasp I. The Safavid Dynasty established Twelve Shia Islam as the official State Religion. Adherents believed in the Twelve Imams and that the last Imam named Muhammad al-Mahdi lived in occultation and would reappear as the promised Mahdi, the male descendant of the Prophet Muhammad. Sheikh Safi-ad-din Ardabili was a mystic who founded the Safaviyya Order, which gained military and political power. Sheikh Haydar solidified and politicized the Safaviyya Order and his son, Shah Ismail I, further strengthened the Safaviyya, Twelver Shia Order, and founded the Safavid Dynasty in 1501. The Safavid Dynasty became the leading state of Shia Islam that opposed the Sunni Ottoman Empire.

The region of Iraq was contested between The Safavid Dynasty and the Ottoman Empire, which led to several battles lead by Suleiman the Magnificent and his Grand Vizier Grand Vizier Ibrahim Pasha. This resulted in Ottoman victories and the captures of cities including Bitlis, Tabrizm, and then Baghdad in 1534. Shah Tahmasp I retreated and initiated a scorched earth policy. After the alliance between King Francis I and Suleiman the Magnificent, Emperor Charles V allied with Shah Tahmasp I and the Safavid Dynasty, reestablishing the Hapsburg-Persian Alliance that Charles V had previously created with Shah Ismail I. King Henry VIII, Emperor Charles V, and Shah Tahmasp I successfully opened a second front in their wars against the Ottoman Empire, allowing Charles V to strengthen his own. On September eighteenth, 1544, the representatives of Charles, Henry VIII, and Francis signed the Truce of Crépy-en-Laonnois.

Emperor Charles V also faced enemies among German princes and their Protestant Reformation. The German princes supported Martin Luther and his statements against the Catholic Church. In 1516, the Dominican Friar and papal commissioner for Indulgences,

Johann Tetzel, travelled to Germany to sell indulgences to fund Saint Peter's Basilica in Rome. The Roman Catholic Church stated that faith alone could not justify man but charity and good works such as donations to the Catholic Church, which had become abusive, were also needed. In October 1517, Martin Luther wrote to his bishop, Albert of Mainz, protesting the sale of indulgences. He enclosed in his letter a copy of his *Disputation of Martin Luther on the Power and Efficacy of Indulgences*, which became *The Ninety-Five Theses*. Martin Luther challenged the Pope and the Roman Catholic Church, stating that forgiveness was granted by God alone. At the Diet of Worms, Emperor Charles V punished Martin Luther for not renouncing his writings, which resulted in political ramifications with Francis I and German princes.

The German Peasant's Revolt erupted from 1524 to 1526 between the peasants and supported by the Protestant Clergy and the Swabian League that represented the Imperial Estates. This resulted in the slaughter of roughly 100,000 peasants and farmers. Peasant leaders who initially sided with Martin Luther, including Thomas Müntzer and Florian Geyer von Giebelstadt, turned against him, as he had sided with Protestant aristocrats that only desired clerical reforms. The Schmalkaldic League was subsequently formed, creating an alliance between the Lutheran princes within the Holy Roman Empire that began calling for the League to replace it. Amid rising tensions, Holy Roman Emperor Charles V delegated his brother Ferdinand I to handle Germany. In 1545, The Council of Trent initiated the Counter-Reformation and after the death of Martin Luther in 1546, Charles V outlawed the Schmalkaldic League. Martin Luther had made enemies among the Jewish people by urging for their persecution and removal and among the peasants who initially supported, which helped Charles V in his political ambitions. Holy Roman Emperor Charles V defeated the League as his forces drove the League's troops out of southern Germany and defeated John Frederick, Elector of Saxony, and Philip of Hesse at the Battle of Mühlberg, capturing both.

Charles V continued to expand his territories in the Americas as the Spaniards founded several cities in New Spain such as Puebla de los Angeles in 1531, as well as the settlements of Colima, Antequera, Guadalajara in 1532, and the city of Querétaro, Bajío, and Guadalajara. The Spaniards also founded the settlement of San Francisco de Campeche, which served as a trading town with Veracruz. After the Lord of Mani converted to Christianity, he encouraged the surrounding leaders to submit to Spanish rule in 1542. The eastern Mayans launched an attack on the Spaniards in 1546 but were defeated as the Spanish Empire continued to increase their territory in the Americas.

In 1536, Gonzalo Jiménez de Quesada was chosen by De Lugo to lead an expedition inland along with de Quesada's brother Hernán Pérez de Quesada, his second in command Juan del Junco, Juan San Martín, Lázaro Fonte, and Sergio Bustillo with a support fleet of six ships and over 900 men travelling south through the Magdalena River. Only two of the ships completed the entire journey and only 166 men survived after suffering through the dense jungles, diseases, and surviving on a diet of frogs, lizards, snakes, insects, and leather from their harnesses and the scabbards of their swords. In March 1537, they reached the Muisca Confederation ruled from the capital cities of Bacatá and Hunza (or Tunja). The southern ruler was Zipa Tisquesusa, who ruled in Bacatá, and the northern ruler Zaque Quemuenchatocha. Using superior weaponry and over eighty-five horses and taking advantage of rivalries between the native chiefs, de Quesada and the Spaniards defeated the Muisca Zipa Tisquesusa. Other regional chiefs submitted to the Spaniards, including Chía and Suba, as the Spaniards continued to defeat the army of Zipa Tisquesusa.

Zaque Quemuenchatocha tried to appease the Spaniards while hiding his gold and emeralds from them, but his strategy did not work and on August twentieth, 1537, the Spanish conquerors led by Gonzalo Jiménez de Quesada found Quemuenchatocha sitting on his throne decorated with gold, emeralds, and wearing precious cloths. Zaque Quemuenchatocha fled once again, but later perished and his nephew Zaque Aquiminzaque assumed the northern Muisca throne. Zaque Aquiminzaque was later executed by decapitation by Hernán Pérez de Quesada in 1540 in Tunja. Zipa Tisquesusa was alarmed at a prophecy stating he would perish "bathing in his own blood" and was soon captured and executed. His general and successor Zipa Zaquesazipa would also suffer defeat at the hands of the Spaniards and died after extensive torture. Other caciques were captured and executed from territories including Toca, Motavita, Samacá, Turmequé, and Sutamarchán. On August sixth, 1538, the city of Santa Fé de Bogotá was founded on the remains of the former Muisca capital of Bacatá. The New Kingdom of Granada was formed and led by Governor Gonzalo Jiménez de Quesada, followed by his brother Hernán Pérez de Quesada. The Spanish Empire also continued their expansion in South America, creating the Viceroyalty of Peru and establishing its capital in Lima, Peru in 1542.

Manco Inca Yupanqui had suffered abuse at the hands of the brothers Juan and Gonzalo Pizarro and ultimately rebelled in 1535. Manco Inca Yupanqui capitalized on a disagreement between Almagro and Hernando Pizarro and attempted to recapture the city of Cuzco. He gathered an Incan force of 150,000 warriors with additional reinforcements that defeated Hernando Pizarro's initial attack. Manco Inca Yupanqui surrounded the city of Cuzco and successfully penetrated the city as the Spaniards retreated within two large buildings near the center of the plaza. The Spaniards were aided by thousands of Indios auxiliaries or native allies and over 200 of their own men as they desperately initiated a counter attack towards the Incan base of operations in the walled city of Saksaywaman. Juan Pizarro led fifty horsemen and cavalry in a frontal assault of Saksaywaman as Incan arrows rained upon his cavalry. For several days, the assault continued successfully, however a large stone struck Juan Pizarro in the head, resulting in his death several days later as the assaults on Saksaywaman continued.

After resisting several counterattacks, the Spaniards scaled the walls of Saksaywaman during the night. They had captured most of the city while several Incan Commanders like Paucar Huaman, along with the Inca High Priest Willaq Umu, fled two towers in the main plaza, leaving the Incan noble Titu Cusi Gualpa in command. Titu Cusi Gualpa was defeated and the city of Saksaywaman was captured by the Spaniards, which relieved the pressure of the Spaniards during the siege of Cuzco and ultimately forcing the retreat of the Incas from Cuzco. The Incas would stop fighting to observe their religious traditions during every new moon as the Spaniards continued to attack, demoralizing them. Francisco Pizarro decided to lead a direct attack on the Incan Emperor Manco Inca Yupanqui at the city of Ollantaytambo. Manco Inca Yupanqui organized an army of over 30,000 warriors from various tribes lead by their own tribal leaders called kurakas.

The Incan soldiers fought on rugged terrain and dug pits like their Mayan counterparts to hinder the potent Spanish Calvary. Francisco Pizarro led over 100 Spaniards consisting mostly of cavalrymen and relying on over 30,000 native auxiliary troops made up of the Cañaris, Chachapoyas, and Wankas tribes and nobles opposed to Manco Inca Yupanqui. Despite superior weaponry and their vast native auxiliary force, the Spaniards suffered losses at the terraces under a hail of stones and arrows while the plains were flooded with water, rendering the Spanish cavalry ineffective and forcing Francisco Pizarro's retreat towards Cuzco. Manco Inca Yupanqui attempted an attack on Cuzco, however his army was defeated in a surprise night offensive by the Spaniards and Manco Inca Yupanqui retreated into exile to the city of Willkapampa or Vilcabamba Peru. The Neo-Incan state would be ruled from Vilcabamba Peru but would not be able to defeat the Spanish power after the additional Spaniard troops led by Diego de Almagro arrived to the city of Cuzco.

Diego de Almagro was called El Viejo (or the old

man) and had lost his left eye in a battle against the natives. He took a native wife named Ana Martínez from the isthmus some called Panama and had a mestizo son named Diego de Almagro II (or El Moro, meaning "the lad"). The withdrawal from Chile was violent as Diego de Almagro ordered executions and the theft of native property and pushed natives into slavery, forcing them to carry heavy equipment as he returned to Cuzco to take the territory Francisco Pizarro had claimed for the Spanish Empire. Upon his return, Diego de Almagro imprisoned Francisco's brothers, Hernando and Gonzalo Pizarro, on the night of April eighth, 1537. Francisco ordered an attack led by Alonso de Alvarado, which failed at the battle of Battle of Abancay, on July of 1537. However, the Pizarro brothers defeated Diego de Almagro, forcing Almagro and his supporters (the Almagristas) in the battle of Las Salinas in April of 1538. Diego de Almagro was later captured and humiliated by Hernando Pizarro as his requests for an appeal to Emperor Charles V were denied. He was then executed by garrote and decapitated in July of 1538. The Viceroyalty of Peru was formed several years later in 1542 with Francisco Pizarro as the leader.

Diego de Almagro's son, Diego de Almagro II or El Mozo, swore to avenge his father and on June twenty-sixth, 1541, he and his followers managed to get into Francisco Pizarro's palace in Lima and attempt a coup d'état. In the subsequent battle, Francisco Pizarro died and Diego de Almagro II was named governor, but the populace did not accept him and he fled to Cuzco where his forces lost in the battle of Chupas when Vaca de Castro's forces killed over 200 Almagristas and executed captured supporters of El Mozo—including El Mozo himself—in September 1542. In 1542, Cristóbal Vaca de Castro became the governor. In 1544, Blasco Núñez Vela y Villalba, a Knight of the Order of Santiago, became the first Viceroy of the Viceroyalty of Peru. The Viceroyalty of New Spain and the Viceroyalty of Peru strengthened their occupation of South America, Central America, and initiated further expansion into North America. Charles the V expanded his power in Europe while maintaining his African territories such as Mazalquivir, Peñón de Vélez de la Gomera, Oran, Algiers, Bugia, Tripoli, and the Canary Islands. Charles V also moved into the Eastern Indies in the territories previously explored by Magellan.

In 1544, peace between Francis I and Charles V put a temporary end to the French and Ottoman alliance, however Suleiman the Magnificent continued his warfare with Emperor Charles V while expanding the Ottoman Empire in Northern African territories like the Barbary States of Tripolitania, Tunisia, and Algeria while maintaining control of Egypt, Somalia, Yemen, and the Islamic Holy sites of Mecca and Medina. Suleiman attempted to wrest control of Western India from the Portuguese Empire and establish a trade relationship with the second Mughal Emperor Humayun. Holy Roman Emperor Charles V continued to expand as he battled Suleiman the Magnificent and establish his power in the Americas and the islands.

Charles V maintained a strong alliance with King Henry VIII, however the king's mental stability had degraded along with his physical condition. King Henry VIII had strengthened the position of the king and the Protestant movement within England. He oversaw the unification of England and Wales with the Laws in Wales Acts in 1535 and 1542; he became the first English monarch to rule as King of Ireland after the Crown of Ireland Act in 1542. King Henry VIII's six marriages—which began with his efforts to have his first marriage to Catherine of Aragon annulled—led to a disagreement with Pope Clement VII and the start of the English Reformation. He then appointed himself as the Supreme Head of the Church of England, resulting in his excommunication. King Henry VIII's subsequent marriage to Anne Boleyn produced no male heir and she was executed and beheaded before King Henry VIII's marriage to Jane Seymour. Jane Seymour gave birth to Edward VI and died from postnatal complications at the age of twenty-eight in October of 1537. King Henry VIII's fourth marriage to Anne of Cleves was declared never consummated and annulled, which created additional friction between Henry VIII and his Chief Minister, Thomas Cromwell, the 1st Earl of Essex. Thomas Cromwell was a former ally with Anne Boleyn and had aided in her downfall as well as a proponent to King Henry VIII's marriage to the German princess Anne of Cleves. He was a prominent advocate for the English Reformation but quickly fell out of favor during the annulment of King Henry VIII and Anne of Cleves. King Henry VIII married the sixteen-year-old Catherine Howard on the twenty-eight of July 1540, at Oatlands Palace, however Catherine was beheaded several months later due to accusations of treason and adultery.

Henry VIII married his sixth and current wife, Queen Catherine Parr, in July 1543. He had grown unstable in his war and claims of French lands as well as his previous annulment of his marriage to Holy Emperor Charles V's aunt, Queen Catherine of Aragon. Thomas Cranmer was appointed Archbishop of Canterbury and had moved against his rivals, including the Roman Catholic House of Norfolk and helped promote the English Reformation and the idea of Royal Supremacy, giving the king sovereignty over the church within his realm. Henry VIII had suffered a jousting injury on his leg which became an ulcer and his weight steadily increased. He had once boasted an athletic physique, standing six-foot-one-inch with a thirty-two inch waist, thirty-nine-inch chest, and weighing about 200 pounds, but now the king had close to a sixty-inch waist and weighed over 300 pounds. Henry maintained a delicate relationship with the stronger Francis I and Charles V, however the English Reformation created additional tension between Henry VIII and Charles V. Henry defeated the Scottish army of King James V in November of 1542 and King James V died that December. King Henry VIII desired to unite England and Scotland through the marriage of his son Edward and Mary I Queen of Scotts, but war continued between England and Scotland. He also improved the English Navy and fortified the south and southeastern English Coastline. Holy Roman

Emperor Charles V was informed of King Henry VIII and his failing health. At the age of fifty-three, King Henry was covered in foul smelling boils and his mental capabilities were rapidly declining, although he had strengthened his military England remained weaker than the Charles V's Holy Roman Empire.

Charles V had initiated the exploration and conquest of North America, building upon earlier voyages into Baja California by Francisco de Ulloa. In 1542, Juan Rodríguez Cabrillo left Navidad in New Spain and explored the greater northern California regions, naming several areas and stopping in a region he called Bahia de los Pinos. Juan Rodriguez Cabrillo later died on the third of January 1543 after suffering from gangrene after falling into the rocks and splintering his shin in San Salvador as he attempted to defend his men from Tongva warriors.

The Spanish Empire increased in strength after the death of King Francis I of France in 1547 and during the reign of his son King Henry II as France suffered from internal turmoil between the Catholics and Protestants. King Henry VIII died in 1547, leaving England under the rule of Edward VI. Holy Roman Emperor Charles V strengthened Santo Domingo and his dominion over the island of Hispaniola while the islands of the south remained unconquered. Radamés Cesar Milfuegos had sold the few sugarcane fields he had and he used the gold he had managed to acquire, to get other Spaniards from the lower class to fund a small expedition towards the smaller islands southeast of Hispaniola. In his effort to finally find some respect and obtain new lands for his son Maximo, he had convinced over 150 other Spaniards to join him in his efforts. Radamés Cesar Milfuegos also believed he could find Amanex, the man he had grown to hate more than any other, and kill him, his family, and destroy his community. The Spanish Empire was the empire on which the sun never set and Radamés Cesar Milfuegos planned to bring that empire upon Amanex.

CHAPTER 24
A VENGEANCE IN ANTIGUA (1546)

Amanex advised his eldest son Simon Pedro Haübey about the coming danger of Radamés Cesar Milfuegos. At the age of sixty-one, Amanex only desired peace for himself and his family. With his ability to fight steadily decreasing, he believed this would be the last opportunity to confront and kill Radamés and his followers. For several months, Taino scouts had informed Amanex that Radamés had gathered a crew and had acquired a ship for the purposes of exploiting the smaller islands in the southeast of Hispaniola. After several years, hundreds of African slaves had escaped to the smaller islands and joined the Taino and Kalinago people. Amanex, who had some initial trouble with the Kalinago, had found unity with them against the common Spanish enemy. Intermarriage between Amanex's community and the Kalinago also helped to strengthen this new alliance into a larger community which blended the cultures between natives and Africans. Amanex's community in the island of Saint Vincent had grown to over a thousand people with hundreds of warriors willing to fight any Spanish incursion.

He had been informed of events occurring on the island of Hispaniola, including the death of Cacique Enriquillo and other caciques who had resisted Spanish rule like Cacique Tamayo. Amanex learned that African leaders who fought alongside Cacique Enriquillo, who subsequently joined Cacique Tamayo, also perished in battle. This also included the brave Onyekachi. Amanex had learned about the destruction of Cacique Enriquillo's community in Azua and the horrors committed by the Spaniards, particularly Radamés Cesar Milfuegos. He feared that if Radamés was to successfully conquer any of the smaller islands, it would encourage other Spaniards to shift their focus away from the mainland and into establishing permanent colonies on all the islands. Amanex was also informed that many of his friends had perished either in wars against the Spaniards or within the settlements in Hispaniola. Guaikán, the Taino adopted son of Cristóbal Colón who was called Diego, had passed away several years prior. Guaikán had fallen out of favor with many of the Spaniards over accusations of wrongdoing, including an involvement with the death of a Spaniard named Manasa many years before. Amanex doubted the accusations against Guaikán and the insufficient evidence against him however, Guaikán's high place within Spanish Catholic society sheltered him from most of the dangers that befell the average Taino.

Amanex called for a meeting between the elders of the Tainos, Kalinago, and African tribes to discuss possible offensive and defensive battle strategies against the incoming Spanish. He now wielded a high level of authority over the Taino groups after the death of prominent caciques among the islands of Cuba, San Juan Bautista, and Jamaica. Some began regarding Amanex as an informal cacique despite the fact he had no royal blood. However, he learned strategy from observing Spanish as well as Taino warfare.

Elombe Masombo had also risen in status among his fellow Kikongo Africans and held a high level of respect and leadership. His daughter Malundama Masombo married Amanex's eldest son Simon Pedro Haübey upon their arrival to Saint Vincent, cementing Amanex and Elombe's friendship. Malundama was now showing signs of pregnancy and Amanex and Tayamari were overjoyed with excitement although it was tempered by the looming threat of invasion. As Simon Pedro approached the age of twenty-seven and Malundama Masombo became twenty-three years of age, they expected their first child. Simon Pedro was advised to remain in Saint Vincent as his father prepared for a possible confrontation with the Spanish forces led by Radamés Cesar Milfuegos. Amanex asked Simon Pedro to protect his brother Adán Hatüey, his mother, and his wife despite Simon Pedro's request to lead his own force against the Spaniards. Amanex believed he could defeat the Spanish forces, however there was a strong chance he might perish in the encounter and he did not wish the same fate for his children.

As the month of March came to an end, Taino scouts had informed Amanex that the Spaniards led by Radamés had a galleon ship on the southeastern coast of San Juan Bautista with a possible smaller second ship. Amanex and Elombe called a final meeting to discuss a larger offensive. He believed the second ship was not part of the expedition, but he began planning a war strategy where both ships engaged the native and African alliance. Amanex called for the Kalinago people to request aid from other Kalinago leaders throughout the islands and African maroons to supply additional weapons and warriors. He believed Radamés had largely funded his expedition largely from his life earnings in a desperate attempt to attain a higher class in Spanish society and perhaps obtain retribution. Amanex understood that a swift victory against Radamés would not bring other Spaniards to retaliate against him, since Radamés had numerous enemies among the Spaniards. At the beginning of April, Amanex had received responses from native leaders of the surrounding islands that they would join him in his fight as he demanded more canoes to be built to transport his alliance north. Amanex planned a major offensive during Holy Week, as he believed the Spaniards might possibly halt their advance in observance of the holiday. He called for warriors to guard the island of St. Vincent, leaving some warriors behind—including Mamadou Dieng to guard the island and recruit more Kalinago in hopes of defending St. Vincent and Saint Lucia against a possible invasion. Mamadou Dieng desired to join the forces of Amanex and Elombe, however Amanex successfully convinced him to concentrate his efforts towards a defense of St. Vincent.

Amanex and Elombe led their warriors north, increasing their numbers as they landed on successive islands approaching the incoming galleon now sailing past the island of Bieke. Radamés Cesar Milfuegos had landed on the island the natives called Malliouhana and the Spaniards called Anguila due to its eel shape. Radamés had spent nearly all his lifetime wealth to fund his expedition towards the smaller islands of the southeast. Radamés believed his expedition would give him lands, riches, and titles which would lift his class in Spanish society and give his son territories which could elevate his family name. Radamés had outlived most of his Spanish enemies despite his lower status and questionable heritage and he would express his frustrations in unbridled brutality on the native islanders he initially encountered in Anguila. Radamés brought several Taino and Kalinago slaves as translators that he used when he encountered the people of Anguila. For several days, he demanded to find gold and began killing the natives, allowing his men to rape the women and children until he was confronted by hundreds of islanders. Radamés ordered the Spaniards to fire into the advancing native warriors, killing many and forcing them to retreat in fear as the Spaniards shot many of them in the back. He subsequently advised that they should sail southward towards the island named Liamuiga (meaning "fertile lane" and now renamed Sant Yago), which was two miles north of the island named Oualie (meaning "land of beautiful waters" and renamed San Martin).

Amanex had sailed north past the islands of St. Lucia, Martinique, and landed in Dominica where he received information of the massacre which had occurred on the island of Anguila. He had now increased his forces to over 300 warriors led by Elombe, himself, and a Kalinago leader from the small island of Dominica named

Maruko. Maruko had been elected to lead his people in the offensive against the Spaniards by Kalinago chiefs and elders and he agreed to do so on the island of Sant Yago. He would launch from the island San Martin while Amanex and Elombe would bring a second wave of attack that would drive the Spaniards out. Maruko witnessed as the people of Sant Yago flee south towards his position in San Martin. Radamés and his son Maximo had brought their brutality against the natives to two consecutive islands and just as Amanex predicated, the Spaniards were overconfident as they settled in Sant Yago to celebrate their Semana Santa (or Holy Week).

Amanex had learned much about the Catholic Religion and understood the importance of the month of Lent which began on Ash Wednesday and ended roughly six weeks later on Easter. He knew the purpose of Lent was to prepare the believer through goodwill, discipline, rejection of materialism, penance, intensive prayer, some would fast, repentance of sins, and other acts meant to draw them closer to God. Lent, according to the Gospels of Matthew, Mark, and Luke, was when Jesus Christ endured forty days and nights of fasting in the Judean desert where he was tempted by Satan.

Satan appeared and observing Jesus' hunger, asked him to turn stones into bread, to which Jesus replied, "One does not live by bread alone, but by every word that proceeds from the mouth of God.'"

Satan asked Jesus to jump from a pinnacle and rely on God's Angels to save him, and Jesus replied, "'You shall not put the Lord, your God, to the test."

Finally, Satan brought Jesus to a high mountain where all the kingdoms of the earth could be seen, promising that all would belong to Jesus if he worshipped him. Jesus replied, "The Lord, your God, shall you worship and him alone shall you serve."

Amanex had explained the story of Jesus and Satan to his people as he called the Spaniards hypocrites for their brutality, greed, materialism, lust, and disrespect for their own God. Perhaps their defeat in battle would offer proper punishment for their hypocrisy.

As Holy Week began on Palm Sunday, the Spaniards feasted and celebrated their recent conquests. Radamés Cesar Milfuegos was now a sixty-four-year old man who had outlived many of his Spanish enemies and now believed that he would gain the lands, riches, and titles he deserved for himself and his twenty-four year old son Maximo. His abuse towards his own wife Paulina had led her to the arms of other Spaniards according to several rumors circulating in Santo Domingo, which only increased his determination to search for wealth and power. Radamés drank wine along with other Spaniards while a small group kept watch, however as the night progressed, in their confidence the Spaniards became careless.

Radamés exclaimed to his son Maximo, "Perhaps I should have been given a title and commissioned by the Viceroy of New Spain Antonio de Mendoza y Pacheco to conquer these islands for myself. Perhaps I should have been given an opportunity by the governors of the West Indies to lead men as I am leading them now. Conquest has been difficult but I have always executed the demands of my superiors and never have I benefitted from the spoils. Now I have shown how easy it is to conquer the feared Kalinago and take these neglected islands for myself. If I cannot have a piece of the American mainland, I will carve out my own lands in these islands and you will carry my name to glory."

Maximo, who always felt somewhat disappointed with his father, began to believe in his vision and his own greed began to increase.

As the celebration raged through the night, the Spaniards were unware that Maruko and over 100 warriors were now planning an attack. Maruko was advised to wait the additional forces by Amanex but feared he would be discovered by the Spaniards before Amanex's arrival, leading him to launch the attack on the night of Palm Sunday. Palm Sunday celebrated the triumphant entry from the Mount of Olives to Jerusalem of Jesus Christ after he raised Lazarus from the dead as well as the beginning of his

Passion and the last moments of his life on earth. Through translators, Maruko was informed by Amanex and the other Tainos about the beliefs and customs of the Spaniards. He thought an early attack would symbolize the arrival of Jesus and the Spaniards would realize the irony of their own actions as different from their own beliefs—as men who now worshipped gold and brutality and caused their own defeats and deaths. Many large dugout canoes carried the Kalinago army, who awaited their leader Maruko. Maruko encountered the Spanish galleon docked near the beach and did not see a second one, which reassured him about his decision for an early offensive. Maruko gathered archers with arrows poisoned by the manchineel tree near the large Spanish camp while sending twenty warriors close to the shoreline in case of a Spanish retreat. As clouds obscured the light of the moon and stars, Maruko signaled to his archers to fire into the main section of the Spanish camp.

Poisoned arrows ripped through the flesh of the Spaniards as they ate and drank wine. The Spaniards stumbled to find their armor as arrows continued to rain on them. Some reached for their arquebuses and began firing blindly into the darkness. Maruko screamed for his men to charge the camp before they could put on their armor, forcing the Spaniards into a tactical retreat into a position near the beach where they lined up in three long rows and began firing at the advancing Kalinago, killing many. Maruko ordered his reserve Kalinago units to attack from the rear of the Spanish lines, disrupting the Spanish offensive and forcing Radamés and his son to retreat into their galleon as their troops killed the remaining reserve Kalinago units and retreated into the galleon as well. Over fifty Spaniards and nearly all the Kalinago were killed. Radamés ordered the captain to open and aim the galleon's cannons on the retreating Kalinago in a fearsome show of power. Maruko and fifteen other Kalinago fled the island south towards St. Martin to gather additional warriors and await Amanex's Taino and Kalinago coalition.

As the sun began to rise, Radamés and his son

sailed southbound towards the island firing his canons towards the shoreline of Saint Martin to strike fear into the native resistance which had killed over fifty of his men. Maximo advised his father to request help from the other Spanish galleon near the southeastern coastline of San Juan Bautista, however Radamés desired the glory of conquest for himself. Amanex and Elombe had gathered their Kalinago and African forces, which had grown to over 200 warriors, on the island of Antigua as they began preparations to sail westward. Some of the Kalinago fled eastward to warn Amanex while Maruko decided to stay and draw the Spaniards out into the island of St. Martin. As Monday came to an end, Radamés advised a raid into St. Martin on Tuesday morning, leaving his son Maximo along with twenty other Spaniards guarding the galleon.

As the sun began to rise, Radamés and over eighty Spaniards travelled inland into the island of St. Martin. Many of the Spaniards believed the Kalinago had fled possibly with the aid of Tainos towards Antigua or Montserrat. The galleon circled the island of St. Martin as Radamés and the Spaniards marched eastward. After travelling for most of the day, Radamés and the other Spaniards completed the trip. As they stepped on the eastern side of the island, Radamés encountered the leader of the Kalinago named Maruko and his remaining forces, and he ordered his men to fire on him. Maruko, unwilling to retreat and to stall the enemy, charged forward, disabling some of the Spaniards and breaking through their lines to reach Radamés and his son. The armor of the Spaniards blunted the Kalinago and Taino attack and although Maruko could reach Radamés, he was finally cut down by his son Maximo. Celebrations erupted among the Spaniards as they extinguished resistance in St. Martin and found evidence of Taino and Kalinago escape eastward towards the island of Antigua. Radamés swore to not repeat the mistake he made at St. Yago, choosing to move forward on Holy Wednesday towards Antigua. Full of confidence, he believed he could successfully conquer more islands before returning to Santo Domingo to ask for reinforcements.

Radamés had captured some Tainos who he questioned about Amanex and believed his adversary was on a nearby island. He desired to capture and make an example of him and with added motivation, he reorganized his efforts towards Antigua on Holy Wednesday.

Amanex sent a message to his son Simon, who was now on the island of Guadeloupe, about the battle situation and the impending Spanish attack on his allied position in Antigua. Amanex was informed regarding the number of Spaniards and believed his coalition and Spanish weaponry his warriors had gathered throughout the years would stun the Spaniards and overwhelm them. Amanex warned his son not to engage unless he and Elombe decided upon a retreat and advised him to recruit more warriors to increase his numbers. Simon Pedro followed his father's instructions to gather more warriors committed to fight the impending Spanish attack on his father's forces in Antigua. Simon Pedro Haübey began to think of his mother Tayamari and her cries for him and his father to stay on the island of St. Vincent. He began to think about his beautiful wife Malundama Masombo and their unborn child. Simon Pedro yearned to be back with his family, however he loved and respected his father and was determined to find a way to help him in battle.

As the morning of Holy Wednesday began, Radamés Cesar Milfuegos approached Antigua. Holy Wednesday told the story of the Jewish Judges called the Sanhedrin that plotted the death of Jesus Christ who was in the house of Simon the Leper. As they sat at the supper table, a woman named Mary anointed Jesus' head and feet with expensive spikenard oil, which caused disciples to question Mary for not selling it. One of the twelve disciples named Judas Iscariot plotted against Jesus and subsequently met with the Judges to negotiate a deal. This would be the day the Spaniards would confront Amanex and his allied force and Amanex could have his revenge. The Spanish galleon finally appeared with its three masts and sails over ninety feet in length. Radamés made sure to keep the ship's cannons pointed toward the shoreline as he and eighty other Spaniards began to explore inland. The rest of the Spaniards and Maximo would remain near the galleon. Amanex positioned over fifty Kalinago archers on the treetops within two miles inland from the beach and sent Taino warriors within eyesight of the Spaniards to pull them in. Amanex and Elombe separated into two units armed with arquebuses and Spanish swords; Amanex led 100 men to the left and Elombe led over fifty men on the right in front of the Kalinago archers to box the Spaniards in.

The Spaniards were led inland by Radamés and a twenty-man cavalry and sixty men on foot right into a hail of poison arrows. The fully armored Spaniards were better equipped to handle the initial assault; however, some were pierced with arrows and fell sick and weakened, unable to fight. The Spaniards began to fire upon upward into the trees, killing many of the Kalinago who began to climb down and begin a full-frontal assault. Initially the Kalinago could push the Spanish line backwards, but Radamés organized his lines into four rows ready to fire upon the Kalinago. The lead Spanish line retreated, leaving the secondary line with clear sight as they began firing. Amanex and Elombe ordered their respective forces to fire upon the rear lines of the Spaniards in a devastating hail of violence. The Spaniards were alarmed and the cavalry was cut in half as Radamés ordered a tactical retreat towards his galleon. Maximo Milfuegos and the reserve Spanish units fired upon the native and African alliance as they chased Radamés and the retreating Spaniards. In the confusion of battle, Amanex demanded a retreat inland away from the Spanish galleon's cannons to no avail. Radamés managed to get aboard his ship with less than fifty men and ordered the cannons to open fire, killing most of Amanex's warriors.

Through the heat of the battle, Radamés now realized Amanex was the leader of the alliance and shouted, "The Taino savage known by his Spanish name Abrahán and better known as Amanex is here in the island of Antigua and I want his head!"

As night approached, Radamés was advised by Maximo to seek help from other Spaniards on the island of San Juan Bautista or await any Spanish galleon which might pass through the area for additional support. Radamés feared Amanex's escape and believed if he did not complete his victory he and the Spaniards would lose an opportunity to conquer the smaller southeastern islands. The expedition would continue the following day on Holy Thursday with the purpose of capturing, executing, and putting an end to Amanex's offensive. Amanex's forces received most of the damage and Amanex and Elombe were now leading thirty-five warriors against sixty-two Spaniards led by Radamés and twenty Spaniards aboard the Spanish galleon which included Maximo Milfuegos. Elombe argued that they should await the reserve forces led by his Amanex's son, however Amanex did not want him to face a superior force and desired to engage the Spaniards to weaken them before his son's arrival. As the sun rose to the highest point, the unbearable heat tired the Spaniards as Amanex and Elombe awaited them within the Antiguan forest. Amanex wanted to engage the Spaniards in close combat to limit the effectives of their arquebuses, choosing to hold fire until they were within roughly fifty feet.

Holy Thursday (also called Maundy Thursday) celebrated the Last Supper of Jesus Christ and his twelve disciples. It was where Jesus identified the son of Simon Iscariot, the disciple Judas Iscariot, as the man who would betray him. Judas later betrayed Jesus for forty silver coins because Satan had entered his body—the same Satan Amanex believed had entered the spirit of Radamés and the Spaniards who were filled with greed, lust, and the search for power. For the first time, Amanex was within 100 feet of Radamés and he along with ten other Tainos and Africans separated from Elombe to pin him down. Elombe ordered his warriors to fire upon the Spanish as Amanex discharged his weapon upon Radamés, who fell from his horse. The Spaniards were struck by the fire of the arquebuses as they desperately returned gunfire. Elombe engaged the Spaniards in close combat and Amanex charged upon Radamés as he reached for his sword. The bloody battle continued as Amanex cut through the Spaniards, killing two men before reaching Radamés. Their swords clashed, both men seething with hatred for one another. Amanex and the Tainos were now defeating the remaining Spanish cavalry, but Elombe was fighting a losing battle and he retreated to reach Amanex.

The Spaniards were now attempting to push the Africans and natives into the galleon's cannon range. Maximo and five others cautiously observed the fighting, deciding whether to bring the rest of the Spaniards into battle. With most of the crew's attention inland as they stepped off the large galleon, they were unaware of over fifty Africans and Tainos approaching by canoe from the island of Montserrat led by Simon Pedro Haübey. Just as Spanish victory was close, Simon Pedro landed on the island of Antigua, attacking the Spaniards as Maximo retreated and boarded the galleon. Simon Pedro and his men boarded the galleon as well, disabling the Spaniard's last line of defense and capturing four of them as Maximo and several others escaped into the island in a desperate attempt to reach Radamés. As the Spaniards advanced towards Amanex's position, Radamés and Amanex continued their fight.

Radamés struck Amanex with a glancing blow on his right thigh as he exclaimed, "Your family has brought pain and anger into my life. I have done much to subdue the savage races of the Indio and African and their mixes. These lands are for us the Spaniards not for the Indio, the African, or any of the mixes created from the Spaniards and savages!"

Amanex angrily replied, "You are the savage! A people who only have brought strife, disease and greed to our peaceful way of life. You are hypocrites in the views of your own God which you claim to follow, and I will live to see your death. My desire is to see the rule of those Spaniards that are vile come to an end. You are called El Moro, a man not even considered a Spaniard as you are considered a moor, yet you speak as if you are better than us. Your own people have never accepted you and all your life you have searched that by treating the Africans and natives as below you. It may be an act of the gods that you have been denied the ability to father any more children."

Radamés' was overcome with rage as he attempted to kill Amanex, disregarding his original plan to imprison him. Amanex evaded his strike and got to his feet as the Spaniards approached his position. Amanex thought of his wife and children, believing death was certain as attempted to kill Radamés.

As the Spaniards approached, Radamés laughed. "Your death is near, savage! I will enjoy the destruction of your family and community."

Suddenly, Elombe along with the retreating natives and Africans reached Amanex in a last attempt to overcome possible defeat. This allowed Amanex to disable Radamés and overpower him, slicing off his hand and striking his leg.

Elombe shouted, "Strike that animal down and complete your revenge!"

Amanex exclaimed, "The Spaniards may win the day but this is the last day Radamés will ever see." He thrust his sword into Radamés' chest as he struggled to reach his weapon. The remaining Spanish forces were rapidly approaching Elombe and Amanex's position and they were informed that Simon Pedro had arrived. Radamés, Elombe, and the remaining fifteen Africans and Tainos retreated towards the galleon.

The Spaniards laughed, believing Amanex and his alliance would face Spanish cannon fire and certain death. They hit Elombe and he fell from his horse, however as the Spaniards rapidly approached Amanex and the beach, Amanex sharply turned away from the galleons cannons, leaving the Spaniards open to cannon fire under the control of Simon Pedro Haübey and the native African alliance. The Spaniards ran in fear as they were killed by their own galleon with the remaining few shocked at the rapid turn of events. Few Spaniards escaped into the forest along with Maximo Milfuegos, prompting Amanex to order a search of the island and execution of any Spaniards before the possible arrival of another Spanish ship. As the sun began to set on Holy Thursday, Amanex's worst fears came to fruition with another smaller Spanish ship approaching from the island of Barbuda. Amanex ordered his son to take control of the galleon and stop any Spanish escape from the island of Antigua.

Maximo and several other Spaniards raced on horseback towards the arriving galleon named Concepción, leaving the others behind to be cut down by Amanex's forces. The captain of Concepción, Samuel Guerrero, was surprised to see the desperate Spaniards fleeing and desperately asking to board. He was also shocked to see Maximo Milfuegos drenched in blood along with four others defeated by the natives and Africans. They were informed that the rapidly approaching Spanish galleon La Redención was now controlled by Africans and natives. Maximo demanded Samuel Guerrero to engage the much larger and powerful Redención, believing the Tainos and Africans were incapable of naval warfare as La Redención finally lived up to its namesake as The Redemption.

Maximo exclaimed, "My father is still in Antigua. We need to destroy their ship and find my father and the others."

Samuel Guerrero's ship took heavy bombardment as it attempted to maneuver its cannons towards The Redemption. Samuel Guerrero opened fire on The Redemption as Simon Pedro maneuvered the ship away aided by their Spanish captives who feared for their lives.

Amanex approached Radamés as he lay dying on the ground, witnessing the naval battle from a small hill near the coastline. Amanex observed his stolen necklace around Radamés' neck and he struck him until he relinquished the precious item. Amanex took a poisoned manchineel arrow and pierced Radamés' mouth and lower regions and he writhed in pain from the injuries and poison rapidly circulating through his body.

Amanex said, "You are now suffering just a fraction of what you have personally caused to hundreds of

Africans and my own people! You are below your peers and any other man no matter if he is African, Spaniard, Asian, or native and thus you suffer a death not fit for any respectable man."

As night fell, the sounds and lights from the large explosions during the naval battle continued. Both ships were on fire, but the smaller Concepción took massive damage as it sailed northwest, escaping certain destruction. Radamés Cesar Milfuegos lay in his own human waste, quietly pondering the fate of his son and asking for death. Amanex, who was not as cruel despite a life of cruelty placed upon him and his family, took his sword and plunged it into the heart of Radamés Cesar Milfuegos, finally bringing his reign of terror to an end as he whispered, "Happy Good Friday."

The Redemption returned battered but victorious and the remaining Spaniards were quickly executed after Simon Pedro gathered intelligence from his prisoners. Amanex returned and sat next to the dying Elombe, whispering, "We are now free, my friend. Rest easy, for your family and my family are one and I will always take care of them. I will speak of your name and our great friendship so our descendants will tell our story and through them we will always live."

Elombe smiled as his life escaped from his body, which brought great pain to Amanex even as the natives and Africans celebrated their victory. Simon Pedro Haübey was reunited with his father as they gathered Spanish weaponry from The Redemption as it continued to burn through the night.

Tears rolled down Amanex's face as he held his, son proudly stating, "You have sown an honor and bravery to the levels I never have exhibited. Never have I been so proud of you than at this moment. Amanex prepared to leave the island of Antigua the following day on the morning of Good Friday as The Redemption sunk under the sea.

The Concepción limped back towards San Juan Bautista, barely making the trip as Maximo continued to request a return to Antigua to avenge his father. However, Samuel Guerrero and the other Spaniards who never liked Radamés Cesar Milfuegos and his small band of degenerate followers did not care enough to return and face the feared Kalinago resistance. Samuel Guerrero was secretly sent to tail Radamés against his own will as the Spaniards did not trust him, however they desired to capitalize on the small possibility that Radamés Cesar Milfuegos was successful. Radamés failed in his expedition and his family name sank with him along with the status of his son Maximo Milfuegos, who seethed in anger in San Juan Bautista. Maximo was now penniless with his father's savings and dreams beneath the Caribbean Sea.

Good Friday was the day commemorating Jesus Christ's crucifixion after Peter denied him three times as he predicted during his trial. The Roman Governor Pontius Pilate deemed there was no basis to sentence Jesus despite the accusations of the Jewish High Priests and King Herod. Pontius Pilate washed his hands, declaring Jesus innocent, however he handed Jesus over for crucifixion to avoid a riot. Amanex told the story of Jesus and how even in death he stated to his father, "Forgive them, for they know not what they do." They conversed about the Spaniards—their culture and defeat—as night fell and Saturday approached. They decided to rest on the island of Dominica, where Amanex spoke about the death of the valiant Kalinago leader Maruko. Amanex spent the Holy Saturday or the Great Sabbath with the Kalinago people. He enjoyed his time on the beautiful island as he prepared for his arrival to Saint Vincent.

Easter Sunday arrived and the Kalinago, Africans, and Tainos celebrated their victory. Amanex understood the Spaniards' tactics of divide and conquer throughout the Americas and was proud that through his, Elombe's, and Maruko's leadership they could see beyond their small differences and realize they shared more in common—especially against the enemy. It was a hard-fought battle that saw the end of Spanish expansion into the eastern islands— at least temporarily—and a strengthening between the communities. Amanex finally landed on St. Vincent, where his community eagerly awaited the details of the battle. The body of Elombe was carried out, adding to the sorrow regarding of all those who nobly perished in their battle against the Spaniards. Tayamari was overjoyed to see her husband return injured but alive and her son Simon Pedro Haübey honored with a hero's welcome while at the same time, she was melancholic over the passing of the brave and well respected Elombe. Mamadou Dieng was left by Amanex along with his son Adán Hatüey and others, including Arjana Dieng, to defend the island of St. Vincent if the Spaniards were victorious. Mamadou approached Amanex with feelings of happiness for the victorious alliance and dejection for Elombe, who he had respected as an uncle. Mamadou, his sister, and the community joined in mourning for the death of Elombe and the success of Amanex.

Elombe's mistress Magdalena was inconsolable as they arranged Elombe's funeral. Elombe's daughter Malundama cried over the death of her father as her husband Simon Pedro Haübey consoled her as best as he could. Amanex spoke to his people after the funeral about his life and Elombe's and how he had grown to respect his culture and beliefs. Amanex thought just as Jesus had died and rose on the third day, now through bloodshed, freedom was reawakened.

As the months passed, Amanex' community grew stronger through intermarriage. He and Elombe's family also solidified with the marriage between Simon Pedro and Malundama and the birth of their son Matondo Enrique Haübey. Amanex and Tayamari celebrated the birth of his first grandson Matondo and Adán Hatüey celebrated the birth of his first nephew. Despite being surrounded by death, Amanex and his family found joy in a new life born into freedom—a freedom that was precious and delicate in the age of Spanish Empire. Amanex enjoyed greater respect among the Africans, Kalinago, and Tainos who sometimes referred to him as cacique. He was voted as an official leader of his community within St. Vincent and would sit among the Kalinago and African leaders to discuss the affairs of the island. As the years passed, Amanex realized he had finally achieved peace and freedom, although he sometimes pondered the dangers of a possible retaliation by Radamés Cesar Milfuegos' son Maximo Milfuegos. Tayamari would calm his fears, yet Amanex nevertheless sought to prepare his community for possible attacks from the Spaniards, French, or other Europeans now arriving in the Americas.

CHAPTER 25
RISE OF THE LATINO IN THE AMERICAS (1550)

Scouts kept Amanex informed regarding the changing world of the Americas as well as the transformations of economics and culture of the region. The place the Spaniards had often regarded as the New World was always the one Amanex understood, however a new people were rising throughout the islands and the Americas, incorporating different backgrounds through their cultures and backgrounds. Amerigo Vespucci and his explorations influenced the naming of the New World as America. America was used frequently to refer to the lands of South America since the early 1500s, and later became the name for the landmasses of the north as well. The Spanish Empire continued their expansion throughout the Americas as the social dynamics changed.

The armies of New Spain were victorious in the Tiguex Wars led by Conquistador Francisco Vázquez de Coronado against the thirteen pueblos of Tiwa natives as well as other Puebloan tribes in 1541. The Spaniards also engaged in the Mixtón War fought between them and the Caxcanes and their native allies, including the Zacatecos, from 1540 to 1542. Initial contact with the Caxcanes occurred in 1529 when Nuño Beltrán de Guzmán set forth from the capital of New Spain with over 300 Spaniards and more than 6,000 Azteca and Tlaxcalan allies as the

Spaniards attempted to put the Encomienda system in place. Guzmán followed policies of unprovoked killing, torture, and enslavement as he founded several cities such as Nueva Galicia and Guadalajara. The Caxcanes were led by a brave and charismatic leader named Francisco Tenamaztle who mounted a strong native alliance against the Spaniards. This led to the Viceroy of New Spain, Antonio de Mendoza, to call on the brutal conquistador Pedro de Alvarado. Pedro de Alvarado had participated in the conquest of Cuba, was involved in the Juan de Grijalva's exploration of the coasts of the Yucatán Peninsula and the gulf, and in the conquest of the Aztec Empire under the leadership of Hernán Cortés. Pedro de Alvarado would participate in the subjugation of most or Central America, including Guatemala, Honduras, and El Salvador, which led him to become governor of Guatemala and Honduras. Pedro de Alvarado planned a westward expedition to China governed by Emperor Jiajing of the Ming dynasty and the Spice Islands. He was to organize an armada of thirteen ships and approximately 550 men for the expedition set for 1541, however he received a letter from Cristóbal de Oñate, who had been besieged at Nochistlán by native forces led by Nueva Galicia. Pedro de Alvarado was later crushed by a spooked horse and died days later on July fourth, 1541. He did not produce any children with his two legal wives, Francisca de la Cueva—who died shortly upon her arrival to the Americas—and to his first wife's sister, Beatriz de la Cueva—who would become Governor of Guatemala after Pedro de Alvarado's death. However, Pedro de Alvarado had children with a native Nahua noblewoman named Luisa de Tlaxcala, daughter of the Tlaxcallan Chief Xicotencatl the Elder, which produced three children named Pedro de Alvarado, El Mestizo Diego de Alvarado, and a daughter named Leonor de Alvarado y Xicotenga Tecubalsi, who was married twice to two Spaniards.

The death of Pedro de Alvarado called Tonatiuh (or the Sun) further encouraged the Mixtón leader Francisco Tenamaztle and his army of over 15,000 warriors to attack the city of Guadalajara. Viceroy Antonio de Mendoza organized a force of over 450 Spaniards and well over 40,000 thousand Aztec, Tlaxcalan, and other natives and invaded Caxcan territory and later defeating the Caxcanes in 1542 and ending the Mixtón War. The Caxcanes and their native allies were killed, tortured, and torn to pieces by Spanish war dogs and the remaining natives were absorbed into New Spain as slaves or members of the native auxiliary forces. Leading guerrilla campaigns against New Spain, Francisco Tenamaztle escaped until 1550, when he was captured and sent to Spain to the court of Holy Roman Emperor Charles V. New Spain had suffered many setbacks from the native groups as well as the violent weather of the Caribbean. In 1553, a hurricane sank three large vessels filled with Aztec gold and other precious metals while the remaining seventeen ships suffered massive damage, resulting in over 1,700 people dead while the remaining 300 Spaniards were forced to fight a losing battle against the Karankawa or Comanches people—three Spanish survivors were all that was left. Nevertheless, the Spanish armies continued a successful campaign against the native people.

Francisco Tenamaztle was imprisoned in Valladolid Spain and would later reside in a Dominican Monastery and would be defended during his trial in 1555 by Bartolome de las Casas as they presented his case in from of Emperor Charles V and the Council of the Indies. Francisco Tenamaztle and Bartolome de las Casas argued that Francisco was the rightful leader (or Tlatoani) of his people and that the brutality of the Spaniards—particularly Nuño de Guzman, Cristóbal de Oñate, and Miguel de Ibarra—led him to the just war of the Caxcanes people against the violence and exploitation. Francisco Tenamaztle also requested to be reunited with his wife and children, but he would be refused and denied justice before he later died in Spain.

The Spaniards had continuing conflicts with the Yaqui people and had now initiated a war against the Chichimeca Confederacy located in a desert region in an area of over 60,000 square miles north of Guadalajara, which included the states of Guachichiles, Zacatecos, Tepecanos, Caxcanes, Pames, Otomis, Guamares, and Tecuexes and boasted over 50,000 warriors. The Spanish outpost of San Miguel de Allende was attacked, resulting in fourteen deaths and later another raid on Tlaltenango resulted in the death of over 120 natives friendly to the Spaniards along with some Spanish deaths. As the war progressed, the Spaniards began a policy of Fuego y Sangre, meaning "fire and death", promising torture, enslavement, and large-scale massacres of the Chichimeca people. As the Spanish expanded in North America, they also spread throughout Central and South America.

The Viceroyalty of Peru was now led by Antonio de Mendoza, Marquis of Mondéjar and Count of Tendilla, after the deposition of Viceroy Pedro de la Gasca in 1550. Antonio de Mendoza had served as the Viceroy of New Spain before serving as Viceroy of Peru and had amassed a sizeable army after his initial arrival in Panama in 1546. Gonzalo Pizarro, brother of Francisco Pizarro, had killed the first Viceroy of Peru Blasco Núñez Vela in battle in 1546, however Pedro de la Gasca could diplomatically win the support of the Spaniards and repealed the New Laws, which won him support from the Spanish landholding class. Most of the Spanish officers joined Pedro de la Gasca during the battle of Jaquijahuana with the notable exception of Francisco de Carvajal, infamously known as the Demon of the Andes. Viceroy Pedro de la Gasca would subsequently surrender his power to the Audencia in 1549 and leave Peru for Spain in 1550 when he was made bishop of Palencia by Emperor Charles V. He soon fell ill and died in 1552 and Viceroy Melchor Bravo de Saravia, Dean of the Audiencia, became Viceroy of Peru.

In 1547, Melchor Bravo de Saravia y Sotomayor was named to the Audiencia of Granada and the President of the Audencia of Lima as well as interim Viceroy of Peru. Melchor Braco de Saravia defeated a rebellion led by Francisco Hernández Girón, imprisoning and later executing him on December seventh of 1554. Melchor

Bravo de Saravia later was succeeded by Viceroy Andrés Hurtado de Mendoza, third Marquis of Cañete in 1556. Numerous battles continued to be waged south of the Viceroyalty of Peru in the general captaincy of Chile which had previously been established in 1541. The Battle of Tucapel in Chile—between the Spaniards led by Pedro de Valdivia and the Mapuche natives led by warrior chiefs Toqui Caupolicán and vice Toqui Lautaro— began after the conquistador and first Royal Governor of Chile, Pedro de Valdivia, marched to Quilacoya. There, he gathered his forces of over fifty-five Spanish soldiers and over 4,000 yanakuna natives against the allied Mapuche forces of over 10,000, clashing in the territory of Arauco.

Pedro de Valdivia quickly built forts such as the fort of San Felipe de Rauco (or de Araucan), however the Spaniards faced trouble when the forces of Gómez de Almagro were cornered near fort Purén due to Mapuche war strategy. The Spaniards repelled an initial attack, but Spanish Caballeros were dragged from their horses and killed and a third Mapuche led by Toqui Lautaro defeated the allied Spanish forces. This culminated in the deaths of nearly all of the over 10,000 allied yanakuna forces and all the Spaniards, including the capture and death of Pedro Valdivia. He attempted to compromise with Toqui Lautaro, promising the return of Mapuche lands, but Mapuche natives did not trust the Spaniards and Viceroy Pedro Valdivia was clubbed by a Mapuche warrior named Pilmaiquen. The Spanish succession was now in conflict between three Spaniards named Francisco de Aguirre, Rodrigo de Quiroga, and Francisco de Villagra, weakening the Spanish Empire's power in Chile as the greater Arauco Wars raged on.

The Spaniards continued expanding into the pacific as the reign of Charles V was coming to an end. In the Pacific Spanish, exploration continued following the expeditions of Spaniards including Ruy López de Villalobos, who had sailed and encountered islands in 1542 on his way towards the islands soon-to-be named the Philippines. Some of the islands, such as La Desgraciada, were named and documented by sailors like Juan Gaetano. Some island chains were unofficially named La Isla de los Ladrones (or the Islands of Thieves) after the Spanish accused the native Chamorros ironically of theft and began to attack them after Magellan's ships arrived. The islands were also called Islas de las Velas Latinas (or the Islands of the Lateen Sails) and would later be called the San Lazarus islands. The Spanish Crown was in position to increase the expansion of their empire and envelop the world under Hapsburg hegemony.

As the wars went on and the Spanish Empire expanded in the American mainland, the islands continued to experience increasing neglect by the Spaniards. They continued to seek the Spanish mainland in their effort to gain land, slaves, and silver and gold. The smaller islands in particular were neglected due to the failures of Spanish expeditions, including the embarrassing and ignored failed excursion led by Radamés Cesar Milfuegos which resulted in two Spanish galleons lost and over 150 Spaniards defeated and killed with only a few surviving. Maximo Milfuegos had barely survived himself, arriving to the island of San Juan Bautista where he was promptly summoned to the city of Santo Domingo on the island of Hispaniola, where he was disgraced by the failure of his father and his own poverty. Maximo was ordered to arrive at the Alcázar de Colón in 1548 by high Spanish officials trying to analyze the failures of his father and the loss of two Spanish galleons. The judges questioned Maximo regarding his father's recklessness, brutality, and in his attempts to conquer all the islands of the southeast Caribbean. Maximo, disgraced and drunk in front of the Catedral Primada de America, the first cathedral in Santo Domingo, quietly sought an answer from God through the heavy fog of despair that had surrounded his mind. Maximo's mother Catalina, who was rumored to have shared various romances, had left to the island of San Juan Bautista to the city of Puerto Rico and married a noble Spaniard by the name of Don Jerónimo Molina. Despite her pleads, Catalina could not convince her disgraced son to join her in San Juan Bautista as Maximo sought to re-establish his family's name. Samuel Guerrero had become an enemy and when he left for Cuba in 1553, Maximo followed him, desiring to reach a higher status. Stripped of all his father's lands and acquired wealth, Maximo left west to the island of Cuba to work, gain wealth, and possibly attempt to travel to the Americas and afterwards back towards Antigua and the southeast Caribbean to avenge the death of his friends father.

American society was changing through the expansion of Spanish power upon the native lands. The Spaniards and Portuguese continued to bring Africans mostly from West African kingdoms into the Caribbean and the Americas. Various Spaniards advocated for the increased migrations of working class Spaniards into the Caribbean and Americas to increase the Spanish population and help balance against the growing numbers of African slaves as well as the increase of mixtures between the different races. In the mainland, there was an increase of Spanish and Indigenous mixed people called Mestizos, some taking leadership positions. Other mixtures between Spaniards and Africans began occurring within New Spain and regions of Central and South America. Mestizas like Hernan Cortés' wife, La Malinche Doña Marina, helped the Spaniards diplomatically in their conquest of North and Central America while Hernan Cortés' son, El Mestizo Martín Cortés, was educated in Spain and became a page in Emperor Philip II's court. Although he was not the eldest, Hernan Cortés' full Spanish son, Don Martín Cortés y Zúñiga, Second Marquis of the Valley of Oaxaca, would assume titles and land because he was of full Spaniard blood. Other conquistadors had children with native women, creating an increasing mixed population while many of the free Africans also mixed with the indigenous populations and contributed to a growing populace largely opposed to Spanish rule.

The Spaniards, Portuguese, and French would begin identifying the mixed offspring, labelling them to help enforce a racial hierarchy in the Americas. At the higher levels of government were the Spaniards born in Spain called peninsulares, while the middle and lower levels of government were occupied Spaniards born in the Americas called Criollos, who were sometimes mixed with natives or other groups. The Spaniards and the other European colonizers believed a hierarchy would help maintain Spanish power while socially and economically influencing the other races to bitterly fight among each other. The idea of divide and conquer had continued to aid the Spanish Empire as they used tribal conflict to help topple the Aztec and Incan Empires and continued to be effective in the Spanish and native wars in North, Central, and South America. Disease also helped cripple numerous native societies. The Neo-Incan Empire continued to survive and resist against the Spanish Empire in Peru; however, the Incas had steadily decreased in size and power. After the murder of Manco Inca Yupanqui and his wife Cura Ocllo by Spanish conquistadors, their son Sayri Túpac succeeded as Incan ruler in 1545 with his brother Paullu Inca as a puppet of the Spanish Empire. The young Inca Túpac Amaru later discussed his hopes of re-establishing a true Incan Empire.

In the Caribbean, the Spaniards began advocating for increased Spanish migrations into the island of San Juan Bautista (which was frequently called Puerto Rico), limiting San Juan to Puerto Rico's capital and primary port city. This was a policy of improving the race which they believed would help keep a racial hierarchy and their belief in an orderly society with Spaniards remaining in high leadership positions and retaining their power and wealth. What the Spaniards in power feared was a unification of the lower castes, including the Spanish poor, to form an alliance against the nobility in power. The Caribbean islands of Cuba, San Juan Bautista and particularly the island of Hispaniola were now mixing between the African, Tainos, other natives, and Spaniards at a higher rate. The neglect of the former Spanish power center of Santo Domingo in Hispaniola was causing a blurring of the tribes and people. Native revolts progressed and marooned societies throughout the Americas, the Caribbean, and the island of Hispaniola continued the struggle for freedom. In the island of Hispaniola, the fight against the Spanish encouraged marriage between the Africans and native groups creating a distinct African and native culture which would later include intermixing between the mixed native and Spanish and Spanish and African people within the island.

Amanex and his family lived free from Spanish control on the island of St. Vincent in their growing African, Taino, Igneri, and Kalinago community. Very few Igneri had participated alongside Amanex and Elombe in the war against Radamés Cesar Milfuegos and the Spaniards choosing to defend the island, however they contributed largely to the St. Vincent island community. Through Taino scouts, Amanex learned about the events on the island of his birth Ayiti (now Hispaniola). Amanex understood the Spaniards and their tactics of divide and conquer and he would often speak to the Kalinago council, advocating for the need to stay unified against the Spaniards. He spoke about the importance of respecting the cultures within their community and the need to recognize their unified struggle for freedom and the new culture being formed.

Amanex was informed of similar things happening in the Americas and on the island of Hispaniola as well as the Spanish neglect of the islands—including Hispaniola—as they shifted their focus towards the American mainland. In Puerto Rico, the blending of the people of the Canaries, Portuguese, Spaniards, and Tainos created an increasing Andalusian and native Taino Jibaro culture. The wealthy Spanish class had reduced in Hispaniola, leaving a large population of poor Spaniards and increasing amounts of free Africans and natives such as the decreasing Taino population which had mostly merged with the Africans. In Hispaniola, as poverty increased, the poor Spaniards had children with natives and Africans which Amanex believed could improve relations between the people inhabiting the islands. However, Amanex also believed that Spanish power would continue their practice of divide and conquer to create a racial and economic hierarchy within Hispaniola and the surrounding islands of Cuba and Puerto Rico.

The city of Santo Domingo continued to maintain a stronger racial and economic hierarchy among Spaniards, Africans, Tainos, and the various offspring each produced while the rest of Hispaniola experienced a reduction in racial heirachy as the different communities merged. A new culture of people began forming, combining the African, Spanish, Taino and other natives and their religions, languages, and practices as well as the common language of Castilian, which many spoke easily to others despite their respective backgrounds. Amanex did not know what the new culture and its people would be called in the upcoming generations. He did not know if they would continue to fight among each other or unite as a new people opposed to the Spanish, Portuguese, French, and the other European empires to come. Amanex was critical of these new societies, however he hoped these people and their culture would learn to live in peace in an egalitarian society like the one he worked to build in St. Vincent.

In the smaller islands of the Caribbean—St. Vincent and St. Lucia where Amanex often visited friends among them—a true egalitarian society had formed. It existed to a higher degree than Spanish and other native societies and had continued among a solidified new society between Africans and natives in the smaller Caribbean islands. Amanex enjoyed the similarities in beliefs between the Taino and Kalinago people and how they respected and honored their ancestors in hopes of achieving harmony and peace. The Kalinago believed in the evil being named Maybouya who had to be appeased for the Kalinago people to escape harm. Bones of their ancestors would be kept in their homes. They believed it would bring protection and peace to themselves and their descendants. The shamans (called buyeis by the Kalinago) were highly respected for their ability to cure the sick, ward off evil, and placate Maybouya. The buyeis underwent specialized training to serve their communities and they came to respect Amanex and his family and accepted him as a leader.

Amanex would soon limit his visits to Saint Lucia when he was informed that over 300 French pirates led by a man named François le Clerc (nicknamed pata de palo because of his peg leg) had used the island as a base of operations. Amanex had considered an attack on François le Clerc and his buccaneers, however he believed they did not pose a major threat.

Encouraged by the solidifying of his community through the merging of cultures and marriage, in 1556 Amanex and Tayamari agreed to the marriage of their shy and youngest son Adán Hatüey—who was now thirty-four—to a beautiful, young twenty year old Kalinago woman named Kashiri, who was the daughter of a Kalinago council leader. Kashiri was named after the beautiful moonlight her parents observed on the northern coast of South America when she was conceived. Adán Hatüey and Kashiri would have a beautiful son in 1556 named Mabey Elombe after the Cacique leader who fought alongside Hatüey and Elombe, Amanex's closest friend. Amanex also enjoyed the birth of his first granddaughter in 1556, produced by the union of his son Simon Pedro Haübey (who was now almost thirty-eight) and his wife Malundama (now thirty-four) named Dulce Anacaona, after the Cacica Anacaona who Amanex continued to admire and the sweetness she reintroduced to her family.

Amanex and his wife Tayamari, despite the pain they had endured throughout their lives, were now experiencing a new form of happiness as their family grew alongside their community in freedom. Amanex was informed that several Spaniards had escaped death, including Maximo Milfuegos, and his return to Puerto Rico and his possible residence in Hispaniola or Cuba. It distressed him; he did not have the forces available to mount an attack on any of the three major islands of the Caribbean. Thoughts of Maximo Milfuegos and his possible attempt at revenge over his father's death continued to plague Amanex's mind as he feared for the safety of his community and family. Amanex desperately tried to keep his thoughts from Tayamari and his children, however they manifested in increased conversations with the Africans, Tainos, and Kalinago leaders.

CHAPTER 26
THE LAST OF THE TAINOS (1558)

Holy Roman Emperor Charles V was rapidly experiencing failures in his health. Charles V suffered from an enlarged jaw, which reoccurred in the Hapsburg family among inbreeding, gout, and bad digestion because of his inability to properly chew food. Charles V's pain was crippling and he was forced to be carried around in his sedan chair within the monastery of Yuste in Extremadura. He began abdicating many of his territories within the Hapsburg Spanish Empire, including the States General of the Netherlands and the country of Charolais given to his son Philip. Charles V also abdicated the Spanish Empire to his son Philip in January 1556 and handed the title of Holy Roman Emperor to his brother Ferdinand that September. However, the abdication was not accepted by the Electors of the Empire until 1558. Charles V passed away from malaria on the twenty-first of September 1558. His only surviving son Philip II succeeded as Holy Roman Emperor along with his wife and cousin, Empress Isabella of Portugal. Philp II named García Hurtado de Mendoza y Manrique, Fifth Marquis of Cañete, as the Royal Governor of Chile in 1557, while his father Andrés Hurtado de Mendoza y Cabrera, Third Marquis of Cañet, continued his rule as Viceroy of Peru.

Philip II sought to increase his empire and solidify

his reign over the seventeen provinces of the Netherlands. He continued the Spanish wars against France, initiating several battles against King Henry II. In 1556, Philip II signed the Treaty of Vaucelles with Henry II, granting the territory of Franche-Comté to Philip II, but the treaty was broken and Philip II went to war with Henry II in Northern France and in the Italian. This resulted in a victory for Philip II in Saint Quentin and at Gravelines, which led to the Treaty of Cateau-Cambresis, which recognized Spanish sovereignty of Franche-Comté under Philip II. He responded to Pope Paul IV and his criticism regarding the Spanish Empire by initiating a war against the Papal States, acquiring Italian territory. By 1559, King Philip II and Hapsburg Spain was the preeminent power in Europe, however Sultan Suleiman the Magnificent continued to control the Mediterranean and increase the power of the Ottoman Empire.

Suleiman the Magnificent admired the accomplishments of the Macedonian general Alexander the Great and sought to surpass his glory as well as the glories of others in his establishment of a global Ottoman Empire. Suleiman broke from tradition, marrying the former slave and harem girl from Ruthenia named Hürrem Sultan and bestowing lavish gifts upon her and penning various poems under his pen name Muhibbi. Suleiman expanded the Ottoman Empire and constructed many buildings, mosques, and aqueducts through the vision and work of his chief architect Mimar Sinan. Mimar Sinan was compared to Michelangelo and along with Leonardo da Vinci, was invited to Rome to see Michelangelo's plans for the Saint Peter's Basilica.

Suleiman's personal life was filled with domestic conflict and toxic politics, which resulted in the deaths of his Vizier Grand Vizier Pargalı Ibrahim Pasha and the execution of his son by his wife Mahidevran Prince Şehzade Mustafa Muhlisi. Through his grief, his son Prince Şehzade Cihangir also died—later killed by his brother Prince Selim in 1561. Despite his internal political and domestic problems, Sultan Suleiman maintained power in the Mediterranean over the Spanish Empire, prompting

Philip II to create an allied force including the Republic of Venice, the Republic of Genoa, the Papal States, the Duchy of Savoy and the Knights of Malta called the Holy League. The Holy League encompassed over sixty galleys and 140 other vessels which transported over 30,000 soldiers under the command of the nephew of Genoese Admiral Andrea Doria (named Giovanni Andrea Doria). The increase in Spanish naval power in the Mediterranean allowed Philip II to continue Spanish expansion in Europe, Asia, and the Americas.

The islands were increasingly neglected by the Spaniards as they continued to seek land, slaves, and riches in the mainland Americas. Amanex was constantly waiting for information regarding the location of Maximo Milfuegos and his current motivations. The summer of 1558 brought large hurricanes through the Caribbean, however most passed mainly through Puerto Rico, Hispaniola, and Cuba, leaving the smaller islands untouched minus some strong winds and occasional rains. The hurricanes in 1553 were deadlier, resulting in the partial destruction of the New Spanish fleet and Amanex wished other Spanish and European ships profiting from abuse and exploitation the same fate. As the year 1558 ended, Amanex celebrated the birth of his fourth grandchild and the second born son of Adán Hatüey and Kashiri named Comerío Jerónimo. Weddings occurred throughout the year, including the Islamic ceremony of Mamadou Dieng and a Kalinago woman, and his sister Arjana Dieng and a Taino man. The marriages further solidified Amanex's community, much to the happiness of Amanex and the council leadership.

Amanex spent much of his time teaching his grandchildren about his Taino beliefs but the children also learned about the African, Catholic, as well as Kalinago beliefs. The children of the community loved the Kalinago stories, including the one of the two brothers named Maruka and Cimanari, famous for their charms. The brothers would often visit the master named Tete Chien, who was a giant with a crest of diamond on his head and crowed like a rooster. Maruka and Cimanari would take what was now commonly referred to as tobacco and burn it on a paddle in front of Tete Chien, who would subsequently vomit the black Caribbean. Maruka and Cimanari later turned into normal boys with one dying and the other living on the island now named Dominica. Other Kalinago stories were popular—mostly told in Spanish as it had wider usage here. The children learned about the spirit of the rock and the gifts bestowed upon them if they visited the rock at Pagua. Amanex also told Taino tales, which kept the children happy and entertained. on the afternoon before his eldest son's birthday, Amanex learned of the fate of Maximo Milfuegos.

Maximo Milfuegos and Samuel Guerrero were in Cuba for about a year as animosity continued to grow between them. In the year 1554, Samuel Guerrero and Maximo Milfuegos were residing in the Cuban capital city of Santiago de Cuba. Maximo Milfuegos plotted the murder of Samuel Guerrero and received an opportunity during the surprise raid by the French buccaneer François le Clerc. François le Clerc and his lieutenant Sores had previously set out from France in 1553 with three royal ships and privateers under commission from Francis I of France and were supported by the current King of France, King Henry II. Like his father Francis I, King Henry II had a feud with the House of Hapsburg and the Spanish Empire regarding the growing Spanish colonies and the riches they exploited in the Americas and funded French Piracy. François le Clerc raided several Spanish outposts, including Santa Cruz de La Palma in the Canary Islands, San Germán in Puerto Rico, and several ports in Hispaniola and Cuba.

Suspected of launching his raid from the small islands in the northern archipelago of northern Cuba, François le Clerc launched a vicious attack as the French pirates cut through the city of Santiago de Cuba. Samuel Guerrero received a shot in the leg as he tried to escape into the outskirts of the city with Maximo Milfuegos. Maximo Milfuegos took his sword and with the energy of his misplaced anger and hatred over the loss of his father, thrust it into Samuel Guerrero's chest. Le Clerc held the Cuban capital city of Santiago for over a month and stole over 80,000 pesos in treasure before leaving. Maximo falsely stated that Samuel had died at the hands of the French pirates and although some Spaniards suspected Maximo of contributing towards his death, there was little evidence against him and he travelled towards Western Cuba and the city of Havana in 1555.

The great city was named after Cacique Habaguanex and was previously named San Cristóbal de la Habana by the deceased Conquistador Pánfilo de Narváez. Havana was an important Spanish outpost in Northwestern Cuba, however many of the Spaniards were nervous about increased French piracy in the Caribbean. Havana had now risen to prominence in Cuba after Santiago was burned to the ground by François le Clerc with the aid of Jacques de Sores. After several months residing in the city of Havana, it was raided by the French buccaneer Jacques de Sores (nicknamed L'Ange Exterminateur or "the Exterminating Angel"). Jacques de Sores was the leader of his band of French Protestant Huguenot pirates that led over ten ships into Havana, laying waste to the city and the surrounding countryside. Maximo Milfuegos managed to reach the port trying to escape towards Florida but in his greed, he returned to steal some gold and was promptly killed as the French searched the port for survivors. Maximo Milfuegos, who initially tried to fight the French, fled and was killed by a French pirate with a sword to his lungs. He perished in the port of Havana, choking on his own blood. Amanex openly spoke to his sons about the irony regarding his decision not to attack the Northman Francis Le Clerc, which eventually led to the death of his last known enemy Maximo.

Maximo was believed to be childless when he died with probably children by an African slave, however Amanex was relieved that the chance of retaliation was dead with Maximo in the city of Havana. The next day was December fifth, 1558, and Amanex celebrated the fortieth birthday of his eldest son Simon Pedro Haübey with serenity. The celebrations united the community and Amanex was finally at peace with himself and a gentle calm enveloped him as he embraced his only wife Tayamari. Amanex had become a great leader and a man of respect and in his tradition, great men had multiple wives. Although the thought of taking a beautiful, smart young African, Taino, or Kalinago woman had crossed his mind, he felt fully content with Tayamari. She had raised his children and given his family structure and cohesiveness and for that Amanex was eternally grateful.

In the following year, in November of 1559, a massive hurricane in the Gulf of New Spain wrecked Spanish ships, killing over 1,000. Amanex believed the continued strength of his people and the powerful hurricanes could help deter Spanish, French, and other Europeans in any future attempts of conquering the small islands. He understood the importance of a powerful coalition and through his scouts, he was aware of the growing French piracy in the Caribbean. Soon other European kingdoms would seek to exploit the people of the Caribbean and the Americas in a race among themselves to acquire wealth and power. Amanex was resolved in his continuing purpose to provide safety for his family and community and believed if they could defeat an already established Spanish Empire, they could certainly defeat the piracy of the French and other potential European pirates. He focused his energy on creating a community in St. Vincent, which combined the cultures into a strong union that surpassed the sum of its parts. Amanex respected and loved this mixed community, however he sometimes thought about his birth on the island of Ayiti and Kiskeya and the strong, proud, and peaceful society of the Tainos and he could not help but feel saddened; the Taino people had seemed to fade away. Disease and Spanish brutality had reduced the Tainos in the Caribbean and they were now surpassed by African slaves, Spaniards, and even Kalinago in the smaller Caribbean islands. As he rejoiced at a new people rising, he lamented the increasing loss of the Taino culture.

It had incorporated into a greater mixture of people. Through Taino scouts, Amanex learned about the deaths of many of the Taino caciques in the Caribbean and the people they led. Great caciques now dead or removed from their leadership positions like Agüeybaná, Agüeybaná II, Caonabo, Anacaona, Bohechio, Guamá, Guaoconel, Hatüey, Hayuya, Imotonex, Inamoca, Loquillo, Mabodomaca, Majúbiatibirí, Majagua, Manatiguahuraguana, Maniabón, Yacagüex, Yacahüey, and many more. With the death and disappearances of the caciques and rapidly decreasing population of Tainos, Amanex realized the potential threat of his own people's disappearance.

Amanex consoled himself with the possibility that the Taino would survive as a free people and their culture would live through their descendants even if Taino society came to an end. He taught his family and community the importance of respecting the cultures of others and preserving the Taino culture as well. Amanex was given an opportunity to bring policy to the greater Kalinago Council which enabled his community to receive a larger role on the island of St. Vincent. As the years continued to pass however, Amanex began to give a larger share of his responsibilities to his eldest son Simon Pedro Haübey. He believed his community was strong and he contemplated retiring from his role. Amanex would sometimes attend the Kalinago Council meetings, but most of his time was spent with his family or farming and fishing.

CHAPTER 27
THE CACIQUE OF SAINT VINCENT (1565)

After the death of Edward VI of England his older half-sister would claim the throne and rule as Mary I of England after the execution by beheading of Queen Lady Jane Grey. Queen Mary I reversed Edward VI's protestant reforms and her frequent executions of Protestants earned her the nickname Bloody Mary. Queen Mary I married to King Philip II becoming Queen Consort of Hapsburg Spain in 1556 however, she passed away in 1558. Queen Elizabeth I of England succeeded after Mary's death. The daughter of King Henry II of France was now to wed King Philip II of Spain. King Henry II of France was celebrating the marriage of his daughter Elisabeth of Valois to King Philip II of Spain.

King Henry II of France suffered an injury to his eye during a jousting accident when he was wounded in the eye by a fragment of the splintered lance of Gabriel Montgomery the captain of the King's Scottish Guard in June of 1559 and died from sepsis on the tenth of July 1559. King Henry II's son King Francis II of France succeed his father and was also King Consort of Scotland because of his marriage to Mary, Queen of Scots. King Francis II soon died in 1560 from an ear condition and was succeeded by Charles IX of France. The religious wars between the Protestants and Catholics continued to weaken the Royal French House of Valois as the Spanish Empire continued their dominance despite several bankruptcies in Hapsburg Spain.

New Spain was led by Viceroy Luís de Velasco who in 1564 commissioned Miguel López de Legazpi and Andrés de Urdaneta on a voyage towards the Spice Islands into the Pacific in efforts to reach the islands that Ferdinand Magellan had reach in 1521 and Ruy López de Villalobos had reached in 1543. Viceroy Luis de Valasco passed away in 1564 and had not enriched himself during his tenure as Viceroy while he concerned himself and became an advocate of the poor and indigenous. Francisco Ceinos became interim viceroy in 1564 and Viceroy Gastón Carrillo de Peralta y Bosquete, 3rd Marquis of Falces became the permanent governor of New Spain. Allegations increased regarding possible Spanish rebels who wanted to separate themselves from the authority of the Spanish Crown which placed Viceroy Gastón de Peralta as he was suspected of being sympathetic towards the rebel cause. King Philip II sent two visitadores named Luis Carrillo and Alonso Muñoz, to New Spain to investigate the viceroy and the rebellion and to remove from power. Viceroy Don Martín Enríquez de Almanza became the fourth Viceroy of New Spain in 1568 after being chosen by the Council of the Indies. The Spanish Empire continued to expand its territory the capital city of New Spain which was previously renamed México Tenochtitlán continued to increase in importance while the city of, Puebla de los Angeles became New Spain's second most important city serving in between the capital city and the port of Veracruz. The Californias region had been explored but remained of little interest to the Spanish Empire as well as the region of New Mexico which had been previously explored by conquistadors including Francisco Vásquez de Coronado and Francisco de Ibarra.

Viceroy Andrés Hurtado de Mendoza y Cabrera met with the leader of the Neo-Incan state Sayri Túpac in Lima Peru on January fifth of 1560. Sayri Túpac renounced his claim to the Incan Empire and accepted baptism as Diego however, he died suddenly in 1561 and his brother Titu Cusi Yupanqui claimed leadership of the Incan state and resumed his resistance against the Spanish Empire. Titu Cusi Yupanqui subsequently made Túpac Amaru a priest and custodian of Manco Inca's body in Vilcabamba. After the recall and death of the fifth Viceroy of Peru Andrés Hurtado de Mendoza y Cabrera he was succeeded by Viceroy Diego López de Zúñiga y Velasco, fourth Count of Nieva in 1564. After the death of Viceroy Diego López de Zúñiga y Velasco he was succeeded by Juan de Saavedra and then Viceroy Lope García de Castro. Lope García de Castro was sent by the Council of the Indies to the Audiencia of Guatemala for the purposes of attaching that territory to the Audiencia of Panama and had served as the Governor of Panama before becoming Viceroy of Peru. The son of the deceased Andrés Hurtado de Mendoza y Cabrera, the governor of Chile García Hurtado de Mendoza y Manrique had left Chile for Peru, leaving Rodrigo de Quiroga as interim governor of Chile. Created the mita system which regulated native labor in Peru. Under the mita each chief would choose one out of six natives to work the mines while the other five would work the fields and the natives would finally be paid one sixth of what was produced through their labor. Males and females under the age of eighteen or over fifty years of age would be exempt from the mita. Despite the mita system natives would be abused by the Spaniards. García Hurtado de Mendoza would return to Spain to the court of King Philip II where he was subject to the juicio de residencia, to answer for his treatment of Spanish soldiers and the removal of encomienda resulting in being guilty of over 196 charges however, he was absolved and would serve in the Royal Guard in Madrid and later as a representative of King Philip II in Milan.

The Portuguese presence in South America was also expanding in Brazil. Between 1534 and 1536, fifteen Captaincy colonies were created in Portuguese America and by 1549 they were united into the Governorate General of Brazil with the city of São Salvador established as the capital. The third Governor of Brazil was Mem de Sá with Estácio de Sá as the Governor-general of Rio de Janeiro an office which Mem de Sá would also hold. The first Jesuits would soon arrive to the capital of Brazil which oversaw the colony of Brazil and large sugar cane plantations which brought large amounts of African slaves to supplement the decreasing native populations. King John III of Portugal could not compete with the large Spanish Empire in the Americas however, the Portuguese under his rule established colonies in India and were the first to establish contact with Ming China and Muromachi Japan. After the death of King John, he was succeeded by Dom Sebastian I of Portugal in 1557. The Portuguese Governor General Mem de Sá would later destroy an early French colony named France Antarctique in the region encompassing Rio de Janeiro and Cabo Frio. The Portuguese Royal House of Aviz would soon weaken as Spanish dominance continued to increase in Europe and the Americas. The city of St Augustine in Florida would soon be found in 1565 by conquistador, Pedro Menéndez de Avilés who killed French Huguenots who previously attempted to settle in Spanish Florida including Jean Ribault. The Spanish Empire would fight to keep its American Empire intact as the French, Portuguese, and other European nations including England were seeking to profit from the exploitation of the Americas.

The death of Sultan Suleiman the Magnificent in 1566 brought Sultan Selim II to the throne of the Ottoman Empire. Sultan Selim II was nicknamed Selim the Sot for his frequent drunkenness. King Philip II believed the Ottoman Empire was weaker under the rule of Sultan Selim II which encouraged him to expand Spanish power in the Mediterranean region. Most of the Ottoman state affairs were handled by Selim II's Grand Vizier, Mehmed Sokollu who could finalize a treat at Constantinople with the Austrian Holy Roman Emperor Maximillian II in 1568 a member of the Austrian House of Hapsburg. The compromise allowed Maximillian II to pay 30,000 ducats annually to Sultan Selim II and Ottoman authority in

Moldavia and Walachia. Sultan Selim II would suffer a defeat at the hands of Russia and their leader Ivan IV nicknamed Ivan the terrible resulting in a treaty between Russia and the Ottoman Empire in 1571.

On October seventh, 1571, The Holy League organized under Pope Pius V and heavily financed by King Philip II, fought Sultan Selim II's Ottoman Navy in Gulf of Patras, Ionian Sea. The Holy League was led by Philip II's younger half-brother Admiral Don John of Austria, while the Ottoman Navy was led by Sufi Ali Pasha. The Ottoman right was led by Şuluk Mehmed Pasha against the Holy League's Right led by Christian left led by Admiral Agostino Barbarigo which resulted in the death of both leaders and the beheading of Şuluk Mehmed Pasha by the sword of Giovanni Contarini the Venetian. The Ottoman left was led by Occhiali who outmaneuvered his opponent the knight commander of the Order of Santiago Giovanni Andrea Doria who led the Holy League's right and captured the flagship of the Maltese Knights. The overall battle however, was won by the Holy League and the leader of the Ottoman Navy Şuluk Mehmed Pasha was killed in action. Navy Şuluk Mehmed Pasha's flagship galley the Sultana battled directly with Don Juan's flagship La Real resulted in the boarding of the Sultana and fierce close quarter combat which resulted in the decapitation of Şuluk Mehmed Pasha. The Cross defeated the Crescent and the myth of Ottoman Naval superiority was crushed as King Philip II further expanded the Spanish Empire around the world.

Amanex was informed by some of the details of world events but as the year 1570 approached he had decided to finally give all his leadership responsibilities to his son Simon Pedro Haübey. Amanex now expected to enjoy the end of his life as a free man and desired the same for his descendants. By the end of the year 1570 Amanex and his wife contemplated the long life they had both lived despite the dangers faced by the Taino people. Amanex was now eighty-five years of age and his wife Tayamari was eighty years of age. Simon Pedro Haübey was now fifty-two years old and his wife Malundama who was now forty-eight, Malundama's Taina mother Magdalena was now seventy. The children of Simon Pedro and Malundama were a beautiful product of Kikongo African and Taino cultures and their eldest son Matondo Enrique Haübey was now twenty-four and their younger daughter Dulce Anacaona was now fourteen years old. Amanex's younger son Adán Hatüey was now forty-six years old and his Kalinago wife Kashiri was now 32. Adán Hatüey's eldest son Mabey Elombe was now fourteen and his youngest Comerío Jerónimo was now twelve years of age.

Amanex often thought about his parents Maraguay and Ana and his elder brother Amayao and their violent deaths however, he consoled himself understanding that they would be proud of how he helped bring forth a family by instilling the ideals Amanex himself had learned from his parents. Tears still fell from the eyes of Amanex as he remembered the family and friends he had lost through violence, disease, and for those who were lucky, old age. Amanex also experienced joy through his grandchildren and laughed with Tayamari as they prepared for the wedding of their eldest grandchild Matondo Enrique to a beautiful young Igbo woman. Amanex never believed he would live a long life and live to see a grandchild elope and he hoped to live his remaining years with joy surrounded by his family and his community. El Prudente or King Philip II the Prudent was the master of the world even having thousands of islands in the Pacific Ocean named the Philippines after him however, Amanex was the master of his own life, free to live his life as he wished. Amanex was commonly called the cacique by some of the Tainos in Saint Vincent, however his eldest son Simon Pedro had now claimed full leadership responsibilities. Amanex now spent his days surrounded by his family and friends and writing in various languages including writing his Taino language using the Spanish alphabet. When Amanex was not writing, he would read near the beach and sometimes fish with his grandchildren. Amanex was finally free.

CHAPTER 28
FREEDOM

As I sit and watch the beautiful waves and listen to the birds and the winds of Saint Vincent, it reminds me of the beautiful island of Ayiti and the region of Jaragua where I was born. I always remember the words of my father Maraguay and my dearest kind mother Ana and have always tried to uphold the values they instilled in me. I have tried to instill the same values to my children and grandchildren as best as I could. My only desire is that they can improve upon my successes in life while they learn from my failures. As a Taino, I was raised in a free society that had structure, allowing us a large degree of freedom with security—a Taino society which valued harmony between people and nature and nurtured the growth of mutual respect for men, women, and children. There was freedom to love who you wished and live how you wished. The natural harmony was disrupted when I was a young child by the arrival of the Spaniards.

At first, I did not understand the lust and greed of these invaders or their barbaric actions. We understood aggression before but not to the level of the Europeans, which I later learned had been perfected through centuries of warfare amongst themselves in Europe. If were more civilized as they said, then why would they continue their wars and their never-ending quest for precious metals for their own leaders who keep that wealth from their own people? I believe we live in freedom more than the poor Spaniard, poor French, poor British and any poor in Europe. They focus on dividing the people they seek to conquer and yet they usually don't realize they are also divided amongst themselves. In my fear and anger, I became like the Spaniards and adopted their anger and warlike behavior for the sake of mine and my family's survival. Through my violence against my oppressors, I contracted that same sickness they spread among my people and the other native and African people they sought to conquer. I never believed I possessed the innate bravery of my brother Amayao, or the knowledge and perseverance of my father Maraguay; the leadership abilities of Caonabo, Enriquillo, Anacaona, Agueybana II, nor the high level of empathy and kindness of my mother Ana, but through determination I could persevere and carve out our own freedom here in St. Vincent.

The European rulers are now in a race to expand the power of their respective empires in the Americas and Europe, however the poor Europeans do not enjoy the level of freedom that our people experienced in Taino society. The European rulers wage war among our people, the native civilizations of America, and among themselves, sending their own subjects to die while the resources are concentrated in the hands of the noble and royal few. I find it ironic that these kings are related to each other and the wars of the world can be deduced as a large family conflict to obtain wealth and power. The mighty Aztec Empire has now been defeated, a ruin rebuilt as the territory of New Spain. Other empires, including the Incas, were also defeated and in its place, arose the Vice-royalty of Peru and the territory of Chile. The Governorate General of Brazil was an expanding territory belonging to the Portuguese Empire. Other native groups were currently fighting the Spanish Empire and Mayan Empire. I believe the French and the English will also arrive with their own form of colonization and seek to exploit the native people of the Americas.

They have identified certain groups of people simply by their appearance or the color upon their skin and this division will continue with the arrival of new people from Asia under the control of other European kingdoms like the Netherlands and the English. The few Europeans who would desire to live in harmony as equal men and women are ostracized by their own people and set aside as the empirical machines march forward with the agenda of their rulers. Our only hope in the future will be for us to stand united against a common enemy. Other leaders throughout the Americas and in these very Caribbean islands will rise if their freedom is threated and I believe we can triumph if we solidify our communities. Our people and culture will change and with that change I hope that our unity strengthens as we move forward together in a new society free from oppression and brutality. My hope is that we have intelligent leaders that choose to unite us instead of divide us and if our common enemies choose to war against each other that our leaders also use their divisions against them. The poor European, if he chooses peace and unity and goes against the brutality of his own people whether they are Spanish, French, Portuguese, or maybe others such as English and Dutch, will live in harmony in a greater, peaceful society. I sometimes wonder in my old age if some communities which remain isolated will later war with the descendants of our mixed communities, which I know will only serve to keep us from enjoying true freedom.

Our native societies already had levels of laws and freedoms that I believe are more inclusive than the democracy of the Greeks I have read. The freedom for the Roman was limited and many of these prior and existing civilizations provide more freedom to the wealthiest and most powerful of their citizens. Freedom has existed outside of Europe as well in Egypt, Ethiopia, and West Africa, as my friends and now extended family have informed me. Perhaps it will be best to have common laws that apply to all men and women that provide a simple yet full life of freedom and happiness for all people. I don't know what will happen but what I do understand is that freedom is a delicate idea like, the wings of a butterfly. Freedom is important for society and the individual and we must fight for it. Freedom can mean different things to different people who come from different perspectives and different stages of life. All I am certain of are my nostalgic thoughts of Ayiti. I was born free in this island now called Hispaniola in Jaragua and now I believe I have attained freedom once again. As I see the sun set on another day passed on the beautiful beach, I understand how hard one must fight for freedom. My only hope is that my children, grandchildren, and those who follow them will always fight for their freedom and live within true justice, peace, and happiness.

THE END

EPILOGUE:
RISE OF LATIN AMERICAN & CARIBBEAN REPUBLICS & INDEPENDENCE

Amanex and his wife Tayamari lived the rest of their days on the island of St. Vincent. Amanex's descendants predominantly assimilated into the small Black Kalinago or Garifuna community. Some of Amanex's descendants migrated south to the island of Trinidad and some others travelled towards the country that would become British Guyana in the northern coast of South America. Those on St. Vincent would merge with the native Kalinago, creating a group called the Black Carib by the British to distinguish them from the Yellow or Red Carib. Some intermarried with Indians who were brought by the British Empire as laborers. The Spanish Empire would continue to expand in Europe, Asia, and the Americas and compete with the rival powers of France, England, the Netherlands, and the Ottoman Empire.

The Americas would continue to be colonized by the Spanish and Portuguese Empires and subsequently other European Kingdoms would begin to colonize there such as France, the Netherlands, and England. The Spanish Empire expanded under the rule of King Philip II the Prudent, however the Hapsburg Spanish Crown would face several state bankruptcies in the years 1557, 1560, 1569, and 1575. The Seven United Provinces, out of a total seventeen provinces of The Low Countries, would rebel against the Spanish Empire led by William I, Prince of Orange (also named William the Silent). The Dutch Revolt called the eighty-year war included French Protestant Huguenots and resulted in the Republic of the Seven United Netherlands or Dutch Republic, but the southern Netherlands would remain under the rule of the Spanish Empire and Fernando Álvarez de Toledo y Pimentel, the Third Duke of Alba (also known as the Grand Duke of Alba) until the rule of Spanish Netherlands was passed to King Philip II's daughter Isabella Clara Eugenia and her husband Archduke Albert VII of Austria in 1598. After the death of King Sebastian of Portugal, King Philip II claimed the throne of Portugal after Fernando Álvarez de Toledo led the Spanish army of over 20,000 soldiers to victory over the Portuguese forces at the Battle of Alcântara in August of 1580. King Philip II ruled both the Spanish and Portuguese Empires called the Iberian Union and the vast Portuguese and Spanish territories. However, he would suffer defeat at the hands of Queen Elizabeth I of England and the Dutch Republic when his Spanish Armada was defeated in August 1588. The Protestant Queen Elizabeth succeeded her half-sister, the Catholic Queen Mary I of England, upon her death in 1588. The Iberian Union continued under the rule of the Hapsburgs until the Portuguese Restoration War in 1640, which brought the Portuguese Empire under the rule of King João IV of Portugal and the recognition of the Portuguese Royal House of Braganza with the aid of England and France.

King Philip II increased the power of the Spanish Empire towards its zenith, however the Spanish Empire would soon experience a decline in power and influence in Europe and the world. The Spanish Empire expanded its territories in the Caribbean and the Americas, now stretching into north of New Mexico into the Californias and Florida. The Portuguese continued to rule the territory of Brazil and the Dutch had territories in the Caribbean and the Americas, including New Amsterdam. The French held large territory in North America attained from French expeditions such as those of Giovanni da Verrazzano and Jacques Cartier. Samuel De Champlain founded Quebec, which was to become the capital of the fur-trading colony of New France and would later become Canada. The English would capture New Amsterdam and rename it New York after the Duke of York, who would ascend the English Throne as King James II.

Arbitrations had continued between the Spanish Crown and the descendants of Cristóbal Colón. On the twenty-eighth of June 1536, the president of the Council of the Indies, the bishop García de Loaysa, along with the president of the Council of Castile, Gaspar de Montoya, delivered a settlement confirming the title of Admiral of the Indies in perpetuity to the line of Columbus with privileges similar to those of the Admiral of Castile while titles of Viceroy and Governor General of the Indies. The island of Jamaica became a fiefdom for the Colón family, who would hold the title of Marquess of Jamaica and a territory in the Veragua with the title of Duke. They confirmed the descendants of Cristóbal Colón the possession of the lands in Hispaniola and the perpetuity of the titles of alguacil mayor or high sheriff of Santo Domingo and of the Audiencia tribunal. They also ordered a payment of 10,000 ducats annually to the heirs of Columbus as well as 500,000 maravedíes per year to each of the sisters of Luis Colón.

Spanish Conquistadors like Álvar Núñez Cabeza de Vaca continued to expand the power of the Spanish Empire and became one of four survivors during the expedition of Pánfilo de Narváez, dying in 1528. The expedition of Pánfilo de Narváez explored Florida, Mexico, and the Gulf of Mexico. The crew initially numbered at about 600 men from Spain, Portugal, Greece, and Italy and was believed to have been the first time Europeans and Africans observed the Mississippi River and crossed the Gulf of Mexico and Texas. The Pánfilo de Narváez expedition made stops along the way to Florida at Hispaniola and Cuba; they suffered a hurricane and other storms, losing two ships.

After landing near Sarasota Bay, Florida, they were attacked by natives. In 1540, Conquistador Álvar Núñez Cabeza de Vaca was appointed adelantado (or governor) and captain general of New Andalusia, which would later become the Republic of Argentina.

The Viceroyalty of New Spain had created the cities of Puebla de los Angeles, Veracruz in 1519, Colima in 1524, Antequera in 1526 (now Oaxaca City), Guadalajara in 1532, Santiago de Guatemala in 1524, and in Yucatán Mérida, founding the cities of Querétaro in Bajío in 1531. Guadalajara was founded northwest of Mexico City while Zacatecas was founded in 1547 deep in the territory of the nomadic and fierce Chichimeca. This resulted in the protracted Chichimeca War from 1550 to 1590, which began after the previous Mixtón War of 1540–1542.

Spanish expansion would later face threats from the Apaches and Comanches. The Portuguese continued to expand their territories that would later become the United Kingdom of Portugal, Brazil, and the Algarve, after the fall of Louis XVI King of France and the rise of Emperor Napoleon Bonaparte and French power in Europe. The successful war against King George III of England resulted in French victory and the establishment of the United States would later cause a great financial decline in France. This led to the execution of King Louis XVI as the Third Estate helped fuel the French revolution and contributed to the rise of the French Empire under Emperor Napoleon.

Led by Francisco de Toledo, The Viceroyalty of Peru ended, which also ended the indigenous Neo-Incan State in Vilcabamba with the execution the Incan Emperor Túpac Amaru. In Mexico, the African slave leader Gaspar Yanga waged war against the Spaniards in 1609 and finally agreeing to a free settlement for Africans, named colonial government for self-rule of the settlement. This was later called San Lorenzo de los Negros or San Lorenzo of the Blacks, and also San Lorenzo de Cerralvo. Gaspar Yanga was named a national hero of Mexico and El Primer Libertador de las Americas (or "The First Liberator of the Americas").

French expansion in the Americas had also established a western territory on the island of Hispaniola after The Treaty of Ryswick on September of 1697. This treaty recognized the colony of Saint-Domingue (later called Haiti) and the region of Acadia in modern day northeastern United States and Canada. The Treaty of Ryswick was the culmination of the war between France and the Grand Alliance of England, Spain, the Holy Roman Empire, and the United Provinces called the War of the League of Augsburg or Nine Years' War. Throughout these battles, Napoleon Bonaparte needed to finance his army, which allowed United States to cheaply purchase a large region of French territory during the Louisiana Purchase of 1803. The United States would also acquire Spanish Florida and the entire west coast from Mexico after the Mexican American War (1846-1848). After the final defeat of Napoleon's French La Grande Armée by Nathan Rothschild's heavily funded Seventh Coalition, led by the Duke of Wellington and the Kingdom of Prussia led Gebhard Leberecht von Blücher, France fell as a world power and Napoleon was exiled. During the Napoleonic wars, the eastern side of Hispaniola was under the era of La España Boba (or "Foolish Spain") during the reign of Napoleon Bonaparte's brother Joseph.

When Spain previously ceded the eastern region of Hispaniola to the French, many exiled Dominicans returned to the island and defeated the French under the leadership of Juan Sánchez Ramírez and his allied Dominican and Puerto Rican forces at the Battle of Palo Hincado on November seventh, 1808. In 1804, the continued Slave Revolution in Haiti initiated by François Mackandal and later in August 1791 by the Jamaican African leader Dutty Boukman—who was believed to have been Muslim and carried a Koran—finally led to the declaration of the independent Republic of Haiti in 1804, creating the first black independent nation. Toussaint Louverture led the Haitian slave rebellion against the French Empire but was later captured and imprisoned in France, and the Republic of Haiti would arise under the leadership of Jean-Jacques

Dessalines. The independence of Haiti sent ripples throughout the enslaved African world and inspired many black leaders as well as the white abolitionist leader John Brown, culminating in his death in 1859. The leaders of Haiti would also host Simon Bolivar, influencing him to emancipate slaves within Latin America and supplying Haitian troops for the greater Latin American Independence movements. The eastern region of Hispaniola continued to resist European control until forces led by José Núñez de Cáceres y Albor took the city of Santo Domingo, declaring the Republic of Spanish Haiti on December 1, 1821. Spanish Haiti, under the leadership of José Núñez de Cáceres, tried to unify under Simón Bolívar's La Gran Colombia, but it would come to an end under Haitian Unification on February ninth, 1822.

José Núñez de Cáceres soon fell out of favor with the Haitian government of Jean-Jacques Dessalines or Jacques I, who was assassinated in Haiti in 1806, and José Núñez de Cáceres would be exiled and would subsequently relocate with his family to live in Maracaibo, Venezuela. He would later and work in the printing trade in Caracas in 1824, joining the Anti-Bolivarian movement. José Núñez de Cáceres suffered the same fate and he was also forced to relocate with his family to the cities of San Luis Potosi and then Ciudad Victoria, where he would practice law. José Núñez de Cáceres was previously a teacher at the University of Santo Tomás de Aquino in 1795 and would start the satirical newspaper *El Duende*, believed to be the second Dominican newspaper, criticizing colonial Spanish rule. He also found the newspaper called *El Relámpago* (or *The Lightning*) and other newspapers like *El Constitucional Caraqueño* (or *The Constitutional from Caracas*), *La Cometa* (or *The Comet*)—a newspaper that harshly attacked Simón Bolívar—as well as recent issues of the newspaper *El Venezolano*. He would write numerous fables, which led to many honoring him as the first Latin American fabulist.

Haiti would suffer from civil wars and financial strain under French debt, while the Haitian President Boyer's Code Rural and heavy taxation would further strain

Haitian and Dominican relations and lead to war and the declaration of independence led by La Trinitaria of Juan Pablo Duarte Díez, Francisco del Rosario Sánchez, and Matías Ramón Mella. The independent nation of the Dominican Republic was declared in 1844. Pedro Santana would take power and lead the Dominican Republic towards victory against the Haitians including victories against Haitian President Faustin Soulouque, while Santana assumed dictatorial powers. Pedro Santana subsequently orchestrated the annexation of the Dominican Republic to the Empire of Spain. The annexation of the Dominican Republic resulted in the overthrow of Pedro Santana and a revolt by the Dominican populace, which led to the Dominican Restoration War of 1861 to 1865. The Dominican Republic was victorious over the Spanish Empire and Queen Isabella II. The Spanish Empire would continue to face rebellions in the Americas and the Caribbean islands of Puerto Rico and Cuba. Cuba had wars against Spain allied with soldiers from the Dominican Republic and Puerto Rico in the Ten Years' War (1868–1878), The Little War (1878-1879), and the Cuban War of Independence (1895–1898), which would be involved in the greater Spanish American War. The Spanish American war would result in a devastating loss for the Empire of Spain and the Treaty of Paris, which ceded the territories of Guam, The Philippines, and Puerto Rico.

War soon broke out in Puerto Rico against the United States as well as the Philippine American War (1899–1902), which would continue under the veterans of the Katipunan. Powers would arise and World War I brought an end the Ottoman Empire and the Russian Monarchy. World War II would bring allied victory and the emergence of two rival powers: the U.S.S.R. and the United States (the Cold War). On July fourth, 1946, the Philippines declared independence from the United States, creating the Republic of the Philippines. As the Spanish Empire was weakened, various Latin American Republics would arise. New Spain would become the Mexican Empire and later the Republic of Mexico. Other nations revolted and declared their independence, leading to the republics of Belize, Costa Rica, El Salvador, Guatemala, Honduras, Mexico, Nicaragua, and Panama. Brazil declared independence and various states including the Viceroyalty of Peru, Viceroyalty of Rio de la Plata, Viceroyalty of New Granada, the Free Province of Guayaquil, and the United Kingdom of Portugal, became the free Latin American Republics of Argentina, Bolivia, Brazil, Chile, Colombia, Ecuador, the Falkland Islands, French Guiana, Dutch Guyana (Suriname), Guyana, Panama, Paraguay, Peru, Suriname, Trinidad and Tobago, Uruguay, and Venezuela. Some islands previously had become territories of England, including Trinidad, Tobago, and Jamaica, which had been territories of Spain.

In the 1900s, many of the Caribbean islands that were part of the English territories would start declaring their own independence. Latin America made up most of the nations in the Americas and the Latino people were a diverse community with a similar general culture that united them. The Spaniards created a racial caste system in which the Spaniards born in Spain called Peninsular held the highest political positions as well as financial power; Spaniards born in the Americas called Criollos held secondary political positions while Mestizos, Mulattos, Cholos, and Blacks held lower positions. This hierarchy often resulted in conflicts not only among the natives, Africans, and mixed population against the European elite, but also manifested in conflicts between the marginalized groups. Wars like the Caste War of Yucatán (1847–1901) was a conflict between the native Mayas and European-descended population (called Yucatecos). There were also various wars and the marginalization of people such as Africans and natives by European descended people who often held higher economic and political power. After the independence of the Latin American nations, the general racial template remained in place to varying degrees. American influenced dictatorships including that of Rafael Trujillo in the Dominican Republic marginalized certain groups while also improving the economic health of the nation which brought mixed feelings about that specific regime. Leaders in the twentieth and twenty-first centuries would attempt to bring improved economic conditions and promote equity and civil rights towards marginalized populations in their respective nations, however their efforts were often undermined by foreign powers in collusion with their own respective elite classes. A social democracy with reduced income inequality, promoting improved capitalism and social programs as well as respect for all individuals no matter their race, culture, and religion was misrepresented by the elite of those nations to misguide their own people and would suffer from foreign interventionism. Social Democracy exists despite efforts by the elite to misrepresent these mixed economies, perhaps over time Latin America will develop healthier forms of government and societies which will serve to uplift the standard of living for a majority of their citizens or all of their citizens.

At the beginning of the twenty-first century, Latinos became the largest minority in the United States. Views on race in Latin America greatly differed from those of the United States due to the Jim Crow laws passed by Anglo Saxon Protestant elites, simplifying views on race and identifying anyone mixed with Africans as blacks. Latin Americans have a variety of people from backgrounds including Asian, Indian, African, Arab, European, and mixtures between these groups. Nations in Latin America developed high levels of mixed populations like Mestizos, or high levels European descendants, while the nation of the Dominican Republic resulted in a majority mixed population made up of various races and predominantly of Africans, Spanish/European, and Tainos. Other groups such as Asians and Middle Easterners would arrive later in the history of Dominican Republic. The West African influence is great in the Dominican Republic and the Dominican culture was created from that of West African, Spanish, and the native Taino culture, while a diverse community now exists between Asians, Arabs, and other people who migrated to the country throughout its history and would continue to immigrate in the future. This diversity can be a strength or weakness depending on how this reality is used by the political and economic elite who can choose to either promote division or unity. This diversity has also created the beautiful culture and people of the Dominican Republic, also called Kiskeya or Quisqueya. As the population of Latin Americans continues to rise, they would bring various political beliefs, world views, and supplement the complex social tapestry of the United States. Latin America could become a great power in the world as long as its leaders promote solidarity and equity within their respective nations.

(Latin America)

(Caribbean & Central America)

(Coat of Arms of the Dominican Republic)

ACKNOWLEDGEMENTS

I want to thank my parents and family for helping me become the man I am today. I also would like to thank Kim Sierra and members of the native community for helping me with this book. Thank you to my friend Marcos and my other close friends for helping me grow as a person.

ABOUT THE AUTHOR

Rafael Morillo was born in the Bronx, New York. Rafael is of Dominican and Jamaican descent and he studies history and he is an avid reader of history and historical fiction. Rafael enjoys studying about different cultures and their history. Rafael enjoys reading historical fiction, alternate history, science fiction, and writing historical fiction from different points of view that are not traditionally explored. He also enjoys sports and is interested in sharing his perspective and investigating unexplored themes in literature.

CPSIA information can be obtained
at www.ICGtesting.com
Printed in the USA
LVHW091517280420
654675LV00002B/586

9 780692 903469